Robert McLiam Wilson
in Ireland. He is
Manj

Robert McLiam Wilson

RIPLEY BOGLE

published by Pan Books

First published 1989 by Andre Deutsch Ltd
This Picador edition published 1990 by Pan Books Ltd,
Cavaye Place, London SW10 9PG
9 8 7 6 5 4 3 2
© Robert McLiam Wilson 1989
ISBN 0 330 31384 3

Printed in England by Clays Ltd, St Ives plc

For Clare

Contents

Hark, hark, the dogs do bark,
The beggars are coming to town.

It Begins

(Enter man with money. He waits. Enter woman, misclothed and passionate. They rut. Exeunt.)

'Aaaaaaaaeeeeeeiiiiccchhhh!'

The world's disquiet gets underway. Birth scene. The calm cry of parturition. For the one. The incandescent infant. Mrs Bogle screaming her way to the unwilling production of Master Ripley Bogle, the famed. Splayed knees and bucking loins. Dirty, heavyheaded, eponymous bastard shoving his angry way out.

'Aaaaauuuuuuuuuurrrrrrrrccccccttttttttttcccccchhhhhh!'

(Hark at the second coming! The old trick – shout before you whisper.)

Mrs Bogle breaks wind in a loud spluttering rasp. Middle-aged midwife, Mrs Johns, creases her brow in distaste while naughty Nurse Carter tries but insincerely to hide her smirk. Young Dr Poole, fledgling medicaster, vents an eyeless smile of considerable width. Blushing, boyish, he looks at Nurse Carter across that great swollen belly and the messy, wideopen legs.

'Yeeeeeaaaaeeeaeaeaearrrggggghhhthk!'

There is no song, no celebratory ode, nor any rejoicing nor merrymaking in the castle halls of his great Godly Gaelic clan. Bogle unbugled. The pipes are still as he tears and splatters his uterine path into the wilder world. A bawl will come soon, a trumpet of arrival and hardy intent but that will be very much of his own making. His only song. There is no greater sadness than the birth of Ripley Bogle. Ream-isled and poordreamt.

'Aaaaaaaaaarrrgggghhhhhhaaaeeieiiiiikkkkk!'

Little bastard pushing hard now. Has to. Stretching those mother's loins to impossible, inelastic lengths. His first debt. Everquick, he has caught the general fever of confusion and panic in the world and he's buggered if he's going to suffer for it. This is his moment and a pox on the others.

1

'Ooooooooooooooohhhhhhh.'

With a quiet, weary retching noise, Mrs Bogle completes her ripened task. From her parted, stirruped legs plops a son. Unnamed and ugly, he makes little impression on that worldroom. An augury of his rivercatching life.

THURSDAY

ONE

Thank you.

I seem to be spending increasing amounts of my time in thinking about my birth. This is, I freely admit, a futile thing to be doing. The event was, alas, poorly documented and my own recollections of it are ranged upon the impenetrable side of hazy. However, that is probably how it was — more or less. I feel it in my bones.

It must be said that now is not a good time for birthly thoughts. The world is but little like a womb at the moment, for me at any rate. For instance, a slow, inexorable pulse of cold shivering is in the process of threading its way from my coccyx to my liver and I'm damp and dribbling and dank. I've run right out of fags and I have not eaten in rather more than three days. Now, does that sound womblike to you? No, indeed.

June. Lovely frozen June. Curiously enough, a large proportion of English folk tend fondly to think of the month of June as being situated during the summer. This is patently bollocks. Admittedly, the trees mount a spurious verdance and people endeavour to play feeble cricket on a variety of blasted heaths but I can assure you that there is no way in which the term 'summer' can be justified. No way! Only we — we the destitute, the homeless, the vagabonds — only we know the Siberian truth of an English June. We are its allies and confidants. We are on first-name terms with its frozen strangle and frosty grip.

Thus, here I am in the middle of that month, with frostbitten testicles and iceberg feet, doing serious hand-to-hand with hypothermia. I'm so cold I'm not even hungry, for Chrissakes! (Though Malnutrition and Attenuation coyly beckon with mild eyes and smiles urbane.) Yes, the cold is bad but fading slowly. I'm ignoring it as best I can. This seems the sensible course. Anyway, after a while, real cold — the proper Arctic assault — becomes theoretical. Like a disquieting intellectual conviction, it nags but fails to irritate. It anaesthetises against itself. Which is nice of it. All this gives the business of frostbite a kind of grotesque ascetic

5

respectability but I could still do without it . . . that's just how I am.

Just at the moment, I'm sitting on an icy parkbench in St James's Park, grimly satirising the shoddy prismatic glimmer of evening. This is, I concede, a wildly emetic thing to be doing but my menu of alternatives is not exactly encyclopaedic just now.

Two curious things to be noted.

First; despite the arse-numbing temperature and general high discomfort, I can't help feeling rather sentimental about this particular parkbound glide of twilight. I hate to say it but it looks as though the world has really dressed up for me tonight. It must be going somewhere nice. If I knew it a little better I'd try to cadge a fiver or something. Now, that's aestheticism for you. I won't though. The world and I are a little sniffy with each other these days.

The second thing to be noted is the fact that I am sitting on this frozen bench, threatening to flop over at any minute and die of pure poverty and all the while I am less than three hundred yards away from Buckingham Palace. (This thought has an annoying tendency to make me giggle hysterically.) The Queen is in there. Jesus, maybe she's even sitting there at one of those rigid, blinking windows right now, watching me! Laughing at me while I get all Belsenesque and pissed on. (It's raining now. Fucking rain.) It wouldn't surprise me in the least. I mean, the merest mutts in that place are better fed than I am. Well, then again, the merest mutts in most places are better fed than me, for that matter. (Here I giggle again like the true arsehole that I am.) It occurs to me that I am better educated better looking and a nicer person than the Queen and yet I am still starving to death in her front garden. What would Charlie Dickens have said about this, I wonder?

Actually, there is a third curious thing to be noted. The most capricious and witless of all and that is that I don't really mind too much about any of this. Not really. Not desperately. I mean to say, the fact that I am a filthy, foodless, cashless tramp doesn't seem to be bothering me in the way I'm sure it should. I must be off my chump. Since when has indigence been a breeding ground for blithe insouciance? But there it is. In the midst of my poverty and degradation I am strangely, nebulously happy. Prat and irrepressible little cutie that I am, I sense that things aren't after all so very bad. Needless to say, I am hugely mistaken. Things are very bad indeed and set fair for getting worse. Nevertheless, I view myself in this pure, cool moment; chastened and made lean by hardship. The fight is on but I'm standing still. Ducking and weaving is not for me. I leave that to the well-fed, the wise. Okay, so I may well be missing the old bedless, malnutritional, frostbitten point here but it matters little.

Just think of what it gives me, this deprivation, this harsh philanthrope.

Whoops! Rather frantically I scrabble for the recollection of what exactly it *does* give me. Ah! Oh yes, that's it. Of course.

The gifts of thought and memory, that's what. Well, what else is there? Thought and memory. I remember and I think. I have a lot of time and few true distractions. Yes indeed, being a down and out is quite vital to the formation of a truly incisive intellectual mien. Think of Dickens and Orwell. Where would those two have been without all that fruitful early pavement-licking?

Thought and memory. Surprisingly good stuff. I confess that my intelligence is but sporadic in appearance but mnemotechny is my constant, sturdy prop. Replicable moments – these are the sum of my little history. The revision. The milky thoughts and cloudy forgettings. Editor, I greet and shove reality, me and my naughty auctorial caprices.

With these I comfort myself. Wouldn't you?

More of me, I think. Some detail. Some background. Your measure and your gauge.

My height is five feet and eleven inches. My weight is fluctuating and not good at present, not good at all. My eyes are green (and fabulous!), my face is pale and my hair is dark – now pretty indeterminate due to a wily patina of filth and neglect but dark anyway. I am twenty-one years old, my name is Ripley Bogle and my occupations are starving, freezing and weeping hysterically.

I am part Welsh and part Irish. You will excuse my candour if I point out that this is a fucking dreadful thing to be. I can never quite make up my mind as to whom I loathe most ... the Welsh or the Irish (the Welsh generally have it by a slim margin). The Irish side of my family is my mother's side. Now, all the Irish women I have ever known have been particularly hideous and you'll be glad to hear that my mother was no exception. A real old rolling fatbag. She's probably dead now, I like to think. Her father (my granddaddie) is still alive, I believe, pissing his life away on the dingy streets of Belfast. His father, my maternal greatgrandfather, was the only Irish member of my family ever to have held much of a position in the world. This position was one of Official Hero. He attained this eminence by having his legs and most of his testicles blown off at Passchendaele while fighting for the British nation against the German Army – while his brother (my greatgranduncle?) was having his head blown off on O'Connell Street while fighting for the Irish nation against the British Army in the Easter Rising. The rest of the family form the usual cast list of subhuman Gaelic scumbuckets.

My father is definitely dead. This, I know. Though less physically repulsive than my mother, he was much more of a bastard. I remember fondly that he once tried to disembowel me with a broken Bass bottle. I think I was eight at the time. I would probably have murdered the old shitpot eventually if he had not beaten me to it by emptying the majority of his vital organs over the kitchen floor one day before I was old enough or big enough to slice him up on my own account. I don't know a great deal about his antecedents. They were, undoubtedly, rancid Welsh fuckbags like himself.

Harsh? Unconvincing? Yes, a little perhaps. I don't quite know why I bother with all this ballsaching fire and semi-satire. It doesn't really suit me and I'm not terribly good at it. I *was* very good at being cruel and offensive when I was younger. I had a flair for spite and blind condemnation. It all seemed such a good idea then, such a useful weapon and tool. Now, it seems feeble. A demi-truth – the hard half of nothing.

History seems to have come to something of a stop for me. I opted out. I stepped off and bedded down in the crisp comfort of my own failure and decline. I just capitulated to the world and slipped away as silently and unobtrusively as I could manage. Here I am and happy to be so. I haven't been indoors at all this year. Terrible, isn't it? My muscles and sinews wither from abuse and overtime. My flesh is paling to grey with warmth-lessness. I'm much more than a simple tramp. I'm a claustrophobic, a hermit, a prophet, a loser, a cipher! Bejabbers, I'm a symbol of the age! Big deal, suits me well enough.

Now, I *used* to be a success of sorts. I used to be a wiseman, a moneyed, fêted, soughtafter man. Now I'm nothing. Nobody knows me and I barely exist. I'm going the way of all flesh, i.e. fading into reality. The day before yesterday's man.

Happily though, I have at least given up lying, carping and griping. I'm keeping an eye on my invective. I've declined the gage of youth and endeavour. I've backed out of that modern, worldly brawl. It seemed only such a waste of time and I have a lot on my mind these days. I have a kind of purpose now, you see. (Portents, mystery, strange apparitions!) I'm on a quest, you might say. It sounds absurd, I know, but what can a poor boy do? Here in my poverty and my shame, amongst the debris of my aspirations and the rubble of my talents. I have a kind of purpose.

This is for what my story is. This is the sly map from which I shall exhume my goal, my task and treasure. This is where we are all going. You, me and my story (such as it is). That quest. My search for final, fundamental goodness in the world.

There were and are such things as truth, honour, wisdom and beauty to be had. It is just that they are difficult to find. They are furtive and wary of the clamp of recognition, of that proof and loss of faith. They are succubi among the contented evils of nowadays. But that is what I want. That's my base requirement. What other should there be? The evidence and residue of goodness in this one world.

(More, more, pile it on.)

Here in St James's Park, the evening has fallen slowly and dimly. Shadows roll and tumble in the cloudsprayed sky and the pond glows with twilight shine. Oh, I wish to fuck I didn't have to look at this kind of thing!

I stand up. The cold is actually beginning to embarrass me. It is so oddly surplus to requirements. I wink at the trees and flirt briefly with the idea of stoning some ducks. But no, alas. Poverty does terrible things to one's sense of humour. You need a little dosh to chortle adequately. No, it's time to walk. Which I do but gingerly, summoning a little fictional warmth and moistness to the creaky timbers of my legs. This moment of maritime comfort is, however, quickly outflanked and upstaged by a blistering broadside of pain which splinters my spine, boils my brain and pillages my poor, poor kidneys. I wish . . .

I wish I had a cigarette.

9

TWO

> One potato
> Two potato
> Three potato
> Four;
> Jamsticky fingers wiped on the door.

By all accounts I was an intrepidly repulsive infant. Apparently, even the most philanthropic onlooker could scarce suppress the yawing horror that tended to greet the first sighting of my infant self. It has been reported that a prodigious proportion of the nursing staff on the ward I occupied went on to change their careers or at the very least to require psychiatric care. There were nervous whispers about misbirth, lycanthropy, experimental subatomic detonations and the like. I can't help feeling that this was all a ploy, a stream of hyperbole meant to mitigate my parents' immediate and lasting hatred for me.

> Five potato
> Six potato
> Seven potato
> Eight;
> I like the things I like
> And I hate the things I hate.

After my birth, my mother, Mrs Betty Bogle (Can you believe that?) was assailed with guilt. She had been married but one month before I was born, prematurely ending a promising and suitable career as a lowrent prostitute, and she considered that my illegitimacy was a contributing factor to my grotesquerie. My father, Mr Bobby Bogle (It gets worse) was prone to agreeing with old Mumsy. He was a resolutely unemployed ex-baker with a miraculously inexhaustible supply of alcohol and rather felt that he had married beneath him. Well, that's the Welsh for you.

> Nine potato
> Ten potato
> Eleven potato
> Twelve;
> I'm sure I'll wet the bed tonight
> I hope I do it well.

Indeed, as my mother continued to parturate with dazzling regularity, her erstwhile profession and my own dubious pedigree became severe trials to Mr Bogle's feelings. The resulting tempestuous brawls form some of my earliest and fondest memories. These scenes delighted me. Far from having any infantile intuition of conflict or trauma, the rapid, acrobatic brawls and operatic verbals intoxicated me. And soon, amidst the parental yelling, screaming and screeching there would be heard the unmistakable sound of my own gurgles and babyish cries of appreciation and encouragement. A good early example of a basic want of tact that has remained with me ever since.

Ah, my childhood! The mornings bowed and greeted my childishness, honouring it with their own day's infancy. My early life seemed to be composed of eternal mornings, greening trees and hedges, the verdant kiss of child's grass and the beaming wink of the paternal sun. My endless energy, health and indestructible self-confidence stretched timelessly before and behind me.

All good things, however . . .

'Ripley . . .?'
(Picture it – happy Bogleian breakfast, brats and bubs everywhere.)
'Yes, mam?'
'Ripley – I've got something to tell you. Do you know what school is?'
I well remember that when I heard the word 'school', I felt a curious mixture of dread and excitement. I wondered briefly which sensation to adopt as policy but stuck to form and opted for dread.
'Well, do you know what school is?'
'No.'
'Well, school is where everybody has to go to learn.'
Fucking brilliant, eh? There was a brief pause of boyish assimilation.
'Why?' I squeaked.
That spannered her a little.
'Well, so as you'll be able to know how to read and write just like your father and me.'
(Dubious at the best of times.)

'Why?'

'Because you'll have to be able to read and write when you grow up . . . or else nobody'll like you.'

After this Malthusian definition, I calculated briefly before pressing on with my ploy of cute and bewildered child buggering boorish adult about with adorably precocious and unanswerable questions. It had served me well thus far.

'Why?' I repeated. (Though perhaps I could have varied it a little.)

'I told you why, ya cheeky wee bastard!'

I tried to regroup and lead a cavalry charge on the flank of her maternal tendernesses.

'Will you be there, Mummy?'

'Don't be stupid. Of course I won't be!'

I was a little bruised by this but I was in a sanguine mood and considered this bluntness merely a screen for the true turmoil of her conflicting emotions. I gave my pause all the doe-eyed charm of early boyhood before bleating piteously.

'I don't think I want to go to school, Mummy.'

By Christ, I was a jerk even then! Needless to say, this didn't wash with old Mumsy and after putting her boot up my arse, she laid it on the line, so to speak.

'Well, tough titty! And don't get your trousers dirty today, because . . . ' she had been a little lax in informing me in advance of the beginning of my educational career ' . . . because, you're going to school tomorrow.'

'Oh,' I said, reasonably enough.

And so to school. From the intimate improvisation of familial neglect to the more organised version of primary education. I was a child unpunctured. No BCGs, no wimp's immunisations, no forms, no certificates, no doctors and no dentists. Disease could have had me if it had wanted me. (Like everyone else, it didn't.) I had to muck along very much under my own endocrinal steam.

I hate to admit that I wasn't, generally speaking, actively abused. This costs me. I would dearly love to spin out a series of wild, shlocky tales about the mental tortures, the sexual eccentricities and physiological experiments visited upon me in my boyhood. All those characterforming vilenesses that, strictly speaking, I deserved. Unfortunately however, I can lay no valid claim to these incontrovertible qualifications for sympathy. I was merely ignored, neglected, edited, tippexed really. From all I had no word of tenderness, encouragement or pity. I wasn't even worth the effort needed for cruelty or contempt. I made do with optimism and it made do with me.

(I look about me as I trudge trampishly up Constitution Hill. This is only England, sonorous and sweetly chilled. It is hard when here to think of all that. That was the soft, imperceptible end of child cruelty. No social workers for that kind of thing in that kind of place. Ah, those caring professions! Casuistry and camouflage at best. They never had any of that kind of old nonsense when *I* was a battered baby.)

I also trudged trampishly to school on that first day, I seem to remember. All morning my brothers had been indulging in a spectacular riot of mewling and puking and my father had been discovered, dead drunk, in the coal shed. Subsequently, diplomatic beyond my years, I had made no further appeals to my mother's clemency.

I recollect that, as I was dragged towards the end of my innocence that morning, I wondered whether the people who passed us in the street could tell that I was a poor maltreated boy with a wicked mother. I fully anticipated that some gruff, balding old man with kindly eyes and a nice-smelling pipe would stop us forcibly in the street, chastise my unnatural mother and whisk me off to his brightstoned castle where I would be able to eat marshmallows all day and have beautiful lady servants to play with.

(Vomacious, eh?)

Well, I was winked at a couple of times and even saw one or two faces with kindly eyes but there was bugger all in the way of brightstoned castles for me that day.

That was it. Finis. Nadir.

I've said before that my childhood seemed to be all sunny morning. Well, from now on it seems to have been all hazy, anxious afternoon. At the time I wasn't quite sure what it was that I had lost but I was certain that whatever it had been I missed it very badly already.

(Just at this point, a girl passes me shrinkingly. She looks around and about me, carefully marshalling and checking her gaze. She skims the wall, jaw tight with fear and disapproval. Her head is lowered censoriously, her steps, sharp and rapid. She doesn't like me. She doesn't like my vague dirt and my crippled, victim's gait. I embarrass and frighten her and this she could do without. This is made worse for me by the fact that she is young, pretty and has those human, clement eyes I used to love so. She scuttles past me gratefully. Me, the tramp. I am younger than her.)

I learnt of a great many things on my first day at school. I tasted the sour joy and disillusion of knowledge. It was pretty tough going. Christ, if you think I'm looking rough these days, you should have seen me back then! I was practically crookbacked with age and care.

I discovered that I lived in Belfast and that Belfast lived in Ireland and that this combination meant that I was Irish. The grim young bint we were loaded with was very fervent on this point. She stressed with some vigour that no matter what anyone else were to call us, our names would be always Irish.

Wishing to please, I spent most of the morning wondering which arrangement of nomenclature would placate the silly cow best. I felt that 'Irish Bogle' didn't scan and that Mommie Dearest wouldn't be too keen on 'Ripley Irish', obscuring as it did my familial identity. Being at all times a witty and all-inclusive type of chap, I plumped in the end for 'Ripley Irish Bogle'. I remember being highly chuffed with that.

This temporary solution was, however, shattered when little Miss Trotsky herself told us that the occasional Misguided Soul would try to call us British but that of all the wrong things to call us – this was the wrongest. No matter how the Misguided Souls cajoled, insisted or pleaded, our names would remain Irish to the core, whatever that meant.

Well, as you can imagine, this buggered me up no end. I was dazed and anxious. I was worried and confused. But with a precociously fine critical instinct and a juvenile distrust of pedagogical fervour, I decided to consult the maternal oracle upon my return home. In the meantime, in the spirit of compromise (ever with me even then), I dubbed myself 'Ripley Irish British Bogle'.

So, there I was, poor little sod, almost wiped out by the startling array of difficulty and consequence that I had suddenly been lumbered with. Predictably, when I quizzed old mater on the titular proprieties of my situation she tried to stick the kitchen table up my bum. She railed at God-above for presenting her with such a misshapen blight as my good self. I tended to agree. On reflection, it might have been kinder in this Godabove guy to have kept me for Himself.

(Should I show a little more clemency to the past? A little generous revision? No, I don't think so. I hate to think of it getting away with anything.)

THREE

Regent's Park. The particular moment. The hard filament of a thought, remembrance or an augury. The envelope of word and lyric: but most of all, memory, the bathetic dribble of error and reparation. That's it. My cinematic past unfurls again with the hardiness and demeanour of perspective.

This.

Walking, a glance held at a dark, hazel-framed house in this of all my nights. The heliotropic leafspangles in the halo of street lamp above my head.

And?

More. Quick to memory's prompt, the Christmas joy of ten years old and the hope of newer games. The links these moments offer, the frail compensation; the adjunct to the untraceable elusion of all those years ago. Optimism and taintless faith, all unmenaced by the mercature of experience. So, I remember — occasionally, unbidden and fast ebbing. These old aching moments administer the ballast that I sometimes need. Why yes, intermittent digging in the strata of my own past steadies the irrelevant jig of that outside world.

Yup, all that kind of stuff! (Pretty impressive for a tramp, I'm sure you will agree.)

The Christmas vision dissolves and I continue walking. Tired, I am and I'm having trouble with my thoughttrains. I'll try to make them stop.

(Maurice once told me that I thought too much on too little. For Maurice that passed as epigram. He was fond of the terse phrase and he liked to keep me up to scratch.)

The night is dark and very cold. Scantleaved trees sway, their feathery twigs seem to shudder with nerveless apprehension, silly things. Upstairs, the sky holds that black, starpitted allure which I hate so much. Wily and obdurately adamantine, an enemy. A tricky little breeze ruffles my chip-pan hair. My strange and unlovely personal odour drifts away on that merry wind. Ah me, trampnights! How I love them after all.

Well, well – Regent's Park. Indeed. We all know about Regent's Park, don't we? Regent's Park means a great deal to me. For all my times, good and bad, Regent's Park has space for me. Ridiculously beautiful, seething with dosh and privilege, that's my Regent's Park. This is more like the London I dreamt as a boy. I try my several moods here and play them out under the arc and glide of these street lamps. It softens them a little.

How I love Regent's Park and St John's Wood! Cricket grounds whisper to me in words of glamour and promise. Especially at night. This place – green, black and grey. What is really astonishing is the fact that a rancid, fuckpig vagabond like me should be allowed to posh it out amongst all this major money. It's hard to believe. I can quite legally trail my particular slime and cess over these pricey pavements. It shouldn't be allowed. It's just not on. I certainly wouldn't stand for it.

(Well, as a matter of fact, I am here for a reason. I play my part in this opera of wealth and opulence. The role that poverty plays is integral to the success of the greater piece. After a while Money loses its ability to make much of a difference to what has already been bought. At its extremes Money becomes theoretical, impalpable. And that's where I come in. What greater contrast can there be? I service the rich. Wealth is, of course, merely a gauge of one's distance from poverty. It is how much you are not poor. A Croesus only knows he's a Croesus when he can see a vagabond like me shlepping about outside his mansion. He needs me. What would his riches be without me?)

London in general is a funny old place. Yes, it is. You know it is. I like old London. In all its grimegrey glory. Lives live here. Lots of them. In the candletime the snow is dry and whitened, unlike Ireland where winter is wet and brown. Ah, London. Such a city! I've walked it all. So very many casually wealthy people around and so many determinedly poor. The Lordly and the Abject. London lives for them both – in almost equal measure. Their province and their right. Though as Mick as Mick can be, I don't feel at all foreign in traipsing these streets. It's a city of foreigners anyway. Hardly an Anglo-Saxon face to be seen. Good old egalitarian England! Arabs, Africans, Americans, West Indians, East Indians, Germans, Pakistanis, Jews, Chinese, Japanese, French, Scottish, Irish and, doubtless, a liberal deposit of the fucking Welsh. Don't get me wrong. It's no bad thing but compared to that lot I'm St FuckingGeorgehimself!

Now, which is your London? Which is the city that you know? Rich-poor, North-South, East-West, up-down, in-out? Me, I know them all. The lot. All those different, differing Londons. Golders Green, Muswell Hill, Chiswick, Chelsea, Camden, Kennington, Finchley, Fulham, Rotherhithe, Richmond, Notting Hill and Bethnal Green. I know them all.

I know these places as a tramp. As a watcher. That's what trampdom gives you – audience status; the observer's, the artist's overview. We tramps, we watch you all – and listen too. Rude perhaps but we've got bugger all else to do.

London is a whole different, exclusive city for us tramps. The most differing of all those listed Londons. It's much bigger for a start, the trampcity, though, paradoxically, its geography is more minute, more precise. The scale is increased but the mapping is concentrated. Tramps know the city in its smallest essence. They know its stones, its pipes and bricks and doorways and pavements. We sleep on them after all. I mean, think for a moment how well the average person is acquainted with his or her bed. Right? Well, there you are. That's how well we know the streets of our city. That's the beggar's ground-level slice of London, his close-up, his particularised urban view. I've felt the friendliness of the pavement. I've felt the chase and lull of sleep in its impermeable embrace. I'm not complaining, believe me. Eventually, at the arse-end of endurance and hardships most things have their saving graces, their quirks, their own peculiar charms.

Now, most tramps have their patch, their ground. They form grimy communities and rot in precarious union. Me, I wander. I flit hither and thither. I'm not one of these snobbish, conformist tramps. I'll try anywhere once. You could say that I sleep around in my own small way. I stay alone, it's true, but that is the way I like it to be. Anyway, tramp cliques are volatile things. Down and outs are always trying to kill one another for some reason and sometimes they succeed. They're greedy bastards too and I must say that nothing depresses me quite so much as the spectacle of avarice in my fellow-man. They have no conversation either. I don't know if you've noticed but eloquence is rarely their strong point. Pantpissing they can manage but the merest whiff of intellectual debate leaves them helpless. Okay, so it may be that malnutrition, disease and deprivation are not ideal academic aids but these guys don't even seem to try, for goodness' sake!

(The worst thing about tramps is, of course, that they smell so fucking bad.)

Don't mistake me. I have nothing against tramps. It's just that I occasionally feel that they've got themselves into a rut.

The chill of the grubby night now begins to weave its icy threads around my faltering heart. Weatherwise, I'm all heart these days. Temperature falls, depressions and cold fronts reverberate and frolic in my cardiac pathetic fallacy. It's a worry. Summer must come soon. It *will* come! I know that well enough. I mustn't fret myself. Yes. At this welcome thought, the very street lamps assume an amicable, shabby twinkle for my melancholy, for my lonely eyes.

It suddenly comes to me that I am hungry. Well, perhaps 'hungry' is not quite the right word. Bowelwitheringly fucking ravenous might well be a more just and measured phrase to describe what I am currently experiencing. All right, so I'm a young man and, no doubt, prone to the overstatement of youth but this is the real thing. This is the actual, veritable item. Hunger is hitting me hard. Hunger is tickling me with a crowbar and Hunger is enjoying it. Have I already mentioned the fact that I haven't eaten in more than three days? Big deal, you'll be saying, I've had worse than that! Well — four days ago I hadn't eaten for five days and I grew so fucking desperate that I picked a half-eaten hamburger out of a litter bin, cleaned the grit off and wolfed it down with relish. (The enjoyment kind not the condiment kind.) How about that, then? Eh? I bet you wish you hadn't opened your mouth now. (N.B. I was so ashamed and disgusted that I almost immediately boked it all up again and haven't tried it since.)

Anyway, back to my present little pangs. I think I've done pretty well up to now. I've suffered in something close to silence. Which is big of me (and uncharacteristic). Your actual attenuation is a weird and many-faceted thing. It goes in stages. (I've never actually gone more than a fortnight without food so my expertise is of necessity limited. Any more extensive and I'd be blind or mad or dead.)

First, you ache dully for a day or so. Your abdomen is swollen and taut, you belch prodigiously and seem to have more saliva than you know what to do with. We all know that hunger. Between-meal hunger, fast-hunger, travel-hunger, diet-hunger even. It's a doddle. Easypeasy. Just not a problem. Then you hit a nice upward curve of comfort and strength. As your brain chews over the last of its glucose, your wits are sharpened, your mind clears. Your thoughts and words are airy, dashing, pyrotechnic in scope and beauty. You write poems, play probability and find three separate cures for cancer.

This is good. This is fun. But then Agony sticks a knobbly great pole up your arse and waves it around in your already stretching abdomen. Half a day of festive screeching and this passes . . . thankfully. Not stopping for a moment, you move onto another plateau of tranquillity. You are unaccountably happy. Not even the dullard intrusion of encroaching brain death can disturb this new serenity. You know and welcome all. Macrocosm and microcosm. You have a great aerial breadth of wisdom and reparation. You are the Hunger Philosopher with the seer's bowl of vision and sagacity. God comes and speaks to you.

Agony interrupts and rapes you violently. Thirty minutes later you give birth to a combine harvester with blades a-spinning and you cough up what looks like your major intestine. It slithers away to a new life in the sun before you can catch it.

And just as you think you've had it, just as you think you're all finally fucked-up, the calm comes again. It's a slow calm now. A coma-calm. Time stretches and you foray into Hippyland. Perception and intelligence take a little holiday somewhere out of the way and you wallow in feeble peace. You don't care very much about what happens to you at this point and you may well find yourself trying to sleep on motorways, etc. just about now. Don't worry though, with the state that you're in you need all the careless-ness you can jolly well muster.

Whoops! But what's this? Why, stap me vitals, it's old Agony again! He is truly pissed off now and desires to do you harm. He starts off with a spot of resolute bowelboiling before going to work on your stomach wall with a brillo pad. In a moment of inspiration, he ties your pancreas to your bladder with a cheesewire. You crumple and stay that way. Your legs drop off and when you essay to put them back, they don't seem to fit. You improvise and fall over.

It passes. You wouldn't think so but it does.

Having reduced options, your brain decides on a little scrambling. Neurons collide and tumble against your throbbing skullbone. You come over all esoteric. Phantasmagoria is the name of the game now and suddenly Kafka seems like P.G. Wodehouse. The Devil comes to call as a fetchingly giant spider with suppurating boils and diarrhoea sweat. His monstrous, quivering maw pouts invitingly at you as he squats in his own shimmering, steaming obscenity. Aroused now, he snogs with you for a while before lunching on your lungs and liver . . .

Et cetera . . .

Bad, eh?

Actually, the thing about starvation that most people don't realise is that if you ignore your hunger it sulks and goes away. Up to a point. After a while, of course, you die. You really, truly die. I mean, don't try it – it's not much fun.

Wow, that helped! I feel a lot better for that. The vacant claxon of my gut has hushed its noise. For this relief much thanks.

Well, that's just about it for Hunger. Apart, of course, from the terrible endocrinal, subchemical mess it gets your poor old body into. This we can imagine. Who needs to know that? With Hunger such a permanent and stalwart companion, I prefer to ward it off with the extremes of optimism and ignorance. What you don't know *can* actually hurt you quite prodigiously but what you've never *had*, you never do miss. Or, more precisely, what you haven't eaten, you can't chuck up. Anyhow, hunger's horrible but here to stay.

Twinkling, the stars twinkle. Somebody else's suns, I'm told. Other solar systems. Other skin cancers. Sunnily, shine they for others. Starrily, glimmer they for earthly old us.

> Twinkle twinkle, little star,
> Don't give a toss to what you are,
> Up above the world so high,
> Like shiny acne in the sky.

I'm heading for Tottenham Court Road now. This appears to me a more suitable venue for my life, awash as it is with the tack of Japan and America, all unEnglish and steeped in grotbaggery. As I walk, I pass the time by observing the tricky patterns of my legs and feet. I admire the graceful crumpling lines and wrinkles of my old black trousers. My old shoes too. Last of their type, mattblack and toesharp. They fire my feet, these nimble and courageous shoes. (I'm jolly well-dressed for a tramp, don't you know?) As I watch these change-and-change-again feet of mine, a pleasant stupidity begins to throb and glow in the marrow of my brainbone. Hunger has receded and Exhaustion is a keen substitute with a lot to prove. I have a faint and inarticulate desire to go on walking through the night under the cool and restful beauty of all this street lamp. I stumble, nearly ending up on my arse. My mind snaps reluctantly back to life, the optimistic bastard. I walk on.

Yes. Tottenham Court Road. The glisten and electric tremble of the twentieth century. Nearly ten o'clock, I see. Beyond the halogen-halo and the stutter of LED, the sky glows in a splendid moonlit curve, peppered by the blueblack whorls of evil clouds. Under its canopy, Tottenham Court Road suddenly transfigures, growing to a fantastic avenue of squalid mystery and wickedness. A sneaky filament of moonspangled tarmac and paving stone. Upon which walk I, the grateful suscipient.

I'm good-looking for a tramp as well. The blight of deprivation and bad living hasn't yet taken its toll of my appearance. I look rather rough, true, but no more than that. A little casual, a mite shabby, quite dirty. That's all. Tall, young and straight, I contradict the generally accepted image of the all-purpose vagabond. Though pale and more than a little ragged, my face is lean, clean and has low wind resistance, good planes and pleasing curves.

Apart from the stubble, the drag co-efficient is practically zero. It's true that under that stubble I have a haggard look but on me I consider it rather modish, fashionable almost. Blow me, most movie stars would give their false back teeth for the kind of lived-in look that I possess. I've got it sown up. I have.

My eyes are good too. Special eyes, they are. Greenly green. Simply, completely green. They tell another tale, do my tasty eyes. They stun and surprise. They beguile and fascinate. Much is the womanly bullshit that has been spouted about my eyes (mostly by me). You'd like my eyes. Me, I try to ignore my eyes. They can be a drag.

Yes, I sure am a clochard beau. My health has just about held out enough for appearance's sake. I get by, so to speak. I don't look like the sick man I am. Nor like the sick tramp I am.

Oh my health is bad. My health is poor. My health is blinkin' 'orrible! For one so young, I am quite astoundingly in a bad way. I'm anorexic, jaundiced and febrile. I'm toxic, necrotic and inflamed. My mouth is fissured and scaly, my lips stiff and intermittently scabrous. The menu of my nutritional defects is inviting – mouth-watering. My anaemias, beriberi and cheilosis while away many happy hours and I suffer constant epigastric tortures. My belly distends and contracts at will, rather like an accordion. My spongy, alternatively igneous abdomen has invented new diseases and novel agonies. Hypoglycaemia, steatorrhea, gastritis and oesophagitis are cheery chums of mine. These light-hearted fellows combine in arias of discomfort and danger. And, oh, does my poor heart weep at all this! Bradychardia is hardly the word for my snailpace pulse and the soft, distant plops of my vague cardiovascular dithering. My vomit is utterly unspeakable and I'd prefer *not* to talk about my teeth.

Yes, I'm pretty badly off when it comes to the issue of health. I hate to think of what kind of pathological paragon I'll be by the time I'm thirty. I don't like to go on about it like this but this health business is the main thing when you're down and out. This is the vital question, the big issue. This is the staple and foundation of tramply policy. This is our manifesto.

How has this happened? Why have I let myself come to this? Why?
Let me tell you. Give me time. Listen. You'll see.

FOUR

In my boyhood, the sky was bright and clear, spilling its jewelled smiles into my widening windows. Mad September wasps fought lunatic dogfights in my days and suffered, frenzied deaths at my experimental hand. The harboured dust of gravelled paths sprinkled my classroom steps. The Sacred Heart Primary School for Catholic Boys – woodbrown and sunpale. Old blackboards, chalked and musty. The venerable breadth of childhood. The tributes of the many wandering boyhoods that had been tricked out in this place. What gutsy scenarios I played out there! Lulled by the delicious boredom of school. Mind tickled by the once wordly figures of antiquity and legend (I had a youthful crush on Demosthenes for some obscure reason).

The sum of boyhood is always elegiac and patchy. Half-held traces of cloudless aspiration. Quick pictures. Same for me. Dusty days in granite playgrounds when I tried to understand the passing of time but gave myself a headache, so big and strange it seemed. Playing football after school while light grew dim and cast dramatic shadows on those walls. Gritbound lanes, where I waited for my life to form; events to come from uneventful haze of childhood wonder and confusion. Boy oh boy, the endless possibilities and comeliness of inexperience. Epiphanies galore!

You know, it took years for them to discover what a fucking genius I was! Hard to believe but true. I managed to bullshit my way up to the age of eight before they found me out. They were fooled by my adroit assumptions of righteous idiocy, my well-researched autistic eccentricities, my stalwart bedwetting and judicious charades of illiteracy. They despaired at the impenetrable slatemist of my abnormality. They plotted, they planned. Briefly, they sent me to a special school for the Educationally Disadvantaged. I wasn't clever enough and was sent back almost immediately.

It goes without saying that my lice-ridden ratbag of a mother couldn't give a toss. Imbecility was not something to bother Betty Bogle. She had a cloudy presentiment that I was perpetuating clan traditions.

Needless to say, I was a genius all the while. I had read the entire works of Dickens and Thackeray when I was five years old and had spent the rest of that year taping up most of the literary output of the nineteenth century. (Perhaps that's why my style is so florid, so rotund, so fucking courtly.) Then I throttled Shakespeare, Webster, Marlowe and Spenser (propping them up on my nappy while I read). I moved onto that Hellenic thing before dipping into a little amateur astrophysics. My baby teeth were still going strong when I began to investigate Nihilism. Orwell, Camus, Sartre, Mann and Eliot depressed me a little I admit, but I was only six years old so I recovered. I had already researched the Epicureans pretty thoroughly anyway, so I was laughing hedonismwise! Higher Maths caused me one or two problems, I concede, but I decided that it could wait until I was, say, ten. I mean, I had to pace myself. As a seven year old I laughed at Freud, giggled at Jung, sniggered at Lawrence, guffawed at Woolf, cackled at Barthes and gave Bertrand Russell a pretty hard time of it.

Perhaps I was precocious.

Explanations? Yes, I think you deserve some of those. Perhaps my prodigious intellectual gifts do indeed merit a little casual background information. There are two. Explanations, that is.

One

As a child I suffered from a complete inability to ignore the written word. It might have been some quirky visual defect or wily kink in the smooth surface of my brain but whatever it was – I read *everything*. Tout! The whole lot. Shop signs, newspapers, posters, timetables, instruction manuals, cornflake packets, jamjar labels, scraps of magazines rescued from the dusty greed of the street. Everything. I had this febrile, insatiable hunger for script and my mind would bubble and race horribly if I had nothing to read. Perhaps I *was* potty after all.

Two

The second cause is much simpler. First we had the demand then we had the supply. My thirst for words led me to the Public Library on the Lower Falls Road (a surprisingly imposing building). There my literary needs and the light-fingered dexterity that I claimed as a family right combined. Now, I couldn't steal from the Children's Section. No chance! The psychotic hag librarians there were well onto that one. However, in the Adults' Section it was a vastly different story. There, I was above, or rather below, suspicion. What could be less worthy of vigilance than a stunted, noisome ghetto-urchin comme moi wandering aimlessly through woodenshelved avenues bordered with all that's weighty in Literature and Philosophy? You get the picture? Easy pickings. With all my Bogleian adroitness and tenacity, I practically emptied the shelves. By God, what an education that place gave me! Illegal but extensive. When I had read these tomes I would bury them in a neighbour's garden with the aid of a soup ladle and an old, splintered cricket bat. Miraculously, no one ever discovered me in the midst of this operation and I was able to proceed with my underground educational dealings, more or less unmolested. And so I improved myself – which was a bloody good job as no one had the remotest intention of doing it for me. (Gripe, gripe, grizzle grizzle.)

So, you'll say, if I was such a colon-bursting prodigy, why did I take all that trouble to hide it? Why did I pursue this policy of demonstrative imbecility? Why didn't I come out of the closet, do a few game shows, win awards and make a little dosh?

Well, it occurred to me that if they ever discovered what a genius I was, they'd stomp my head off, they'd boil my balls and roast my bottom off. Yes, yes, I know I was a paranoid infant, I know all that – but guess what! Mmm? I was right. When they did find out, they *did* try to do all those things to me. Christ, they hated me. Now, just why was that?

This is what happened.

Classroom. Late morning. There we were, thirty-four assorted hunchbacks, cripples and idiots learning to read under the pedagogical eye of the aptly named Mr Samson. Dear God, that man was a brute! He used to arm-wrestle us for our pocket money, cheat openly and then threaten to twist our heads off if we told anyone. He was a complete bas⁺ard. Anyway, there we were, boiling in the microwave splay of our basement classroom, trudging through some goggle-eyed kiddies' book when all of a sudden the word 'copper' came up. It happened. Mr Fate came a-calling. Samson decided to open up the debate, the bastard.

SAMSON: Does anyone know what copper is?
(Expecting the answer, 'Brown stuff, sir' – 'What you use in pipes, sir' – 'A coin, sir' – 'A policeman, sir'.)
BOGLE (*brightly*): A mineral, sir.
SAMSON (*patronising*): No, Bogle. It's a metal.
BOGLE: It's a mineral, sir.
SAMSON: Bollocks!
BOGLE: It's not bollocks, sir.
SAMSON (*apoplectic*): Don't you back-answer me, you little shit, you don't even know what a mineral is!
BOGLE (*insanity gripping*): A mineral is a naturally occurring, chemically and physically homogenous, inorganic substance in a solid or liquid state,

having a definite, defined atomic structure. They arise as a result of geological processes unaided by . . . man . . . sir . . .

My voice trailed into silence. There was a soft, rumorous hush as my classmates patiently awaited his verdict. I knew what I had done. I shouldn't have let my secret out like that. Adult censure and distaste was going to come round and sort me out now. Samson himself was gazing at me with distended nostrils, popping eyes and gaping mouth (very unattractive). I felt the control of my life's events slip inexorably away. It was all out of my hands now. Samson vented a wild, blood-curdling screech and charged at me with thunder in his eyes and rage in his heart.

(Hackneyed but true. My life's like that. It has no subtle irony, no gloved wit, no satirist's intent. No dash and little flair. I have to settle for the capitals. Writ in large. Brute broad patches of character and discontent.)

Believe it or not, I was whopped into an ambulance and rushed to the Royal Victoria Hospital! Harper, the boss kiddie shrink (consultant child psychiatrist), just loved me to death. He congratulated my school for their prompt action. I was a bad case and worsening. A highly disturbed child. Obviously my unwonted intellectual precocity was just the tip of the jolly old iceberg as far as my neurotic disorders went (which was quite a long way according to him). With pearly eyes and smiling teeth, he began to make therapeutic plans for me.

I was sent to another special school once a week. Here the educationally subnormal and the exceptionally gifted were taught together in a fever of experimental egalitarianism. There we were, morons and geniuses, kicking the shit out of each other whenever possible. Great things were achieved. Kierkegaard was debated with illiterates and precocious polyglots were taught about the English alphabet with the aid of picture cards. All good stuff.

When Mumsy heard about this novel talent of mine she refused to believe it. She had enough humility to be astonished that a product of her low-grade womb could be anything other than troglodytic. When she eventually accepted it, she persisted in seeing it as lasting proof of my reasonless enmity and defiance. Naturally (and perhaps commendably) she used this new grievance as the excuse for a whole new series of vilifications and enthusiastic beatings.

In addition, there were hazardous diplomatic implications at school. I had always been popular on account of my ugliness and this was fading (the popularity, that is, the ugliness seemed there to stay). No one likes a genius. I began to get into fights which, to my surprise, I usually won. Exhibiting pugilistic skill on top of my mental gifts was tactless. I was due for a fall. I was challenged by D. Stark.

D. Stark was the best fighter in the school. Though barely twelve years old he was already five feet and nine inches tall. He had started shaving (I swear, honestly!) and even had a respectable number of hairs on his chest about which he affected a great lack of concern. He was big cheese and he felt that he could scarcely afford to ignore my new fame. There was room for only one School Phenomenon. There would have to be a contest of arms.

So, D. Stark delivered his gage in the traditional manner of the warriors of our school, i.e. by gobbing thickly and wetly on the crown of my skull. D. Stark's mastery of this form of challenge was abetted by the fact that he had been smoking forty cigarettes a day since he was seven years old. His goads were always distinctive and marvellously adhesive.

On the day, I suspect that D. Stark had some qualms about tackling an opponent so much younger, smaller and less psychopathic than himself. As he watched me in my tinyness, dancing and weaving, his scruples dissolved. His honour was at stake. With heavy heart and weighty executioner's hand, he moved in.

It was a debacle. D. Stark was a monster. Even Samson was scared of D. Stark. It was rumoured that he used to hang his father out of an upstairs window when he wanted fag money. The man was a brute. He mashed me. He minced me. He bounced me off walls and tarmac, he cracked my ribs like cardboard and punched my gob into a pulp. He went to town and back again. I was off school for three weeks.

To do him justice, my dad was actually pretty impressed. He felt that this was more like the manly order of things and even Big Betty was less violent than usual. When they learnt that in the middle of all the Bogle-butchery I had, by some incredible fluke, managed to dislodge one of D. Stark's teeth, a little parently pride managed to bluff its way into their grimy breasts.

Back at school, it was more of the same. Standing toe to toe with D. Stark was seen alternatively as the pinnacle of human courage or the very nadir of imbecility. On either count, my peers felt, that made me worthy of note. Even D. Stark himself grew rather friendly. He would give me cigarettes at breaktime and there we would sit – me green-faced and choking, him serenely smokesoiled.

(I suppose at this point I should say something like – 'My word, I wonder whatever happened to old D. Stark' – but that's easy and trim in the telling. After a short but successful life of trouble, crime, squalor and a half-hearted association with Sinn Fein, D. Stark was shot dead by an army foot patrol in the Ardoyne. Like I always say – people shouldn't knock me about.)

Oh yes, those Troubles! Those nasty Irish things! The Northern Irish Conflict certainly did its bit for the decoration of my early years. I made damned sure that I got a good seat. I needed the material and it came to me early and gratis (mostly). They served it up to me and I fell to with a will and a half.

I spent a great deal of my childhood seeing things that I shouldn't have seen and making the acquaintance of uncomfortable notions that certainly could have waited a decade or so for their entrance. Murder, violence, blood, guts and sundry other features of Irish political life tend to telescope one's development a little as you can imagine. You zip along to cynicism – blink and you'd miss it. For me, the beginning was Internment Night.

You've heard of Internment, I presume. No? Well, look it up. It's a good one. I must say, I had a hugely profitable Internment Night one way or another.

In common with the majority of the Catholic working-class population of the city of Belfast, we Bogles were raided on Internment Night. Just before two o'clock in the morning, the front door of our squalid little house was kicked in by four hard-faced, anxious young soldiers. (At least, I presume they were hard-faced and anxious – I was in bed at the time.) Apparently, these soldiers were polite, even slightly diffident as they separated in order to ransack our ghastly, microscopic hovel. Daddybuns was as usual elsewhere and probably pissed and thus the Bogle materfamilias was able to give free rein to her violent indignation. Naturally, she did this with all her accustomed verve and gusto. The unfortunate militia hadn't really banked on this frothing harpy and they seemed distinctly less than chuffed to be there. A miserable young lieutenant was left to deal with the by now apoplectic Betty while the others hurried off to search round the old homestead.

When the combined might of Her Majesty's Armed Forces crashed into my bedroom, my excitement knew no bounds. I looked up as the light was switched abruptly on. Imagine my amazement and joy when I beheld a massive West Indian corporal standing at my bedroom door brandishing a large automatic rifle. My untutored blood raced with elation. I had never seen a real black man before and now I had one standing, albeit rather sheepishly, in my own tiny and familiar bedroom. Boy, was I chuffed or what! He brought a breath of exotic and dangerous glamour to me. The man remained motionless and embarrassed for some moments while I felt my eyes grow moist with love. Uncertain, he tried a feeble wink and his teeth smiled whitely in his tactile, ebony face before he abruptly disappeared from view.

Well, after all this excitement I could hardly try to sleep now. I slithered towards my still open door. I could hear shouts coming from downstairs, the business-like grunts of the soldiers mingling with the insistent bellow of my deranged mother. I felt an instant's pity for the unsuspecting soldiers. Then I heard my little brothers begin to screech and wail in remarkable unison and my pity doubled. Poor old Brits. Not the sort of palaver you expect when you're trying to suppress the natives a little. However, this was all much too good to miss. I slid furtively down the little staircase leading to the tumult.

I paused in the hall. My ragged pyjamas were but thin and the cold air was blowing harshly through the large hole where our front door had once been. I crept towards it. To my joy, I could see the cul-de-sac outside, a swelling hive of activity. The whole string of tawdry little houses that were Monagh Parade were lit up by the implacable glare of the headlights of the army jeeps and Saracens which were lined up at the bottom of the cul-de-sac. And there were soldiers everywhere. Soldiers with blackened faces running into unlit, sleeping houses and dragging half-dressed men out into the waiting Saracens; soldiers crouched behind walls and lamp posts, rifles poised and aimed; soldiers shouting; soldiers punching; soldiers kicking; lots of soldiers doing their soldierly thing while the screams and execrations of frenzied women dinned the tepid night air.

I sneaked gladly into that curtain of din, bustle and glaring light. I crawled along, underneath the little fence of our tiny front garden. I felt a thrill of illicit freedom, never having been outdoors quite so late before. The air and sky seemed foreign to me, nocturnal inhabitant of my own daytime garden. Keenly, I watched the churning maelstrom of arrest and protest through the gaps in the little fence, feeling well-hidden and marvellously secure. It was almost cosy.

Abruptly, the blissful secrecy of my hiding place was in peril. A young soldier ran up to my fence and crouched down on the other side, hugging close to its flimsy white planks. Though he could easily have stretched his hand to touch me, he seemed unaware of my presence. My hardy blood checked still and frozen-calm. My face was scarcely inches from the massy, fatigue-clad figure, weighted and bulky with a vast array of curious, nameless military equipment. I could see the inarticulate knobs and catches on his dull blackandbrown rifle as it was aimed at Sean O'Grady's house on the far side of the open square. We both watched as Sean's father was dragged out to the Saracens. I knew that it was an SLR that the soldier carried because I had heard some boys at school discussing the merits of the British Army's Small Firearms Issue:

'Nowhere near as good as an armalite!'

'Yes, it is.'

'Come on, an armalite can blow your head right off, like squashing an apple!'

28

'But the Paras put dum-dums in their SLRs. Cut you in half as quick as look at you!'

I wondered if the young man whose cold, acrid breath whipped my face was a 'Para'. I wasn't as adept as the other boys in distinguishing the various regiments but many were the tales of relished atrocity that I had heard of these Paras. I trembled violently. The walkie-talkies clipped on the soldier's breast suddenly erupted into a dry cackle. I started violently, as one might, very nearly disclosing my presence. As the young soldier listened to the inarticulate sounds issuing tinnily from his chest, I was over-whelmed by the strangeness of crouching in the dark so close yet unknown to this man. I peered at this supposed enemy of mine. As the mysteries of war and hatred welled in my boy's mind, I felt a dreamy, veiled tenderness for the youth whose soft breath moistened my face. Close enough to kill, I could sense the birth of power and fear in my own warrior's heart. (I think I'd just been checking out D.H. Lawrence again.)

Suddenly I heard a muffled noise coming from the Ginchys' house next door. I turned quickly to see a small, ghostly female figure disappear into the long striped shadows that ran along the side of the Ginchy house. I knew that this would be Muire Ginchy and I knew what she was going to do. To walk her tightrope of barbed wire. Her party piece. She was always showing off to me by walking along the barbed wire on her father's fence. She had never done this in the dark.

The soldier's ears twitched with a doggy alertness when he heard the sound. He froze in fear and shouted to his sergeant. Suddenly, two huge soldiers vaulted out of the darkness over my head, crashing noisily to the ground in front of our parlour window, their guns and boots clattering in a loud, confused hymn of danger and fear. They crouched warily while my soldier joined them. I hid still, undiscovered, inches away from their sturdy, threatblackened boots.

'What is it?' the sergeant asked.

The young soldier answered with an obviously burgeoning sense of his own importance.

'I saw one of them trying to get away. He went along the side of the house next door. I think he had a gun.'

The sergeant took over quickly.

'Right, you go on through the back door of this place. Take the lads inside with you. We'll go round the side ... we'll give you about forty-five seconds.'

My soldier clattered enthusiastically into the Bogle domicile. I felt sick with panic. Forty-five seconds. It was only Muire Ginchy walking her tight-rope of fence and gate. Showing off, that was all. All those soldiers and guns! I realised with reluctance that I would have to speak. I couldn't just leave her to them. I couldn't do that.

'Excuse me, mister . . .' I squeaked.

'Christ!'

An angry torch was flashed onto my terrified face and a panicked rifle butt was thrust into my minor chest. One of the soldiers yelped in terror. However, luckily for me, the nimble sergeant quickly perceived my extreme youth.

'Catch a grip of yourself, for Christ's sake! He's only a kid.' He turned towards me. 'What are you up to, sonny?'

Fear and horror seemed to melt my bowels and I could feel the first warm trickle of urine greeting my thigh.

'It's only Muire, mister.'

'What?'

'It's only Muire.'

'What are you talking about?'

'Round the back there. She's only a wee girl.'

Again the burly sergeant was quick to comprehension and he reacted sharply. He shouted into the open doorway of our house.

'Wilson! Wilson! It's just a little girl . . . Wilson? Oh, shit.'

He careered round the side of the house followed by the other soldier and myself. As we reached our large back garden there was a wild burst of confusion as bright torch shafts streaked the moonless black of the scene. Knowing my own garden well, I was able to cut through the stumbling mass of soldiers to where I knew Muire would be. I saw her. Standing high on the fence, her tiny draped figure stamped against the vague, looming glow of the Black Mountain. I saw Wilson just beneath her, gun raised. For a moment they were both still, their silhouettes framing a slow tableau of weird dusky beauty. Then I heard the soldier's rifle click and shunt, ready to fire and I rushed madly towards him, bellowing with fury. Muire screamed, her body seemed to twist in terror and she slipped, dropping straight down, her open legs straddling the barbed wire.

Of course, because of Internment, the ambulance was a long time in coming. Or so they said as we waited. At least Muire had stopped screaming by this time. Now the only sounds were Mrs Ginchy's dead voice telling her daughter that it was going to be all right and the agonised sobbing of the soldier called Wilson.

'I'm sorry. I'm sorry . . . I'm so sorry.'

His face was spattered with tears, black camouflaging grime and smears of the bright blood of the child he had cradled when she had fallen. The other soldiers were quiet. They stood apart, feverishly waiting for the ambulance to come so that they could leave. One squaddie cradled a furtive cigarette in the crook of his hand.

A captain had arrived on the scene. A handsome young man, crested by the impossible glamour of a peaked cap. He stood near me, whispering to the attentive sergeant who still kept his firm grip on my shoulder. I somehow understood that the nature of little Muire's injuries in some way appalled these men, investing them with a helpless kind of chivalry. I tried to mirror their reactions though in truth I could not see what was so *very* terrible about it. I felt sorry for Muire and all the wet, red blood that she had dripped. Very sorry. But I was confused. I wondered why her mother wasn't angry. Why was she smiling at her daughter like that? No bitterness.

By the time the ambulance had taken Muire and her mother away the commotion in the cul-de-sac had died down and I could see, to my great excitement, paleness begin to seep across the sky from behind the mountain, signalling my very first witnessed dawn. The soldiers had drifted off apologetically, depressed and shaken. Already I missed their brief glamour. In a wonderful moment, the sergeant had told my raging mother that I was a good brave lad and he had even given me a pound. Pride had swelled in my Irish heart though I still felt rather subdued about Muire. When the soldiers had finally left, my mother took the pound from me and threw it away hurriedly. Wisely, I said nothing. Dawn grumbled and spread across the sleepless city, bleating new life into the ragged dustbin-clanging protests of the night. Internment had begun.

I wonder what old Muire Ginchy is doing these days. She's no record-breaking matriarch, for sure. I think we can definitely rule that one out, gynaecologically speaking. Sad – when you think about it. She's probably just a rancid, hard-eyed Irish tart like the rest of them now. Belfast does that to you. Thickens your body and your brains. Chases your soul away.

Pity though. I liked Muire. I even had a vague prepubescent crush on her. She was a nice kid – and cute too. A show off, true, but she didn't deserve the humbling she got.

Who do we blame for that? Young Wilson? Me? Anyone? No, I don't think any of those fit this bill. I prefer to blame Belfast. It's all Belfast's fault. Something should be done. Belfast shouldn't be allowed to get away with this kind of thing. Belfast has to be stopped. Its time will come.

I hope.

FIVE

Embankment. Another bench – another rest. Another caress for arse and woodrot. Benches punctuate my homeless peregrinations. Little wooden harbours of some thing like safety and ease. You know, I *do* like the Embankment. I like the way the bridges strut and glitter over the slop and slither of the sewer Thames. Especially old Westminster Bridge. That bridge certainly has what it takes. A pretty cool bridge – as bridges go. Sometimes, these part-time lights are shining in the under-arches and they illumine slat, beam and water in the most attractive manner. The brown of the river and the green of the bridge merges in this chocolatemintish pool of fluid sparkle. These lights aren't actually switched on tonight but I can live with that.

There is in fact rather a lot of glitter around the Embankment. It's a tawdry reminiscent kind of glitter, true, but these are the nineteen eighties. We've all got our problems these days. Glitter's no real help.

Tonight, the air is sharp and clogging and my orphaned hands are chafed and stiff with cold. I have put them in my pockets which seems to have made little appreciable difference. That's the nasty thing about the night time. It's always so frigging cold. Yes, nights are cold but at least they are dark and wide.

So, who is it that cares about the darkness and the width? Me, I care. These things are important to me. This nightly broadscreen scene gives me my space, my embarrassment of elbowroom. The gap for my memories to fill.

And lo, here they come, crowning and jostling around my moistened bench. They have a grievance, they want to be heard. They heckle and harry. Beside them, live and deadly, the thick water is riverbanked, curdling like cream. On this night, the agreeable, suppedcity is ours.

Listen, I have a series of mental pictures of my changing, nasty self at various points along my climb to and slide from grace. Let me share these snapshots with you. Please. Albumfodder. Three of them, they form a witty, representative trio. This is the first. Me at my boyish best. Childtime.

Limber, dartsharp, he runs and walks. In speckled-brown zip-up cardigan; sky-blue canvas bell-bottoms with stretch anchor-clasp belt; mauve, blue and white hooped football shirt; one grey and one green sock; in cheap, blunt-toed outsize black shoes, he struts his stylish. Carroty head and fluff face. Mean little winkle eyes and opulent warts. He farts and belches recklessly, aiming for volume in both. His knees are crusty and hard from soccer and his arse bruised from the fruits of malefaction. His smile is snaggle-toothed and moronic. He plots over stinkbombs, catapults and moggie tortures. He is free from discernment and experience. He is frankly revolting. He wishes he had been a king with a brother called Richard whom he could insult at great length and never ever suffer for it.

As I did the business of growing, the membership of my family increased apace until, all told, we numbered eight. Seven boys and one girl. My one sister, Patricia, contributed massively to my earliest experiences of death by conveniently dying. She died at the age of three of an ailment mysteriously described as a hole in her heart. I was appalled and unconvinced. It didn't sound very scientific to me. I don't remember much about my sister but I vaguely recall that she was pretty though thin and linenpale. She looked nothing like the rest of us Bogles. We were the epitome of the worst kind of urchin-guttersnipe breed but Patricia was different. Maybe that was why she died. Maybe she couldn't face a Bogleian childhood, perhaps she didn't like the Irish either. I don't know.

I remember the funeral well. In a moment of sympathy, old Ma Ginchy had slipped me a bag of Danish boiled sweets. Mother of Christ, they were delicious! For some reason the wrappers had pictures of cows wandering through meadows, presumably of the Danish variety, and this absorbed me disproportionately. Children's coffins are a piece of cutesie, aren't they? Patricia's was tiny, startling, incongruous. It had a bad effect on all the adults, the size of her coffin. Particularly my mother who, to do her justice, seemed rather more than cut up about the whole thing.

As the other youthful Bogles exhibited no particular tendencies towards following their only sister, I continued to enjoy their unabated companionship. Peter, Patrick, John, Paul, George and Declan. (The latter always seemed the most cruel to me – I had it bad but little beats a tag like Declan Bogle!) They were an unremarkable lot, largely inheriting the traditional Bogle characteristics of preternatural stupidity and petty criminality.

George, the second eldest, broke several family records by having his fingerprints recorded by the police at the tender age of eight. He was always the promising clan favourite.

My father's extensive research into dipsomania also increased with the years. Surrendering even the merest airy concept of looking for a job, he became a full-time and talented drunk, the hope of his fondest years. I liked him better for it. His moods were more predictable – less intemperate and at least he seemed less eager to beat the shit out of me the whole time. I know that I'm hard on my father but then I owe him so very little. The only thing the Welsh bastard ever gave me was my ridiculous, my brilliant name.

So, Betty Bogle continued her struggles against material adversity largely unaided by her husband. She was awfully good at this. Though she had no job, she managed to amass a very respectable income by dint of her many fraudulent social security claims. Here is a probable pointer to the real source of my unusual intellectual gifts. The imagination and creativity which my mother devoted to her deception of the welfare authorities was a highly edifying example to her entire breed and myself in particular. These exercises of imagination mainly involved the nimble use of wigs and false addresses in the maintenance of her various noms de plume. We younger Bogles did our bit by multiplying ourselves in the most alarming manner and retaining enough youthful *froideur* to answer to the multitude of names we had been assigned to support Mrs Bogle's claims to have mothered anything up to eighteen children. Though daring, these claims were generally unchallenged due to the tremendous difficulty in gathering enough of the slippery Bogles into any one place in order to establish a reliable headcount.

The other branches of the Bogle clan were not prospering quite as much as we – partly due to the fact that most of their menfolk (such as they were) had been imprisoned on Internment Night. Goodness knows why the British Army went to such considerable expense and trouble to incarcerate a shower of imbeciles, degenerates and wastrels – but there they were – in Long Kesh. With its barbed wire, its turrets, its cell blocks and all that sort of thing. (At the time I thought it was all because of some obscure parliamentary grudge against Bogles in general. This would have been excusable, perhaps even laudable.) As a matter of fact, in arresting the run of defectives and worse that made up the Men of Bogle, the security forces had actually managed to net one object of legitimate interest in the shape of my interesting uncle, Mr Joe Bogle. Uncle Joe was a layabout like the others but he had once been part of one of the Civil Rights marches and had even been spotted chucking some bricks during a riot on Castle Street.

I loved visiting time in Long Kesh. (Or the Maze to you Brits. Names are important in Ulster, like Derry/Londonderry names show your creed. They're an oath, a cry of allegiance. Aspirate your aitches in the wrong place in Belfast and you end up with a rope around your neck.) Yes, visiting the Kesh was fun. There were strip searches for civilians and I always entertained lustful hopes of being allowed to go through the women's section on account of my tender years. It was, however, not to be. I was always shoved in with the blokes and had to endure the brunt of fat, sweating men with their odours and strange sprouts of hair and flesh.

Like most of the other prisoners, Uncle Joe spent most of his time carving exquisite wooden Gaelic harps. The Bogle domain was littered with dozens of these clumsy emblems of solidarity. They were utterly and spectacularly useless until George, my brother, began to make vast sums of money by selling them to American television crews at hugely inflated prices. The rest of Joe Bogle's time in the Kesh was taken up in being recruited for Sinn Fein by the tiny band of actual paramilitaries that the army had managed to nab that night.

After my adventures on Internment Night I had developed a penchant for the nocturnal life. I would steal out of my bedroom window after dark and prowl our booby-trapped neighbourhood. This was incredibly foolish. Turf Lodge at night was an indescribably dangerous place. The miracle was that after evading the bombs and bullets of the estate my luck extended to escaping the knowledge of my mother whose retribution would have been much more gory and unwelcome than anything Turf Lodge could have produced. Later, I smoked properly for the first time under the shadow of the corrugated iron of Fort Monagh, the army camp near our school. My first whole cigarette tasted of the bitterness of experience, my gestures borrowed from the television I rarely saw. My problem was that I enjoyed smoking almost immediately and was pretty soon on twenty a day and rising – or as close to that as I could scrounge. I realised early that cigarettes would play a major role in my life and that many would be the hymns of gratitude and joy that I would sing to Rothmans, Benson & Hedges, to Marlboros, Gallaher's Greens, Regal Number Fives and Embassy Filters.

Turf Lodge was a vile shit heap but it was a marvellous location for the events of my growing up. It has been said by many worthy folk that the more leprous and deadly the childhood environment has been then much the greater will be the genius in adulthood. I believe myself to be the perfect illustration of this theory. I was surrounded by a mêlée of bombs, guns and Irishmen from an early age and have turned out so very well despite it all. Proof of the pudding, I rather think.

The early confusion over loyalties in Turf Lodge was both amusing and instructive. The IRA at that time was split into two groups, the Provies (or

Provisional Wing) and the Stickies (the Official Wing). One group was revolutionary nationalist in its outlook while the other was staunchly Trotskyist in countenance. I was never told which was which never mind what these awesome terms actually meant. Both wings seemed to share the notion that the best way of achieving their disparate aims was to strike an irrevocable blow to the British War Machine by blowing up Marks and Spencer's every Saturday afternoon.

The general effect of this was that whenever the Stickies were in control of Turf Lodge, the region was patrolled by jeepfuls of Stickie gunmen in balaclavas and Provie shops were destroyed and looted. Whenever the Provies were in control, the gunmen wore tights over their heads and the shops that were looted and burnt were Stickie. Thus the only trader to actually make any consistent money was Mr Painter, the Jewish grocer, who, with the proceeds of this profitable arrangement, immediately bought up two vacant shops on the Protestant Shankill Road in the hope of an equally lucrative schism in the Loyalist ranks.

Turf Lodge was fab, groovy and full of fun. The Troubles were terribly old hat to us urchinish fellows. Our only remotely nationalistic contribution was the occasional gleeful stoning of the massive armoured cars that used to dander up the Monagh Road. It could, of course, be terribly thrilling if there was the odd gun battle at night. My father would drag the mattresses downstairs and prop them flopping against the wall and we would huddle cosily on our uncarpeted floors for the night. It was a pleasantly gipsyish sensation with an agreeable spice of danger which only sharpened the ends of our eccentric comfort.

Turf Lodge was also the scene of my first love. I was smitten early. More than smitten. I was decapitated, disembowelled; I was kneecapped by love. I had it bad.

Jeanette Conlon was the object of my first ardent promptings. The Conlons were a grotty bunch of rejects who had recently left the Short Strand under something of a cloud. Jeanette was far from being an attractive little girl but she was all to me. Anyway, I couldn't help but feel that my own glaring physical deficiencies forced upon me a certain humility of choice. I consider that to have been a nicely judged sentiment for one so young. Young Miss Conlon had a lilac-edged gaberdine which beguiled me utterly. When the object of my desire was not actually before me, the only detail of her being that I could recall with any exactitude was this wonderful garment. Lilac and blue, it seemed to me a soft gateway to another world – a world of glamour and promise. Though I was certain that it was Jeanette that I loved, my feelings about this garment caused me some confusion.

I never really got around to actually communicating my passion and the

36

small damsel concerned remained ignorant of the ardour of my silent gaze and the discreet worship of my lonely hours. I would spend hours cycling in a tight circle outside her window, on a borrowed bicycle, in a Christmas mood. Round and round I would struggle until the sky paled and deepened into the dusty splendour of a Turf Lodge evening. I deemed this a quite practical declaration to the comely Jeanette. A satisfactory consummation of our passion. What else could there be?

In truth, I had a pretty fair idea of exactly what else there could be. I was already having a violently enjoyable recurring dream in which, after being hijacked by a group of hairy Protestant desperadoes, myself and the now-naked Jeanette were tied up and forced to rub our fine young buttocks against one another. Though intended to be the direst form of torture, I'm appalled to admit that I found the whole procedure hugely rewarding. Hot stuff, huh?

(Pervy? Probably. But Maurice once told me about his first sexual fantasy. His infantile turpitude makes my efforts look amateur. He dreamt that he was riding along in a full suit of armour, hastening to rescue his young beloved from something unspecific but unpleasant. It doesn't sound like much until you learn that he was naked under his armour and apparently covered in jam! That is disgusting. Such a nice Catholic boy too.)

Jeanette and I never stood much chance of erotic requital. The greater world was beginning to move in and make itself heard. I had already astounded West Belfast by being the first Sacred Heart pupil ever to have passed the eleven plus, scholarships were flooding in and American universities were offering me lectureships. It was announced that I was to attend the Christian Brothers' grammar school on the Glen Road. St Martha's, this dump was called. It was the beginning of the end of my childhood. I spent a last blissful summer lying in the fields under the Black Mountain, trying to dodge the camera crews who wanted to interview me and dreaming languidly of freedom and Jeanette's lilac-edged gaberdine.

St Martha's was not much fun at all. I was very unpopular. As usual, I excelled in all I did but there was none of the affectionate tolerance of my genius that there had been in the Sacred Heart. Even the respect and for-bearance usually accorded to me on account of my extraordinary ugliness was missing. The other kids queued up to take a punch or two at my objectionable noggin. After D. Stark, brawling held no terrors for me and I usually did pretty well considering the fact that my opponents' friends were generally holding me down at the time.

I only had one year at this shithouse and it was a bad one. My father (or at least, Mr Bogle) snuffed it that year. Bleeding into the sink and dribbling messily away (I'll tell you about it later – later). A bad year.

My sojourn at St Martha's came to its end in truly memorable fashion. One afternoon in late May I was walking home from school when I spotted a boyish fray taking place on the roundabout at the top of Kennedy Way. I considered it better not to get involved but the fracas lay almost directly in my path. I walked on with what I hoped was an expression of indomitable purpose on my face.

As I drew closer, I saw that five or six boys of my own age were kicking and punching another boy who was lying curled up on the pavement, his arms trying to ward the blows from his head. Pshaw! I cursed my luck and searched my mind for feasible reasons for not exhibiting the inevitable and costly gallantry. However, though clever, I was not a subtle boy and really had no other option. I charged the little group, swinging my satchel and baying with as much savagery as I could muster. I hoped that this would achieve such a terrible psychological victory as to render actual conflict unnecessary.

Of course, this didn't quite pan out and the five attackers turned to face this new and unexpected onslaught. When they saw that it consisted of myself alone, they stood their ground with some relish. To my horror, I realised that Fate was on my case again – the boys were from my own school. There was nothing I could do. Talking my way out of this one might have proved a little tricky even for an orator like me so I continued on my noisy and self-destructive path. I used their own surprise at my identity to my advantage and launched a rather attractive, arcing punch to the nearest nose. The owner of that organ dropped like a stone, measured his length upon the ground and discreetly remained there for the duration of the engagement. My advantage receding, I executed a blistering kick to the tallest fellow's knee. The youth in question hopped around in a mad caper of rage and agony, clutching his cherished, shattered limb. I decided that this would suffice as an initial skirmish and hopped quickly out of range, dodging several wild, testicle-bound swipes.

Ripley Bogle ... 2   Sectarian Villains ... 0

It occurred to me that the other three might not oblige me with such neat opportunities. I was right. They set upon me in the notoriously effective configuration of three to one. Things looked black indeed for young Bogle until the fellow that they had been assaulting rose to his feet and began to lend me assistance in the most vigorous fashion, employing the cricket bat he had been carrying with great elan and native dexterity. Thus, under our combined onslaught, my cowardly schoolmates were soon vanquished. His wieldy willow blows and my deft punches settled their hash for them.

When it was over I panted hysterically to calm my racing intellectual's heart. I needed a fag. I glanced at my comrade in arms as he surveyed the Catholic wreckage with grim satisfaction.

'Are you all right?' I asked, adopting my modestly heroic voice.

'Yeah.' A coarse, unforgiving accent. He looked at my school tie in surprise. 'You're a Fenian? From the same school as them bastards.'

'Yes.' I smiled in my best ecumenically harmonious manner before going on, 'It makes no difference when it's five against one.'

I felt epic, cowboyish and stern. The hard-faced boy nodded without expression.

'You'd better get them on their feet before the Peelers come, I'm not hanging around here.'

Smiling at the gruffness of his gratitude, I bent down to tend to my fallen Godkin. This was the second unbelievably foolish thing I did that day. I heard a soft, evil whisper and then fell heavily as the cricket bat cracked amiably onto my skill. Out.

I was expelled. When the police picked us up, the other boys, in a remarkable example of collective and spontaneous creativity, invented a marvellous account of a huge raiding party of Protestant cut-throats led and abetted by my renegade self. Such synchronicity was astounding but the fuzz had their doubts. The school authorities, however, were untroubled by any such equivocation. When I eventually left hospital, with my cracked skull but imperfectly repaired and my forehead graced with an impressive addition in mass and angle, they summoned me. My five school chums were seen as heroic victims of my dastardly Quisling treason. I was banished in disgrace. They had enough clemency to allow me to see out the term. This was an astute piece of devilry which enabled me to enjoy the bracing consequence of several mass beatings at the hands of my outraged peers.

Since I had been booted out of this school onto my arse I imagined that I would be considerably less of a posh choice for other schools but this was not the case. Thankfully, I was still generally acknowledged to be a prodigy. Schools fell over themselves to sign me up. I was top of the transfer market.

St Cecilia's was the establishment fortunate enough to secure my contribution. I tried this secondary education business for the second time. St Cecilia's was a co-educational convent school set deep in the epicentre of the Unionist heartland of Ballymena. It was attended in the main by rustic children, products of the Catholic farms and small towns of the region. With my sharp urban accent and my city-bred ways, I was considered something of an imposition upon the delicacy of their feelings. Once again I was startlingly unpopular. Their witless, yokel machismo goaded me into another depressing series of fisticuffs. The more fights I won, the more I had to fight; until one day I lost my temper and mashed some hapless culchie. He was hospitalised, poor chap, and I was suspended for a fortnight.

The young ladies of this establishment also played their part in my downfall. Co-educationalism was very bad for me — I fell in love ceaselessly, tirelessly. I still tried to choose the plainest girls, always mindful of my own dearth of pulchritude, but still my advances were met with scorn. One revolting young lady, called Soupy on account of her pebbledash complexion, actually went to the Mother Superior to complain about a suggestion I was supposed to have made to her involving the use of a spiral staircase and a pot of raspberry preserve. Again I was suspended.

Now came the turn of Ballymena's Protestant extremism. (Ballymena was more than Loyalist. It was True Blue and proven Orange. The Spanish Inquisition was still causing resentment in this town. Here, Methodists were considered practically Papist and even Anabaptists weren't quite the whole hog. Teenage girls had posters of Oliver Cromwell on their bedroom walls.) By this time I was sick with misery and reckless of consequence. Tired of the tuneless jingoism of Ballymena's amazing array of Pipe Bands, I decided in a fit of youthful pique that enough was enough and that I was bound to retaliate. To this end I had a blotchy tricolour painted on my boyish posterior by the reluctant and inexpert hand of my brother, Declan. I beaked off school on the afternoon of one of the most important Orange marches of the year ...

When I got out of hospital this time, I was dismayed to find that no further suspensions awaited me for my buttocky display of nationalism. In my despair, I stole a bottle of whisky from a local off-licence, got trouserwetting drunk, tried to seduce the octagenarian Sister Mary in the most forceful terms and then crashed the school bus in my attempts to escape when the police had been called. I was too short to reach the pedals, you see.

I was expelled.

My education was beginning to be something of a sticky wicket when I was suddenly offered a place by a school back in Belfast (I was pretty infamous by now, mentions in *The Times Educational Supplement*, questions in the House and so forth, so it was quite surprising). St Malcolm's College for the Education of Catholic Boys was situated at the foot of the Crumlin Road. That is to say, in the pleasant region of Carlisle Circus, forming a lunatic no-man's land with the rabid Catholic ghetto of the New Lodge on one hand and the equally rabid Protestant ghetto of the Crumlin Road on the other. On one side of the school there was the controversial Mater Convent, a hive of rebellious and disaffected nunhood, on another was the Crumlin Jail itself, a prison so incompetent that escaping prisoners would hire coaches to cater for their vast numbers. Behind the school was an army barracks, a rifle range and an army helicopter landing pad. The boss of this joint was The Very Reverend Canon Brendan P. O'Hara. Dubbed Paddy Sniff (alternatively Snaddy Piff) by the boys on account of his excessively prominent hooter, he was imbued with ineluctable, terrifying power. Almost occultish, it was, bedad! (The captains of the priesthood always have this gift. I wonder from where they get it? God knows.) The school cosh (Dean of Discipline) was a priest called Father Murphy or 'Rubber' to us. Rubber earned his nickname because of the elastic properties he induced in his victims as he bounced them off the lockers, walls, floors and ceilings of whatever school building that happened to be to hand. All in all, this looked like the school for me.

Once again my raffish demeanour stood me in good stead in the way of making new friends. The list of these new comrades was long and included such luminous figures as Plonker O'Halloran, Sean 'Missing Link' Murphy, Donal 'On the head' McArdle, 'Abdul' McGonagle (a boy with a suntan), 'Pustules' Brady, Rob the Yob, Mad Rat Johnson and of course my dearest, my closest pal, the strangely named Maurice Kelly. All bad men and false but I was pushed for buddies and they made up the numbers.

Of course, it was nice to be liked but I was having one or two initial problems. These were almost all financial – it was all to do with dosh. My precious cigarette supply had slowed to a trickle. Fiscally, St Malcolm's was a closed market. There was just no lucre to be had. But I needed nicotine. Draconian measures were necessary. I had to get my oar into the Malcolmian Stock Exchange. There was nothing else for it. I would have to see ... (gulp! sob!) ... Geek!

Geek was the financial genius of the school. He ran the illegal cigarette sales to the Junior School and the illegal off-licence to the Sixth Form. He supervised the school bookie and made the (grossly loaded) odds for all of the college's sporting events. He managed the Upper Sixth casino and controlled all the protection rackets, minor and major. In short, he took off the top of every scam, dodge and confidence trick in the entire school. Some even said he was bribing the bursar. He had a car of his own and wore a gold watch. School had been very kind to Geek.

However, the really terrifying aspect of this stupendous young man was, believe it or not, his wooden leg. God only knows how he managed to be lumbered (ho ho) with it in a world of sophisticated, high-tech prosthetic limbs but there it was, for all to see – or more precisely, for all to studiously ignore. For Geek's only apparent insecurity was this quirky arborean addition to his physique. Subsequently, it was very much a taboo subject, for despite his aversion to this appendage, he wielded it with a deadly expertise which left all the boys and half the staff trembling. Life with Geek could be a problem, as the high turnover rate of his closest confidants suggested. He would insist on playing football and swimming in the blithest manner possible, as if there were nothing remarkable about his corporeal dimensions. It was difficult for his cronies constantly to exhibit a perfect ease of manner and anything that could be even vaguely construed as a reference to their captain's state of incompletion often proved close to fatal.

This was, manifestly, not a man to be trifled with. Within a week, I had decided to take my life in my hands and try to muscle in in my own puny way. Believe it or not, I waltzed into the sixth form bogs one day (a capital offence in itself) and informed the psychopathic tycoon that I wanted a slice of the action or something similarly American. In the eight and a half seconds before Geek tore my spine out I managed to blurt out a frenzied precis of my proposals. He stopped in mid-lunge and applied his rabid gaze to my sweating, terrified gob. To my lasting joy, murderous violence did not in fact ensue and I was practically given a partnership on the spot.

Geek allowed me twelve per cent which was bloody generous for Geek. Indeed, I rather think I had managed to engender an unusual partiality in the one-legged mogul who seemed to deem me a likely type and eminently suitable for the vacant position of junior manager of his ever-growing financial empire. Thankfully though, an unfortunate fourth year from Lisburn got that job (he lasted three and a half weeks and ended up with his teeth knocked so far down his throat that he had to stick his toothbrush up his arse to get at them).

So, what had I suggested? How had I swung such an unlikely reprieve? I ain't tellin'. I'm a socialist – commercial adventuring is anathema to me. Besides I might get arrested or something.

Thus with my fags in my gob and my twelve per cent a-pocket I strode happily into a more settled school career. This was fortunate as my darling mother had vowed to boil my head if I got into any more trouble and she wasn't one for hyperbole. On I moved to manhood.

This was my second problem at St Malcolm's. I had no real adolescence as such. It all happened in one week of my fourteeth year. On the Monday I was as I had always been – smooth of face and body – my boyish plump-ness unsullied and uncorrupted by the grossness of maturity. By the Wednesday I was coming over all curious and by the Friday I had started shaving and had an outsize and hirsute gherkin in my Y-fronts. Very indecorous. It seemed to happen in minutes. If I'd blinked I'd have missed it. It was amazing, legendary. The best bit was that I quite abruptly became incredibly fucking handsome as well. Just like that. Genie stuff. Bang, baby – you're beautiful!

Mumsy was most dischuffed by my express ride to manhood. As a manifestation of change it was doubly unwelcome to the old bag – both a beacon of her own relentless ageing and a hint of betrayal on my part. Predictably, I lost little sleep over Mom's difficulties. After all, she'd lost none over mine.

I was pleased to note that at school I became the subject of much envy and conjecture. There were several theories to explain the sudden burgeoning of my full flush of virility but the majority of these could be discounted on grounds of personal, religious or physiological impossibility. It has to be said that my chums took it rather well considering that they were, to a man, busy fighting off the worst sebum attacks of their own troubled, scrofulous negotiations with puberty. They named me 'Zoompubes' in honour of the celerity of my growth and some of them even offered to let me sleep with their sisters or mothers, so zealous was their admiration.

Though I was glad to have side-stepped the carnage of acne, I confess that I rather missed my old ugliness. It was nice to be handsome but unsightliness had been such an intrinsic part of the greater equation that made up this Ripley Bogle that for quite a time I could not consider myself complete without it.

My word, I was something else! Suddenly muscular and trim. Boiling hard with the febrile, energetic victory that youth presents to you. You'd have hated it. Everyone else did.

Well, the middle to late years of my boyhood had proved tricky but I seemed well-set for my merited destiny now. I had my school. I had my cigarettes. I had my little buddies. I had my pubic hair and I had my fate in my own grasp. Soon error, mayhem, despair and catastrophe would be mine for life, I was pleased to think.

Yes, I *was* strong once and firm in body. Fully youthjuiced generally, I was. But now my bones are knobbled, crusty and my belly is slack. My lungs flap raggedly as I breathe and my joints creak and groan with every movement. This is winter's gift to the tramp. My body is aged, querulous, disgruntled. My body seems to have no respect for my youth. My body doesn't want to know.

The river has turned to a vein of cold sweat. I'm freezing my priceless off here. I've gotta move soon. Unsteadily, I sneak to my feet, my eyes scanning the lightless sky. We have a bad bugger of a sky tonight. A mean, griping welkin. Tonight the heavens will have their grudge against us. They're watching sardonically, implacably. It's spectating sky. Mistless, sans cloud and clear of aircraft, the eye is on high. The show. I.e. me. What we want. Poverty and sleeping rough. The youthtime of the gods. Let's investigate.

I think we'll have The Anatomy of a Homeless Night now. Thank you.

SIX

We come now to the hard part of the night. The darkness teems with solitude and comfortlessness. I'm tiring. My eyes are dry and heavy and my skull throbs with despair. Darkly, the pavement distends and shimmers under my feet and even the prospect of sleep renders me dizzy and sick. Where do I find consolation here? My limbs are sandstone and my brain is custard. This is getting to be too much for me. I need to stop. To cease. Not to rest or sleep or die or anything like that. Those stern alternatives are too complex, requiring excessive volition and effort. Just to stop – that's what I need and all I can manage.

I can't though. Not really. I'd like to and would certainly swing it eventually but I mustn't. It's time for me to show you around. To tell you about trampnights, about streetnights. The examination, the setpiece, the anatomy of indigence. Come.

(A brief ripple of applause. Listen. Learn.)

We start before dark. Early evening. Night is coming soon and the sky has paled to monotone – ready-blank for night's brush. Cold it is and miserable. Here you are in beggary. Fun? We'll see. The first point of importance is that you have, say, three pounds and fifty pence in your possession. You wily old capitalist, you! Now, it is imperative that you should keep this in your possession. Don't spend it. Don't eat. Don't drink. Don't go making any wild investments on the stock market. You'll be needing the dosh later on and needing it badly too. You need it *now*, admittedly, but you have to be strict with yourself. (You see, what most people don't realise is that these homeless types generally have at least a couple of quid on them. No one is really completely penniless. No one is that stupid. No one is that unlucky.)

Well done. You've held onto your dosh. Excellent. Prosperity seems just around the corner. You look about you with a newly sanguine eye. Time

45

nudges and badgers you. You're a little bored. At this juncture, boredom is probably your chief enemy. If you're in a capital city, this isn't so bad. Hang around an art gallery trying to look aesthetic. Indeed, an artistic temperament is quite a sturdy excuse for the grubby eccentricity of your clothing. Failing the gallery, get onto the Underground. It's inexpensive, warm and intermittently entertaining. The Circle Line is your best bet here. A goodie – warm and eternal. Its circular motion is its chief joy. You can stay there all day. The other folk always get off after a while – they don't see your destinationless degradation that way. Have a little kip. Stretch out a bit. Scratch your balls (or whatever else you've got). Soon you'll have to move. Sad but true. Sleeping on the Underground always gives you a headache – perpetual motion, stuffythick air, commuter smells and windowed vibrations in your recumbent skull. A recipe for your great discomfort. Claustrophobia, ennui and shame drive you above ground.

Outside, night is closer, a decorous twilight. You would appreciate it if you could but hardship has dulled you. Canine in thought and deed, you shuffle listlessly through the promenade of rush hour trying to ignore your growing conviction that life is pretty shitty. You stare with doltish resentment at the vast straits of the urban outdoors. An idea crops up, rather fortuitously. You decide to go to a railway station.

(Our scene suddenly staggers under a weight of filth and rubbish; half-eaten hamburgers, sodden newspapers, decrepit syringes, used condoms, floating turds, discarded people, tramps, thieves, harlots, runaways, rapists and lunatics. Men slump in seamy corners, slobbering, bawling and pissing themselves. Basically, your average British train station.)

Good, these are places in which you can loiter more or less inconspicuously. Go on, take up your train station posture.

Lots of people wait in railway stations. A great deal of respectable waiting takes place. For arrivals and departures, for appointments, chores and clandestine love trysts. Generally speaking, these are people with money; folk who own homes and kitchens and beds and pillows and sheets. You remember all that kind of thing, don't you? Why, fondly you do! That's it ... hover around them. Be near them. Try to include yourself in their winsome aura of normality and health. Let them rub off on you. Endeavour to look as though you're ordinary – just like them.

In your pursuit of poshery, you keep looking impatiently at your wrist even if you haven't got a watch. That's always a good one. That tells the tale of at least some kind of dalliance with the offices of time and dependence. It would have been nice if you still had your watch. Believe me, a watch is a vital accessory to genteel destitution. Hold onto it for as long as you can. Watches are dilletante and relatively expensive, the whiff of non-necessity.

They are the stamp of careless money – or something like it.

After a while the railway station will become irksome. Don't worry – it's natural that it should. The average chap's mind has only so much capacity for ennui. The city's first population; its homeseeking, workfinished crowds have dribbled away and the station is less populous and bleaker than before. You decide to go for a walk.

This is very foolish. You will have all the walking you could possibly want later on and more. Yes, it is very foolish indeed but still you embark upon your little perambulation. Actually, this does have one relatively benevolent aspect. It will give you some impression of how cold you are going to be tonight. This impression is always wildly wrong. You always underestimate. You are going to have your bollocks frozen. Even if you have done this kind of thing before you will still have forgotten how incredibly fucking cold it gets. The next day you will forget again. It's an unpalatable notion. You give it no room. You show it the door. No one likes to think that they have been sliverclose to expiring of hypothermia the night before. Medic though I'm not, it occurs to me that lack of sleep and abundance of hunger also do their stalwart best in rendering you even more susceptible to cold. An unfortunate conglomeration of circumstance. But this medley of misfortune is the tramp's permanent companion. The expertise with which fate and ill-chance contrive to bugger you about is truly admirable. The delightful and roguish way that your discomforts, aches, trials and setbacks team up for maximum destruction leaves you breathless with admiration.

As you're walking down Charing Cross Road or the Strand or Long Acre or Oxford Street or wherever for the fifth time that day, you are actually (moronically enough) surprised when you suddenly feel an abrupt and hammerfast thump of hunger. That tiny empty bellyscrape. (We've talked about Hunger – we know that fellow.) Ignore it, man! Keep that precious bloody cash. That's vital. Try to forget which pocket it's in. Pass on by those closing sandwich bars. Cross to the other side of the street. Ignore those warm, odorous hamburger joints. Don't lose your head now. Come on, for Chrissakes, show a bit of gumption for a change!

You breathe again. You sigh with deep relief. Well done again. You let it pass. Felicitations, you did good, kid. You didn't splash out on a five-course bacchanalia in the Savoy. You're a hero. Walk on. Walk.

At this point we greet an interesting digression. Must be made, I'm afraid. If the homeless person in question happens to be a smoker (as by some cruel twist of divine pedantry, they always seem to be), then the ordering of the finances becomes a much less complex affair. Say that the fellow in question has something like a five-pound note. Say that twenty Rothmans or Lambert and Butler or Woodbine or Benson & Hedges or Embassy

Regals are about 150p a packet. He will buy three packets of cigarettes and two chocolate bars thus quelling all his needs. You simply can't afford to buy food when you need cigarettes to dull your hunger pangs. If he is a clever sort of chappy he will smoke as few as he lungbleedingly can during the day so that he has as many as possible to drag and fuel him through the hardship and hatred of the night. That's half the reason that you always see tramps and winos hanging around in libraries and places like that. It's partly for the warmth and sleep, true – but it's also because they're not allowed to smoke there. That's the aid their asceticism needs.

Look. Darkness has now fallen and the city is filling with its second population, the Epicureans – the pleasure-seekers. Even more than the workers, the daytime inhabitants, these nocturnal citypeople are galling for you. You watch as they spend their large and their little piles of cash and plastic on booze; meagre restaurant meals gobbed in by the waiters; two hours' brainless diversion with the banal herdhappy coloured lights of a cinema; or the wheedling, egocentric, rantings of some bunch of half-arsed thespian mediocrities. You watch the taxi fares that could buy you a bed for the night. You watch the fat, greasy bastards spending their week's wages on a five and a half minute rut with some onion-breathed, syphilitic old hag.

Oooooh, you get so annoyed! Fair, it isn't. (One of the curious by-products of houselessness is that it makes you so terribly, terribly socialist.)

Here there is a second welter of boredom to conquer. The citypause. The deep urban breath until those slimy shits with their fat faces, shiny hair and clean underwear file doggylike out of their restaurants, theatres, cinemas, pubs, nightclubs and general wanking shops. No problem though, you conquer it. You're nothing if not resourceful. You dream of money, food and the warmth of London's great normality.

But whoops! You've spotted a cheap, crumbling old fleapit showing some cruddy, decrepit B-movie that you've already seen eight times on the television that you don't have. Now, now, resist that feeble impulse, you gutless bastard! Be wise. Those two hours of soft, smelly warmth and comfort will only leave you colder and more alone when you come out again. Don't be a chump! Walk on past. You'd probably be raped anyhow. Who knows what kind of people they get in a place like that?

It has passed: but once rebuffed, Temptation just tries another window. You look around for somewhere to go. Somewhere to take your poor mind off it all. Somewhere untempting.

(Once again our scene is infested with strata of faecal matter, cess, garbage, scum, detritus, slime, sick and general tack and turds.)

Another train station? Why yes indeed. Another railway station. You have so many to choose from. Avoid the modern ones though. Too clean and brightly lit. That sadistic glare and reflection of chrome, plastic and glass is surplus to your requirements. No. Seek out the shamesaving shadows of the ancient ones – St Pancras, Liverpool Street, Charing Cross (as was). Hide there for another hour.

Why don't you buy yourself a coffee? Good man. It rids you of a fifth of your remaining assets but what's life without a little self-indulgence? Drink its sour warmth with fervour and start a little amateur smoking. Careful with the fags though. Try not to enjoy them. Ecce. Beware. It's for this that you tend your poverty. Drink it up, my boy – whop it into you. Coffee and tobacco. That's good, isn't it? Yes, yes it is.

And by golly, silly young spooney that you are, you start to feel a little better. Abruptly, you welter in a little crest of lunatic optimism. Things don't seem so bad now. (Things are lying – they're still as bad as always.) But you're feeling young and sprung and well-hung again. That reasonless adrenalin of yours breaks jail and takes a tour of you. Slim, trim and tricky, you begin to watch the bims. Those girls! Those svelte, monied, travelling sophisticates. And they just might even see you too. Despite your shabbiness, jewel-eyed tributes you get a-plenty. This is fun but dangerous. Yes, oh dear ... a sanguine little fantasy come to mind. All day that furtive thought has sneaked around the periphery of your mental front garden, trying to break in. Oh, here he comes, that dreamburglar.

Come on, you think, cute little sexpot that you are – somebody's bound to pick you up. Some fair, fortyish professional bimbo with a penchant for the young working-class type ... wait a minute, the young pukka type – the young arty type – anything – by jingo, you can do the lot! A divorcee perhaps. With lots of dosh and a cute fringe. She give you a boff and a bed. Lackaday, you dream. You pile it on.

Well, fool, forget it. What do you expect? You know so much about these things. You still believe in these stopgap Victorian benefactors, those miraculous, maudlin men. Where have all the dei ex machina gone to? That's something like what you need. What about the Fairy Godmother with the pied-à-terre and the fabulous tits?

(Here she comes, stepping towards you out of the melee. She smiles.)

FAIRY GODMOTHER (*invitingly*): You are beautiful. You are young. You are poor and hungry and cold. I am very beautiful. I am rich and wellfed and warm. Come with me to my mansion where I will give you comfort, sustenance and roger you to a standstill, see if I don't. (*Exit*)

Is that the sort of thing that you're looking for? Is this what you dream? You, the arch-fantasist! Do you honestly expect that?

Thankfully, all this hope, all those nebulous improbabilities soon fade.

Back to misery. None of that sort of thing ever happens. Not to you. Not when you need it. (That's the thing about Luck, the lazy shit. It's no mug. It only ever shows up when it isn't needed. It likes to be superfluous.)

And here now, what's this? You're approached. Gadzooks! An encounter. Some dialogue, a conversation. Teufel!

Slouching, slobbering, the tramp from Hell moves to you. His eyes glitter with the evil envy of the dead. His mouth creases into formless speech. Wicked smells envelop him and words of nameless evil trickle from his gash of mouth. Your skin crawls, your nails slither and your follicles shimmy. No, not that!

No, you don't fancy that, do you? Whackin' up some scag down the underpass. The man pleads and lauds his wares. Oh, you begin to pray that you won't come to that. The supplication of the provincial pillock. O Lord, deliver me from Narcotics, nasty, expensive and flesh-corrupting as they be.

Zoom! Off you jog, your heart lumbering in panic and your secondhand soul screeching in shame and disgust.

Outside, London is quite black. Created from darkness and ignorance, the sky bears its augur's coat. As your frantic run trails to a stop in this heaving, soiled city, you feel a curious numbness. Your panic evaporates into sour despair. You are useless until your night's end – a cipher. Those obstacle-hours stretch before you, amorphous and menacing. Hours before dawn. Aeons before light and day and their rest.

You slump to a crouch against some streaming wall. You light another cigarette, feeding the clots in your ragged, mountebank chest. With nicotine, you feel the sluggish passing of time pricking your skin. This muskish prayer of Catholic night brings no beauty. Its nighted air beats insistent and windharsh upon your forehead. The building fronts, illumined in the stage yellow of strings of street lights glare at you, accusing and malevolent. This city, built by Protestant and Englishman and prosperity, this city turns its withered face away from you. You are too poor, too dirty and sad. You have sinned against its light.

You slump wearily on the sordid pavement while all around you the world buzzes with its news. You sit alone and cold and friendless. You fade, you wither, you slip away.

In bubbling halfsleep you dream of cloudy, insubstantial dramas. Troubled scenes reel before you; a capering dance of Hell. Caverns, chasms and tunnels vast in horror open onto that dizzy screen. Absurd, terrible figures mouth wordless messages at you. Throughout this whole grotesque vision some kind of dreadful meaning is apparent. But its substance is elusive and you lose its import. You dream of someone you know to be your father, a shadow-figure in the uniform of the Salvation Army, he speaks rapidly, waving his finger in urgent, foreign gestures.

You wake and your pale, ironic face folds with pain. Your mouth is scummed with sleep though you've only dozed for a few minutes. The cold is unbelievable. Your bones seem to groan and swell and your muscles stretch like bacon. Your feet are actually insensate and your paws throb vaguely. It's time to move.

You do so. With infinite, itemised agonies, you clamber to your feet and start to walk. It's midway between midnight and one o'clock. It begins now ... this walking.

With gradual ease of pain, you slither from King's Cross up past Euston, left down Gordon Street ... right into Gower Place where you briefly revile the university ... left into Gower Street itself where you begin again to feel the cold as a sliver of wind spins up that valley ... fighting that, you speed up left into Torrington Place, quickly connecting with Tottenham Court Road ... fifteen minutes of this and you'll be as warm as you want to be ... down Tottenham Court Road onto good old Charing Cross Road ... the Strand ... Waterloo Bridge ...

Now you see how very tedious and lonely this is going to be but you comfort yourself with the thought that in London it isn't as dreadful as it might be. You've seen worse. At least at this time of night, the city's little history comes to life (it's the only time that it does) and it says hello. London parades the corners of its nocturnal past for all to see. But there's no one watching but you and those like you. (Where are they, these folk, these chaps like you, where do they lurk?) You've always felt pretty solitary in your keenness for the splash and quiver of the past. Pompous little thing that you are, you feel that you're the only one left who cares.

Remember that bold old Charlie Dickens did this kind of thing a lot. The nightly perambulations of grotty old London. He even did it when he didn't have to – even when he was all posh and published. For fun – to remind himself. Harkin' back to the Blackin' Warehuss an' all that. Yes, you can never forget. Replicable moments. These once destitute aesthetes. Orwell the same. They always circle around the recollection of their worst of bad times. You and they never lose that poignant little kink of insecurity. Poverty's a bugger. It haunts you when it dies.

This is what you too will do. Even when you're back in some approximation of prosperity you'll do it. Nip out every now and then for a homeless night. A curious syndrome. It's always so nice when you come back to comfort. Those dear little things that suddenly seem so special . . . linen, pillows, food and smooth cleanliness.

It's nice, is it not? The thought of what eminent company you are keeping these days is very appealing. A lot of big literary numbers have traipsed trampishly around London's streets. Dickens, Orwell and your very own chunky little self.

(*Enter Charles Dickens and George Orwell. Their faces are bright with fraternity. They hop madly towards you, their arms flapping wildly.*)

CHARLES DICKENS: It was a cold, bright day in April and the clocks were striking thirteen.

GEORGE ORWELL (*consumptively*): It was a chill dark night with a damp wind blowing . . .

CHARLES DICKENS (*losing the thread un peu*): Oranges and lemons say the bells of St Clement's.

GEORGE ORWELL: Poor thing! Have you no feeling that you keep him out on the cruel streets at such a time as this? Have you no eyes, that you don't see how slender and delicate he is? (*He takes your hand.*) Have you no sense that you don't take more pity on this cold and trembling little hand?

CHARLES DICKENS (*uproariously*): Ignorance is Strength. War is peace. Bugger the Thought Police!

GEORGE ORWELL (*sobbing*): The shame, desertion, wretchedness and exposure of the great capital; the wet, the cold, the slow hours and the swift clouds of the dismal night.

CHARLES DICKENS: Fuck Room 101! I wanna bathroom en suite, ya Irish git!

(*The two great writers collapse into helpless laughter and skip offstage.*)

You smile, viceroy to the reigning calm.

Still you walk, you clatter on regardless. You hobble through the black muchfeared night. Very early on in its progress, you begin to work out the dynamics of this ambulatory business. It's quite easy. The actual physics of the process itself are simple and can be left mostly to themselves. On this automatic mode, you have time and grace to solve its other problems. The dilemmas of distance and destination are easily solved. All you have to do to ease the tedium of all your blanket walking is to set yourself goals. Like a lag, you make the best of it. Break your sentence into its component years. Makes it shorter. As you're dawdling along Bloomsbury, you decide to walk to Victoria or Kensington High Street. When you reach your destination you set yourself another. In chunks, the night shouldn't frighten so. A silly trick which doesn't really fool you but if you adhere to it the night seems less onerous, less deadly.

This walking has limitless advantages. It keeps you nice and warm if you put your back into it. It prevents you from smoking your cigarettes too quickly. It eases the boredom. It distracts you from the urgent tocsin that your health has become. It amuses. It delights.

However, the most important boon that walking brings is, curiously enough, its vague respectability. Yes. Bang! Wahey! That's it. You silly sausage! It makes you look as though you're going somewhere – as though you have somewhere to go. You know that real tramps, the veritable destitute, just hang around trying to keep warm or sane or they erect those great coffin-tubes of cardboard into which they slither for some grieving sleep. Tramps drop on the spot or snatch a drunken slumber in the doorway of some High Street chemist's. They hover, they bed down. They don't give a fuck. But you, you stay mobile. The Peelers leave you alone that way. You keep walking, exhaustively – beyond pain; while legs forget and feet improvise. You walk because ... and this is the major point about the whole thing ... because ... you're so ashamed! Jesus, Mary and Joseph, do you feel degraded! Humiliation, bitterness and shame – all these are yours and more. You'd die rather than let anyone discover. Now or ever.

That shame only hits a few of us. The posh ones like you and me. We crave anonymity and inoffensiveness. The more robust tramps eke out lives of varying comfort. They are boisterous and shameless, the lucky, confident bastards! We, you and I, we are those who starve and wither in shame. We are tortured by the pathetic difficulties of trying to maintain a decent appearance et al. All day you have stretched your meagre soul in trying to appear other than what you are. To look like some kind of student or blue collar eccentric. Or even the regional yokel up to the big smoke for the day. Desperately you essay for a trace of simple shabbiness. Your clothes aren't so very bad as yet but still you somehow don't convince. You have the telltale stain of purposelessness. You'll never pull it off, friend. Don't even try. It will break your heart.

(Incidentally, one of the worst things about these bad days is the influx, the injection of newer and better-bred down and outs. Younger, cleaner and less qualified for trampdom than we, the old hands. These folk are poorly equipped indeed for destitution on this scale. They crowd you out and take your space. Homeless London is filling up. There are no vacancies. Soon perhaps, they will put the rents up. You watch these new recruits with sadness in your empathetic heart. The sudden welter of the unemployed, of the runaways; the evicted, the chanceless. These amateurs have been coaxed onto the streets by the acutely meritocratic nineteen eighties. They have been taught to expect a job and a life and a roof; or at least a drudge and a life and a hovel. To their surprise, they get much less than even that. For the most part they get nothing. Precisely, surgically nothing.

So, what can you do if you're a youthful dolebird from Liverpool, Glasgow or Newcastle? Your mum and dad turf you out. (They're always doing that, mums and dads.) You take stock of your situation, hopes and expectations ... this doesn't take very long, there not being much to compute. You boogie on down to London. Perhaps you get a dolefunded B&B for as long as you're allowed (which nowadays is about seven and a half minutes). Maybe you hit an easy squat, hippystudent digs or similar. You putrify there briefly until you're raped or murdered or booted out and then – and then it's the streets. You know where you've come to and you know why you're there. You slip, you slide, you fade away.)

Well, back to you and your problems. After reaching Victoria or Chelsea and getting lost for a handy half hour in Belgravia, you turn back and drift into the sour, nightbussed babble of Trafalgar Square. In Parliament Square you saw that it was still only half past one. Damn! Still much, much too early. Time is slouching. Time is stopping to get its breath back.

You lurch aimlessly in a moronic circuit of Trafalgar Square, your walk-walking feet confusing your fuddled brain, your eyes watching from the incline. The lighted twinkle-city. Lamps stuttering red, yellow, white and green. Nightish folk working their sleepingcity functions in the bright squares of office windows. Peoples untouched by day, smugly snug. You wonder at this darker world of theirs. You grow querulous and bewildered.

Cars sailing by. Curious how they always seem quieter at night. Fewer of them, you adroitly conclude. Through clack and tap and squalid tumult, you seek the clemency of solitude. Your heart trips and stammers horribly. Fear and loathing grip you hard. The trickling, incandescent city palpitates as your ghostwalking heart recoils at speed. Desolation, panic and despair. Oh, it's hotting up. Fast approaching your nadir, your bluegreenbrown eyes slowly close. You're dying a death. You clutch your chest as the wind blows cold. The cars fade to silence and the people dribble to inconsequentiality. You stop and close your eyes. You breathe deep against your enemy lungs. That's it. It's not a problem. You breathe.

Urban equilibrium reasserts itself and the cars return, drone-growling. Hands on steeringwheels, pointing headlights in graceful arabesques. You wonder how the city never sleeps. Or maybe never wakes. You're tired – these things seem profound to you.

You ebb away from the square. In an intrepid moment you effectively write off the next couple of hours by nipping over to the Barbican and back. The backs of your knees are beginning to grumble rather. Soon you'll be too weary to walk much more. But fuck it, you think, you'll come up with something.

You kick and struggle through that sludge of pain and reluctance. You're brave, you're hardy. Give yourself a round of applause and walk on.

By the time you get back to the Embankment, you're spent. You've had it. You've been walking all day. You haven't many steps left in you. The strip of the Embankment ribbons feebly towards you, patchlit by straggling rows of ornate white lamps and bulbstrings, sheening the greyed tarmac. All appears comfortless and harsh. These fripperies seem tactless to you. You look over to the South Bank. You ponder. The South Bank is actually quite a good place for your purposes. The stairways, walkways and all that are pretty sheltered and sporadically discreet. Private and quiet – almost. The latter is becoming an increasingly important consideration. It's very late now and by this time you are pretty familiar with the third group of London's shifting inhabitants. Those like yourself. The tramps, the down and outs, the whores, the rent boys, the criminals and muggers and rapists and lunatics and gangs and bad boys and general weirdos. Yessir, around about this time the fucking scrambleheads really hit town in a big way! They stake their claim. And you don't like it. You don't like it at all.

Now, you're a pretty tough kid/bloke/girl. You've been around, so to speak. But these people are fucking crazies. They'll drink your blood and dine on your offal. You simply cannot win with folk like that. Not unless you join their camp. You see, the thing about this violence business is simple (so much is, or seems to be). It's not a matter of how big or tough or expert you are. It is merely a matter of how *mad* you are. How much psychopathic talent you possess. If you can perform a plausible scramblehead impression, you're safe, you're laughing. Nobody wants to tangle with that sort of nutcase. You must scream and froth horribly in warning – contort your face and let your body kick and flail. Leave your sanity traces well behind. If you can do all that, muggers and the like will probably give you money to go away. Few want the action that you're promising. (Incidentally, do not attempt this little ruse with a real crazy . . . he won't be fooled, he will *not* be impressed.) Increasingly, it's these crazy fellows who are winning the well-documented wars on the streets of all our cities. Your own courage, though it makes the effort, is a polite and rather faltering thing. It needs encouragement and cultivation. It needs to be right and just. It hasn't a chance here. These people will do everything to you – without pause, cause or scruple. No matter what you do to them. (Not that you could ever do very much to them that is going to bother them a great deal.) These are the folk who run your nightmares and categorise your phobias. Leave them to themselves. You're not in their league. At least, I hope you're not.

You've watched them tonight, haven't you? With popping eyes and rebellious gut, you've seen their show. The tale of their less-than-picaresque. Earlier on, near Holborn Circus, that crazy guy, that strip of mad euphoria, kicking the shit out of those two Salvation Army geezers. A Sally woman lying on the pavement, blood streaming from her nose. Her hair matted with the street's mud and piss. And the two philanthropes just standing there being kicked in the face by Mr BrucefuckingLeehimself as you passed shrinking on the other side of the street.

And Charing Cross Bridge. That woman. That bag lady unhurriedly wiping her bottom on this cold night. Unbelievable. She scraped, gouged, ferreted for hygiene. Her pale, porridgy arse glowing under the street lamp against which she discreetly leaned. Her wrinkled face, querulous and aggrieved. Quite soiled you, it did. You tried not to look. Her spoiling the world for other people. Her aged, rubbing hand, her dappled, pudding flesh, her mad old eyes. Pah!

The girl. Her hard hatefilled hair and carious, fuming mouth. Her voice. Tight, thin with insistence. Her pain, your grief – both your accusations. A commercial transaction. The might and right of erotic commerce. Caveat emptor. No, not that – not with her. Not with her scrawny, pallid thighs and her scant, sharp breasts. Her tracks, her rickets, her miseries and her arsenal of gurgling, malevolent venereal afflictions. And her sadness, her pain, shame, crime. Her little death. No, not with her.

(Other people's uninvited madnesses are always much madder than your own explicable, excusable little insanities.)

Montages of drunkenness and vice play themselves out in every street, court and alley. The screeching revellers of London disport themselves wildly. The very bricks and trees mutter under their garish stripes of light. The night is disfigured and obscene. Noise. Darkness. Hell. Everywhere you go, people are shouting, laughing, screaming, weeping without restraint. The faces you see are deadened and blank, murdered by drink and feeble lust.

(These pictures, these scenes are quite mild compared to the riot of insanity and vigorous horror that you might see on any New York night. Nonetheless, they are still enough to unsettle your faltering soul. Anyway, the worst that you could see, you will never see. These are hidden away, private, furtive. In the places that you don't know and to the people you've never seen, worse things are happening. What you're seeing now is the posh end of these things. You're having it easy.)

Yes, I think the South Bank is a good idea. Shift your buns sharpish.

There, that's better, isn't it? You sit more or less comfortably on one of the cheerless staircases that crawl up the arse of the National Theatre. You ferret in your coat and rescue your last few cigarettes. You've been expiring for want of a fag and you feel you owe yourself a little consideration. You light up, charmingly. You shift your numbedmeat buttocks a little. Your muscles flood with blood, oxygen, pain and relief. You lie back against the hard ridges of the stone steps. Why, you're in clover!

You know that you will be moved on sooner or later but you don't particularly care. In your better times – when you used to watch the drama-stuff here – you would see the South Bank security guys at work. You know their form. They've always seemed like a fairly decent bunch of chaps. Embarrassed by having to kick out all the tramps: by having to keep the place clean and guiltless for all the pampered unlovelies sipping their interval drinks. Management policies and all that. Can't have some fleabitten old turd coughing his intestines up over one's nice patent leather shoes. 'Pon my soul, no! Then of course, these poor security blokes are harangued by some obese theatrico bastard with a villa in the South of France, a milky-breasted girl from an escort agency on his arm and temporarily egalitarian notions.

Yes, you like these security fellows and no doubt, they'd like you too. But they will come. They'll move you on. Have to do it, son. More than my job's worth. You understand that, don't you? Of course you do. You're big enough and ugly enough to take it. A little humanitarian consideration is all that's needed.

The coppers will get you in the end anyhow. They will shift you PDQ. They can't let you sleep. It's against the law. You can sit; you can stand around; you can loiter as much as you like but sleeping on the streets is illegal. What kind of law is that? Do they seriously believe that if sleeping on the streets is legalised there will be a sudden influx of City men, civil servants and millionaires, all frantic to do a bit of legitimate dossing? Does this sound likely?

Anyway, as you sit on those arse-numbing steps, watching the dirty river slide past, teartwinkling the lights of Somerset House, you begin to notice the cold. Yes. It's time for this long-awaited trial. By fuck, it is *freezing*! When you were walking, it hadn't seemed so very bad. Remember? Well corblimeystrikealight you thought, this is no major deal! I can take this. I've got what it takes. You were wrong, weren't you? Giggling as it goes, your corporeal temperature begins inexorably to slide. Your feet just light out – without even saying goodbye – and your fingers start to sting and scrape with bloodlessness. Your nose becomes a wet, squeaky mess and your eyes clang and warp. For the first time in your life you become intimately acquainted with your innards, your entrails. You can actually *feel* your liver and your kidneys and they can actually feel you. (They aren't very happy about it either.) Your bladder stretches and quivers, summoning a whole series of tiny, short-lived, joyless pissings against convenient walls. You hear and sense the serpentine slither of your major intestine. Wow, is that major intestine a grumpy big boy!

More. Your joints become frozen punctuations along your several channels of quaking, shivering limbs. Your knees, elbows, ankles and wrists capitulate almost immediately, the gutless bastards. To your surprise, you find that you have one vague patch of frothy warmth just south of your navel (which for some reason is unaccountably moist). You stick your icy paws under your belt and tuck them under the warm, amorphous mass of your genitals. This is a horribly bad idea. Your hands are too far gone to benefit much and the iciness that they impart threads its way through your pelvis until it reaches your bladder. The poor old pissbag grows confused again and you stand for another symphony of frostbitten, fictitious micturations. You've pissed all you can piss and by now you are thoroughly miserable. You begin to understand why folk try to avoid this kind of thing as a general rule.

While your body is amusing itself in this edifying fashion, the gods of poverty and sleeping rough play yet another cruel trick upon you, you poor bastard. You light another fag, more for heat than enjoyment. After the first few experimental puffs, you realise, to your sphincterflapping horror, that you are not enjoying it at all. Not in the least – in no wise. This is you. Mr Nicotine. The fag fakir. Not that! Not my smokes, please! A few ragged and unsuccessful coughs later, you try again. Jesus, it's even worse now! The smoke scrapes at your frozen chest. You can feel the dull thump of the amateur smoker's headache greeting the back of your skull. Ah, fuck it all, lads, not that! You pray to St Christopher for the might, do you not? Aye, that you do. You beg for clemency to all the saints of the sepulchres. Not in order of preference neither. Indeed no. Strictly alphabetical. One must at all times remember one's devotional diplomacy. In all the tongues you can muster, you ask for an estimation.

And get none. No answer. Not a sausage. It's not on, mate. Not on at all.

You see, you have to be comfortable and pretty healthy to enjoy a really good smoke. Above all, you have to be warm. You just gotta be hot.

So, now what do you do? Cigarettes are out and that *is* bad. That is awful, ghastly, appalling. Get a gun. Shoot yourself. Splatter your brains onto the pavements and warm your hands in all the steaming grey goo before you die. Ah, you would if you could, wouldn't you? Yes. Wouldn't anyone in your position? Damn right they would.

So. Towards an end.

It's not even four o'clock and you're beginning to think that if you don't get some warmth pretty damned quick, you're just gonna fuck it all and jump into the filthy old Thames. Be quick at least. You'd be poisoned before you drowned. You're oh so cold! Your pubic hair is standing on end and your eyeballs have started to rotate. Fuck this for a game of soldiers, you conclude. You've got to move before you die. A quick, painful, stiff-jointed clamber to what were once your feet. Walking is tricky now that the soles of your shoes are the least numbed part of you. God knows how you're managing but you're managing. Come on, try – push hard. Make an effort. You must keep moving. That's it. Good. Rightleftrightleftright. Try not to think about it and your legs might do it of their own shaky accord. They're pretty used to this walking lark by now. Leave them to it. Delegate.

You have fallen and the sky grumbles darkly at you as you measure your length upon those stones. You think you detect a rumour of dawn trickling over that fluid, shallow sky, shedding a ghostly light on all that you see. But you're wrong. You realise that it is your eyes, dying.

Rotted by malnutrition, scaly teeth and rancid breath, you stand. Rotted by time, cold and despair, you look out across the river at your city. Greasy with exhaustion, your mind slows to its stop. To an end. You wait there. You fade, you wither, you slip away.

And the city?

The city. Crouched in the night. Urban deity. Black as death. Make obeisance to it. Worship. The dull, soft, thunder-rumbling, godly-mumbling car words drone on, lost in the dark. Little moving lighthouses with friendly shining dashboards, nice coloured lights. Red, yellow, green. Late now. The vast morning of darkness awaits its sunny sentinel.

Wait.

SEVEN

(South Bank — au coup de soleil. He sits in huddled, fuddled mid-repose under the lee of Festival Hall. Damp and solitude creep through the stiffness of his sweat-caked limbs. He listens to the riverdribble, weeping sweetly to himself, a concrete face of withered grief.)

Ah! The night has deepened briefly to a sour purple envelope. The chilly perfection of frost crinkles my hair as the sluggish minutes grind to dawn. The world has been remote and forbidding tonight. It has given me no good time. A flurry of dirty, inconsequential rain begins to stud my face and hands. It's hardly worth moving. Indolently, bludgeonthick, I watch as the lampfed sparkle of the tiny drops ribbons and dries on my frozen slablike hands.

Dawn soon. The creak of daybreak and the joist and heave of sunlight. To my left the railway bridge hums festively. The rustle and whine of tracks and slats. The weary trainsong, sleepsoft and dulled. Soon to rumble and clatter. This is fun. I like the way it gets the day moving. Stir and bustle. Switching on. Feeding the networks of electricity, gas and radio signals that try for warmth, light and noise. There's something very sociable and public about all this. Heating, water, power. Running under the streets — snaky and sinister, patch-holed by tubelines, like a rotten cheese. All fall in.

The dawn is beginning to glow into the feeble promise and benison of daylight. Cold light has just begun to filter over the trees, roofs and river, grey and liquid dawn — still a bereft limbo before day. In houses all around England, rude radios are switching themselves on. Early men are shaving, curtains raised, each one hoping to stock up on the benign beauty of daybreak, a general augur to their different days. Universal thoughts plague me, leaving me mild and kind. The underside of tenderside. Feel old, do I at such times. Though young, I see the emptiness and banality of my new true life. The tramp-dilletante. It has crushed my heart.

Come dawn, I usually get all platitudinous and semi-universal. Sweating out my days how I do, I'm untroubled by the world of contemplation. However, the night addles my wits. I consider the toils of the world. Honour, justice, truth, charity, power, strength, death and God all make their best contributions to my confusion. I chew dyspeptically on the cumbrous meal they make up. I should leave it alone. I'm barely out of my teens for goodness' sake! I can do without all that.

Ah, listen. The morning is filling with noise now, losing the deepwelled silence that had so comforted me in the night. Birds grumble in the cold air and I can hear the distant rumble of the awakening town. Light coming. The darkness has a cloudy, opaque sheen and my nose shines sharp and red in the gloom. I peer inhospitably at the rumpled, greying prospect, at the dull blinking windows, at the soft drizzle that has fringed the scene in its gentle, wispy embrace.

By God, I'm getting tired of this kind of life. The hours of my fucked-up days don't fade away as the recent past should. They pile up and clutter the streets. They set up a demo, the bastards. It has to stop soon. I've got to get this life of mine working. Walk outside the city. See that old sky and sea again. Meet those golden women I see in my dreams. Move. Change. Live. Before I crust and wrinkle and wither.

The drizzle falls harder now, that welkin pressing heavily upon the earth. Grey burgeoning light is splayed wide, squatting slowly over London.

I view the morning with much alarm.

It's in these corpsehours that my thoughts turn to my women. The history girls. In all my life, you women seemed the gravest main priority, each one a spray of godliness, a crutchhole in the shingle. My women, thinking them all out always cheers me up. Don't know why – women have generally crapped on me from as great a height as they could manage. Still, there you go – that's just me.

There have been two major women in my life. Two top bims. Neither granted me much of the thing known as happiness. On the other hand, they were both very handy at dishing out the misery. For this I can thank neither enough. Deirdre and Laura. My bims, Irish and English. Laura and Deirdre.

Of a bad pair, Deirdre Curran was the first and worst. I met her on an ill-starred Thursday afternoon when I was fifteen – an evil chance. I find it hard to believe that I ever got myself into all that. When all is well, susceptibility counts for such a lot. In my young Ireland I'd been from Killibeg to Dungiven, womanseeking, talking shite all the while ... being both Irish and young, you understand. I had, however, almost completely failed to fall into the rowdy rigmarole of youthful love. Too old and too nasty too soon, as I liked to think to myself. Deirdre spelt the end of that. Yes indeedy! Her sonority and sang froid pulled my wings off sharpish. She clipped them for me. She toned me down.

When you're young, it comes to you as the simplest of reflexes. Wham! There you go. You're in love, you bugger. The juicy jolt of recognition. She's for me ... or so I'd like to think. Everything conspires to aid the incontinence of your years. The echoes of soppyseeping pop songs blaring from rogue radio stations. The preponderance of romantic sentimentality in the nineteeth-century tracts that you adore so. The empathy, the clemency, the joy – the simple weight of your billowing, indulgent ego. Someone playing sillybuggers with your emotional discernment. Pish! Love! How we do wilfully disguise that grisly ganglionic stimulus. Love is the silken cloak that backs the witless levitation of the penis.

Hey, get a load of all that bollockwithering cynicism! Pretty impressive, oui? Looks and smells like crap to me. I'm no good at cynicism. I haven't got what it needs. It's waste of time, I never had the gift of being casual.

Love and benediction. Wellwish and all that. To confer good without sympathy is all you have to do, I'm told. Poor old romantic (erotic) love is having a rough time of it these days. People seem to consider it a little foolish, rather quaint, faintly David Copperfield, anthropological almost. Subsequently, it comes well behind lust, jealousy, greed, the pornopulse of modernity and (especially in my case) infatuation. True. I hate to admit it but I'm nearly always in a state of bovine infatuation. If you were ever to meet me (O lucky chance!), I am more or less bound to have conceived a youthfully maddened desire for some remote and frosty object. It would, no doubt, bore you titless. You would deem it immature, a sad waste of time. Curiously enough, I'd tend to agree with you. That is, as I've said before, just the kind of fellow I am.

Deirdre Curran – that Deirdre! Deirdre Curran was short, stumpy, Protestant and rich. Oh yes, she was also surprisingly stupid. I fell in love with her like a shot.

(That's the trouble with being an auto-didact. For me, as for all the self-taught, mistaken impressions tend to be tenacious, unshakeable.)

Dear me, how I wanted that girl! I used to pray to St Jude, Patron Saint of Lost Causes. I planned, I plotted, I dreamed the dreams of sanguine extravagance. I conjured her image and sweated out gutsy, improbable dramas of abduction and rescue, with me doing my Tom Jones and her doing me. I anticipated abject failure but tried it on notwithstanding. I made my move.

And would you believe it! She didn't jump on my bones. As a matter of fact she was so far from jumping on my bones that she told me (verbatim, I swear), she told me that she wouldn't piss on me. (Had I asked her?)

I was a mite crestfallen.

Nonetheless, I persisted. I was always topped up with resolution at that time. I asked her out to dinner. (Me, Mr Cool – I'd never set foot in a restaurant in my life – I'd never even *heard* of tablecloths!) She turned me down.

I ploughed on:

ME (*winningly*): Lunch then.

DEIRDRE: Can't ... sorry.

ME (*ardently*): Breakfast? Tea? Supper? Elevenses, 'tweenie snacks, fridge raids, midnight munchies, dormfeasts ... anything?

(Boy, was I cool or what!?)

DEIRDRE: I told you – I can't.

ME (*urbanely*): You'll die if you don't eat, you know.

DEIRDRE: Oh really?

ME (*brightly*): Yes. Believe me, I know about these things.

DEIRDRE: I can imagine.

(Pause. Dontcha just love this?)

ME (*anxiously*): Is it to me or the food you object? It would be equally hazardous to deprive yourself of me. Really it would.

DEIRDRE: I don't think so somehow.

ME: Ah, so cold, so harsh!

DEIRDRE: Look, I have to go.

(She tries to move off. I stop her. I wish I wouldn't but I do.)

ME (*energetically*): What is it then? My lack of reserve, my egoism. My rudeness, pomposity, my immaturity ... Look at me – I'm gorgeous! Don't you think.

DEIRDRE (*grudgingly*): You're not bad.

ME (*vigorously*): What can it be then? I must confess that I generally consider myself in the light of a gift from the Gods. All wrapped up and proffered to you.

(?)

DEIRDRE: Well, it's not my birthday.

ME (*reprovingly*): Did your mother never tell you that it is impolite to refuse gifts.

DEIRDRE: Yes but she also told me never to accept sweetness from strangers.

(Long pause. The only clever thing that Deirdre will ever say and it was probably accidental.)

ME (*facetiously*): She sounds like a nice woman, your mother.
DEIRDRE: Oh yes, she is ... very nice.
ME (*primly*): And fond of her favourite daughter, no doubt.
DEIRDRE: Dotes on her. (*Exit*)

Wasn't I something else! Why is it that adolescent boys talk so very much crap? I was certainly sticky with the blemish of the banal. I mean, I was bad but by no means unusual. Well, come now – I was young. I *am* young. I beg to plead callow immaturity.

Well, anyway, unaccustomed to the brush-off though I was, this looked suspiciously like it. But at least she hadn't threatened me with her urine this time. This led me to aspire further. I tried again.

And again.

And guess what! In the end I succeeded. A couple of weeks and about fifteen dismal seduction attempts later, I actually brought it off, so to speak. I trapped her at a school bus stop and made my final fruitful effort. I did well, very well. With all due modesty, I can claim that I was fucking incandescent and made bloody sure that she knew it. I danced for inspiration within my own uncharming circle ... and it worked.

She agreed to take me with her on a shopping trip the following Saturday. A shopping trip! Well now ... my heart swelled immoderately, as well it might. Wasn't I the fortunate fucker?

Predictably, she didn't even turn up. (I had nicked a fiver especially and was deuced peeved.)

I should have guessed something from this kind of behaviour. I should have been warned. I wasn't obviously. My myopia when it comes to my own fate can be extraordinary. The projected carnage of my future with her was there for all to see – except for me. Futility had tempted me. Disaster had set its sights on me. I should've known. I should have checked back on my previous track record fortune-wise. (One always seems to reserve one's greatest omissions and blunders for oneself.) I really should have left it at that.

Needless to say, I didn't. I tried her once more. Her reluctance was doing a stirring job on my resolution. To my surprise she seemed quite keen this time and returned my extravagant desire in her own fettered, Presbyterian manner. I honestly don't think that she'd ever met anyone quite like this particular Catholic boy. I diverted her. I amused. I surprised, I bewildered. I was also much better looking than she could have reasonably expected. This is probably what won the day for me. My ace beauty being the only trait to which Deirdre could really apply her rudimentary perceptive faculties. She was hardly one for spiritual or cerebral love, old D. Curran.

We met in Ormeau Park on the next Sunday. I did the bit again. I did magic for her. In the splash of twilight I made the soppy old church bells ring for her. I coaxed and cajoled their pealing iron. I made them sing and dance. (Lyricism came easily to me then.) I dusted off my soliloquies and made the most of my tawdry talents. I agonised feverishly over whether or not I should risk trying to kiss her. Without much ostensible agonising, she shoved her hand down the front of my trousers.

I asked her what she was doing.

She asked me what it looked like.

Something very rude, I suggested.

(Christ, even now I blush to think of the prawn I once was.)

Well, obviously I wasn't about to have that sort of thing clogging up my sentimentality. I pointed out the error of her Protestant ways, of her licence and lack of modesty. I evoked the ideals of purity, virginity and mutual respect. She asked me when I was going to pork her.

I was fifteen. You understand what I am saying? Fifteen. I tried to bolster my innocence. I tried to think of fidelity and erotic continence. I tried hard: so very hard. I was fifteen. I had had a permanent erection for nearly a year. Fifteen. Sex was ever in my thoughts in guises more or less enticing. Fifteen. I could sense the admonitory shade of Agnes Wickfield keeping her steady eye on me. But I saw frothing, writhing ballets of buttock, belly and breast. I was fifteen. I hadn't a chance.

I was forced to concede that, despite my jealous regard for her honour, I was going to have to shtup her. Therefore I made my plans. I swallowed my integrity and talced my penis. In mutual impatience and heat we awaited our chance.

Oh, there was already much to mourn in my youthful decision, the gim-crack solution to all of her obfuscating principles. Her bed I wanted now, more for the necessity than the desire, though there was in truth a residue of that as well. I was bewildered, uncertain. (Youth, youth!) I needed advice but where was I to get it? I was a son to myself but it was a father that I required and pretty damned quick too. Virginity was both our problems for though I was a hero lad, I had not yet dipped my pen into that most necessary of life's inks. For her part, Deirdre, though a voluble advocate, had lacked a suitable launch into her intended career of debauchery, or so she said. Me, I was unsure. Fool too, I trembled at its advent and certainty for us both. (Was there ever youngster did not?) My maiden thighs were like fucking jelly, I can tell you.

Despite these fears and scruples, I tried with vigour to concoct the stage for our Grand Passion. It would be touch and go. I was wealthy with will but lacked that little execution. Notwithstanding, I was fairly confident of my caddish purpose. Where were the snags and hazards with such a violently willing partner? I thought of her maidenhood. I smiled. Nothing like a spot of deflowering to give yourself that titillating sense of your own muscular wickedness.

In the end, at the final squalid conglomeration of parents out and plonker in, gates open, manhood waiting, her eyes closed and ready, her chest heaving and my pulse leaping, in the end – in the end I just couldn't do it! It was her clothes that did it. That schoolgirl array of improbabilities and compromise, not made to be shed. Not made for me to see the inside of. They glowered at me as they slipped off her swelling limbs. They reprimanded me. They rapped my knuckles. They told the tale – of her. Little Deirdre. That girl, that child. Human being and all. Hey, I thought, hold on! I don't want this. She is tits and arse and aperture. Go to it, bold Bogle. Stick it into her. Give her a good one. Fuck her bendy! But there they lay, those garments, crumpled, formless, the badge of her youth. None of that, they cried. Get off! Voleur!

You see, combining the act and fact of tenderness and rutting is a difficult task, achieved only through great study and application (or alternatively, by growing up). Quite impossible at my age and stage. I had looked at the mantelpiece while stoking the fire. Fatal. I was thwarted though stiff and desperate. All of a sudden, I liked her. A big mistake when it came to the callous indiscrimination of boyish porking. I liked her too much.

I lit a fag.

I don't think that Deirdre really understood. Short of functional impossibility (the failure of my rodlike, are you serious?), she couldn't see any hindrance to our objective. I explained my position. You know, I have to admit that I think she was pleased, touched, probably relieved. We had a cup of coffee and talked about abstinence and its little joys.

Implausible perhaps. Not quite what you would have expected from Ripley Bogle, the bold and cruel. The precocious boff-merchant. It's true though. Absolutely bona fide. As I look back, I can't help feeling rather sentimental about myself. All that selflessness and regard. I rather congratulate myself for my consideration. I was, fundamentally, a nice kid. Considering what eventually happened with old Deirdre, it's ironic, it's tragic, it's just sad. Confused? You'll see. You will understand.

Ah now. Here it comes. Morning. Anaemic light has stained the sky, dripping its misty glow over my recumbent, nostalgic self. The whisper and hiss of morning throbs across the soupgrey river. Day sets out its seedy stall. People have begun to dribble citywards, rested and ready. London adopts the mode matutinal: it lounges, it slouches. London is happily impassive.

I am tired and will sleep now. Yes, sleep. That will be a novel experience. Sleep. Day has come. It's here. Friday has arrived in full. It's my birthday today, you know. Or at least, I *think* it's my birthday today. Who can tell? Not me, that's for sure. I'm calling it my birthday for lack of evidence to the contrary. Well, twenty-two today. Huzza! Laud the day! I never liked birthdays anyway. Fatewise, in terms of luck, they seem to be asking for trouble.

Ah, close your eyes, Bogle. Sleep it off.

Suddenly, the city sparkles hard in a brief shaft of morning paleness scything down from the doomy bowl of clouds withering the corpselike sky.

FRIDAY

ONE

The grit-gravelled path crunches under the creaking blackbrown shoes of Ripley Bogle, disturbing the morning's sleepy hum. He, born twenty-two years ago this day, gazes hard at the awakening prospect around him; as he walks, he pokes the long greenless privet hedge with a stick.

Twenty-two. The ghosts of his life parade through his mind, capering sarcastically. An anniversary masque. Twenty-two. None of the child he had been.

He clears the crest of the long, gentle slope and catches sight of the morning river glistening quiescent, torpid water under the early sky. He holds his breath, diligently absorbing the morning. This is his trick. To sense and steal. Comfort lives where it can be taken.

He issues his pent-up breath in a long imperceptible sigh. An early, straying gull careers overhead, squawking a shrill seacry – beachcry.

Ripley walks slowly the tidebound riverbank. Coffee soon, he thinks. Warmth and steamsour comfort. Cigarette – one or more. He smiles hardily. He takes his time in the thought. He almost always does. Sensual proficiency demands his time and care. Invariably. He crunches out onto the tawdry river-shingle. The air is cold and raw. A rimy mist squats over the sparse trees and hills of the city. The sky is patched and stained with thick banks of dingy white cloud. There is little wind and the dulling vapours muffle what little sound there is. The fading, arcing cries of gulls, shrill yet soft.

He approaches the rocks at the outer rim of the bank that lead a mossy, river-washed path into the water itself. He picks his way thither, loitering amongst stones and fetid pools, riverward walking. Breathing sea air memories of bitter salt water. The shock when a child first tastes the juice of the flat sea that looks so friendly. Yuk! He still remembers. The burning tongue cured by ice cream and he philosophically put it down to experience.

The ragged young man approaches a large smooth rock about twelve feet from the river's edge, stepping on its brothers, stepping stones. He sits on the yet dry stone, gazing green eyes, wrinkled riverward as the yellow morning sun makes its appearance, belching over London like some ethereal milkman, bringing fruits of the earth in chinking bottles. Wakey, wakey.

Sensually satisfied, our hero returns to his thoughts. Twenty-two years ago, he was born. As he has been informed and believes. Ripley Bogle, successful tramp and sometime complete man, is twenty-two years of age today. Felicitations. Congrats. Been years since he saw the inside of a birthday card. Tsk tsk! Keeps himself to himself since his life died. Misanthropic. Very fickleominous.

Lonely birthday boy Ripley Bogle (Oh, that name, that name!) gazes skybright eyes at the skybrightened river partly punctuated by tide crests.

He thinks again. Soon he will smoke. A brief light flickers in his paling face. In anticipation his disreputable lungs ease their tightness. O noble Benson & Hedges and your ilk! With your cute little cellophane wrappers and your golden hues, regal and imposing. With your cricket sponsorship and your tricksy advertising hoardings! Ah, you usher of pleasure and calm, you!

Enter.

Not far off, rounding the pebbled curve, a stunted, stiltfigure clambers rickety over seep and shingle.

Qui va la?

Perry.

He comes.

Ripley sits with the sibilant, hissing river. It whispers and sighs. It gurgles its secrets to him.

Perry ambles woodenly towards Rock of Ripley. Slow, steady crutches à tâtons over the riverbank stones. Click kick hick scrape scratch. Like a tortoise. Tortoise head too. Pushed slightly forward, stiff hair sticking out at neck's nape. Tortoise tuft.

'Morning, Perry.'

'Hello, boy. You're looking good.'

Perry manoeuvres his crutches and hobbles fantastically to a seated position. Ripley offers no help to the old man and feigns to be unconscious of his pain. You see, Perry likes to pretend. As does Ripley.

The ancient speaks. Solicitude. Enquiry.

'Bad night?'

'Aren't they always?'

'True enough.'

There is a smileless silence of concord. Ripley shepherds his greedy gaze from the old man's satchel. Hand presses chin of bristle.

With querulous, quivering hand, the aged cripple roots in the ragged canvas shoulderbag. It parturates. Thwunk! First the flask. Tatty tartan cylinder of hopeless promise. Then its twin, the raggedbaggedy tobacco tin. Clink, clink. Breakfast for the boys.

'Will you have a little, Ripley?'

Old sageface assumes with studied ease the diplomatic visage of courtesy. Young foolface couldn't care less.

'I think I might indeed. Thanks.'

Smiling upon each other, they prepare. The tasks are divided. Youth pours treacly black coffee into lidcup for both. Elder, with nimble, with knotted fingers rolls secondhand cigarettes for both and each. The sun, it shines cold and pale through its sombre membrane of clouds.

The cup is passed. Perry sups deep. His withered lips pucker to savour. He returns the cup to his acolyte. The boy, too, drinks deep. His belly leaps and shudders in alarm. Curious, unsymphonic sounds bellow from his startled stomach, from his neglected innards. He blushes. Perry ignores. They still like to pretend.

Again they smile, old and young, upon each other, upon themselves.

They sup again. In turn. It is welcomed now, that sterling coffee. The advance party has laid good ground. Ripley's intestines slither though noiselessly this time. The thing called Pleasure makes its slightly shame-faced bow.

'Thanks.'

Perry sweeps his aged arm on the rasping rock and a matchflame spits and hisses to angry life. He lights two sparse and crooked cigarettes and surrenders the larger and straighter of the two.

'There you are.'

With reverence, devoutly, Ripley Bogle pulls hard and long, fingers and lips warming. Of this has he dreamt in his sorrow. He senses that old, grateful catch of lung, moistening as he rolls the ball of damp, acrid smoke in his placid chest. By ChristourLord, that makes the difference of the day!

'You like that, yes?'

'Very much.'

'I know ... me also.'

'Yes?'

Ripley stalls. The poetic interrogative. A useful device – leaves you listening. Though mostly to yourself. In mouthblue smoke, Perry issues his next.

'It doesn't go well with you?' he asks.

'Not very.'

'You're young. Much you can do. You shouldn't be like this.'

'I know.'

73

Both watch the lazy grey river. Dead, seamless liquid ploughing past the massy, rusty bridges. Ripley mouths his cigarette with dab hand and happy lips. He soils his desperate, quivering lungs once more. The silence drips like fog, dulling the weird screams of the satellite gulls. Minutes pass. Morning lengthens. They are silent. Suffered phrases speak to them, starkly indefensible. The wind in their hearts.

'Have those men come back?' Ripley asks with a fair assumption of solicitude.

'They came yesterday.'

'What did they say?'

Perry's benevolent tortoise eyes shine mildly at his friend. Perry meekly waits to inherit the earth.

'They say the hut does not belong to me.'

'But you built the fucking thing!'

'That's what I said.'

'Are they going to evict you? They probably aren't entitled to, you know.'

'They're entitled to do whatever they want.'

Old eyes full of amber and plumtreed gum slowly close. Meekly.

'What will you do?' asks Bogle.

'Wait.'

'What for?'

Perry's lined and holy old face turns to the river winding at his side. He smiles.

'I sometimes wonder how there can be in this good old world so many bastards.'

Ripley ponders with the speed of youth. Ohoh! Old Perry's getting senile. Touching eighty probably. An old man. Searching for gravefriends. His pitiless family. His six sons. Bastards all. Vigorous untroubled men with their ancient trampfather heading for the high jump. Depressing. By fuck it is. Must remember. Discourse with the aged is conducive to morbid speculations on mortality.

He tries to keep the small talk going.

'They'll never move you. They can't.'

'Well, it doesn't matter.'

A pause. They smoke.

The morning has broadened its pallid grin. The city fumbles with sleepy life and doltish movement. The stranded gulls wheel and dive in hungry panic, their clamour louder, more insistent. The silent trees fringing the river stretch their meagre branches into the soft, misty fur as if seeking warmth. Scantleaved and drooping, they disdain the evergreens with their

74

uncountried breath of green and promise. Around them London straggles damply grey, darkened and menaced by the lowering sky.

In a mad fit of daring Ripley begins to remove his overcoat. Perry stirs with slow surprise. He gestures to the growing blankets of mist that roll off the slimy river.

'Why are you taking your coat off?'

'I've been wearing the fucking thing for weeks on end. It smells revolting.'

'Taking it off won't make much difference.'

'It's the principle.'

'Oh.'

The young man drapes his discarded garment over a nearby, brother rock. He has kindled to sudden anger. The act and fact of his own odour shames and angers him. His jaw tightens with displeasure and he is close to ill humour. He inhales the fetid fumes of his lessening cigarette, pulling the last dregs from the grimy stump of paper and weed. He colours deeply.

'You want another cigarette?' asks Perry.

'Thank you, yes.'

Abruptly, the young man's ire dissolves in the tendrils of clammy fog that envelop his head. Again, Perry's crusty hands are busied with his tobacco tin. Ripley throws his used cigarette into the arcing air. It plops in the river mud where it hisses in dying.

The mist has gathered and banked around them now. A ponderous curtain of diaphanous fog and subtle drizzle. Mist glitters on the hair of both men, thick and thin. Perry speaks.

'Why do you do this thing?'

'What thing is this?'

'Being a tramp, you know, that thing.'

'Oh yes, that.'

'Well?'

'My career plans are a little uncertain at the minute, Perry.'

'Funny.'

'Yes.'

He strikes another match and lights both paltry cigarettes.

'This is no good for you. You look like a dead man.'

He gives the mortal remains of Ripley Bogle another cigarette. The corpse thanks him.

'You don't want to be like me when you're an old man.'

'Why not?'

'Don't be a fool!'

Perry's tortoise eyes pierce our hero's blush. Satisfied, he continues.

'Believe me.'

'I do, I do.'

There is silence. Discord and unease is exhaled in windwhipped tobacco-smoke. In that silence, the cold seems to sharpen and bite deeper. Ripley watches a train of sopping worms snaking their way past his rock towards a large clump of dock leaves. They are slow and silent, coiling and uncoiling with their strange untracked motion. He laughs.

'You might be right. Maybe it's time I gave it a rest.'

'Get yourself some money. Get a place to live. You could do that easily enough. Couldn't you?'

Ripley's merriment burgeons.

'Oh yes. Not a problem nowhere.'

His laughter fades and his face grows bitter with the mild amusement of despair. His future does not trouble him. He'll mix a kind of hope, knead it and bake it in experience.

'Ah, we understand each other, Ripley. There are things we don't have to say.'

Oh dear. Ripley smiles a flushed, embarrassed smile. My my, metaphysics at this time of the morning. What to say? Don't you think Marvell conjures that notion of grateful despair so well, Perry old fellow? Why, absolutely, Ripley my dear chap. Where does he look? Riverward as a longer and higher surge splashes the foot of his rock. He wiggles his toes. His socks are wet. They were wet already.

A very, very long pause indeed.

Water lapping rockbase. Ripley's soaksocked right foot, oblivious of further immersion, dangles in the fetid, oily foam. Perry starts in surprise. Older. Slower to notice.

'The tide's rising. We'd better move.'

Ripley rising, hising trouserlegs. Watch him splish splash along. Feeling young again. Let's hear it for Spontaneous Rejuvenescence! Perry hobbles the dry way. Poking deep crutch holes in the shingle. Pins a tiny, wandered crab, scuttling home. Dead. Ripley watches the death throes. The single witness. Perry bringing everyone with him.

Cripple and tramp limp bankward, wet and dry, chased by the green-brown riverrise. Perry's cacophonic hobbling grating the air. Riverwracked bank and drying silt reached. Sprayed with irregular tufts of sickly bankgrass in a dismal state of wet conglomeration. Here and there spotted with the shite of dog and bird, squelching under foot and crutch. Ripley stares back at his watery rock.

'Bugger! Where's my coat?'

With fumbling crutchhand, Perry hands the garment back to Ripley. The young man dons it quickly, his flesh pricked and pimpled with soggy cold.

'I must be getting on, Perry. Are you going back to the shack?'

'I think I'll just sit here for a little while more,' Perry gainsays, indicating a damp, grassy mound near by. 'I like to look at the river in the morning.'

Indeed. The two men stand in awkwardness, not knowing how to end. In wetted fogbreath, Ripley looks to the old man. His face is framed close in the fluff of mist and drizzle, his eyes bought and troubled.

'So ...' he begins, soon to stop. A sentence dies and lies unburied. (Never a good idea – comes back a traitor in someone else's mind, all sonly duty gone.)

Ripley struggles with his stammer. He thinks too quick and leaves behind the need for dramaturgy.

'I'll see you tomorrow, then,' he manages.

The old cripple smiles.

'You certainly will.'

Ripley knows that this is doubtful at Perry's best. Each morning these days stands a betterthangood chance of being his last. Perry's, that is.

Still, they stand. The corruption of rain and fog seems to be lifting now. Wicked shapes loom suddenly through the clearing air. On branches, birds recommence their lazy twitter. Vile and leprous, the city grins its grimy appreciation. Ripley summons his resolve. Demonstrate consideration with conviction. Shelley's glass dome staining his cathedral floor.

'Well cheerio, Perry. Take care,' he advises.

'Goodbye.'

Perry shuffles and scrapes to his earthy seat.

Riverhiss. Morningbreath.

Ripley slopes off over the torpid grass. Wonders whether he will see old Perry again. Hard to say. He knows where he is going though. No mistake. Downhill with his wheels greased.

He puts his chafed hands in his pockets. His right hand feels a curious, half-familiar crinkle and curl of thin, leaflike paper. He stops, head bent. The grass glows up between his feet. His fingers fumble and he almost drops his prize. Slowly, with infinite care, he opens his stiffened fingers and peers at the ten-pound note that lies in his dirty palm, rustling slightly in the breeze.

His trick is not to think. Shame and guilt – crouching dwarves – bleakly determine regret. He walks on, straining for the safety of that privet hedge. He tries to ignore but still looks back. Looks now:

Perry sculptured, moundseated, surrounded by the morning that encircles his sea. He meekly waits.

TWO

Putney Bridge Road. I light another cigarette. Another mountebank to bleed my chest anew. Christ oh Christ, that's the thing! Forty fair Benson & Hedges will see me through the half of my dirty day. Thanks to those pounds. Those ten crinkly, wonderful, socialist pounds!

Here we go. Happiness settles on my limbs like dew. By God, there's nothing like a little dosh to chuff you up. Thanks to Perry, smoke slithers around my clogged innards, a harbinger of joy and relaxation. Smoke cleans me up, it gives me my medical, it reads my horoscope, it solves my problems. Oh Lord above, how I love to smoke!

Eighty a day, did I when I had money. Oftimes more. Lungwise, I was all macadam. My breath was sulphurous, my tongue tasted of rotting seaweed and beach sewer and my belly was copperplated. Smoke was my natural habitat and my chiefest sustenance. Fresh air made me puke and oxygen gave me a headache which only nicotine could cure. Fifteen minutes without a fag was enough to leave me clambering up the walls. One year, I practically financed Essex County cricket team!

I was some smoker.

But what about the good red blood that I coughed from my lungs every morning, eh? It wasn't the blood that worried me. It was the other stuff, the blancmange, the industrial adhesive, the dead creatures. My insides were rotting and mucus-ridden. That firm slithery phlegm that I manufactured every day was getting darker and more substantial. Happy little blobs of it, sitting pertly on the table, shining and squirming. Like an augur, I used to inspect its entrails for signs. Brown was good and green was better but it soon became yellow and black if not candy-striped. All very inauspicious. Thicker too, jellied and elastic. My good two ounces of matutinal lungbung.

In the offices of the Benson & Hedges marketing boys, I am a legend. Soon their advertisements will refer to me specifically by name.

I turn up Armoury Way, heading for York Road. South London is particularly dingy this morning. York Road is a wonderful example. Squalid and damp. The crumbling pavement and creeping grime slither underfoot and the air is stale with local debauchery. The stretch of shop and hovel parades its misery and filth. The people slouch with shame and abnegation. My kind of place all round.

That's the problem with Putney. It's miles away. A real Tolkientrek! Nonetheless, I usually waltz out here of a morning to see the bold Perry. Old Perry's exceptionally groovy for a crippled old Polish bloke. He's got a verminous old shack on some infested wasteground near the river. He built it himself about a century ago. He lives there. I mean it's not a nice place but he lives there. It's a dump, a kennel, a frigging privy but he still lives there. He doesn't want be a tramp, that Perry. He's too proud and posh and Polish.

Perry's a very handsome old bloke. It's a funny thing about these Polish guys. They may look like shit when they're young but, goodness, do they get handsome when they're ancient! Perry's like that. Once, he showed me a picture of himself as a young man during the war. He was a gimp, a complete spastic. But now, he's gorgeous! He's a craggy Adonis. He's just so sage and distinguished. Like a cross between James Mason and Blake's God paintings. All grey and piercing. I swear to God that I almost fancy old Perry! I really do.

Perry is Polish. You'd never guess and he rarely talks about it. He hates Poland and the Poles. Rather like me and the Irish, I suppose. He believes that Poland has only ever dumped on the Poles. According to him, nobody hates the Poles as much as other Poles. He was a pilot during the war. (Weren't they all?) When he escaped to England he was asked to join one of these expatriate Polish squadrons that the British had set up. (Ah, that's what I like about the British. They're so polite, so hospitable.) Perry refused. He didn't want to know. I think he would rather have signed up with the Luftwaffe. However, in the end he learnt that the Krauts had minced his mum and dad, his brothers, his sisters, his grannies, his girlfriend and aunts and uncles and all that kind of stuff. Perry was so annoyed that he conquered his better principles and joined this Polack RAF outfit. (Ah, those tactless German chaps!) He then spent the next two years single-handedly blowing the shit out of half the Nazi war machine. (They're a grudgebearing race, the Polish.) Towards the end of the war, he got his pelvis flakked to pieces. (He still managed to land his plane, would you believe!) He went to hospital where he contracted influenza and lost the sight of one of his eyes. An army surgeon cocked up his operation so badly that his pelvis remained completely rigid for the rest of his life. When he left the army they gave him a medal and some crutches.

Perry's had a bad old life. That's what I like about Perry. He's never going to embarrass you with his success.

Perry is my friend. I rather think he's the only one I've got. He's a strange sort of friend for me to have, don't you think? Where are the shared experiences, where is the common ground between an Irish vagabond and an ancient Polish cripple? Still, Perry's the last of my friends. The one. Any day now, I'll have none. You see, the sad truth is that Perry is going to die very soon. There is no doubt whatsoever about this. It is a certainty. No one will give you odds on this one. Perry's going to pop his clogs. I *know* Perry will die soon. Perry *knows* that Perry will die soon. Everybody knows it. It's old hat. The news has done the rounds.

It's not that he is particularly unhealthy. I mean, apart from the fact that he's a half-blind ancient cripple, he's in pretty good shape. He buzzes with bronchitis and has been marinated by hypothermia but that's not what is killing him. To tell you the truth, I'm not quite sure what actually *is* killing Perry but something is, that's for definite. This sounds like crap, I know. It used to be when I read all those soppy old books where the image and presentiment of uncaused death featured a lot, I would be unconvinced. I thought that this Victorian notion of the incontrovertible mark of imminent demise was all guff. For me this mummerstuff was patently bollocks. You know what? – I was wrong. It is like that. You can actually tell. You simply know, just like in those books. That's how it is with Perry. Don't ask me how but I just know it.

I've straightened onto Battersea Park Road. Closer now, the city rumbles in the morning haze. The greying sky looks down on the south of London. Down on dirty rooftops and snaky roads. Churches dotted optimistically amongst the grime.

He has wisdom too, has Perry. He doesn't dish it out a lot but it's there, you can tell. Maybe that's how he got to be so handsome in his twilight years. Who knows? He was a little querulous this morning but you've got to allow old people their intermittent crankiness. (I mean, have a heart ... he's dying after all!) He told me off for being a tramp. He's snobbish that way. He thinks that I should do better for myself. Well, he's winning no prizes for that one. Still, it's nice that he should take the interest. It must be difficult to do that when you're his age. When you have so little invested in the world. You know, I do think the old man cares about me. It's soppy, I know, but that's where these old guys win the day.

It's with decency that they win the day, these old ones. Decency. Yes oh yes. It knocks me dead, does decency. It lays me out. Hard to believe but true. Picture me here, striding this road. Tall, strong, witheringly gorgeous and snake-deadly. I may be a tramp but I'm a triumph of youth and sap. I'm a sneerer. I'm vicious, volatile and I love myself alone. I'm a high priest in the creed of acid youth. But the one thing that really fucks me up is decency.

That deliberate calm, that fucking equanimity. Pit me against a truly decent man, a short-arsed tubby middle-aged mediocrity with an overdraft and scraggy teenage daughters and I'm useless. I'm massacred by all that mild wisdom, that relentless charity and experience. The consideration, the tact, the placid acceptance. Christ above, the sheer unnecessary goodness of these people makes me sick! I get all humble and I stammer ... me for chrissakes! Gorgeous, gregarious, grabber me! When I was younger I used to beat the crap out of them, rape their wives and piss on their toupees – all that kind of thing. But it never made any real difference. I still had the feeling they were winning whatever prize our contest held. I couldn't take it. With their pot bellies and their fleshy necks. What did they have that I didn't?

Don't answer that!

That's age for you. That's what it's got. It's a funny old thing, is age. Just like death, I try not to think about it a great deal. But boy oh boy, is it going to come soon and then where will I be? Oh, that gap. That well-sentried wall between the old and the young. They hate us and we hate them. They do, however, rule the world and all its youth. All those geriatric national leaders that keep our feverish little globe wobbling on. What do they know of the modern world? They passed menopause during the Second World War. They're out of date. They're frigging obsolete!

(On the other hand, I wouldn't want some half-arsed kid running the country from the recipe book of juvenile trial and error. That would not be very clever. It's a difficult one, to be sure.)

The thing about the old is that they're old. They are pompous, intolerant and cantankerous. They have no spontaneity and no vigour. They are terribly sentimental about being old.

The thing about the young is that we are young. We are obstinate, vain and insolent. We have no wisdom and no judgement. We are terribly sentimental about being young.

You know, I think I'll probably become quite good at being old as time passes. Well, I'll have to, won't I? Pretty craggy and distinguished looking too, I hope. I haven't made my mind up about age yet. I'm no gerontologist. I'll think about it more when I'm a little older.

(Passing the power station, I give it a friendly little wave. I like to keep the scenery happy.)

Perry gave me some money this morning. A crafty little tenner. He obviously slipped it into my coat pocket when I wasn't looking. (Light-fingered diplomacy too! The man's a saint. He really is.) I must admit, I rather baulked at that. I surrendered a little more dignity then. I haven't enough left to dismiss the loss. Don't get me wrong. I can definitely do with the dosh but it was just a bit of a blow to what's left of my pride. Pride indeed! Isn't it a marvel of tenacity that I retain something of that venial vice? Scrounging from a crippled shackdweller at my age! I'm on the downward slide now. Perhaps, I should relax about it. Claim its inevitability as my own. Honour its advent.

Perhaps I should learn from the dashing Perry himself. Humility is what I need. In my situation it would seem to be a pretty vital accessory. Well, I've got a lot to be humble about. But then again, there's always my ruling maxim – be strong before you are humble. Obviously, I'm short on strength these days. Videlicet, my weakness feeds my hubris. As is always the way. It's not fair. Perry gets the best of the starting grid on humility. He's odds on. My problem is my pit stops.

Nine Elms Lane now. My sparkling, crackling matchflame hisses anaemic sulphurflame onto my crinkly fagtip. Puffsuck and smokeball. That little mist has returned now. It's making the last of its day's efforts. It's aspiring to be a latemorning blanket of dingy haze. It is succeeding, rather. My filthy hair is further moistened and my noxious lungs are sticky with condensation. The cold, too, has staged a comeback. It is a nipping and an eager air. A strangler's knot of sleeplessness and fatigue tugs at my ailing heart. Man dear, I am tired! Terminally tired. Dreamtired. My renegade concentration is wavering and my thoughts are flaking into hardy gossamer strands. They are taking reasonless flight in this grubby cloak of sky and air. I've got to have a nap soon. A little baby parksleep. Some dosh, some fags, some kip and some grub. Isn't this the life for a likely lad comme moi!

Yes, old Perry is certainly tremendously cool. He has got what it takes, the photogenic honour of the underdog. If I ask him nicely, he may even give a little of it to me. Perry's not greedy.

Maurice was also tremendously cool. He was littered with gaping armour chinks, it's true, but then again he was young. He carried it off. You know I truly liked old Maurice. Affecting, huh? Agape. The schoolboy's love.

Maurice Kelly was the eldest son of a prosperous academic family from the relative splendour of the Malone Road. His father was an Economics Lecturer at Queen's and his mother taught history at St Mary's, a fuckbag girls' school that tries hard to posh it out on the Upper Falls and fails badly, mostly due to the infelicity of location. He had two elder sisters, neither of whom provided much onanistic inspiration, try as I might. The mum and dad were pretty reasonable people, insultingly normal almost, but the various offspring were all highly fucked-up. That sounds callous but I have no time for these high-strung siblings and their PMT and tampon moods.

They're a pain in the arse. Maurice shared this view. Compared to the others he was relatively stable.

Maurice was a major Catholic. He was practically papal. The tenets of the Holy Roman, Catholic and Apostolic Church played a starring role in the formation of his moral code, a code which was rigorous in the extreme. He was ineluctably, irretraceably Irish.

Mixed with this Catholic business were his witless politics. Maurice was a passionate Nationalist and Republican. He was capable of the most bewildering stupidity and barbarism in his support of Catholic Celtism, just like all his badbastard compatriots. The Catholic Church and Irish Nationalism. Lovely. Subjects indivisible in nature and import.

I know well that this is bad for Maurice's image but I'm sure you'll give him a chance. What you must remember is that our particular generation of Irish folk were born into all that crap. We knew nothing else. Think about it. Picture it. The mid-sixties, the birth of Maurice and myself. There aren't actually very many bombs and guns around as yet – just a lot of jobless Catholics getting the shit kicked out of them and having their homes burnt down on Protestant feast days, adding to their well-stocked catalogue of hatred and injustice.

Soon, however, will come the Civil Rights marches. The Protestant lot will get annoyed. They (reasonably, I feel) would rather like their civil rights to remain exclusively Protestant. So, the British Army will be drafted in to protect the Catholic minority from the brutality of their Proddie countrymen. Maladroitly enough, the British Army will then shoot a little bunch of unarmed Catholic civilians, clerics and toddlers on Bloody Sunday. In their turn, the Catholics grow rather peeved and start exterminating a whole plethora of soldiers, policemen, prison officers, UDR men, Protestants, Catholics, English shoppers, Birmingham pubgoers and men who make the mistake of editing the *Guinness Book of Records*.

Tsk, tsk, tsk! What chance did we ever have? For a piece of normality? Not much.

You see, they made a very big mistake with the Catholics. They really shouldn't have pushed them around like that. It was bound to break sometime. And break it did. The Catholics of Ulster may well have been a dreadful collection of drunken, wifebeating, educationally disadvantaged, bastardguttersnipes but it was soon discovered that they had another talent to add to their knack of repeatedly impregnating their foul hagwomen beyond the bounds of obstetric probability and their bewildering capacity for talking shite. That third talent was, of course, killing people. Damn right. Few do it better.

There you have it. That was the Ireland of our birth and growth. It affected us differently. All that Gaelic, nationalist, Celtic superiority bollockspeak. Because he had known nothing else, Maurice saw it as his birthright and treasured its insanity as his own. Because I had known nothing else, I disclaimed blame and didn't want to know. I began to memorise the ferry timetables for Holyhead, Stranraer and Liverpool. It was somebody else's crime and thus somebody else's problem. My answer would be my exit. This used to drive Maurice potty, I'm glad to say.

We used to have these wonderful juvenile arguments on the thing called Irish Politics. This vexed theme was a real scratching post for my oratorical claws. I told Maurice that he was talking bollocks, that he was full of shit and that his opinions were a pile of piss. (Rhetoric was always my indulgence.) Maurice comforted himself with the thought that I was politically naive. I comforted myself with the thought that I couldn't give the vaguest toss either way.

We tried to avoid politics.

Despite all these bony little contentions, we were major bestbuddies. Maurice was the silent type. He pursued a policy of taciturn isolationism. Nonetheless, he usually unbent a little for my good self. I was pleased with that. I was always rather proud of having Maurice as a pal. I considered that it reflected well upon me and hinted at depths of character I might otherwise have seemed to lack what with being such a picaresque scallywag and all.

The great thing about Maurice was that he was just so incredibly handsome. I myself am pretty damned cute but young Kelly was in a different league. He was like one of those svelte guys you see in glossy women's magazines and immediately accuse of being queer. Like one of those ... only better looking.

All you mindsleuths out there will probably be thinking that I had some kind of adolescent homoerotic prompting for the bold Maurice. Well, you're probably right. You would probably have felt the same way if you had seen him. Tall, blue-eyed and with that glossy, thick black hair that makes me spit what's left of my teeth. I think he'd tickle your fancy if you saw him. I'm certain of it. You won't though. Not now. They shot young Maurice. They killed him. Yes, they did. Those bad, those beastly boys. They huffed and they puffed and they blew his head off. Those boys.

It was ironic really. There was me, Ripley Bogle, from out of the less-than-working classes, child of the Falls and son of a gun, breaking my supra-spermbound balls to get out of all that and there was Maurice, child of ease, silvergobbed and pretty posh, trying to be Che Guevara.

He should have left his politics in the realms of theory – polite, debatable and not actually hazardous to life. But he had to delve into the practical side of things, the fatal side of things.

They killed him. I knew they would in the end but what could I do? I was young, a boy. I had problems of my own. It wasn't my fault. There was nothing I could do.

All that's left of Maurice are the anecdotes I choose to tell. What a thing to die for! Then again what else is left of anyone? Your dead are the mute justifications of your lies, misunderstandings and inaccuracies. Very soon, Perry will join that backlog of narrative, recollection and anecdote. Oh, me and my dead or soon-to-be-dead friends! That's their fate. My stock of remembrance. Like short stories without conclusion, they'll glide upon my memory.

That's the trick! Get clannish and dynastical with the deaths of your life. Make 'em count. Those you knew who were but are no more. Tracing back to age and history. That's the ticket. Filling out your backward life with other people's deaths.

The threnody, the dirge, the song of lamentation.

*

Maurice and I were wealthy in areas of disagreement and many would be the furious, screaming rows we would have on a multitude of topics. However, the only issue over which we actually came to blows was the issue of Deirdre. Maurice wasn't keen on the young Miss Curran at all. He claimed that she meant trouble and that she would only give me a bad time in a variety of unedifying ways. Goddamit, he said, the dame jus' ain't no good! Being morbidly sensitive on this of all subjects, I naturally tried to twist his head off. Predictably, Maurice kicked my pickles in for me, he knocked the welt out of me.

I shouldn't have wasted my blood and sweat like that. Maurice was right (unusually for him). As he predicted, my dear old mother soon began to demonstrate the extremity of her objections to my ecumenical romantic choice. She said that Deirdre was a Protestant (i.e. a heathen, a pagan, a Godless one), and though she was a nice enough girl, she was still a Protestant and thus she'd have to go. If I persisted in my treasonous infatuation, my mother would be under the unwelcome necessity of tearing my bollocks off. It simply had to stop. All that corny love-across-the-barricade stuff only ever worked in screenplays and pop songs. In real life I'd soon be graced with a headhole that was, strictly speaking, surplus to my cranial requirements (probably donated by a staunch member of my extended family). Anyhow, argued Mom, she was just a little Proddie tart — hardly worth all the bother.

No doubt, you can clearly see that this was not the correct way to influence me. My heart was full of righteous indignation and my head was full of empty spaces.

*Accordingly, I protested. No dice, I said, not on, get away, I should cocoa ...
absolutely not!*

*This was very foolish of me. Mother dearest asked my interesting Uncle Joe to try
and talk some sense into me. Uncle Joe certainly argued his case with some vigour.
He threatened to blow my knees off if I didn't do what my mummy wanted me to do.
He showed me the gun he was going to do it with if I didn't comply. It would hurt
him a lot more than it would hurt me what with me being family and everything. I
had my doubts.*

*So, what could a poor boy have done? I lit out, of course. I buggered off sharpish.
I hit the road, Jack. I faded, as they say. I bade farewell to that family of mine. I didn't
have anywhere else to go, or any money and that kind of thing but I wasn't breaking
my heart, believe me! Family is family, true; but on the other hand, I was fond of my
knees and keen on keeping them.*

*(I have to hand it to Maurice. He had forecast that she was trouble. Afterwards,
he didn't once say 'I told you so' or 'See what I mean?' or 'What a jerk!' In his
position, I would have had a field day. But Maurice couldn't have been more
sympathetic. He stopped warning me about Deirdre. He left it out altogether. God,
I wish he'd kept it up! I wish he'd taken me to task.)*

THREE

(Hyde Park. An unshaded scuffed green wooden bench glistens and buckles in the sudden sun. We see the light of day descend upon the recumbent form of Ripley Bogle. He is sleeping heavily and sonorously to the tune of wheeze and gurgle, wrapped tightly in his thick, grimestreaked overcoat. His chin and cheeks are tracked with the snailmarks of his own escaping slobber. He twitches and stirs in the heat and a pulse throbs visibly in his temples. His sleep is troubled, populated by monstrous imaginings and foulest memories. He groans and cries out in a small voice.)

No! *(Awakening. It begins.)* Aaaggh! Umph! Blleeuuurrghh! Whoooo! Hrmth. *(He stirs.)* Whhhuughh! *(He asks. He searches.)* Whharrgh? *(His feeble brainstir signalling the juicy stimulus of consciousness.)* Yynneeaakkttchhk! *(And fruit will bloom on that braintree.)* Whaa? *(Though slowly.)* Christ! *(He pulls himself to a slouch.)* Jesus! *(The priestly sacrament of righteous slumber recedes from him.)* Ooooh! *(And he cries out for its benison and warm oblivion.)* Where the fuck . . .? *(The treasure of forgetting.)* How did . . .? *(When little else is left.)*

Ach! *(He coughs and spits kaleidoscopically.)* Acgthk! *(Look and listen. Streaming with mouth mucus.)* Ach! *(Disgusting. All gob and snot.)* Acthk! *(Like sleeping in aspic.)* Athcktk! *(He passes filthy hand across filthy face. He moans. He groans. He wipes away the pain. Scrapes it off. Ready, he sits up gingerly.)*

Oh, my God!

(Awakening)

Ooooh. Ow. Ouch. Christ!

My eyes are streaming and my head is bunged and heavy. I feel like shit. Poverty and sleeping rough.

You can always tell that things are going badly with someone, you can tell that their life is really crumbling, when sleep becomes inordinately precious to them. Almost sacramental. That soft escape and gentle abdication of responsibility. That's a bad sign. Watch out for it. The treasure of forgetting. When that's all you've got.

(And now I sing a little paean to the death of my sleep. The insomniac's lament. As you might have guessed things don't go well with me. It's not looking too spiffing down here at Bogle Mansions.)

Guess what! The day has turned to warmth. Can you believe that? I nearly crapped myself, bedad! After freezing my little gonads all night, I come upon a belter like this! Where's the justice in that?

Here I am in Hyde Park. There are a lot of little boys around. I think fondly of rubella, smallpox and sub-machine-guns. The broad expanse of the lifeless park swelters and heaves in the lunchtime sun that bakes the dusty ground and a sharp scent of promise shimmers in the stifling air. (Not for me, it doesn't.) The wheeling anarchies of the lunchfreed boys are listless and sporadic, soon quelled by the moist blanket of heat and discomfort. On the extreme left hand of the bench adjacent to mine, a small, newly brace-toothed boy is struggling to soothe the agony of his gashed mouth with a warm, dripping peach. I watch his silent tears run into the mess of his untasting mouth. This is one of the reasons why I hate the summer.

Having said that, I must confess that I am beginning to feel rather good. I feel that I'm reaching something of a peak here. It's warm, I've slept, I have cigarettes and money in relative plenty and the imminent prospect of food. Why goodness, you're seeing me at my zenith.

I am a little dirty perhaps. Well, very dirty as a matter of fact. A wash would be nice but it's a little difficult for someone in my position to be as scrupulous in his personal hygiene as he would like. Anyway, what people don't realise is that after a little healthy neglect, one's hardy little body gets used to dirt. It starts to fight back. It self-maintains. Strange but true. Look at me, for example. Now, I blush to think how long it has been since my last bath or wash and yet I don't smell so *very* bad. My hair is winning few prizes but it's vaguely presentable, in half light, with a paper bag over my head. Apart from my agricultural armpits and my fertiliser feet, I'm pretty inoffensive. Still, I admit that a wash would be welcome.

You'll be glad to hear that I've been a clever boy. Since I left Perry this morning, I have bought two packets of Benson & Hedges and nothing else. I've managed to resist the impulse to blow the remaining seven quid on a Lamborghini or a partnership in a major merchant banking group. This is what is called discipline, asceticism. I've got a lot better at this asceticism business of late.

Those crafty seven pounds are cheering me up. They are imparting style and dash to my calculations. Airily, I think of all I might purchase. Not a great deal, perhaps, but every little counts. One of the useful by-products of having one of those handy deprived childhoods is that it gives you an almost limitless capacity to winkle joy from very little. I'm easily pleased.

Contentment lurks around the least imposing of my corners. I'm lucky. It's one of the things I like about me.

Despite my brinkmanship, I'm pretty certain that I should eat soon. I consider it advisable, judicious. My breath is dragonbreath and my gut is coated with gritty tar. Collapse and beriberi are on the agenda so I think I'd better call it a day with the old self-immolation. I'll have to be careful though. My digestive system is a little flummoxed by inactivity. Eagerness might be hazardous – that way dysentery lies. My digestion needs a gentle course of revision before I can move onto anything as ambitious as solids. It needs a few trial runs.

(I once knew a tramp called Crusher Grotbag or something like that. He was a smelly old bastard from Glasgow with completely black teeth and a startling array of skin diseases. I hated that bloke and then some. Anyway, he once went eight days on the bad bend and without eating. On the ninth day he ran out of diesel or whatever it was he was drinking and he ate the good half of a stale cheese sandwich he found in a parkbin. He died of shock. This, I want to avoid.)

Soup. Soup's the thing. Or some coffee and a careful sandwich.

I stand up. I congratulate myself on that one. It seems like a pretty dynamic thing to be doing. From up here on the top of my feet, the fire of the day seems to have increased and homed in on me more than ever. My hunger for smoke grips me in the lowering heat.

Quickly, I light a cigarette.

I sit down again. I over-estimated my rested energy. I'm still well-fucked. I am disappointed in myself. I should make more of an effort. I'm losing the difference. The difference between what I am and a real tramp. I'm slipping into veritable trampdom. Proper vagabondage. I'm not one yet, though. I'm still much too bloody posh. I'll allow the fact that people seem to avoid me in the street but it's a general dread, not the fevered specific of trampfear. My clothes are at least making the effort at respectability and I've never actually begged.

Some are born to destitution and some have destitution thrust upon them. I'm not very sure which was the case for me. I think I had both. I'm a butterfly, socially speaking. I'm homeless but I'm careful with whom I mix. I don't want to let myself down. I've got to be careful. I'm different. I'm not like those other tramps. No.

I ease back and down. I lower my sorry body into the embrace of aching wood and blisterpaint. I am much more comfortable prone. The sun toasts my stubbleface and I sizzle gently in my own fragrant sweat. Now, this is what I call animal luxury! I close my sluggish eyes and my eyelids perform those sunny kaleidoscopes we all know and love. Splash and streak of ocular purple, yellow, orange, amber and black. I wiggle and squirm to settle. The park noises increase in volume and decrease in importance. My mind rolls at rest. My feet are terribly grateful and my dear old belly opts for patience. After so long, it can wait its turn. This is nice. I make the most of it.

Obviously, we're lacking action here, we're losing thrust and pace. I search my surplus of theory and reminiscence. It occurs to me that I have been too quick in running through that childhood of mine. Neglected the genius of epiphany and detail. I drop theory and plump for reminiscence.

Two boyseen incidents. Small and separate but interesting still. I hope you like them.

I remember that when I was a brat I once saw a soldier killed on the Falls. I was about ten. It was my first death and I have since grown attached to it.

My deranged mother was dragging me along to consult the various vampiric shrinks whom I still had to attend at the RVH. It was a typical day on the Falls Road. The dusty squalor of that street cooked in an endyear haze of dirt and cold. The usual Falls stuff – arrests on spec, public strip searches and half-hearted riots. All good fun for me.

Anyway, as my mother and I neared the old hospital we heard several bursts of tinny gunfire. Everyone dived for cover in the generally accepted tradition for these occasions. An army foot patrol had been tortoise-trailing its way up the Grosvenor Road and now split, panicked, in all directions. A couple of massive squaddies huddled under the wall of the Eye, Ear, Nose and Throat Clinic with my mother and myself. There was a sniper on top of the Divis Flats at the bottom of the road. It was obviously perfect sniping ground, giving the perceptive bastard a marvellously unrestricted view of the entire length of the Lower Falls. There was a brief pause while my mother harangued the two soldiers for endangering her with their proximity. Patriotically, she felt that they should present a target less inimical to her own life (and mine too, doubtless). A few speculative volleys zinged harmlessly into the brickwork punctuating the wait nicely. The Brits had radioed for a helicopter and seemed well content to wait it out in the interval. Several minutes passed in blissful silence, apart from an occasional sanguine report from the persistent sniper. I was having a fucking brilliant time and keenly awaited some carnage.

Suddenly, this fat nurse came trundling down the Springfield Road on her bicycle. The traffic had all stopped and there were scores of pedestrians lying flat beside walls and doorways but this obviously didn't say a lot to the silly cow!

The soldiers shouted for her to take cover but the fatarse was wearing a pair of huge, furry earmuffs and obviously couldn't hear a thing. They shouted again, the silly sods. She heard this time but panicked and came to a wobbly, rabbitblind stop, slap bullseye in the middle of the crossroads. There were more frantic shouts and a few shots ripped into the tarmac close to her bicycle. He'd have been doing us all a favour if he had hit her.

One of the prepubescent squaddies near us chucked his rifle away and set off in a great, loping, weaving run towards the terrified nurse. Another riflecrack and he was flung, sprawling backwards through the air at a tremendous height. He crashed to the pavement, many yards from where he had been hit. He was screaming in agony, not really wanting to die. I was surprised and ghoulishly disappointed that I could see no gouts of blood and organ. That sniper must have been some kind of fucking rifle genius. What a shot! Fully three-quarters of a mile away and at a moving target. Boy, was I impressed!

The choking nurse crawled unethically away from the dying man, her eyes wide and incredulous. The soldier's colleagues couldn't go to his aid. They were still pinned down by the invisible sniper and probably thought that he had proved his marksmanship sufficient to the task. So, we waited. Soon, we heard the fatuous grumble of distant helicopters. The soldiers brightened at this and advised their chum to take it easy and hang on in there and similar tactless nonsense.

The sniper evidently noted the arrival of the helicopters and more shots zipped into the walls. The wailing soldier gurgled briefly deep in his chest and tried to raise himself. There was another shot, his body kicked back into the tarmac and flopped still.

He should have stayed where he was, the jerk.

Later, I learnt that they had shot the sniper when he was trying to make his getaway. The Security Forces were rather embarrassed by the fact that he was only thirteen years old. A talented kid.

You know, I always felt rather sorry for the British in Ireland. They didn't want to be there. The Protestants had originally wanted them there but got browned off when their presence began to interfere with traditional Loyalist rites of Catholic killing. It wasn't strictly Britain's problem though to be fair, they had committed some worthy cock-ups in the preceding four hundred years or so and Bloody Sunday *had* been a little tactless. Still, it was no reason to have to keep dying all the time.

The British were onto a very bad thing in Ulster. They couldn't win: if they left there was civil war and if they stayed they got crapped on from all sides. It couldn't have been much fun.

They were always getting into this kind of trouble, the British. In India, those Indians and Pakistanis were always kicking the dung out of each other as the dear old Brits tried to pull out. They were asked to stay a little longer. They did and got crapped on some more and slagged well off for their trouble. It was the same with Palestine after the war. The Jews and the Arabs have never really been the best of buddies. So who suffers? Trying to keep the peace. Trying to play the game.

Let's face it. Most European countries have had their empire at some time or another. Eventually, they crumble and another one comes along. This is what interregnums are – brackets of history. The British got it wrong. They grew all philanthropic and noble. They were the only imperial power ever to try giving their empire back. That was their mistake. We wogs, us wogs, we didn't like that. Not at all.

Of course, little hiccoughs like Amritsar, Bloody Sunday and the Velt Camps didn't help. But nobody's perfect. It's hard to like the British but I try.

I've seen someone tarred and feathered as well. It was about the same time though this was a little strong even for my steel-plated stomach. My boyish voyeurism didn't extend this far. The victim of the tarring was a girl. (Most of them were.) Mary Sharkey. Apparently, Mary was having a little lamb through the fructile offices of some corporal from the Royal Engineers. The folk of Turf Lodge were jolly peeved. (I must have been a clever little sprog to winkle out all that strictly adult truth.)

Some patriotic youngbloods decided on punitive action. They nabbed young Mary and tied her to a lamp post at the bottom of our cul-de-sac. They stripped her and shaved her head. To my surprise, I wasn't enjoying it at all. Mary had very small breasts which seemed to make it worse for some reason. I wasn't prepared for this. It was a Sunday and I'd been reading Trollope all afternoon! The bastards actually boiled the tar in front of her. Even I could see that this was undiplomatic.

To give them their due credit for philanthropy, the locals thought that this had gone far enough. Public humiliation was enough. Brutality was over-doing it. The neighbours stood at their doors in their Sunday suits and dresses, uneasy and reluctant. Of course, none of them had the bollocks to try to stop it but at least the thought was there. The women were weeping bitterly and the men stood, mumbling together in anxious little groups. Mary was utterly still and completely silent.

Soon the tar was ready and two of the men simply chucked the nasty stuff over her. Now, human screaming can be horrible. Not like the cinegenic, kinky stuff you get in the movies. Real throttled-cat belches of outrage is what I'm talking about. Mary was well up there in the screaming league. She was first division and pushing hard for the championship. The deathly wails that she set up had a bad effect upon my youthful sensibilities and I became hysterical. My mother chucked me, screeching and choking, into the back garden to cool off a little.

For ten minutes I had a quiet and rather enjoyable little fit to myself.

When I came back to the scene a startling development had occurred. Bobby Bogle, my nominal father and actual scourge had got in on the act. He made his entrance.

Goodness, would you believe it but my old arsehole papa, that wicked Welsh wanker looked as if he was going to make a stand on behalf of the now sizzling Mary. My mother was bellowing at him in an access of fury and contempt but on he strode, my old dad, to the astonishment of the neighbourhood and, no doubt, himself.

In a surge of filial pride, I escaped the bony grasp of my witchmother and belted on after him.

Mary was in bad shape now. Her hair, now matted and clogged, had been roughly shorn into violent, spiky tufts. On the few patches of visible skin between the steaming great gouts of tar, I could see that her flesh had already blistered and cracked horribly. She had stopped screaming and was now weeping inaudibly to herself. The ragged feathers that still dotted her head obscured her face but I could sense that she was having a bad time.

I watched my father approach the little group of young men around Mary. Anger and ragejudged pride burnt hard in my boy's heart. One of the youths called something to my dad and he stopped just short of them. I couldn't see his face but I saw that his great, lazy shoulders were trembling uncontrollably as if he were trying to hide secret, swelling laughter. The same youth spoke again. He was about twenty years old and had a sly, handsome countenance. Unlike the others, he was well-dressed in a vulgar manner and his sleek black hair was combed back carefully over his small neat ears. A wispy moustache disfigured his upper lip like a little strip of fluff or smut. He touched it often, as if to ensure that it was still there.

'Now then, Bobby. Just you go back up there to your own house. This here doesn't have anything to do with you.'

Bogle didn't answer. Creeping closer, I noticed that he was carrying a short plump lath, like a baseball bat. I saw him grip it tighter and stiffen and ease the vibration of his shoulders.

'C'mon now, Bobby, you know we don't have any quarrel with you. Go home like the wise man you are.'

Again there was no answer. I was shitting myself with terror but it was undeniably exciting.

93

Now, the other men began to lend their voices to the weight of friendly advice being meted out to my da. One of them, a big bastard with a harelip, was in his element. Oily and repulsive, he seemed to have a grudge against my poor pops and saw the time for a spot of retribution.

'Go on, Bogle, fuck away off! What do you think you're going to do with that wee stick? Mmm? Fuck off, you don't want the kind of trouble we can give you.'

My father spoke for the first time as he moved slowly towards the sobbing girl.

'I swear to Jesus, if you open your mouth again, little boy, I'll break your fucking back, big as you are.'

Thrilled to the new power and danger in my sire, I saw the jaundiced arrival of fear in Harelip's ferrety eyes. The men exchanged uncertain glances. The youth who had spoken first barred my father's way. Bobby stopped again. This youth was different. He threatened less but promised more. I felt (correctly as it turned out) that he was dangerous. He spoke softly, almost reasonably.

'Look, Bobby, stop this nonsense. You know what she did. Don't get yourself into any old trouble for her sake! She's not worth it, Bobby.'

Still grasping the sliver of timber, my father stepped past him and began slowly to untie Mary. Gently, gingerly, he whispertouched her tarred and wounded flesh, hopelessly struggling against the heat and the smell. Silence. Icy fear. His bent and ministering back was blind and unprotected against any onslaught the young men cared to make. He seemed aware of this and awaited attack. Suddenly, the cocky bastard with the fucked-up kisser made an abrupt movement towards him. I screamed in filial warning. Sparkspeeded and rapid, my father turned to face him, sporty stick swinging. He hooked hard and knocked the creep's harelip down the back of his throat. (He could've been a cricketer, my dad!) The youth crumpled as you might expect. At a nod from their mustachioed generalissimo, the others stayed where they were. My father turned his apoplectic face to me.

'Go home! Now!' he bellowed.

(Well, what about that, eh? Who'd have thought it of my rancid father? Courage. Chivalry. Style. He certainly came out strong that day. I was dead chuffed. It's nice to be able to admire your father every now and then. Perhaps he wasn't such a shit after all.)

So.

Unforgettably seen and remembered, pictured from behind the rickety gate of our postage-stamp front garden, I watched with conscious sonly pride as my father trudged slowly across the dimming cul-de-sac. Towards his home he walked, carrying the weeping girl, in his strong father's arms. Amongst the coward's stillness of his inactive, unbraved, fully Irish neighbours.

Of course, Bobby Bogle paid for this piece of poetry in the end. It was obvious that he would. The guy with the harelip and the bad boy with the 'tache were both in the Provies. They were pissed off with my father and received their satisfaction by shooting him twice in the abdomen as he was walking home from the pub one night. That was a dirty trick. A nasty place to shoot someone. It took my father an awfully long time to die and he did it all on our kitchen floor. He just dripped away, all sticky and warm. By God, there was tons of the stuff. Thick, oozing pools of scarlet gore formed on the cracked linoleum, streaked and muddied by boot and shoe. The ambulance didn't come for three hours and by that time his flesh yellow and cold. He was well dead.

It's strange to watch someone die . . . especially if he's your dad. To know that his next few moments spell the end for him. Watching him say his goodbyes to himself. It's hard to make his last moments special. You can't exactly throw a shindig.

I'm pretty cool about it now but at the time I was insane with horror and grief. I was only a kid and he was my dad after all.

Warmth. Heat. Comfort. Park bench. Sunlight. Odours fresh and odours stale. Weariness. Melancholy. Tumult and hubbub. Eyes closed, upward gazing into darkness. Lightless. Sleep. Doze. Snore. Nap. Sleep.

FOUR

Yes, they booted me out, my family did. I was summarily ejected from the maternal bosom, dried and withered as it was. My crime was the attachment erotic to a woman of the persuasion heretical. Deirdre was a Protestant and my mother objected. I was sixteen. I left home with three pounds fourteen pence and a green canvas bag with three pairs of sporadically soiled underwear, a toothbrush, an apt copy of *Hard Times* and a small piece of unwrapped Ulster Cheddar.

That first night, I slept on a bench in Ormeau Park. It was August so comfortwise I was laughing. Notwithstanding, my first homeless night was a bit of a shock to my sensitive nature. Next morning, I tried to conjure the sustaining potential of my self and youth. To my surprise, it worked. It was the resolute Epicurean in me.

That day I realised that I had better start looking after myself as no one else was going to bother. I know that it's the same for everyone eventually but I was young and the notion was something of an affront. So I cheered myself by sitting the day out in the Central Library reading the gigglepacked speeches of Winston Churchill.

The second night was much colder and much longer. I discovered that the musculature of destitution ages and creaks gradually and I was wracked with loneliness and benchpain. I smoked the darkness away thinking of Deirdre, warm abed, comfortably numb and unaware of my trials. Puerile tears dribbled freely. I felt no envy or resentment. I was sorry that she didn't know. She would be hurt. Though, it has to be said my sufferings always rather offended Deirdre. She would ferret out my troubles as if they were squalid crimes. Still, I resolved not to tell her that I was homeless. Not just then, at any rate. She was much better in ignorance. Happiness lay there. For her, that is.

This prosing helped me pass the second night. My solitary awareness of the distance between us enveloped me with bleak relish. Her general inadequacy pained me no longer. Why should it? It all rather cheered me up than otherwise.

Next day I wandered round Botanic Avenue trying to look like a student and pissed away my last fifty pence on a cup of coffee and three bourbon biscuits in the coffee room of the museum.

That night I couldn't get into the park. I dossed in a sewerstreaming alley just off the Newtonards Road and cried myself hysterically asleep. When I awoke the next morning, I'd wet myself.

From then on I went into a decline.

It was all a bit tragic really. I mean, I deserved better than this. I couldn't help feeling wildly sorry for myself. I was a nice kid. I was a budding genius. So polite, so considerate, so ballsachingly charming, malleable and undemanding. I thought of all the middle-class parents with their drug-addict, drop-out, pervert, poofter sons. They would have given their front and back teeth for an ace offspring like my commodious self. I would have been quiet, done my homework, charmed aunties, washed the dishes, peeled the spuds and wiped Granny Nora's old arse for her. I would have been an asset. The perfect apple for any discerning eye.

I'm good with families. I was designed to be a clan figurehead. Any family would have welcomed me.

And I had to be lumbered with my criminal, lycanthropic collection! It wasn't fair. All that hardship, that lack of tenderness or appreciation. Nobody deserves that and especially not me.

Well, life certainly did prove to be a hilariously complicated affair just around then. The problems of finding a job and a place to live and going back to school were tremendous. I couldn't get a job unless I had a permanent address. I couldn't afford a permanent address until I got a job. I wasn't entitled to supplementary benefit if I went to school because then I wouldn't be 'unemployed'. I was too old to be taken into care and too young to be classified as a distressed adult. My mother was still being paid my fucking Family Allowance while I was eating my own stools in desperation. It was against school rules to have even a part time job during term time and they didn't want me back without a parent or guardian anyway. I was too young for the YMCA and had too much testosterone for the YWCA. I could receive not charity, not state support, not wages for my work, not a part of pity.

I was all fucked up. I was in a welfare state loophole. I had a whole legal grey area to myself. I had no adult's rights and no minor's entitlements or indulgences. I was in no man's land and I was jolly browned off to be there.

Well, the cheese was hard and the titty was tough. I was growing Belsenesque and my poor lungs were behaving in the most revolting manner. In short, I was living a mite on the hard and bad side.

However, the worst was yet to come. I had been ostracised by my wicked old family. I had been sloshed and steeped in the mire of degradation and poverty. My mother had threatened to have me kneecapped if I showed my face again. I had endured all this for my refusal to end my callow, senseless love affair with the Presbyterian Miss Curran. After all this, I was really quite annoyed to find her disowning me after a roughly similar (though less actually perilous to life and limb) ultimatum from her own family.

Now, this was a bitter blow. Chuckbrain that I was, I had rather preened myself on the nobility of my gesture and was crushed to see it devalued in this way. It was not her faithlessness nor cowardice that stung me most; in fairness, I could have expected little else, she had much more to lose than I. No, it wasn't this that bothered me. It was the paltry fact that I had ended up looking so juvenile. My zeal and ardour were worthless. A youthish gesture.

And so, lamentably, I had to face my little pile of problems all on my poor own alone. My coltish buoyancy and self-belief evaporated tracelessly. There was nothing for it. With a rough hand I gripped myself hard and pulled my lonely face solutionwards. I went to work – breaking balls, stringing paths and spitting blood and spume. I blustered, harried, scraped, whined, begged and bullied my way through. Grudgepacked, I stored up my hatreds and petty failures for future reference and revenge.

On I went, sixteen, penniless and naive. Cutting down the foliage of reason, doubt and argument with the machete of resolution in my best Davy Copperfield manner. I pulled through.

Deirdre and I eventually got back together again. All she had to do was momentarily query her father's Bogleian embargo and we were away. They didn't have the balls to defy their precious only daughter, those Currans.

(It didn't occur to Deirdre that she might have tried to defy her parents' injunction a little earlier. What am I saying? It didn't occur to me either.)

With Deirdre's (vicarious) support, I began a two-year tour of the worst grot mansions of the leprous old city of Belfast. I couldn't stay in one place for very long. I was alternately robbed, conned and persecuted by a long train of psychotic, filth-bound landlords. In one place I had near the beginning in Indiana Avenue, the landlord Raymond Murphy calmly informed me that he was an undercover Special Branch man working to infiltrate the IRA. I nodded very carefully at this and looked impressed. (Belfast is full of these fantasists, these lunatics.) When he started shooting the wasps off the wall above my head with his Smith and Wesson in a William Tellish proof of his marksmanship, I decided to leave.

Poverty, solitude and filth is not a pleasant blend at the best of times but when added to the condiments of exhaustion and despair, the effect is almost heady. I attended school (I had bribed the bursar to let me come back), worked in three different pubs, (to pay my rent, pay my debt to the bursar and occasionally purchase a modicum of foodstuffs), worried, slept, worried and starved. I had no money and few friends. The friends I had were schoolboys and could hardly help past the donation of their embarrassed goodwill. Goodwill isn't such a bad thing, though and I got it in plenty.

Did I slip, did I slide and fade away? I most certainly did not. In fact all this narratival indignation has been rather wasted for despite the distractions of poverty and malnutrition and despite the hazards of schizophrenic, gun-toting ex-policemen, I was, perversely enough, happier than at any other time in my life. Youth is a marvellous thing. Hope isn't bad either and the perfect companion to these attributes is the imperturbable blindness of optimism. I was in Easy Street.

To give her her due, Deirdre had been impressed by the magnitude of the sacrifice I had made for her. She understood such gestures and felt herself to be a fitting recipient for such adolescent homage. She kept a toll on my suffering and humiliation, they were her tribute and she made the most of them.

If, however, any of my tricky difficulties got in her way, if for instance I couldn't attend her to some mediocre movie because I was working that night like every other night, she was much miffed. I didn't need so many jobs, according to her. I tried to point out the necessity of such fripperies as rent, food and clothing but Deirdre accused me of being self-indulgent and turning my troubles into an 'issue'. She considered that I was in the throes of a pernicious downward spiral and led me to understand that she could not be expected to go down with me. I understood completely. Me, I was like that.

By God, I still loved her. More than ever. In the midst of all the squalor she was my comfort and aspiration. I would buy expensive gifts for her (God alone knows how!) to prove that, given half a chance I could be worthy of her. Deirdre felt that this was entirely laudable. What irked her was my continuing reluctance to sleep with her. This she could not understand. She was seventeen and full of the fun of libido. She suspected my strange chastity was evidence of some sinister, bloodless Catholic prohibition on the act of erotic love. She couldn't have imagined that it was only a naive respect for her and her purity. She would have thought it bloody silly, I imagine. And would have been right too, the sensible girl. I was just a boy who couldn't say yes.

So what with my difficulties, disasters and depressions, this part of my life was a little telescoped. Having missed the boat on Puberty (done it in a day) Adolescence passed me by.

FIVE

I eat without relish. My late attenuation squats heavily upon my belly and my bowels. The uncouth noise and hunger of the other tramps makes me feel queasy. I watch as they shove the drab grey potatoes mouthwards and my stomach heaves. One after another, gobfuls of mash are gobbled up. Some use forks like spades, others cut out the middleman and use their smeared fingers. The thin, grease-daubed gravy splashes as forks and fingers trudge and clatter through plates of messy cooling slop.

Some of the attendant clerics are making a show of eating with us. This is an extravagant and foolish gesture. One of them seems to share my fasti-diousness. A liverspotted, balding young man, he gulps palely, his eyes watering and his face greying. He tries to seem unconcerned and struggles gamely with his cutlery. Although this place is cool, he is sweating, a cold patina of moisture has settled on his forehead and upper lip. His egalitarian notions surely don't extend this far? He watches the tramp at trough, swilling, slurping, grumbling, belching and farting. He is drowning in disgust. I watch him and wait for the vomacious exclamation. Whop! Splat! Back onto someone's plate. It doesn't come.

I'm in a rubgrub shameshop. A churchified little hall of Charity and Brotherhood. Sad, eh? We pray in trendy prose monologues and then we get some pukenosh. Pathetic. A bunch of shamebound, oozing tramps and rejects dribble over their shrinking plates courtesy of Lord God Almighty and the Church of England. It's a grisly sight. The active components of the extremes of charity are always grisly sights. The assembled vicars, or whatever they're called, know this. They are fighting a losing battle against their own distaste. I shouldn't bring you to these places, I know. But I want to show you the entirety of my new world. My birthright, my inheritance and my deserts. In the interests of narratival depth, you understand.

Abruptly, silence descends on the lowceilinged, highminded refectory. More prayers, bejasus! They probably don't do this as a rule. Not so many devotions. They must have sussed that I'm a Catholic. Used their

100

ecumenical antennae or something. I've already had a few funny looks. Christ, maybe they've laced my food with strychnine or dog crap or something! You can never tell what might happen with these pagan types.

Swallowing my objections to these heathen (i.e. non-Catholic) rites, I lower my head in mystified sympathy. The darkened, scuffed and stained table stares back at me with indifference. I close my eyes and hear those old whispered enigmas fill the slopfed silence. Outside, I know that the torpid London air is rumorous with the advent of summer. Newbudded trees are growing heavy with leaves. The city is drying its coat of dust, ready for the sudden blinding little winds of summer and I'm sucking dog bones in a soup kitchen!

The thing is . . . I couldn't work up the courage to go to a cafe, a shop or even a dirty old hot-dog stall. I have enough money but nowhere near the confidence I need. I kept thinking that they'd wonder where someone like me had got the money. I couldn't enter into transaction. I couldn't enter that normal kind of world and have its normal kind of values brought to bear on me. I was too ashamed even to spend my money. That's very bad, the first time I'd really thought of myself as a tramp proper.

This failure plagues me now. Here I am. Me and the other tramps. I hope for no difference between us now. I don't want to kid myself. Here we are taking our charity, our humiliation and our reject cat food. It was distressingly easy to come here. I just joined the queue. I've swallowed my pride and it has spoiled my appetite.

I look around at the lowered faces of the still-praying clerics. Their porridgy, sallow complexions conjure to me the faces of all the priests and monks I have ever known. Their jealous piety revolts me. An unwholesome secretion from the small souls of men who are fit for nothing else.

I look to my plate. It swims merrily in its own legion grease. The hashbeefandbean sludge settles and wallows comfortably. It looks so happy that I haven't the heart to disturb it. Gratefully, I conclude my repast.

Aptly, a brief warm glow spirals through the low round windows of this poky old chamber. It transfigures the humble forms of tramp and man as they rise from their meal. The room fills again with discreet, shiftless noise. The clerics move gently, tidily shepherding their trampflock into an adjacent anteroom. (Adjacent sheep dip would be better, judging by the vileness of our conglomerate odour.)

We shuffle, we tramps, we slouch as and where we're bidden. Bidding adieu to the less than groaning tables from which we supped we find ourselves in a larger hall populated by benches and tables piled neatly with dun-coloured mutt blankets and exhumed secondhand clothing, and by nervous groups of Christian Youth. It's their turn now. This is where we get our individual pep talks, moral guidance and scriptural counselling. This is where we are given our cast-off coats, bulbous old shoes and horsehair underwear. It is supposed to do us good both emotionally and sartorially. We accept this kind of thing meekly, we tramps. There is always the chance of some fags being doled out at the end.

Instinctively, the down and outs cluster in the middle of the room. A burping, gaseous nucleus surrounddotted by the satellite vicars, students, television crews and Christian youth workers. One of the wittier tramps near me whispers that there is going to be a gang-bang. We giggle, chuckle or cackle, according to our age, sanity and the condition of our teeth.

The pastors of this bastardchurch move in now and dissolve the epicentre of destitution. They branch off and form squat little groups around the laden tables. The student types start doling out the ragged, graceless garments. Who on earth could have come up with this stuff? The point about trampclothes is that they are not like other peoples' clothes. Tramp-gear is not made – it is grown. Cultivation rather than tailoring. It is a strange agricultural process of fermentation and assimilation with the natural scum and muck of the tramp's person. Tramps' clothes come from some weird draperless region which no one can trace. Honestly, it's a fact.

I hang back with the hard core of proud, disaffected tramps. I'm itching to leave but a hopeful whisper has gone the rounds about these putative cigarettes. I'm sceptical of course but I would kick myself if I missed out. I'll sacrifice any amount of dignity for fags and anyway, as I've said, my seven quid is not going to be enough to retire on.

The room is warm and stuffy and I try to work up the courage to light a cigarette. Who knows? It might be a useful hint. So, I stiffen my sinews, summon up my clots and torch a B & H. The other tramps peer jealously at me as the fragrant smoke billows around my selfish head. They don't ask for one. They know they haven't a fucking chance.

I feel better suddenly. With my mouth on my fag and my pocketed fingers on my dosh, I'm in the pink, imperturbable. To pass the time, I survey the assembled do-gooders. Mostly young faces. Nice boys and girls. Mostly about my age. Their clean, sinless faces are illuminated by the English Christian glow of moronic zeal and innocent banality. The girls with their ostentatiously untonsured hair and makeup-free faces and the boys with their much-patched woollen sweaters and those wispy gingerfluff beards that speak of sensitivity. They minister and they patronise, their expres-sionless faces obstinately cloaking the possibility of unchristian distaste.

(Wowsie! Boy, am I whipfucking cynical and misanthropic today! What harm are they doing . . . except to my pride?)

Ah, such tolerance, such wisdom, such precocious breadth of understanding!

Oh! Mmmmmm. Yes. Uhuh. Ah, yes. What have we here? A girlie, a bint, a bird, a bimbo. In the corner to my left, I've just noticed a real girl in the midst of all this titless, hairy-thighed, barren Christian womanhood. Goodness, she's neat! What is she doing amongst all these godly folk? She's pretty impressive and looks posh as well. Yes. Indeed. Uhuh. She's seen me now. Yes, that was a shock, wasn't it? She looks again. Whoops! Affirmation and reciprocation. She panics and pales markedly. The poor girl is obviously unaccustomed to finding down and outs attractive. She tries to ignore me by draping an almost medieval garment over an incredibly damp and glistening tramp in her vicinity.

It is, however, useless. My relentless, lived-in gaze draws her eyes inexorably to me. A curious, pleading frown wrinkles her brow. She hopes for mercy. She's lucky. My clemency is infinite.

Dear Christ, I'm falling in love here! As I've said, it's very easy when you're young. Gosh, I'm awash with sentiment. Clownish tears spring to my eyes. I forget my degraded position and begin to construct elaborate scaffolds for seduction.

No. Stop this foolishness. Don't be bovine. Don't humiliate yourself any more than you can help.

I look at her again. She's beautiful, this girl. Dark wisps of carefully straggled hair frame those grave brown eyes. A tight, slender mouth, sombre and impassive. All that impossible and reluctant allure. That gravity of demeanour I used to love so much. She's winning me over. Her frank, melancholy return of my poseur's gaze and her soft shield of richly bought clothing, covering that heretic whisper of nakedness and desire. Lunkhead, I offer her the dishonest tribute of my eyes. I'd like to smile but feel with rare sensitivity that this would dispel the frangible web of sadness and longing that links us now. Less can I talk to her. I can't violate the silent submission of those eyes.

I practically choke on my own facile lyricist bullshit. What a joke! Slimy, cheesydicked tramp tries one on respectable young Christian beauty! The Erotic Highstyle lives on! Mock me. I love and deserve it.

This has humbled me further. My short burst of baseless euphoria goes in search of a nicer neighbourhood. The odd, impractical passion wasn't such a bad thing when I was younger but it's disastrous nowadays. I feel a happy welter of acrimony and self-pity winging its gentle way hither. Fuck the fags, think I, I'm off.

I skulk away, furtively easing my way through the groups of grumbling tramps. I try not to attract her attention. I do not wish my retreating ignominy witnessed. I slither out of the room into a holymusty hall. At the end, through the open door, I see the street, streaked with light and bellowing invitingly. I trudge sadly outwards.

'Excuse me ... wait, please!'

A female voice. I swivel sluggishly round. And whaddyaknow, it's Miss Browneyes and Slendermouth herself! She stands uncertainly in the ochre gloom of the little hall. Her lips are parted and her breath stammers. I must say, I'm not surprised that she's nervous. From where in the name of Christ did she gather the courage for this?

Doggedly, in serf's silence, I wait for her to speak.

She smiles ingenuously, white perfect teeth bright in the healthy sheen of her skin. Her voice is clear and posh. Yes indeed, how I do love these toff bints! Her uneasiness becomes contagious. My brain begins to buzz and bubble, unused to these social niceties. Take a look at the liquid shimmer of her flesh! Cherished and madly beautiful. The tale of nice parents and only daughter. Time and money invested in her. Grow and prosper. Lovely mummy and lovely daddy. Their lovely daughter. Their hope and pleasure. Schools and holidays have built her. And who am I to argue?

The silence has stretched and groaned to the limits of its elasticity. She speaks.

'Are you leaving?' she regrets this little fatuity immediately, God bless her. She looks at me, her beauty pleading pain and confusion.

I'm a sucker for this kind of thing.

'Well, yes ... I was just about to.'

Hardly epigrammatic perhaps but this is me being nice. For that, one's intelligence and pampered rhetoric must be diluted. It's only polite.

She smiles. I wish she wouldn't but she does. Adding to my desire and despair. I drown while I can and her unattainability leaves me to my grief.

'It's pretty awful, isn't it?' says she.

'Yes, it is.'

She glances at my well-employed fag hand.

'They're giving out some cigarettes later. Don't you want to wait?'

She cringes creditably at that one. Her anxiety floods rapidly back.

'I can manage, thank you.'

Unhappily, she searches for the insult in my words.

'I'm sorry. It's probably none of my business.'

'No, probably not.'

'I'm sorry,' she murmurs. 'I didn't mean to interfere.'

Antagonistic as always, I damn myself for being a silly bugger. There is a momentary flash of embarrassment and then she smiles.

I feel a little silly standing in this dim, unsunned hallway, swapping inanities with this fabulous woman. Obviously she isn't feeling too clever either. She speaks without confidence.

'I can't help feeling that I've seen you somewhere before.'

'I doubt it. Do you move much in homeless circles?'

She pauses uncomfortably, her brown eyes not understanding. I should be hanged for the crap I'm talking.

'No. But I'm nearly sure I've seen you before.'

Awkwardly, she continues. Her face showing the strain.

'What did you do ... before ... ah, before you ...?'

'Before I became a tramp, you mean?'

Whimpering Jesus! This girl may be undeniably gorgeous but she's hardly choc-a-bloc with tact.

'I'm sorry, I didn't mean ...'

'Some are born to destitution and some have destitution thrust upon them.'

'Sorry?'

'Ah ... nothing.'

'I hate it when people say that.'

'What – ''nothing''?'

'Something, then nothing.'

'It was nothing, really.'

Christ, Oscar Wilde would have been proud of me! This is pretty seductive stuff. We look at each other with mutual, differing idiocy. Her smile flickers briefly and my hunger rises again.

'Do you come from London then?' she asks, rather desperately.

'Well, I lived in Tooting Bec for a while,' lie I extemporaneously.

'Tooting Bec?'

'Yes.'

'That's nice.'

'Not really.'

She is stumped by this and flounders horribly.

'Oh, I thought the pubs in Tooting Bec were full of poets and painters.'

'Well, they're mostly full of stoned black men, actually.'

'Oh.'

The poor mite tries to drag this drivel back onto the track of relevance and comprehensibility.

'Where were you from originally?'

'Up north. That's why even Tooting Bec was a lure.'

'Really.'

'Well, it's pretty tragic living in Worksop.'

'Worksop?'

'Yes, Worksop.'

Pause.

I'm rather good at this, don't you think?

To my unstinted surprise, she now produces a packet of twenty Silk Cut King Size. Who would have thought that these Christian types smoked?

'I've been desperate for a smoke all afternoon.' She sighs conspiratorially. I smile guardedly and she offers me a cigarette. I toss my stunted butt into a nearby vase of dried flowers. Courteously, I accept her offer. She lights my fag for me before handing it over. This girl has obviously seen all the wrong motion pictures. Nonetheless, the gesture intoxicates me. Her posh, clean lips on my soon-to-be-soiled fag. I must look and smell less repulsive than I thought.

'What are you doing in such a frigging woeful place? You don't look like the other intrepid philanthropes.'

I say this to impress her with my distinctly untramply vocabulary. I hope it works.

'I could say the same of you and your smelly chums back there.'

'Perhaps.'

Isn't that the limit? 'Perhaps.' I'm cool, I'm chic. I'm urbane, enigmatic. I'm a ship passing in the shite.

She pulls smoke gently into her chest. Obviously a part-time smoker. I watch her. I've rarely seen a woman smoke elegantly before and I'm all agog. I remember the hobnailed hoydens of Belfast with their stained Regal butts drooping from their croquet-hoop mouths. This is a different sex altogether.

Sudden, cinematic sunlight speckles through the arch of the doorway and dances with her eyes. The glow filters and the hall smoke billows brownly, swirling adventitiously around her. I feel a short tear of pain at the extremity of her beauty. Soppy tit!

'The only reason I'm here is because a friend asked me to come and I was curious, I suppose.'

I run my cleaningrough tongue over my ruinous teeth and smile carefully before saying:

'I came because I was hungry.'

'Yes.'

She smiles in her turn, her eyes adorned with the indifference of beauty.

'I suppose I walked into that one. I'm sorry.'

'Don't apologise.' My smile and conscious, affable charm. I'm picking up these posh habits.

'It's Boggy or Bogey or something like that, isn't it? I remember it was something unusual.'

Her brow knits with pastiche concentration.

106

'I beg your pardon?' I squeak primly.

'Your name. It was something like that. Oh, I remember – Bogle. That was it. That was your name.' Her voice trails off and her face kindles.

Well, stap me vitals! Steeling my rioting, my saddened heart, I smile with studied urbanity.

'No, I'm afraid not.'

She eyes me doubtfully.

'You're sure?'

'Well, I would be, wouldn't I?'

'Yes, I suppose so.'

There is a pause while she doubts and I flounder. My roguish heart races at her generous suspicion. She is claiming her bond. You are confused, aren't you? Me too. My discomfort worries me, spilling my disordered thoughts. Maybe she's KGB ... or CIA. These bastards get everywhere these days and want everyone.

I'm getting bogged down here and she's staring at me with renewed certainty. To my shame. I don't want you to see this. My naughty auctorial caprices again. I resolve, as I always do, to bluster out my exit.

'How could you possibly know me? Look at me and then at yourself. Mmmm? See it? Our paths are a long way from crossing ...' I check myself with editorspeed '... except by the grotesque combination of largesse and neediness that we see here. You aren't au fait with the delicacies of Tramp Society and I hardly flit around the pukka end of town.'

I pause with dick-orator's delight. 'It's hardly likely that we have met before, now is it?'

I'm very calm now. Unruffled and impressive. I think that this has done the trick, if temporarily. Now the boot is very much on the other foot as far as uneasiness goes. I look at her fruitlessly beautiful eyes. They are saved from iciness by this slight waver of uncertainty. On that tiny flicker do I base my youthful trumpery.

The girl blushes a livid scarlet, pinktinged and cute as fuck.

'Perhaps, you're right,' she agrees.

(Phew!)

At her words I feel a sudden witless dart of joy and unschooled terror. This eerie, improbable encounter fills me with a sudden splash of profane, screeching power. Under her jewelled gaze, I flood with youth's blood. My lungs suck the tincture of her golden air. This moment of bliss, of virtuosity. This is what I'm about. This is youth's story.

I look at her lightsoaked hair, her epic eyes and her tragedian's mouth. It chuffs me. I suck hard and pointlessly on the thin, unsatisfying, clogless fumes of her weaktarred cigarette. My face is washed in a dun, dimming haze. I'm conscious of my own burgeoning enigma.

I smile.

SIX

The man is insistent, demanding. Harsh and confident in his grievance, he harangues her mercilessly. She struggles to remain tearless and unperturbed. It's not working. Harrowed she glances round at the onlookers, me included. She is ashamed. His wheedling grumbles increase in volume.

'You promised! You gave me your word.'

Her tears have started to tumble now, bubbles of silent salt. Why doesn't she answer him? Nut the bastard. Kick him in his pickles. This isn't on. Not in public anyhow. I'd interfere if I could. I'd do my heroic knightly best for her. I'd duff him up a bit. I would if I wasn't a tramp. I can't really, things being how they are.

'Well?' he demands, his sharp suit bristling with indignation. He seems to have right on his side, this man. He seems pretty sure of that. I don't like him. I dislike his well-shaved tanned cheeks, his crisp white shirt, his brash money and his romantic complications. She likes him though, I can tell. Her fat tears tell me that and her silence backs it up.

'Well?' he repeats.

She makes a tiny gesture, a small inapt moue of discontent and compromise. A group of youngsters waiting for the telephone start to snigger openly. The man flinches. Come on, I think, don't throw it away. You've got it made here, you're well in. Smile. Chuck away righteousness and discord. It doesn't need much effort. She'll take any kind of apology from you. She's for you, she's heaving with concession and admiration. Don't throw it away.

Abruptly, the man turns from her and stalks off, his hard heels drumming with annoyance. The youths snigger again, louder this time. The woman remains pinned down by her remorse and loss. She looks around her, her cheeks glassy with tears. Her hair flops onto her hunched shoulders, hiding her as best it can. Her eyes meet mine, her stare is blank and dull. Her mouth trembles convulsively, weakly, so weakly. I look away, my poor heart leaping. O misere, he threw it away. I tried to tell him. He just threw it away.

When I look back she has gone. I stare at the width and vulgarity of Leicester Square but cannot spot her amongst the dawdling, changing crowd.

Leicester Square. This is a place of monstrous eccentricity. Cinemas push their boxy bulk from all sides and giant hoardings affront the general eye. The tiny rectangle of grass and tree is staked out in the centre of all this, like a patient enemaed upon a pavement. Starlings, hundreds of them, crowd the air with their rowdy tumult and the spindly trees and benches are coated thickly with their black, bobbing omnipresence. There is bird shit all over the place. The square is polka-dotted with the excrement of English bird and Yankee culture. I think I prefer the birdies' contribution.

The falling sun slants great patches of light and dark over the obstacles of roof and wall. It is growing cold once more. Folk idle and folk busy parade this square in similar pace – a slow, meandering dodge and shuffle. No one looks like much in Leicester Square. This place flatters none. Here, everyone looks, more or less, like a scumbag.

A lot of very slimy people inhabit Leicester Square. Not tramps as much as homeless youths, juvenile pickpockets, amateur prostitutes and scabrous groups of punk and prat. They seem to want what Leicester Square has to offer them.

I'm not very keen on this square but it's a nice place for me to have a break. I come to Leicester Square because in Leicester Square even I look respectable. By the standards current here, I'm prosperous, posh and well-ordered. It's nice to shine occasionally. If the pond is small enough, I'll big-fish it with a vengeance. It's hardly admirable but I feel I should allow myself my little pleasures and small satisfactions.

Having itemised the tramp's nocturnal experience yesterday, I now have a little to say about his daytime life.

The daylight hours are relatively simple for the tramp amongst us. They pose the comforts of sleep, sustenance and sociability. Night time poses only suffering. This is an edifying reversal of normal practice, when it is evening that brings food, rest and intercourse while day time is taken up with the various forms that work takes. Work is a man's trial, his suffering, his nearest equivalent to the tramp's night-time horrors. Inevitable, de rigueur but hardly much fun.

Trampdays are mostly composed of sleep. Naps and dozes are stolen with abandon. (The coldest of days is for some reason always warmer than an average night.) Sustenance also features during the day. Happily, a tramp's nutritional requirements are usually humble and directly related to how much he drinks. The more he drinks, the less he needs to eat. There is still a fair selection of charitable institutions in London willing to fuel a vagabond for his wider pleasures. You saw me in one earlier today. The grub's not up to much but who's fussy?

Sociability is a less tangible feature of the tramp's daily business. As you know, my tramp acquaintance is not large so I'm not really qualified to say very much on this point but I'm fairly sure their society is a relief to them, a bulwark against their isolation and undesirability. Still, I hardly think that there are many great things done or said.

The main drawback of a tramp's day is that this is when his health really gets to work on him. During the rigours of the night, he is too busy in the business of survival to lend much thought to his physiological conundrums but when the relative comfort of daytime comes along he is at the mercy of his multitude of illnesses. Tramply ailments are encyclopaedic and diverting. I would tell you about them but they are too disgusting.

I suffer from a wide range of ill-effects myself. I am aged, exhausted, bursting with infections and disabilities. I'm not tip-top but I don't really mind. I have a greater health problem and it takes up all my time.

Cancer fascinates me. I have a true admiration for Cancer. It scares the shit out of me but I respect it. It's a hard master and I feel I know it well. I've put a lot of thought into Cancer. I don't want it to catch me unprepared.

I don't actually have Cancer. It hasn't been diagnosed anyway. But with what I cough up and void from my sad body, I have my suspicions.

It's just that Cancer is such a total bastard. It is not like other diseases. It doesn't obey the doctorly rules. It cheats. Normal cells are unpretentious little beings. They cause no rucus and want no fame. Normal cells are alike, they're ordered and democratic. They bow to the body's bureaucracy. They're like Swedish people. Neoplastic cells are a different kettle of micro-organisms. They differ, they're unalike, they're bad and ugly and cruel. They are vandals. Marauding maniacs. They are perfect for the disorganisation, the anarchy, the wild pillaging of Cancer.

No one knows what to do about these bodily terrorists. No one knows why they hate life so violently. No one knows how to make them go away. They are deadly guerrillas, implacable and always victorious. They have got humanity taped. They've pushed our backs against the wall.

You may think I'm paranoid but this worries me. In the twelve or thirteen years during which I have smoked I have managed to plough through, at a conservative estimate, very close to a quarter of a million cigarettes. And I'm pretty certain that this has not been doing me much good. Cancer likes to do the unexpected, it likes to let eighty-a-day men live to ninety. But I'm sure it could hardly resist such an opportunity as I provide.

I have a funny feeling about Cancer. I'm quite sure that even if I didn't smoke it would be mine anyway. I've always had the impression that I'm marked down in Cancer's voluminous book of grudges and targets. With a history of ill-fate like mine, the conclusion is inescapable.

Cancer used to terrify me. It's not so bad now. Intimacy doesn't breed contempt but it helps to dispel superstitious horror. I'm high in pessimism and low in lymphocytes. I dream of adenoma, leukaemia and rectal unpleasantness. My thyroid keeps me frantic and my larynx I try to forget. Spongioblastoma, squamous cell carcinoma, tongue and jaw rot. All make me shudder and quail. Me, my bone marrow and my fibrous tissue, we're all touching cloth.

I worry about chromium, cobalt tar, soot, asphalt and the nitrogen mustards. I worry about the hydrocarbons in Benson & Hedges, the fibreglass in Marlboros and the cowshit in Woodbines. Everywhere I look there lurks some form of carcinogenic agent. Burnt toast, for the love of Christ! Burnt fucking toast! What chance do we have?

In my dreams I see endless rows of skinhead neoplasms, stoked up on cider, singing songs and wrecking phone booths. They know my name and want my custom. I'm an attractive arena for the gladiatorial excesses to which they conspire. They're out to get me and they haven't failed yet.

O, here they come, those neoplasms.

THE NEOPLASMS
(singing rowdily)

We're the boys from Deathsville
The lads from Cancer Alley,
We dogfight with the cellular
And add them to our tally.

We laugh at radiation
Chemotherapy leaves us cold,
We are the Bold Incurables,
We're Canker, Rot & Mould.

There's rabies, spina bifida,
The Hep and Parkinson's;
We rule the endocrinal waves
And give medicine the runs.

We are the greatest malady,
Our death rate's far ahead.
With Polio, you get crippled
With us, you just get dead!

You smoke your little ciggies,
You munch your blackened toast.
Hurrah for carcinogenics!
They'll pip you at the post.

So, look out for Melanoma,
Watch out for Dermoid Cyst.
If you meet Carcinoma,
You'll quickly not exist.

(See what I mean? These guys are bastards.)
If one is going to be a hypochondriac one might as well be a well-informed one.

As you may have guessed, death and decay haunt me – the two to do. Both in the same stiff, unlovely attitudes. They lure and repel me with their hollow, necrotic appeal. Of all the vices and traps of life, it occurs to me that Death is the most uncaused and unmerited.

Close to me, the glut of local birds scatters wildly, screeching with vexation. From the clearing, flapping mêlée there stalks a small blackandwhite cat, imperious, unconcerned. It approaches my bench on soft, sneaky pads, dot-bummed and sleek. It vaults onto my seat and nears me without fear. I reach out my hand to stroke it. The animal pauses minutely before deciding to allow me that liberty. It rubs its spiky forehead against my palm. It hopes for food. Cats like me. I like cats. Nice cats. Clever moggies. Not like dogs. Foolish beasts.

The cat purrs sturdily, its little frame vibrating hoarsely in my hand. I have no food to give it. It continues its friendship and rubs its perioral glands against my thumb. It is a happy animal and looks well-fed. I wonder how it manages that.

Whoops! I stand up quickly. I shudder and move rapidly away from the bench. The blackandwhite cat bounds away, unbothered by my exit. I rush madly towards the gentlemen's lavatory in the corner of the square. I hurry through the obstacle throng, charge down the shallow steps into the underground convenience. Bugger! It's a pay toilet. Frantically, I fumble in my trouserpockets and produce a ten-pence piece which I give to the obese geriatric manning the little tollgate. The tiny barrier is raised and I am admitted into the porcelain bowels. Dodging the hovering homos and undercover policemen, I manage to nab an unoccupied and festering cubicle all to myself. Safe in my rancid booth, I bend and prepare. Briefly, I stare close at the stained toilet paper and pissdrunk cigarettes clogging the crusted bowl and then I start to vomit.

Oh God! There it goes. (Blekthgh! Splish.)

Jesus! (Hrrnnggnnhh! Splash.)

Oh no! Stop, please. (Whynjjcklth! Splosh.)

With a final splash and slip and drip, I conclude my business and spit brownly. The last of the mucus still hangs from my mouth by a stalwart, stubborn thread. I spit again and hiss and blow hard. The tiny rope of slobber remains loyally attached to my lips. I drag my hand across my mouth and wipe it on the wall with the other snot and muck.

Better. I check the bowl for misplaced intestines before flushing the toilet gratefully. My head pounds with pain and disgust as I exit. One of the shuffling grotesques eyes me hopefully. He thinks I look awful enough to be interested in what he's offering. He's wrong – just about. I slink out, grateful that I didn't make too much noise or get arrested on suspicion of bog faggotry.

Upstairs and outside, the concluding day has no use for me. The crowd flows past the tiny dam that I present. I look back to my erstwhile bench. It is already occupied. A duo of flea-bitten tramps squats there with a paper bag full of moist chips in the space between them. They pass an unlabelled bottle of blue liquid between them and the little blackandwhite cat crouches at their filthy feet, watching them keenly.

I trudge out towards Charing Cross Road. Charing Cross Road is shabby but at least it houses a few bookshops and their spurious air of scholarship and leisure. I could do with that swift illusion of respectability. I've had enough of Leicester Square.

I don't want to tell you about what I just puked up. It wasn't very nice. It hurt. It was horrible. Perhaps those neoplasms have already been to work on me. It certainly looked like it – and smelt like it too.

I think I might be dying. In a way, I hope I am. I mean, if I live through this kind of thing then death must be a hell of a lot worse. The thought worries me. I like to get the nasty stuff over with at the beginning. I don't want any surprises.

All this suffering. All this intransigent self-immolation. How does it strike you? Does it convince? Does it appal or irritate? Why do I bother to endure?

Am I practising my stamina? Why don't I just take it easy for a while? Put my feet up? Have a bath, don my slippers, pull a chair before the fire and have a little nap? Why am I so snobbish about the affability of comfort and docility?

I'm not. Not at all. Indeed, I used to be a vigorous champion of ease. It seemed to be the sensible, democratic thing to do. I didn't quibble. I didn't crave excitement or educative suffering. I wanted my progress to be plush and painless, unlaundered by the vagaries of incident.

Nothing pissed me off quite so much as the tracts of self-inflicted (or at least, submissive) trial and disintegration that makes up personal progress through the twentieth century. This unchallenged self-destruction seemed meretricious. All that coercion in your own disarray and capitulation. Booby-trapping your own trenches. That pride in humiliation and shaky theorising. I abhorred the virtuosity of these people. The new nobility of degeneration: their dreadful, inexplicable content. This was bollocks and it got me down.

Naturally, I was wrong about all this. My vigorous opinions were, as usual, daringly misinformed. Suffering, when it has had a good chance to tire you out, roll you up and litterbin you, then, suffering justifies itself. It becomes its own raison d'être. It is at least some kind of function, some kind of life. Grotesquely, it amuses and diverts. It's a role like any other and better, dramaturgically speaking, than some.

In other words, when you're all buggered up you'll take any trembling, lunatic solace.

*

I suppose I should really fill you in on what happened with that girl back there, that charity bimbo. I could scarcely get away with that kind of omission. She insisted that she knew me. Which was, of course, quite impossible, what with me being so resolutely lowlife and all. She must have heard one of the tramps say my name. Or else, it was a lucky stab. It would have had to have been a very lucky stab indeed! Bogle is not like Smith, it's not a fair guess, is it? Well, I can't explain how she knew my name but don't let that raise any suspicions. I'd never lie to you.

Anyway, she thought it was tragic that I had come to this. She was appalled, poor girl. She felt she had to do something. This led me to consider trying to cadge some dosh off her. I didn't though. It would have been embarrassing.

She said that she was going to try to fix me up with somewhere to stay. One of her friends had a vacant house in Enfield. She said that she would try to swing it for me. She gave me her telephone number and told me to ring her on Monday. There was no need for me to be homeless she said. I didn't belong on the streets. And once I had somewhere to stay, I'd soon get myself back on the rails, whatever that meant.

Well, what do you think? Personally, I have my doubts. I mean, it was nice of her to bother and all but I have the feeling that she's after my pert little buns, the rascal! I can't allow this prostitution of myself. I think I'll give it a miss. I can look after myself, thank you very much. Chortle. Chortle.

SEVEN

Exterior. Early evening. Draggled, frowsy market stalls nestling in the lower cradle of Covent Garden and Southampton Street. Files of tourist youths issue from the arches in the market frontings, noisy and foreign. The dripping evening doesn't seem to dilute their vivacity and their kittenish antics are unaffected by the drabness of the oily sky and the sudden swelling of drains and pavements.

As you can see, the weather has turned shitty. I knew that this was going to happen.

I watch this moist, splashy scene from the tacky shelter of one of the spurious little terrace cafés that litter Covent Garden. I spectate with relish. I savour the blight of the overarching sky. I like it when it rains.

This is very foolish of me. When it rains I have to improvise shelter amongst the muck and clutterbuck of the city. Rain's no friend of mine. My ankles are wet and my verminous socks cling to my flesh. Rain is doing me no good. Nonetheless, I admire rain, impartially speaking, I love the way it pisses everyone off.

This wicked little belt of precipitation is a good example. It falls like shards, darting and piercing dust and dry. The sky is obdurate and in-hospitable. It deflates the trumpery of this shoddy urban twilight.

Again, I have slept. I nodded off in my chair. Doubtless, I sizzled and gurgled with autonomic snot and catarrh but, surprisingly, no one had the heart to disturb me. People can be nice if they take the time to think about it. I have woken, broken and sad. My spine is rigid and hot with pain. It is the only part of my poor body that remains unfrozen and it is making up for that in the discomfort department.

I shift warily in my seat. Nothing haemorrhages or drops off so I'm quite cheered by the robustness of my health. I fish a friendly fag from the bestforgotten murk of my old overcoat. The packet is mangled and useless.

116

I have two cigarettes left. One has torn from its filter whence it hangs by a stalwart wisp of paper. I pull the filter off and smoke the remainder. In its way, it's nicer without the filter. Cutting out the middleman and all that. I snort hardfresh, harsh tobacco and feel that old answering call of gratitude from my petrified body.

I'm in clover here as I sit in Covent Garden amongst emptying sandwich bar clutter. I have a table and two chairs to myself. Four empty, sugarsoiled coffee cups lie on my table like stains of despair. I have drunk them all and the waitress leaves them there to keep me company.

The dilapidated terrace of this vulgar little establishment serves as a neat frame for the ochre, bedraggled misery that greets my applauding eyes. The rain is heavier now and drums with pleasing sarcasm on the nasty canopies of this impromptu market. People huddle, wrap and run or wait. Their umbrellas suffer the jokiness of the wind and elaborate coiffures are defoliated in a cruel instant. This might have been quite cosy if it wasn't so sodding cold. I rub my hands to produce a little warmth. Bloody June!

Four cups of coffee! This folly has cost me one pound sixty. I needed it though. That coffee was vital. I panicked. Suddenly, after all that throwing up, I felt that I was going to die if I did not have precisely four cups of coffee. Precisely four cups of coffee was what I had. I binged. I whopped it into me. I recovered. I live on. It was a false alarm.

And here they sit, my four coffee cups. Into which I've stared. Bollock-scared. The names and numbers of all my sins. My nemesis. My day of the coffee cups. The day of my meagre reckonings. Truthtime. When, after a quick spot of carpentry, my eyes have opened and I see the joke that I am – what a sorry shambles it has all been for me.

The sop and clownish grime of my rancid little life. In coffee grounds I see that. Profundities by the dozen am I spouting today. All in a quartet of coffee cups.

(Everyone has their off days.)

The sky spits. The pavement is carpeted with the muckyslippyslurry-sludge of a boy-trodden rainy schoolday. The patina of filth and grease is so treacherous that a burly, circumambulating policeman slips and almost falls. There are no giggles, furtive or otherwise.

Rain. Rain, harsh and cold. Dull, greying mudflecks ring the pavements and walls. All is oily and mobile, fluid and dribbling.

This is, as you might already have guessed, perfect weather in which to relate what I intend. This is suitable mud, apt rain, mood-reflective intemperance. This is the pathetic fallacy at its flailing, pissed-off best!

Because.

This is the bit I won't enjoy. It's sadness time now. Time to trawl out my little tragedy. The point where I should engage your sympathy. The soppy stuff. The romance issue. The Deirdre Dilemma. My worst of bad times.

So, I had continued to dribble on through my lack of adolescence, working, scraping, thinning and improvising. Times were tough but I was tougher. I admired myself for this. With careful, gardener's hands, I resolutely nurtured the various chips on both my shoulders. Where I lacked a grudge, I would cultivate one. I tried hard to be embittered, downtrodden and vengeful. To a certain extent and with some justice, I succeeded. I piled my grudges up like coins and counted my bitter hoard on every greedy night. I sure was suffering and someone someday would pay and pay hard. This thought cheered me up no end. It incited me to further survival and defiance. Vengeance is very good for one's self-discipline.

My problem was that my grudges and resentments were largely object-less. Someone was obviously doing me harm but it was someone un-corporeal, someone without a telephone number or a daughter I could rape. Fate was my fruitfilled foe and I had no hope of retaliation. When I kicked against the pricks, they kicked back. I was dysenteric Misfortune's personal private latrine. Ill luck, cruelties, terrors, trials and disasters showered me from all sides. I was permanently drenched in slapstick calamity. My misadventures were alternatively airy, dashing, complex, predictable, surprising, squalid, miserable, pathetic, epic, implausible, well-researched, extempore, necessary, futile, malignant and virtuoso. My stock was low and my shares were crashing.

I used to comfort myself with the notion that things could get no worse. They always did. You could put the kettle on for my obscene and punctual mishaps. Hysterically, I would giggle at my residue of mischance. I lay down and gave up. I rose and struggled on. I accepted meekly and resisted savagely. I consulted a social worker and an exorcist. They both considered me a hopeless case. Misfortune soon ran out of appalling things to do to me. I became briefly optimistic. Misfortune went back to the beginning and started again. I grew bald, wrinkled and impotent. Friends fled screaming if they saw me in the street. My reverses defied the very laws of probability itself, as several eminent mathematicians proved. Humanists had nervous breakdowns on my account and theologians cited me as the proof of a God, albeit a rather sardonic one. I became incontinent, nihilistic and developed a twitch.

Things got worse.

Not that I was completely without actual living figures whom I could actively thank for nothing. Landlords and pub-owners categorised exploitation and humiliation in my lexicon. Deirdre's parents also did their persistent best to thwart and destroy me. They hired private detectives, sent anonymous defamatory letters to my school and planted bombs in my bathroom. The usual in-laws kind of thing. Yes, they were absolutely tireless in their hatred of me but they were never really that much of a challenge, poor ugly, vulgar folk.

Their lovely daughter's unconscious barbs were infinitely more galling. Her casual intolerance and her inconsiderate prosperity scourged me with ease. While I starved and sank away, she grew frumplyplump girlie fat. While I had more hole than shoe, she draped her unremarkable figure in ever more lavish fashion. She had a chubby, sprouting little bank account while I kept a slim album filled with photographs of all the fivers I had ever seen. It was a tricky little discrepancy. (Aren't they always?)

Deirdre's daily lunch box averaged more calories than one of my better nutritional weeks but she betrayed bugger all awareness of this knotty little inequality and obviously expected me to return her discretion in full. Like the soppy dickhead I was, I did actually preserve a diplomatic silence upon the grotesque horrors which I suffered. My seemly lips were unblemished by anything of riot or controversy. If I passed out or accidentally puked up some of the grass I'd been munching, I would pass it off as another hole in the shoe of my shoddy existence.

When you are comfortable, when you are prosperous and content, other people's wild misadventures are the worst kind of embarrassment. I knew this well enough. I didn't want to be a conversation-stopper.

Deirdre was my love, my life, my everything. She was my comfort, hope and best of handicaps. Mopy spooney that I was, I drowned in eyeless passion. Romantically, I was in my nonage but I refused to believe that Deirdre was other than the end of all erotic striving for me. I was set fair. All seemed possible with her at my side. Her bulky figure obscured any vision of an independent future. If ever my mutinous thoughts lingered on her stupidity, greed or selfishness, the moment was brief and easily conquered. Soon quelled. My darling girl could not merit such obloquy – least from me. For me she was light, beauty, strength and rest. It did not occur to me that she might be blight, pestilence and murrain.

(The satirist must be aware of the folly and vices of that which is satirised but

must avoid moral superiority or hypocrisy. Satire has a function: the censure of folly and evil and the stimulation of reform. It should be corrective
not vindictive. It is a deflating weapon which should be employed upon
only that which is mundane.

Is this true? Is this the whole story? I think not.

We are all victims of satire. We suffer under wit, sarcasm, irony and
ridicule. Cynicism, invective and the sardonic plague our doings. The
trouble with our trials is that they are flippant, mischievous and mimic-
nimble. Some kind of drama or tragedy would at least give us an agreeable
consciousness while we endured. But no, satire is feculent and relentless. It
molests us in everything we do and stamps our disasters with its farcical
opprobium. Irony and ridicule bite deep and often. We make a tasty meal
for Mockery.

What it boils down to is this; at our worst we are a joke and at our best,
litotic.)

My eighteenth year was not a good one. A series of very bad things
happened to me in that year. (It wasn't a great year for Maurice either –
what with it being the year he died and all that.) Maurice's death was only
one of the bad things that nasty year. There were an awful lot of bad things
just about then but one particular bad thing stands head and shoulders
above the rest of the bad things that happened to me in that year. Listen.

On the seventeenth of February of my eighteenth year I was, as usual,
working behind the bar of the Shannon Inn during my school lunch hour.
Lunchtime in the Shannon Inn was an education in itself. A superb scene.
Ragged, verminous old men, just beginning to feel human after the first few
pub-fed hours of their day. A low, depressed murmur of voices hidden and
muffled in the tawdry snugs. A dingy envelope of smoke and deleterious
human fumes hanging heavily in the stale atmosphere of the public bar.
Much fun to be had.

Tom Mullen, my vile gag-toothed employer, told me that there was
someone outside who wanted to see me. Mullen was peeved. He told me
that he wasn't paying me good money to fuck about outside with my mates.
Dodging his maladroit imprecations, I rushed outside. I saw that it was
Deirdre's father who had summoned me. I was surprised. He was hardly a
bosom buddy nor a great fan of mine. He looked grim. When he turned
towards me I saw that his face held no greeting.

He told me something very bad. He told me something very unpleasant indeed. It hit me hard and fast. I cracked up rather. Luckwise and clever, however, I had an immediate solution. I got drunk – on the spot. Very, very drunk did I get.

Apparently, Maurice found me later that day, sleeping on the altar of the school chapel, sacrilegiously enough. I carried two bottles of whisky as reinforcements just in case Sobriety tried any rearguard actions. I was completely plastered but taking nothing for granted. I had a lot I didn't want to think about.

Maurice was surprised to find his erstwhile teetotal chum so poleaxed in such a place. He tried to discover what it was that bothered me so. It took much time and patience and quite a few encomiums from my intolerant self before he learnt the truth. To his credit, even Maurice was shocked. So he said afterwards. He hadn't banked on that. It must have been embarrassing.

Deirdre's father had told me that Deirdre had had a miscarriage. It was, by all accounts, the result of a botched backstreet abortion which had occurred some weeks previously. Deirdre had nearly died apparently. She had been a long time gone as they say. It had been the usual bog job – the miscarriage, that is. In other words, the rejected, mangled foetus had been voided and deposited in the family toilet bowl. Not a nice way to go. I think that this was probably the grisly little detail that did for me. I saw the ungodly spoor dying its toilet death, sticking to the porcelain walls of its piss-and-watery coffin, precious limbs and membranes akimbo. As a ducat. Poor kid, I thought. Though I supposed that I couldn't really call it that. Poor whatever it was. I remember that this struck me as an interesting point at the time. A semantic difficulty.

Oh, it got me down. It saddened and depressed me. Despair, grief and shame came round for the weekend. I got so griefstricken and drunk that I neglected to tell Deirdre's father that the responsibility for this obscenity was not mine. I hadn't got a mile near porking her after my initial failure of scruple. I simply forgot to mention that it must have been someone else, not me. It didn't occur to me and since he had accused me of this fertile misdemeanour, it was obvious that Deirdre had neglected to mention my innocence.

It was trebly sad because the whole reason I hadn't boffed her had been my overweening regard for her chastity and my youthful respect for her virginity. I must say, on reflection, I really missed the boat on that one!

It was her suffering that bothered me most at the time, though. It cost me dear. Horrified, I was. The whole fantastic business made me retch and the drinking helped remarkably in that department. Maurice was tremendously upset, splendid fellow! For some grotesque reason, the humour of my situation struck me suddenly and forcibly. I was demonstrably, ludicrously abject. My acceptance of the blame; my cuckolded ignorance; my feeble good intentions and hapless casuistries. It was a giggle and a half, believe me. My mirth was deadened, meagre and the little chapel echoed to my laughter. Maurice was creditably revolted by my behaviour. He couldn't see the joke.

I wish that I could adequately describe how awful I felt (and perhaps how awful a time Deirdre was doubtless having). It's difficult though. I'm not quite equal to the task. I just crumbled, messily. I disintegrated. I broke up for the summer. My head was a snotfilled sponge of sobbing pain and my heart dripped great gouts of blood and misery. Menaced by tears and grief, I capitulated to the insurmountable hatred of my fortune. I drank hard. I had no redress and no appeal. Despair was the order of the day. It's difficult to get the tone right at such times. I slipped, I slided, I faded away.

(Oh, satire is a bastard! Satire will get some of his own one day, I hope.)

The week end following my discovery of Deirdre's gynaecological mishap was, to say the least of it, less than all-round fun. The Friday night was spent in drinking the two pub-size bottles of Pernod that I had managed to add to my sudden alcoholic collection. Saturday was largely spent in trying to fish the more necessary vital organs out of the purpletrimmed puke that spewed uncontrollably from my indignant throat. On the Sunday I tried to cut my own throat with a blunt paperknife but was too drunk to manage even that. I sliced myself up pretty well though. I was harrowed, horrified and hit hard. I cried acid, sparky tears onto the dirty window of my ruinous hovel. I shed bowlfuls of bitter, neckly blood. Oh, all in all, I had a bad time.

My, my, things had gone hugely wrong. Life had turned nasty. Life's like that – it likes to display its versatility. That's what I like about life: its ostentatious, unscrupulous showmanship.

I was in dire straits. I was living in a microscopic kennel bungful of all that's interesting and voracious in the insect and bacteria world. I was working thirty hours a day licking pub floors for a few coppers with which to pay my exorbitant rent and my girlfriend had just had a miscarriage, the sowing of which had not been my task and joy. Poor old Bogle – he always had the pain without the pleasure.

And didn't I scream to the Gods above for a modicum of justice and forbearance. I was barely eighteen and felt that I merited special consideration. As I began to dribble, bawl and bleed my youth away, I pleaded my innocence, my harmlessness, my poverty, my youth and my mortality. Fuck to the use it was! I wasted my breath. I shouldn't have bothered.

*

From this inauspicious beginning, I deteriorated rather badly. Deirdre maintained her silence on the subject of my lack of contribution to her unfortunate pregnancy. I had few chances to clear my name and was curiously unbothered by shouldering the guilt, anyhow. Compared to the other things that were going on in my life, guilt and blame didn't seem to matter very much. Drunkenness pervaded my life. I got a rubber mallet and hit the bottle. It helped me when my life confused me. Which was always. Drink and more drink. My misery came to me in liquid form.

Working in pubs was a great advantage. My supply of alcohol was almost unlimited and as my taste and tolerance improved my pilfering grew more daring. I would leave work with armfuls of dodgy liquor and happily stoke myself up to face the terrors of my sleepless nights. As I slid further into the mildew of my degradation, my increasing intoxication and theft during working hours became difficult to ignore. Pretty soon I was booted out of all the pubs where I tended (about forty by now). True to form, Tom Mullen was the first to jettison me. He gave me his good heart's benediction and persuaded his two enormous, boneheaded sons to give me a rare old kicking. This pair went to it with a will. They stomped on my head with vigour and virtuosity, leaving me with eighteen stitches on my gob, a broken collarbone, concussion and three crushed ribs. (You know, I never liked that Mullen family.)

None of this deterred my stalwart boozing. I sold what few embarrassing belongings I could sell. I borrowed from friend and enemy. I culled and fished for the money I needed to feed my febrile thirst for drink.

In its turn, my accommodation became a tricky issue. I hardly bothered to disguise the sad effects of my intemperance. As I thundered down the ill-health and vice staircase, my last hagbag landlady booted me out. Once again I was beaten up – by the landlady's sons this time. Though not as big as the Mullen boys, they were infinitely more inventive and they gave me a very bad time indeed. (Why is it that these people always seem to have such mutant, psychopathic offspring?) My kaleidoscopic array of contusions, subluxations, dislocations and haemorrhages burgeoned visibly. My fractured and saddened bones varied in damage and agony. (Ah, my bones, my dapper, my daring bones!) They were simple, compound, partial, complete or linear, longitudinal, oblique, spiral, displaced, comminuted, transverse, articular, intra- and extra-capsular and they hurt like billy-o! That stentorian lady of property nabbed what was left of my belongings to cover the rent which I had invested in drink. I didn't really care enough to complain and anyway my bones hurt too much.

Frightening, isn't it?

*

For the first month or so, I continued to attend school for some obscure reason. I can't think what good it was supposed to do as I reverentially embarked upon my apprenticeship in dipsomania but still I went to school. The educative impulse must have been yet strong in my faltering heart. My schoolmates were generally puzzled by my excess but were for the most part, sympathetic. Only Maurice knew the cause for my relentless deterioration and he was keeping it to himself. (He was having thorny little troubles of his own at the time, largely involving his imminent death.) Spotty McGonagle ran a book on my chances of lasting out the term. I was five to one against but had a lot of moral backing. McGonagle made a fortune. (He slipped me several sneaky bottles of gin to improve his chances. I always knew McGonagle would go far.)

It wasn't easy for them. They were mostly the sons of Catholic prosperity and I was fast becoming a tramp as well as a drunken scumbag. Creditably, they felt the inferiority of their position and were anxious to please. In their limited, parented way, they endeavoured to help as best they could but apparently I persisted in telling them to go and fuck themselves. I even took a swing at one or two of them, including Maurice. I was a stubborn bugger at the best of times and my drinking fuelled my obstinance. It seemed that I could or would not be aided but still my charitable chums persisted, the jolly dogs!

I used to pass out in class and would spend a prodigious portion of each schoolday trying to vomit my intestines into the bitter-scented urinals of the upper sixth bogs. 'Plonker' O'Halloran nicked a tin bucket from the caretaker and they would take it in turns to follow me around with this receptacle for my beastly bokings.

At first, the teaching staff furiously ignored my behaviour and despite my hostility my peers were quite successful in covering for my more outrageous follies. They would confiscate the myriad bottles and flasks that I habitually brought into school with me. (Being a wily fellow, I always managed to keep one or two safely secreted. They were too big to stick up my arse – I know, I tried – but I established several neat coverts in the hurling team's changing rooms which I kept bloody well-stocked for my frequent emergencies.)

When I was too blootered to stand, some of my fellows would drag me into the showers and, at the cost of many blows from moi, they would freeze me into some kind of coherence. Once, they even shaved my three weeks' worth of dark and dirty beard for me ... slicing me badly in the process but it was kindly meant.

Those guys practically rogered me! On reflection, I'm kind of touched about the way in which they all rallied round me to a man. At the time, I wasn't at all keen!

Needless to say, I soon became much too disgusting to ignore. The college could no longer afford to disregard my growing wildness. Old Snaddy Piff was informed. Before he could bring his canonical wisdom to bear, I had already passed the stage where I was too pissed to remember which school I was supposed to go to. A problem dissolved.

Well, boys and girls, what can I say? This was a dark time. Yes indeed. My decline did not abate. My decline burgeoned, my decline sprouted, it grew horns and did press-ups. With no money and nowhere to live, I took to the streets (my bestest friends). My eyes clouded and my pride drained away. I didn't try to pretend this time. I didn't care who saw my degraded state and I slept where I could. Ghost, I haunted the stale, dirty streets of Belfast and turned my paling eyes from hope of any kind. Other tramps and drunks began to form my society and my smooth body began to breed filth and vermin. My teeth rotted and crusted in my head and my brain was addled though slitsharp with bitterness and grief. My injuries were left half-healed and my health nose-dived with breathtaking speed. Deirdre haunted me no longer. Boy, was I pissed off, young as I was! My life seemed already concluded and in my sottish, joyless fashion, I revelled in the godless squalor of my future. All fucked up. Me, Ripley Bogle. Ballocky Bogle. Mr Incomplete. All fucked up!

Another snapshot; another picture for my album. Summing up that best of years. This was me. In polaroid. Lowtime:

Hunched, crooked, patch-kneed, he slouches through the puddles. A splatblack, cheap plastic mackintosh three sizes too fat is draped over his battered, boneless form. A crumpled blue pyjama-top serves in the office of shirt and jacket. Ripped, mud-spotted school trousers drip from his wasting legs. His shoes gape. They flap wetly on his miry, sockless feet and crusted toes. His hands are inchthick with dirt. His hair is greasy unkempt, his chin disfigured by spiky stubble and drying dribble. His face is ravaged and stretched. His nose mushy, his cheeks hollow, his brow creased and his oldeyes dull. All is stained and mouldering. The stench of his own ginbright piss clouds around him. He yells and whinges to the world. His head is numb and his heart is hard but he's happy with a sudden, sodden joy. He feels the friendship of the sun and moon and laughs in company with the stars.

Maurice found me about four months later, sleeping under a bench in the

Botanical Gardens. By dint of pledging me with an abundance of alcohol if I complied, he managed to coax me into a relatively scumless boarding house in University Street. There, he cleaned me up as best he could. I'm led to believe that this was no easy task. According to young Maurice I was horribly filthy, caked in my own detritus and pickled in the nameless obscenity of the streets and all that kind of thing. It must have been a real litmus test for Mr Kelly's philanthropy. Anyway, he sluiced me and chucked me a full bottle of Bells (Mecca, heaven, White Hart Lane!) and thus mollified, I soon fell asleep.

Maurice stayed with me that night. He could hardly bring me back to his parents' home in that state. I believe his parents generally expected his schoolfriends to belong to vaguely the same species as their son. He couldn't leave me on my own in case I did a runner; so he stayed. Lucky boy, he slept on the floor and listened to me gurgle, whine and fart the night away.

Predictably, this caused many frowns on the part of the landlady next morning. She obviously suspected us of the foulest kinds of poof debauchery. Poor old Maurice had to endure a long tirade of righteous abuse from the voluble old hag before he could drag me out. Of course, I was hugely unperturbed and generously offered to shaft the old hag to prove my heterosexual rectitude.

Eventually Maurice extricated me and began to marshal me (bottle in hand) towards St Malcolm's. He told me that it was exam day and that we were to sit those things called A levels. Apparently, I was distinctly un-impressed. So much so that I immediately lay facedown on the pavement and stoutly refused to go any further. A levels could fuck away off for all I cared.

Here, Maurice committed the error of summoning a taxi cab which I soon liberally sprayed with my discoloured, whiskeyed vomit. Naturally, the driver protested and Maurice had to give him a tenner to make him go away. We walked the rest of the way.

It is not without a certain juvenile pride that I state that my appearance at school for the first time in months caused one of the biggest sensations in years. It was a major event. I was treated with delicacy and some awe. Some perspicacious fifth-formers even asked me for my autograph.

It was something of a surprise that in my loathsome and disreputable state I was allowed to sit any exams at all. That Paddy Sniff waived various rules and granted me the priceless boon of being allowed to enter the examination hall. I went in. I sat down. I picked up a borrowed pen and eventually after an hour's nap, I started writing. Maurice was dead chuffed. He thought he'd saved me from myself or something like that. He was wrong. I wrote a surprisingly good piece of vitriolic doggerel on the subject of examiners and promptly buggered off back to the business of being a tramp, to the ruination of all Maurice's hopes. Sad but hardly surprising.

The rain banks and eases off. The rapid patter of drip and splash fades slowly. The darkening air grows clear, sharp, lucid. The cold is mobile, it vents and swings in dry corridors of air. Covent Garden shivers and draws close in that cold. The sky hisses the last of its rain and the sodden pavements gleam with hard, wet shine. High above, the sanguine, popping lights of an aircraft slip noiselessly along. Up there, there is warmth and comfort, gin and stewardesses. People being ferried cheerfully, restfully through flights of air.

I've had it! I'm growing sad. All this makes me melancholy. Suddenly lonely, I stare at the last shuffle of dispirited townsfolk. They shift and hurry, seeking their various warmths. I find no comfort there. So sad, Misere. I have a need for the sonority and catchpenny oblivion of alcohol. I need a drink.

I'm sad. I'm so sad.

EIGHT

A dark low-ceilinged chamber; wall mirrors reflect other fictional chambers, conjuring wide spaces bereft of glamour and generally confounding the eye. The cluttered butterthick air is filled with long troughs of tobacco smoke which curls and spirals around the groups of drinking men like some ghostly foliage sprouting from the mangled, match-thin stubs of rolled paper clamped between their wicked yellow fingers. There is a constant clamour – the sottish riot of Irishmen arguing, bawling, singing and shouting in rational, national disharmony. The odour of the place is a verminous, cloying blend of stingsweet whisky fumes, stale spilt beer and rotting carpets. It is heady and warming – a homely fragrance. Confusion is nourished; stomachs bubble and babble burgeons.

A young man enters from the left-hand side of this diverting scene, skulking through the lower and smaller of the two street doors. He is shabby and hunted, his face is pale and unshaven. Grime rings his collapsing shoes and his eyes are hollow and mirthless. Ripley Bogle, he is. On dead feet, he slouches through the Celtic mêlée, heading obliquely towards the bar. Mingling imperceptibly, he lifts his eyes and speaks slowly and bitterly.

'So, what do I do?' he asks. 'Get a job? Find somewhere to sleep? Retrieve my sliding life? No, of course not, I come to Kilburn to see if I can cadge a few drinks off some Irish dickhead like myself!'

There is a short pause. Eyes turn from him, bored already. The swell of pubmen have listened and dismissed. Now, they cackle and guffaw malevolently, with true arsehole joy. A nasty sound. A cacophony of woozy witless noise. Sottish laughter and beery japes. The young man speaks again, his voice leaden with feeble irony.

'A Kilburn pub! S'blood, I'm back home already! A little piece of Ireland. There is a corner of some foreign pisspot that is forever Ulster.'

The barman-landlord cranes his fat, greasy torso Ripleywards. This is Martin Malone, he of the thin head and the fat body. God's gift to Ireland.

'What can I do you for?' he asks in whingeing Derry tones, his eyes bright with greed and invitation. The young man is confused and he mumbles inaudibly. Malone encourages him with his gracious usher's smile.

'Stuck for choice are you?' He sweeps his arm to indicate the proud geography of bottles at his back. 'We'll have whatever you want. An embarrassment of riches. Look and learn. What you want, you'll get ... depending on the dosh, *bien sûr.*'

He smiles again, pleased with his rhetoric and amiability. The young man is yet troubled and continues to prevaricate. Ringmaster, umpire, legion-seller, Martin Malone moves into the gear authoritative.

'Allow me, my young friend.' He mugs and winks to his growing audience of regular drinkers and publifes.

'Alcohol! What is it else? A simple, silly thing. Joy for all. Pure spirit of wine. A class of compounds composed of carbon, hydrogen and oxygen ... some of which are solids (tedious fellows!) ... and some of which are liquids (O lucky day!)'

He laughs stagily and there is a brief ripple of mystified applause from his lowlife acolytes. His anxious eyes scan his young customer's wavering face. He presents some bottles with dab, practised hand. Proffering. Pandaring.

'Gin? Gin. Equals the second best thing about England. Squeezes in between women and cricket – though who's to say in what order of importance. Juniper bubbles in your head – that elusive lightness. What do you say?'

Amongst the greater din of the larger pub, a small group has gathered to watch this exchange. To see this sale and fall. They glance keenly at Ripley. He colours under their gaze and speaks with clumsy care.

'Sadness has come to call. All on account of me and my big bad story. It was all yesterday's fault. What can I do? My past I come to drown but my present cannot swim.' He titters, 'By God, I hope my future floats!'

There is little amusement amongst the onlookers. They had not expected this. They mumble amongst themselves, confused and discontented with the young man's answer. Malone moves quickly, holding out his next bottle batch.

'Whisky perhaps? Fountain spew. The ballsache to contemplation and discretion. No messing about with anything as nebulous as flavour here. Puts fur on your tonsils. Not for the health-conscious or the conspicuously happy. How about some whisky?'

'My tacky little tragedy. Where's the discernment and anecdotal charm in the bad bits of my life? Bad yankee fiction. Oh, for a modicum of originality or a dash of style!'

He looks around upon their incomprehension. Malone tries again. He is panting with effort. He feels the need to sell, to receive coin.

'Vodka? Mmmm? The Russki grudge against the stomach wall. Volatile, inflammable, toxic. The bevy of the connoisseur. In addition, useful for exterminating rodent life. Would you like to try some?'

Bogle doesn't answer. He faces the little group of dipsos and wastrels. He is explanatory, sombre.

'Her love queened it for me. For all that was worth ... which was less than I'd hoped. So sad! I'd try again but I am young and can postpone in confidence.'

Again, the young man's words have not greatly pleased. The tension and displeasure amongst the listeners is building fast. Anxious to calm and eager to please, Martin Malone steps up the selling.

'Port, would it be? Yes, of course, Port. My personal favourite. The only stuff I really like. Yummy slurp! Tastes of dead things, so bound to be posh. Like pheasant. Wine perhaps? Hope not. Not manly. Not Irish. For poofs and women only. Headache juice. Not recommended. Beer! Of course, beer! Bier. Boozy beer. Gottilagear. Lottabottill. Beer. Coloured water and gas. Hopscotch in Yeast of Eden. Piss for piss, probably your best bet here. Relatively undeadly and always handy if you need to regurgitate in a hurry. Getting back to basics with the dishwater brands. Yankee fizz and Aussie burp. Guinness makes you crap an evil blackness. Abbott makes you pee in sugarlumps.'

He pants to a stop, rabbiteyed and breathless. His nostrils twitch. All eyes now rest on Ripley Bogle. The silence is expectant and doomladen. He speaks.

'Growing old is finding that last residue of tenderness. Not a naughty boy no more. Here, I leave my selfstemmed arsehole youth behind ... I hope I do, that is.' He turns to Malone, facing him for the first time. He frowns at the publican's pleading liar's eyes.

'Alcohol. Boose. The deeming drink. Trumpery. Nothing's worth that. Leave it.'

From the tables come general cries of 'Why don't you then?' and 'Fuck off, shitehawk!' The watchers are distressed and begin to grumble loudly. Malone makes his last stand in bluntness.

'What will you be having, sir?'

'The unusual, please, Martin,' replies the boy.

'Certainly, sir.'

There is grudging applause for Bogle. All are glad and merry again. He joins the fold. The tubby Malone slopfills a dirty beerglass, enmity and distrust lined throughout his sluggish countenance. Ripley, the hireling, awaits his master's pleasure. He exchanges coin for slops and quaffs deep in greed and dread. His young, paling, stubbleface light, with brief, feeble fire. He speaks to them sadly:

'And King Finn said "Let there be light" ... and there was darkness.'

He slouches off through his now tolerant audience. Martin Malone slopes off to other duties and the little group disperses heavy with the anti-climax of the aftermath. Malone cooes and beckons to his larger clientele, his fleshy face disfigured by cupidity and vice.

'Stump up and drink up, you impecunious Hibernian louts! Finest lager in London. Best beer in Britain. Drain your draughts of Rhenish down. Slurp it up, my buckoes! The piss in your pan is the pound in my palm.'

He giggles and capers. The scumbags cheer.

'Wip, wip, wahey!'

'Two more here Marty and a bucket for me brother!'

'Keep it rolling, the bold Malone!'

'For he's a highly shrewd fellow which nobody can deny!'

(Much hilarity.)

Martin Malone grabs an armful score of misty beer glasses. He ducks underneath the bartop and has a private moment, then incants urbanely.

'Begod, I like to dribble,
It really cheers me up.
Because I hate to waste it
I keep it in a cup.'

He coughs, gobs and dribbles the worst that he has into the beer glasses. They fill slowly, vilely with his beercoloured spittle. He stands and starts to sell his wares to his greedy customers, an evil twinkle in his goggle eye.

A shabby, heavily rouged middle-aged woman approaches Ripley. She is spectacularly overdressed and sports a hugely stained and diseased fox fur. She walks unsteadily, fuelled by the liquid results of her last social security cheque. She sits rockily beside the young man and leers inaptly at him –uxorious and girlish.

'What's your name, handsome?' she asks.

'Armand.'

'Armand what?'

'Lefevre. Armand Lefevre.'

'Funny name.'

'It's French.'

'You don't sound French.'

Ripley drinks deep and hard, coming near the end of his beer. The auto-biographical details have confused the old harridan somewhat. She struggles to sort out her sluggish thoughts before continuing brightly.

'Well, Armand, what's a lovelylooking young fella like yourself doing wasting your time in a dirty old dump like this?'

'I'm looking for love.'

'Oh.'

A smile, a wide truthbond graces the young man's lying face. The old lady is very much affected by this. An incoherent glance of tenderness trails its muddy way across her thick, coarse features.

'Haven't you got anyone to love you then?' she asks with dark, grisly intent.

'You could say that. No one to buy me a drink when I need one.'

There is a pause while she looks at him with something resembling shrewd distaste.

'Would you like me to buy you one, my love?'

Bogle's face is careful and sad. He is living a little through the medium of his deceit.

'That's very kind of you. I won't say no.'

Leaning towards him, the woman cups his young face in her decaying hands. Her face is creased with triumph and her laughter is chill with intent. She veers that crumbling, sticky-painted visage close to his and kisses him slobberingly, her maw quivering and wet. Ripley Bogle feels no disgust. A man of the people after all.

'I'll only be a wee minute, darlin',' she says as she stands. She wanders off barwards, groggily excited. After a pause, Ripley wipes his snailtracked mouth and contemplates his beery reward, the fruits of his imagination. The assembled barstool kings ogle him in contempt and he dies several shameful deaths while his new friend haggles at the bar. He is heavy, he is unhappy. Oh, he is deep in misery! His fished-in, his filthy beard is a good food guide for all of his griefs contesting.

Around a table set in a far and musty corner of the public bar, the seven Murphy brothers sit in cockeyed conference. They have noted the new presence of Ripley Bogle and their bricked-up, brotherly eyes glitter with drunken spleen. They know him one and all. From out of Ulster they remember Ripley Bogle. All of them. Paddy Murphy, Billy Murphy, Frankie Murphy, Danny Murphy, Mickey Murphy, Marty Murphy and Mobadingwe Murphy. They know him one and all.

Paddy speaks as he ogles Bogle with growing conviction.

'Ach look, isnat whassisname over there? You know ... yer man ... thingy ... Ikey Moses ... him.'

'What? The beardy tramp drinking with the old tart over there?'

'Ay.'

132

'I don't know.'

'Yeah, it's him. You know the one I mean.'

Billy is quick to agree.

'Shitface the Third as he was known to all who loved him. What's he doing here, I ponder?'

'Nothing good for none of us, that's for sure.'

Danny Murphy interrupts. He is much drunker than the others. He is rowdy, rumpussed, his combative face is graced by a constellation of bruises. He makes his contribution.

'Ah, will you three shitehawks shut your gobs – you're causing a draft. What say you we go over there and kick his pickles for him!'

Paddy Murphy; elder, augur, seer, grabs his sibling's gonads and gives them an audible, admonitory wrench. Marty Murphy, *raconteur, bon viveur,* japist *extraordinaire,* tells a joke. (With conscious brilliance.)

'I say, I say, I say . . . how long does it take an Englishwoman to have a shit?'

General consternation. Vague mutterings of 'Dunno' – 'Difficult to say' – 'Who gives a shit?' Marty auto-answers.

'Nine months . . . and then she names it! Ha ha ha hee hee!'

(*Laughter*)

Mobadingwe is mystified. His dark eyes crease as he looks at his pale-skinned laughing brothers. He frowns portentously.

'Ba zan ci dankali ko doya ba!'

'What did he say?'

'He says he won't eat sweet potatoes or yams.'

'Oh.'

'Well, there you go.'

In his corner, with his woman, old Boges is swinging the lead. Mr Drink is doing his work and the mood is good. Two-handed, eager, he sticks the booze down his poor neck. It gets there quickly. It moves mountains, it improves. Bogle's harridan plies him hard. She is working on the principle that if she gets him drunk enough quick enough, she stands a fair chance of getting her old hands on some young phallus. She is mistaken. Probably.

'What has Mummy got for her ickle babba?' she asks, her eyes ironic and her fat face a-wobble with jocularity.

'Something pretty unpleasant, I imagine,' replies Bogle with growing hauteur.

'Mummy's got a little kiss for baby.'

'Oh good.'

'Now, now; don't be a nasty little infant.' She adopts a more serious tone – confident, hectoring. 'Come on now, a snog for a drink – fair's fair.'

They kiss.

'Handsome is as handsome does,' says Bogle as his gaze loiters towards the bar. Adopting his hint as her own, his gross companion lurches towards Martin Malone and his League of Bottles. A shout of scorn and discord issues from the Murphy corner.

'Muffhound!'

Bogle ignores it with some élan. He's good at this. He's had the practice. The Murphy brothers get back to the business of Bogle. Paddy speaks with fine bitterness.

'Do you remember him poncing around Dungannon with that titless Proddie tramp on his arm . . . he was never no friggin' Irishman.'

'And will you take a look at him pretending for all he's worth that he hasn't seen us, the cunt,' says Billy with drunken venom.

'Sure his head's so far up his own arse that it's not a bletherin' wonder that he doesn't see us,' says jackanapes Marty.

Billy tries to recall the lady in question.

'She was a right one, she was!'

'What was this her name was?' asks Paddy, making the enquiry a general one. The replies are immediate and enthusiastic.

'Fido.'

'Rover.'

'Lassie.'

(*To great guffaws and hilarity.*)

Bogle, now rejoined by his drink-laden, ancient paramour looks their way. His brow creases in loathsome recall. As the old lady slobbers and gropes over him, he whispers sadly to himself, eyes glassy with tearless misery.

'Deirdre Curran. Girls' Model Secondary School. Their finest. Fat arse and thick head. The source where my passion once burned.'

He is ironic, he is sarcastic, he is vindictive; he knocks back his beer and tweaks the old woman's left breast, quite gently.

Paddy Murphy, judge, mediator, statesman.

'Curran! That was it. Heathen bitch! Ulster will shite and Ulster will be trite.'

'Oh, they deserved each other, those two. The spoiled Orange tart and the half-arsed Fenian mediocrity,' says Billy, unkindly.

Mobadingwe's dark eyes have been stapled to the form of Bogle. His gaze clears and turns to his brothers with a gesture of contempt and dismissal. 'A bar kaza cikin gashinta,' he suggests. Paddy's reply is mild, wise.

'Ah, so I've heard, son. I don't doubt you.'

Frankie Murphy belches and farts simultaneously and with great volume. He cries out in triumph.

'Ah, pick the bones out of that one, Bogle ya bastard!'

The general publifes take up this cry and a round of Bogle-abuse begins. The filthy taunts thicken the air.

'Go on, shitforbrains!'

'Wankstain!'

'Son of a monkey's dickbone!'

Bogle smiles airily and waves away their compliments. He is very nearly naked now and is engrossed in trying to thwart the worst encroachments of his vile concubine. He gestures provocatively at the Murphy clan. They taunt him in reply and increase the volume of their slander.

'Him and his dirty Protestant whoor! Who did he ever think he was?'

'Ay, Miss Discernment herself! And her da only a jumped-up shopkeeper from off the Shankill Road. By Jesus, he was social-climbing there!'

Danny – something of an expert on all things sexual – makes his contribution in allusive manner.

'I'm told that the wee bitch liked watching cricket.'

'Oh aye?' says Paddy.

Danny is quicksilver, dartsharp.

'And many's the commentary position that she's taken up at the members' end ... or so I've heard and I've not heard wrong.'

(Laughter)

'He said that she was a help to him in his bad time,' sniggers Marty.

'You never said a truer word,' his brother replies. 'She gave him a helping hand and, if I hear rightly – which you know I do – a fair supportive suck or two into the bargain ... if you know what I mean.'

As one, they all intone: 'We do.' They all rejoice in the knifeblade of their nasty wit. Their lips drip with intolerance and their eyes are whitehot with xenophobia. Danny continues.

'Fellatio was her talent, vocation and major pastime. The girl just loved her work. Like a carwash she was!'

'Only cheaper,' says Billy.

They erupt.

Paddy looks over to Bogle with direct, unflinching hatred.

'He's the nasty son of nasty father.' He waves at his victim whose mouth is now being pressed against the old bag's huge, flaccid dugs. Bogle, breast blind to the irony, begins to blubber and sob for his mother. The Murphys take up his cry.

'Oh aye, Mommie dearest,' shouts Paddy venomously. 'That foul bitch of a mother of his. Bargain Betty, the Tuppenny Tart. The incontinent, syphilitic old hag herself!'

Billy agrees but noddingly.

'With her blather and her bullshit ...' he concurs, '... lipstick and mascara. Basement boffs at a quid top whack. And half of Turf Lodge already scaled her inner thigh free of charge.'

'The picture of motherhood, that! Bogle the pro, two bob a go; it's not worth it, Joe!'

Paddy smiles his witty Irish smile. Applause rings out around the room. Suddenly jealous of his brother's acclaim, Marty leaps upon their table and strikes a classical pose. He thunders splenetically.

'Hark at Caruso! The floating turd that never flushes!'

(*Boos, catcalls, hisses.*)

Disappointed, Marty vomits hugely. The other brothers recoil in disgust and the table swims. Glasses clatter and beer is spilt. Paddy, Billy and Frankie gather round their leaking brother and pummel with jovial, tolerant fists. Marty shrugs off their gentle blows and rises, messymouthed, to his feet. He speaks:

'Here, fellas, hold the fort now. I'm going down to the latrines for a slurp. Defecation's the name of the game.'

Marty exits, fardelbearer, to his appointed task. A ponderous walk of unsated fullness.

PADDY (*admiringly, brotherproud*): He's always crapping, that boy.

BILLY: The man's a marvel. A wonder of biology.

(*Various satellite groups sing the praises of Marty Murphy's epic, mobile bowels.*)

Bogle steps back into the fray. He tears his shrinking lips from the old lady's bosom and lurches towards the bar, under his own limited fiscal steam. His abandoned moll screeches at him indignantly before going in search of someone more accommodating. Pulling her clothes about her wrinkled form, she marches unsteadily to the centre of the room. Martin Malone sees his opening:

MARTIN MALONE (*auctioneer*): Who will start the bidding on this well-tried piece of feminine fatuity. I have forty shekels reserve price. Any advance on that? Which of you fine gentlemen will say fifty? She's droopy but she's cheap. Come now, milords!

MICKEY MURPHY: Forty-five and two camels!

MARTIN MALONE (*encouragingly*): Forty-five shekels and a pair of desert mammals I am bid. Any more? Gentlemen, please? Such a fine example of all that was fashionable in womanhood. Look at her, my friends. Brainless, docile, grateful – what Irishman could want for more. Surely a snip at twice the price.

MOBADINGWE (*riotously*): Dare rigar mugu!

MARTIN MALONE: Thank you, sir. (*He scans his customers with wary, unblinking profiteyes.*) Going once … going twice … gone! Sold to the Irish Ethiope for whatever it was he just said. Stumps!

(*Applause and some minor disgruntlement. The harridan veers towards the Murphys' table. She is grief-stricken.*)

THE HARRIDAN (*glancing sadly at Bogle*): Who will love me? Who? None to see and all to slaver. The three ends of the same sharp stick.

(*Confusion*)

FRANKIE (*mildly*): Shut up and drink up.

(*Suddenly, post-auction, there is much comforting gangman obscenity and jocular ribald suggestion from all parts of the heaving, Catholic, man-infested pub. Bogle sobs to see it. He has slumped in a foul urinous corner with his beer on his belly. He nearly laments his ingratitude and lack of ardour. But not quite. Marty Murphy returns from his evacuation, his oblate countenance swelling with pride. He sees the vomitcoloured table, the ruined glasses, the wasted beer. He sobs bitterly and calls out to Martin Malone in his grief.*)

MARTY (*keening*): Hey Malone, gizza bit of service here, you rancid bastard! (*He keels over, bouncing chairs and spilling what's left of his brothers' beer. He flops into a pool of his own sop and spillage. From where he belches and vomits occasionally. The Malcontent.*)

PADDY (*doublechecking*): Honour us with your attention, Mr Malone. Same again sounds just right.

(*Suddenly, unexpectedly, miraculously, a beer tray materialises, hovering three and a half feet above the Murphys' puke-and-beer-stained table. All grasp a glass and drink deep. Wits are sharpened, trousers splashed and brains agreeably dampened. The emptied tray wavers slightly and then banks off into a high climb. It cruises home, weaving through smoke, fume and sudden ack-ack. The distant sound of Martin Malone's cabbalistic incantation drifts across the churning air.*)

MARTIN MALONE (*winking eye and dapper smile, the vampire barman*):

> These necromantic books are heavenly
> Lines, circles, scenes, letters and characters:
> Ay, these are what Malone most desires.
> Oh, what a world of profit and delight,
> Of power, of honour, of omnipotence
> Is promised to the studious artisan!

(*Meanwhile, Frankie Murphy, aka the man for the mammaries, has sidled up to Mobadingwe's purchase, aka the old bag. His plump, antic face splits into an uxorious smile. His eyes glitter, his voice glides.*)

FRANKIE (*erotically*): Darlin', let me be the Clerk of Works on the building site of your emotions!

(*She sobs, not ungratefully.*)

FRANKIE: Ah now, you'd have found no fun with Ballocky Bogle there. It's me you want.

(*Bogle shouts a loud objection. Frankie ignores while all the other Murphys various retort obstreperously.*)

THE OTHER MURPHYS: Shitface! Prawn! Gilbert! Bumbogie!

FRANKIE (*blithely, to the bag*): Show me your labia. I'll pay. Go on, live dangerously, why dontcha? Sell some peeps. Give me a little looksee. A fiver for a glimpse of the glandular. A tenner for the tits. A pound for your perineum. Trust me. My interest is purely scientific.

(*Seduction complete, Frankie shoves his hand up the woman's skirt. Fist and pudenda connect with a dull, hairy thud. She smiles beatifically.*)

THE HARRIDAN:

> You know I love my naughties
> And my naughties dote on me,
> We're playful and romantic
> The perfect company.

(*They fall to and begin rutting vigorously. Ripley Bogle watches with conscious, ignored envy. Mobadingwe smiles a dangerous, African smile and gestures Boglewards. He sees something he dislikes and his white eyes glitter in his ebony skin.*)

MOBADINGWE: Ga Ripley Bogle can!

(*Bogle springs to his feet, his eyes alight in his stubbleface. Wild applause and cheering.*)

PADDY (*astutely*): Hark, a tumult on the mountains. The Lord of Hosts is preparing for battle ...

(*Paddy Murphy and Ripley Bogle face each other square over the rutting couple. Hours have passed and Bogle is well-watered by now. His face is shaped by a fatuous, drunken moron smile. He has lost his script and fears to improvise.*)

RIPLEY BOGLE (*Sad. Explanatory.*):

> I was once a student
> I used to be a gent.
> I used to have a chequebook
> And always pay my rent.
>
> But now I sleep on benches
> I scrounge from passers-by,
> I smell of cess and pisspot
> And affront the general eye.

> Yes, I'd like to have some money,
> Some grub, a roof and bed;
> I'd like to sit in comfort
> But sit in shit instead.

(*There is no applause.*)

BILLY (*parodic*):

> I used to wet the bed a lot
> It made me quite unhappy
> But now my wee is more controlled
> I keep it in my nappy.

(*Ironic cheers.*)

PADDY (*twinkling*):

> He chews the crust of hardship
> He masticates on grief
> Poverty's his mission
> Starvation is his brief.

(*Wild hurrahs and sobs of gratitude. Cries of joy and appreciation break out spontaneously.*)

THE DRINKERS (*sobbing to a man*): Bravo! Encore!

(*The Murphys make their modest jovial bows. Flowers, emeralds, gold bars and high-denomination coins are thrown at them by their bawling, grateful public. Frankie and the harridan finish their rut with mixed results and the Murphy clan stand as one man. Their collective, vindictive might in square stance to face the sad and lonely Bogle.*)

THE MURPHYS:

> Now Bogle is a shithead
> He's the world's worst tosspot
> He's keen to be a loser
> So far, he's lost the lot.

(*The Murphys raise their glasses to the growing rumour and swell of applause that spreads around the room. They smile inwards, upon themselves, their family and traditions. Paddy steps forward through all their avenue of acclaim and congratulation. His left eyebrow lifts and trembles roguishly, his Irish eyes twinkle and his mouth puckers to scallywaggerie. He pauses minutely. This is his moment. Time for his spokesman's message. He speaks.*)

PADDY (*profoundly*): If we cracked open the face of the world, would it be smiling?

(*Pandemonium. The Drinkers mob him joyously.*)

PADDY (*modestly*): Oh please! Really, boys it was nothing. Thank you. You've all been wonderful. A big hand for the band. Thank you. You're all beautiful. Thank you.

(*The Murphys disperse, dispensing patronage and autographs to all who ask. The harridan trails along, wiping her skirt, her arm around Frankie's. She leers at Bogle in triumph. The other Murphys receive offers of marriage, endowment policies, lacrosse sticks, dark chocolates, reggae albums, pornographic magazines, model aeroplanes, duty-free cigarettes, small Pacific islands, donkeys, Oscars, Nobel and Pulitzer prizes, kitchenware of all kinds and a variety of subcontinental gastric ailments. The Song of the Murphys is heard to fade away as they mingle with the myriad starstruck Drinkers.*)

THE SONG OF THE MURPHYS (*trailing to silence*):
>We are the Brothers Murphy
>Our talents are diverse
>We vilify in meter
>And castigate in verse.
>(*Exeunt*)

Without the Murphys, the pubbub becomes general, unaesthetic. The Drinkers are forced to speed up their consumption, such is their sense of loss. Martin Malone does a roaring trade, feeding their tense, grieving thirsts. Bogle heaves to his numbed meatfeet and dithers drunkenly to centre stage. He hovers hopelessly. All his windows are broken and the rain is getting in. He turns his beerless attention to Martin Malone.

'Ah Mr Malone. A bevy if you please. Cashless am I but my name is good for a fiver through half of the city. The other half? – well, I admit that's touch and go. But come along now, take the risk. We must maintain the view dystopian.'

Malone looks up from his slops and coins. His reply is brief, concise, but a precis of his greater wit, terse with double meaning.

'Watch your lip, boy, or I'll blot your copybook for you and no mistake!'

Bogle's failure is roundly mocked. The Drinkers caw in triumph.

'The golden thread of poetry,' retorts young Ripley, 'what would you lot know of that?'

Some of the Drinkers take exception to this. There is much clamour and the general anti-Bogle feeling increases markedly. Bogle stands firm in its face.

'The cold magic of ignorance,' says he. 'Oh, that never fails.'

There is an answering shout from the crowd which Bogle ignores at his happy peril. The Drinkers are displeased. They think little of his performance after the Murphean tour de force which they have just witnessed.

This, they feel, is less than Irish. A rising cadence of booing begins. Bogle gathers his selfhood and tries again for another drink. Martin Malone is impassive, impervious. A silent battle of will beings. Malone and Bogle inter-stare. Hours more pass and the night drags slowly on. It is useless. Bogle cannot win. Malone's implacable gaze leaves him gibbering drunkenly on the floor to the accompaniment of jeers and hisses. He is beaten. All hands down. He had it once, that victorstuff, but it's long gone now. In growing up, he lost the sight and now can catch only etching marks.

A bell sounds. Clear and imperative. A hush descends, some of the men begin to sob and all look anxious. All eyes are turned to the charismatic, wobbly figure of Martin Malone. All await his dread command and opprobium. The barstaff make vague gestures towards clearing up. Cleaners, charwomen and suchlike arrive and commence their work. Some customers drift off but the hardcore drinkers remain almost unperturbed, few deserting their stalwart ranks. They feel they are secure. Malone has never left a penny unturned yet.

'Time, gentlemen?' asks Malone teasingly. 'I think not. I most certainly disagree. Time is no absolute. Boil my buns, who am I to disrupt such an evening of glad festivity?'

(Cheers, joy, knighthoods and gratitude.)

Malone continues in heroic fashion.

'And now we'll be having the Gathering of the Ghosts if you please! Patrons are advised to keep to their seats and drinks will be served throughout the haunting. Thank you. Let's hear it for the supernatural!'

Applause. The Drinkers settle to comfort and await their entertainment keenly. Bogle clambers to his feet. His arms lift above his head and his knees bend. He begins to dance, Graeco-Turk fashion. First up we have the Ghosts of his Former Loves. The room swells with their multiple spectrepresence. There are hundreds of them. All dead, all gone. Bogle smiles, unembarrassable. He begins to reel off their names. He greets, he charms. Dancing.

'Well now, hello Catherine, ah, Carol, how are you, my dear? Goodness, Judy! Sarah, it's good to see you. Hi, Maggie. Diane. Oh Marion, darling Tess, Lesley, Vicky, Siobhan – cad e mar ta tu? Tina, hello. Beryl, Emma, Fiona, Jane, Elizabeth, Georgina, Mary, Alice, Julia, Susan, Debbie, Claire, Celia, Jenny, Anne, Annie, Annette, Anna, hello. Charlotte, Rachel, Thérèse, Frances, Iris, Natasha, Suzy, Muire, Norma, Queenie baby! Philippa, Lucy, Miranda, Olive, Lisa, Tania, Sally, Samantha, Susannah, Sonia, Madeleine, Geraldine, Les, Tes, Justine, oh Erica, ça va Henriette? Roisin, Matilda, Joanne, Vanessa, Nicole, Helen, Jocasta, Kimberley, Harriet, Josephine, Yvonne, Zana, Ingrid, Jodie, Wendy, Ursula,

Thomasin, Rosemary and Agnes, sisters both, Roberta, Victoria honey! Maria, Lucinda, Patricia, Paula, Pamela, Amanda, Quita, Christine, Karen, Rhoda! Valerie, Denise, Melissa, Camilla, Joan, Laura, Hermione . . . hello. How goes it, girls? You were always special to me.'

The men boo. They doubt the total. Bogle smiles impartially. He surveys their ghostly ranks. His brow grows troubled. He speaks.

'The girls I like and love
Are never meant to see
The totting-up/arithmetic
Of which appeal to me.

There they queue in happy ranks
Their faces dark with hope.
It's hard for reasoned judgement
Discernment cannot cope.

I do my best for tactful maths
I try to keep it fair.
The figures are imponderables
The outcomes debonair.'

He smiles as the Drinkers' displeasure burgeons.

'Or . . . as some would say – fair field and no favour.'

He grins roguishly, his hands clapping softly. The Ghosts of his Former Loves begin to wail and moan their own protests. Their fiery womanly eyes smoulder with claimed injustice and they cry for retribution. Bogle is calm, professorial.

'And who, you ask, is the lady that I love still?' says he. 'Why, yet it is of course, the fair Louisa . . . wait, what am I saying? The cruel Laura is who I mean. Goodness me, who's Louisa when she's at home?'

He pauses nostalgically, sadly. Answer.

'Oh . . . just a girl who drew stars on my heart . . .'

The pub explodes to laughter. Great crowlike screeches of mockery and abuse. The Ghosts of his Former Loves totter off, giggling madly. Malone and his acolytes circulate rapidly, dispensing alcohol to all (though not free), the Drinkers sup, mock and jeer. They await the second act. The habitués of nightmare.

Enter Maurice Kelly, hobbling grotesquely towards Ripley. Sudden silence. Bogle stands rigid in the centre of the room, paralysed, terrified. The Ghost of Maurice is repulsive to behold. Gaping, blackened goreholes litter his temple and neck. One festering eye hangs from its mutilated socket by a slimy string of nerve and tendon. His spectre clothes are stiff and black with blood wet and blood dry. He drips dark scarlet mess in his wake. He weaves his way through the happy, appreciative Drinkers, his hanging eye implacable and stern. His eyes hard with grief and accusation, he speaks to Ripley.

'You!'

Bogle is terrified but he attempts to bluff his way through.

'Yes, that's right – me. So what?'

Maurice's deathly anger is dreadful.

'I died for you, proselyte! You led me dead and slimy. You left me to rot in death and ignorance. Just how much do you think you'd like a touch of that yourself? Not a lot, I'd bet.'

In his rage, mouldy patches of his face and neck begin to fall to the ground where they stain and slither. Bogle is dismissive.

'Crap to that, cheesychops!'

'Traitor! Turncoat! You were the one! You killed me!'

'Oh, bugger off and bore some worms!'

There is general muttering. The Drinkers grow hostile once more. They are outraged by Bogle's treatment of this ghost. One of the larger quaffers punches the young tramp on the nose. He bleeds. The spectre of Maurice strikes a classical pose.

'O Ripley,' he intones pompously, 'what a falling off was there! They, in the porches of mine ear did pour a leprous distilment in the form of three lead composition cartridges fired at a barrel velocity of 874 miles per hour decreasing at a rate of 10mph/220ft from a 1925 Army Issue Webley 38 calibre repeating revolver with scratched barrel and rusty hammer. The skull split, the brain burst and the blood bled. Hurt like the bejasus! Why don't you try that little delight the next time you've got five minutes handy?'

'Aw, tell it to the Marines,' scoffs Bogle.

The Ghost scuttles away picking up his bits as he goes. Some of the Drinkers help. Enter Bobby Bogle, father to Ripley, bottle in hand and pancreas on lap. He too is pretty gory but he preserves a lackadaisical, cheerful mien. At his entrance the Drinkers' spirits revive somewhat and there is much abrupt good humour as they settle down to listen to this next exchange. Bobby Bogle (as was) is sodden, mournful.

'What have you come to, child of mine? You've soiled my memory. There was no welcome in the hillsides. Your fault that was. How do you expect me to create a favourable impression with you as my guarantor? Mmmm? You were born a little shit and a little shit you'll die.'

'Sling your hook, pal,' says Bogle neatly, with confidence. 'I'm son to you in shame only.'

Bobby Bogle appeals to the crowd.

'Now, I ask you – what kind of a question is that? Do you see what kind of a son I'm cursed with?'

The Drinkers are sympathetic but Bogle is adamant.

'Go on, sod off!'

The late, lamented Bobby Bogle begins to slope off grumpily. He calls back as he slithers.

'You'll pay, my child. You'll see the error of your ways. I know you, boy. Your secret's unsafe with me.'

Though worried for a moment, Ripley laughs coarsely and the second spectre sobs in maudlin pain. His bottle leaps from his hand and vaults onto the bartop. It confronts Ripley, stopper off and label showing.

THE WHISKY BOTTLE (*roguishly*): Ripley, I am thy father's spirit!

There is much laughter and applause. A little humour was welcome. The Whisky Bottle receives telephone calls from various London theatrical agencies. It rolls off to a press conference. The next act comes on. Deirdre Curran steps forward with hard confidence. Bogle is surprised to see her. She has changed little and improved none. She speaks in tones of thwarted mediocrity. Her grievance is plain and Ripley is less at ease. He challenges her sanctimoniously.

'And what do *you* want? You're not dead. You'll never die. I never loved you. That wasn't love. Don't kid yourself! That was something else.'

'You know what I know,' she replies in bitter mystery. 'You know what I can tell.'

Bogle is frightened now. He grows pale, his lips thin and he turns his face away. Catcalls ring out once more. They are all expecting a climax here and they are not impressed with Bogle's dearth of valour. They want some action. Deirdre is cheered on and encouraged volubly. Nonetheless, Bogle dismisses her peremptorily.

'Go away. You have no place here. Go!'

To the surprise and disappointment of the Drinkers, Deirdre does actually leave quite meekly, her only defiance in the form of a small, wicked smile. There is a short pause. All eyes rest on the bloodied-but-victorious form of Ripley Bogle. An expectant hush fills the vile, sweaty room. The final apparition is due. The Last of the Ghosts. Tension and anxiety drift amongst the sheets of smoke which stain the air. Suddenly, a clean, newish porcelain toilet bowl appears in the middle of the room. Ripley starts in horror and all are worried. The young man's face begins to stream and drip with sweat. Tiny, desperate splashing sounds are heard issuing from the lavatory. Some of the women start to whimper in nameless fear. More frantic splashing and then a tiny, horrible, red hand appears from the toilet bowl. It clutches the rim desperately. A little voice is heard screeching wildly, crazed with fear, agony and death.

'Daddy, help! Father, help me, please ...!'

The screeching ends in a ghastly sob and choke and the tiny, bloodied hand splashes back into the water. Pandemonium breaks loose. The Drinkers, men and women, scream in terror. They bolt wildly for the door. Many bodies are trampled in the wild rush to escape that horror. Several crazed old hags slit their own throats with broken beer glasses. The tumult is dreadful, hellish, obscene. Death shepherds his little flocks as heads are crushed, split and trampled by maddened feet. The screaming increases to a terrible pitch. Then, quite suddenly, all is quiet once more. The Drinkers have fled and all is calm, or very nearly so. Dust settles gently on upturned chairs and tables, on the cadavers of the stampede victims. Ripley Bogle reclines on the floor, his bleeding head lolling in a pool of dark, frothing porter. He moans and grumbles to himself, obviously reviewing some highly unpleasant private experience all of his own devising. Martin Malone, spent, ready for his bed, approaches the young man irritably. He kicks the boy hard. He is a busy man. Ripley's use is done. The landlord kicks him again, with growing anger.

MARTIN MALONE (*impatiently*): Come on, you lazy bastard. You can't sleep here. Get out! Go home and sleep it off. Come on, out of it. Slope off home before I stick my boot up your backside. C'mon move!

(He kicks him again.)

145

SATURDAY

ONE

Big riverbend here. Passing now under the crumble of Putney Bridge. Putney to Barnes. Yes. I dribble away from the city. I check out the Fulham Palace on the other bank. It wobbles and jives in this heat-shimmer. That way Parsons Green and Brompton lie. Not for me, they don't.

Well, it's another belter today. Hot. The active, superluminous sun poaches me in my own sweat and grease. I have to pant and wheeze to catch the stale, warmed-up urban air. In the circumstances, I feel it's hardly worth the effort.

Perry is getting worse. This morning was bad, really bad. I'm not in the mood for the startled confusion of the aged underdog. After last night's wickedness, I'm finding it hard to play upon my sympathies. Perry's getting worse, though. He really is.

It's so hot at the moment that the heat haze is about eight feet high and four feet distant. Or maybe it's because my eyelids are all cocked-up. Alternately crusty or slimy and constantly painful. Perhaps it is close-up goo and not heat haze that I am, in fact, seeing right now. It's surprisingly hard to tell. I should clean my eyes up a bit, I know, but I just can't find the courage.

Notwithstanding, it is still very, very hot. What is going on here? I don't know what it is with the weather these days. I suspect that it has some obscure meteorological grudge against me. It sounds potty, I agree, but I'm almost certain. I've worked it out. I know all about the weather. I'm au fait with the physics and chemistry of the upper air, its temperature, density, motions, composition, chemical processes, reactions to solar a.٨d cosmic radiation, etc. I've done my homework.

The perfect trampweather is that mild autumnal dullness that we get in September and early October. No cold, no heat, no rain and little wind. The happy medium must be struck and struck hard. Tranquillity and quietude are what we chiefly love. Summer's too hot and dry and dirty. We simmer in filth and corporeal corruption. We thirst and we croak and we catch really

149

unusual diseases. Winter is, predictably, much too cold. We freeze and
thaw and freeze again. Hypothermia, frostbite, bronchitis, pneumonia and
gangrene all say hello. Bladders pack in all over the shop and pauperdeaths
litter the seamier sides of town. Spring is too wet. Getting pissed on
becomes depressing after a while. That's the season of trenchfoot,
exposure, rigor, polio, cystic-fucking-fibrosis and the bubonic plague! (I
nearly crapped myself this morning when I discovered this monstrous
bubo on my neck. Fuck me, I thought, this is it! The big B. The plague no
less! Of course, it was only an outsize pimple, a semi-boil. A tramp hill. It
was big though, really enthusiastic, a yellow-topped baked bean, an
astrobleme!)

As I was saying about the weather: the seasons are all buggered up at the
minute. If I'm not fighting with frostbite, I'm struggling with sunstroke.
There is no intermediate stage – it's straight from polar pain to tropical toil.
Every hour the weather winds up some new inclement gimmick to do me
harm. Perhaps it's on account of this new Ice Age that all the boffins are
wetting their trunks about. Yes, that might be it. However, I still can't help
feeling that it is simple supernatural malice. Someone up there is no fan of
mine.

Christ almighty! Last night was a stinker! Lardwit, I got plastered and
blew the sad remnants of my treasured dosh. I'm a cretin, I declare to God
I am. Six final, necessary quid pissed away on soapy booze! And what did
I get? A pound of pain in my brainbone and a slap on the gob from some
crazy Irish bastard who claimed to know me. A fiver and more for that!
Where am I keeping my brains these days?

Subsequently, what I'm experiencing on this fine June morning can
scarcely be described as a hangover. Dear me, no. Alcoholic excess is but
one of the Attendant Lords in the Revenger's Tragedy that my grumpy
body is enacting. Chronic Emphysema plays the virulent, inexorable lead,
well-supported by the superslim Scurvy as the anorexic usurper who lusts
after the luxurious Gynaecomastia, Queen of the Hormonal Confusions.
Melanoma steals the show as the fresh-faced Chorus while Subacute-
bacterialendocarditis toothily disappoints as the Romantic Interest.

I feel a major headache heralding its cruel intent. My neck aches bitterly
and my spinal ropes groan and creak. This is Migraine Time. This is going
to lay me out. My brain will bend and stretch in agony. (You would not
believe the extent of my cranial elasticity when it comes to pain!) The sky is
boiling already and the air is heavy, deplorable, weighing down on the
burgeoning pain in my skull. The atmosphere is tense and attentive.
Stormwaiting. While my own personal tempest rages unabated.

Wheeeee! I feel a clumsy ball of nausea unfurl in my throat and I have a strong and sickening urge to defecate. My abdomen is swollen and taut. Hiding gurgling, bubbling slime and obscenity. I've got to move a motion. Cessbag to latrine. Brother to brother. I need a crap. That's it. All too familiar. Shitting. Migraine. Strain and pain. Nausea. Eggs-in-thorax. Gloom.

Penniless, fecal, nauseous, I trail off the riverbank onto the Richmond Road now. Why am I moving away from the city, you might justifiably ask. What possible joy can I find in the leafy glades of Roehampton or Mortlake? None, I freely admit. I am escaping the city because today is Saturday and London Town on Saturdays gets on my tits amazingly. The whole weekending business. The shoppers, the Salvation Army, the housewives meeting each other for their monthly visit to the choirboy brothels, the nose-eye-ear picking adolescents, the Saturdayfreed schoolgirls strutting their precocious prepubescent stuff, the daytripping hickprovincials gawping at the metropolitan mayhem, the happy, shirtsleeved policemen, the park-playing families, the youthful couples (bastards!), the sportsmen, the grotbags, the promenaders, the people, the people!

Worst of all – the tramps, the beggars and the cripples. The rejects, the drop-outs, the addicts and the tragedies. Saturday is their best begging day. The period of optimum fruitful scrounging. It's an abhorrent sight which I try to avoid. Saturday is everyone's good mood day. People grow charitable. They give in plenty from their plenty. Nice enough but still gets me down.

This is why I tend to hang out on the fringes of the Saturday capital. It probably seems pompous but like I say, I hate to see my homeless colleagues letting the side down.

(Actually, the real reason that I avoid the greater populace on Saturdays is because I'm terrified of seeing someone I know. Someone from my past. Someone who doesn't know I'm a tramp. The mere thought makes me gibber in terror. Cheap, huh?)

I slouch wittily along, young and carefree. I can feel the noisome juices in my belly percolating moistly through my squirting bowels. Shit!

Yes, old Perry's deteriorating. (Rich, coming from me.) He was practically sobbing this morning. Usually, he's a very strong sort of old bloke. I don't know quite what was wrong with him – though I suppose being ancient and about to die is a pretty good starting point. His old face was very grey and stiff which, combined with his sneaky tears and brave poverty, really got me low. I think Perry is bored with struggling and wriggling free of reverse and setback. He's too old. He can't be bothered anymore. This is fatal. Perry's deathdate will have to be brought forward now. In the current of homelessness, youth is vital to insouciance. When you're a young tramp, that kind of despair gives you a headache; when you're an old tramp, it kills you.

He didn't bring me any discreet coffee or fags this morning which is a very bad sign. It's the first time that he has omitted that little politesse. It bodes ill – not to mention depriving me of one of my few daily comfortable moments.

> Me and my selfishness
> Go tripping down the lane;
> The loveliest of couples,
> The ball without the chain.

I tried to comfort the poor old guy but found myself short of wisdom and overstocked with platitudes. You would have loved it. Perry sobbing out the last of his bad old life and me spinning out the television dialogue, all liberally laced with the crap of youth. I should go to hospital. I need the script treatment.

I was choked. I really was. It was undeniably embarrassing and in my state I could certainly have done without it but I felt I owed it to the bold Perry to try to help out a little. For one so young and insensitive, I'm all heart, wouldn't you agree?

Anyway, how can you actually help someone who's had the kind of shitty life that Perry's had? Mmmm? Problematic, is it not? There is not much you can say to cap a tale of hilarious woe and trial like that. I know.

As I've said, he'll soon be dead anyhow, so it will all be academic presently. Derek Death is coming for Perry any day now. I'll miss him. Perry, that is. Goodness me, I'm missing him already. Bye bye Perry. Large was his bounty and his soul sincere. Melancholy buggered him up all about the town. Bye bye Perry ...

(Just like Perry, I'm coming to a junction, a crossroads. Perry's choice is between imminent death and present despair. My choice is between Mill Hill and Rocks Lane. I've got the worst of it. I look around me at the guerrilla grass and trees, at the brickplump walls, the cricket pitches and the grave-yards and ... I choose ... Mill Hill! Phew!)

Twelve cigarettes left. Twelve good fags and true. I must be careful. I must plan. Frugality is the sort of thing I'll be aiming for tobaccowise. Nonethe-less, I light one now, as a reward for my foresight. That's better. That's good. Smoke.

I wish that this heat would lay off a little and the swelling pain in my head would bugger off and leave me alone. I wish the burbling, liquid filth staining my guts would solidify. Most of all, I wish to fuck I had some money!

(Perry wasn't slipping me any sneaky tenners this morning. Hard to believe but true. I felt that I could hardly ask – what with him dying and all.) I walk. Yes, I do.

So, you want to hear about last night? A drink list and a regurgitational inquest? The repeated past of all my family's leak chinks. My destranded and wetseparated kinsfolk. Like Big Bobby Bogle. Dear dead pa, drawn from life. You want to see me do the Bogle? To demonstrate my cultural and biological headstart when it comes to the booze? An update on my inheritance. A few misinformed sideswipes at the clan you little know but greatly loathe.

So allrightalready! I got blootered. Pissed, plastered and poleaxed. It was that story. That sad old tale of mine! Those memories.

(I mean, allow me my sodden sentimentality. It costs little and harms none.)

You wouldn't want to hear about it anyway. That would bore you blind. All that spastic hilarity, that hopeless, helpless Gaelic beeriness. The palaver, the crap! Who needs it?!

It's my story that matters and we now turnface to that. Back to the business of bathos.

When we last left the youthful Ripley, he was in a pretty bad way. A tramp, a drunk and a nihilist all before the age of eighteen. He was one of those sturdy young dipsos you see lying on the pavements of provincial towns. With their scraped, windwhipped faces, their mad yells and bloody eyes. He was scum. The dregs. Bottom of the least of barrels.

Unbelievably, I got out of it. I managed to be pulled away before my ticket to iniquity was irrevocably stamped. By rights, I should have stayed like that for the three or four years left to me in that kind of life. I should have faded away to end up as giddy corpse in a cirrhosis lecture for the strong-stomached amongst medical studentry. I was lucky though. I had a fortunate escape. I was *fucking* lucky.

One night in late summer, four RUC men picked up a young tramp trying to break into an off-licence on the Lisburn Road. After several complicated taunts about the prevalence of the love that dare not speak its name amongst the ranks of the RUC, he proceeded to try to beat them up – all four of them. When they had knocked him about a bit, they managed somehow to get a smattering of autobiographical detail out of him.

They drove him to St Malcolm's and knocked old Paddy Sniff out of bed.

The young fellow had mumbled something about this luminary. The policemen offered Canon O'Hara a charitable alternative. Either, he took the boy off their hands or they arrested and charged him. Luckily, he did the noble thing.

You know, I was bloody fortunate – for it was me, that tramp chappy – I was bloody fortunate that the four coppers didn't knock my nuts in. Conscienceless, they could have pulped me without too many questions being asked. I was a lucky boy. People can definitely be nice on occasion.

It must have been fun for the Reverend O'Hara. It must have been a bundle of laughs. Me smelling to high hell and him fighting down his rising nausea and sleeplessness. I wish I'd been there, so to speak.

Next day, to my shame, Paddy Sniff gave me a whole lot of money and packed me off to a Cistercian monastery in Portglenone to dry out amongst the monks. With a suit of monkish grey and a pair of stout, priestly shoes, I trained it up to Portglenone and entered upon the life monastic.

When I returned to Belfast three months later, I still had my holy suit and shoes but I'd left my drunkenness behind. I had a few other things as well. No longer the old cute ineffectual Ripley Bogle with his bravery in misery, his amused shouts of outrage at what life conspired to do to him. I had hatred and strength now. And I had a kind of purpose.

I found a very nasty bedsit just off Downview, borrowing the money from a loanshark whose son I knew from school. It was one of the awful places. The landlady, Mrs Collins was a revolting old drunk who hadn't seen the inside of a bath for years, or so she smelt. When intoxicated, she had a penchant for telling the same interminable tale of her husband's life and death. I had to sit there and listen to this maudlin account of chemotherapy, hair loss and flesh-rot, or else I'd have been out on my arse. Though in truth, eviction would hardly have been a blow. The place was incredibly insanitary. It oozed filth and vermin and smelt as if there were syphilitic corpses buried under the floorboards. The kitchen, in particular, was unspeakably vile, swimming in grease and weird, incognito life forms. I was already somewhat etiolated after my recent privations but in the face of all this salmonella potential I gladly underwent further degrees of attenuation. Better to starve than having to fight the fungus for your food. This suited the shrewd old harridan well. A starveling boy made a very inexpensive lodger indeed.

I needed an address now. For my purpose I required the merest locational stability. I sorted out my finances and my educational dilemmas. I managed to persuade the DHSS to help me out by threatening to write to the President of the United States or something like that and with boyish charm and deep humility I coaxed the bold Paddy Sniff to let me go back to school. I had a purpose. When I told him about it I was surprised that he didn't laugh, boot me out or call the giggle wagons. He let me go back to school for a little while – for as long as I needed. That man was a saint. Pope soon, I hope.

And what was this purpose, you ask? What was I about to do? Well, you must understand that I was at this time the filth of the world. I had no money, no family, no friends, no job, no qualifications, no chance and no hope. The merest of the proletariat looked down on me, tramps and beggars avoided me in the street and outcasts of every kind considered me beyond the pale. I was vermin, pest, failure.

Naturally enough, I decided that I would have to go to Cambridge. I was going to be a varsity man!

Snigger not, you cynics! It occurred to me that if I was going to drag myself out of my cess, I might as well do it in one fell leap. Straight from scumbag to Cambridge undergraduate. From one extreme to the other. This appealed to me; tickled my sense of the absurd. Quel arriviste!

This was what had stopped my drinking. It wasn't the monks with their humanist platitudes and humble aspirations. It was the extremity of ambition. The alcoholic down and out waltzing along to the premier university in Europe. I liked that.

I went to it with a will. I was desperate to succeed. Though I never really envisaged my grimy feet actually treading Cambridge pavements, I was vaguely confident. I had to be, what with it being my only chance and all. Failure was a thought untenable.

After her miscarriage, Deirdre's parents had packed her off to visit her fat aunt in Germany. When she returned, she threatened to kill herself if she was not allowed to see me again. Her family complied as they always would. They deserved their daughter, did Mr and Mrs Curran.

(I should point out that Deirdre had still neglected to tell her parents that I hadn't shtupped her and was therefore innocent of any fatherish offence as regards her unfortunate condition. Prat, I hadn't cleared up this little misunderstanding either. It simply hadn't occurred to me.)

When I saw her again all my hatred and fine new bitterness deserted me – just when I needed it most! It had served me well and I didn't really need it anymore. Perhaps I grew up a little then. Saw what manhood was and is. Then again, perhaps not. Deirdre had changed – much for the worse. Any pretence of normality had been surrendered and she was, quite obviously, off her rocker. Now I slept with her. I had to really. Refusal would cause further hysteria and besides, I still had a furtive fancy that I loved the girl. I thought that this love was the stronger for being tempered in the harsh fires of adversity. Very cute. Very neat.

Nonetheless, Deirdre's insanity was becoming difficult to ignore. Her erotic pleasure seemed dependent on the infliction of pain and I was perturbed by the violence of her tastes. Once, in the very act itself, near the culmination of that rut, she started relating the story of her miscarriage with a surprisingly keen sense of narrative detail. At the point of joyous cessation she concluded her tale by saying that the 'baby' had looked just how any baby of ours would have looked. Bogle the diplomat tried to hide the sound of his gagging as he vommed the night away.

She would attack me with my own cricket bat; she would spit on me, revile me, punch me, scratch and throttle me in her transports of licentious ecstasy. It was a nasty business. She had an amusing habit of turning up on my doorstep, semi-conscious and claiming to have taken a lethal overdose or two. I would have to drive her to hospital in her car. (She had her own car now, poor girl.) This was diverting in the extreme. Cars and me have never mixed well. We are a disastrous combination. Deirdre was in more danger from my eccentric driving than from any of her narcotic cocktails.

Once, when Deirdre's parents had gone away for the weekend, she and I spent our only ever complete night together. After copulating vigorously and joylessly in her parents' double bed, we both fell asleep, as one does. After a couple of somnolent hours I grew sleepily aware of an odd tickling sensation on my naked back and shoulderblades. The placid surface of my slumber was barely ruffled and I was falling back into a deeper sleep when I heard a series of dull metallic clicks. Soft and secret. I wrestled lengthily with the weariness of my body. I felt so wonderful and warm, you see, in this huge clean bed. So very, very tired. With great effort, I eventually roused myself. And bloody good job that I did.

When I confiscated the scissors from my interesting young lover I hurried to the bathroom to wash the blood from my back. The rips in my flesh were not very deep – she had evidently been toying with the notion initially. However, they were long, numerous and stung like fuck. I tended to my wounds, left quietly as I could and walked the fourteen miles back to the city. I decided that it would be better if I did not see old Deirdre for a little while.

That is not to say that I finally relinquished all my attempts at love and tenderness. I loved her still. Her imbalance was understandable, excusable – her ordeal had been a terrible one. Somehow, I managed to ignore the vibrant claims to my selfishness and egoism that were cropping up. My inheritance of the guilt in Deirdre's impregnation should have troubled me, for instance. I was ignoring the actual fatherhood of her abortion mess. I never seemed to get round to asking the identity of her impregnator. Indeed, the notion that my supposed lover had shown her sexual incontinence in this nasty fashion didn't prey on my mind half enough. From start to finish I was a poor soppy sod without the wherewithal for anger.

So, despite everything, I continued to love Deirdre and her image was only very slightly tarnished in my mind. Not much but at least it was a beginning.

I sat the Cambridge Common Entrance Examination in November of that year. Three fifty-pound bombs were detonated in a garage just up the road whilst I was writing. This was cool. I wondered how many other ex-dipsomaniac down-and-out Cambridge hopefuls were sitting these exams to the accompaniment of proximate explosions. It was a cheap thought but it made me feel special.

I sat those exams. I wrote in hope and trepidation. I prayed that I would somehow get the sympathy vote. I wrote for all I was worth and more.

And of course, I did it! But you could see that one coming a mile off, couldn't you? I got the letter when I returned to my hovel in the early hours of the last Friday before Christmas.

Dear Mr Bogle,
   We are pleased to inform you ...

Utter, stunning ecstasy flooded my veins. Christ almighty! Think of what I had done. What I had managed to pull off. From out of this squalid little house with its sordid drunken landlady I had beaten a path to Cambridge. The act and fact of my achievement was scarcely to be believed. Deirdre and all her like, with their loving parents and helpful money and expensive schools – they, with all this, had failed. And me, destitute, disowned, disreputable, had beaten them all – on my own – with none to thank but myself and a handful of charitable priests.

And the cunty Currans! The bastards who had despised my poverty, my religion and my class. I was now superior to them by their very own diseased system of evaluation. A Cambridge undergraduate, no matter how poor, was a lot bloody posher than a jumped-up shopkeeper and his spawn, no matter how wealthy! The sweet bliss of revenge lit upon my body – the thought of my long parade of enemies and oppressors. I dedicated my success to them. I saw, enjoyably, the gall and wormwood that would fester in the hearts of those who hated me.

It was nearly dawn before I recovered from the receipt of this friendly epistle. My head still swam with giddy happiness and I could hardly go to bed. I went for a walk.

Outside, the night glistened gently, welcoming me, whispering my news among sleepy houses and tall, nuded winter trees. The Antrim Road, an old friend, ribboned grand and beautiful before my poorshod feet; a tarmac carpet of congratulation. The Cavehill called its distant approval through the dark electric breeze. My ticket to prosperity flooded me with insane bliss.

I wandered into Alexandra Park, open and dozing underneath the black, early morning sky. An early milkman chugged past, a gentle song of matins. I called an unheard greeting. I walked through that bower of leafless trees, a patchy roof on darkened ground, towards the small blackwatered lake. Grey, sooty swans glided regally over its surface, disregarding the happy boy following their progress. All one to them.

Dawn was breaking by this time, slowly filling the wintered park with cold grey light. My eyes shone as points of happy glitter in the gloom. I turned back. Bye bye Ireland. As I walked onto the Antrim Road once again, it seemed to me that the familiar, dilapidated house fronts awakened and revered me, their onetime son. I walked home through the avenue of their silent applause, blushing modestly as I passed.

I was chuffed. I was pleased. I felt I deserved this kind of thing. I began to make my plans.

(When I rang Deirdre to tell her the brilliant news, she was so furious that she hung up. She thought I was copping out and couldn't face the real world. Deirdre was able to face the real world because her dirty old father had paid her first year's fees at a private art school in Leeds.)

The only thing that spoiled the next few months for me was Maurice's getting bumped off. It cut me up rarely but Cambridge was a consolation. The nasty business was a confirmation of why I was leaving in the first place. I didn't want to be done in. I didn't want to die. Not the way my dad had died. Not the way Maurice had died.

And so I came close to the end of my Irish term. Merrily (apart from my Mauricegrief), I prepared to depart, to embark. My eyes were green again, I had younged up again. I was feeling trim and tremendous once more. All was ready. My city was packed up and labelled. Nothing there nomore. All was ready now. Departure. Bye bye Ireland.

By God, I wish I was feeling trim and tremendous now. These obscure

London streets have dwindled from grisly order to placeless confusion. I don't know where next to go. A little lost am I here. I look round at the heated, mouldering roads and the matterless, marmoreal air. On a nearby wall, I spot a piece of pert graffiti. The draughtsmanship is competent, skilled. It reads thus:

D.H. LAWRENCE FUCKS DOGS!

I'm glad to see that the twin tides of wit and discernment have not entirely ebbed from South London. I smile a secret smile of accord and my pain takes something of a backseat. This is the little humour I needed. My poor head pulses with less excoriating rhythm now. My bowels slow their slide and my eyes clear of heat and crust. A little puking and I'll be right as rain. I'll rest soon. I'm coming to the pleasantest part of my story. To the bits I enjoy. My varsity years will cheer you up too. It's not all been trial and tribulation. I've had my halcyon patches. Laura. You'll hear about her soon. Some lyricism, some romance. I'll just nip off for a bit of vomiting first.

TWO

And Ireland? What about old Ireland? I can't just leave it at that, can I? Before fleeing my beastly birthplace where should I have stood on that?

We Irish, we're all fucking idiots. No other people can rival us for the senseless sentimentality in which we wallow. Us and Ulster. The God-beloved fucking Irish, as they'd like to think. As a people we're a shambles; as a nation – a disgrace; as a culture we're a bore ... individually we're often repellent.

But we love it, us Irish fellows. We just slurp it up. The worse we are, the better we like it. We love old Ireland and it loves us.

Oh yes, begorrah! Belfastard! Cities to use with our voicey badges of accent unIrish. Ulstermen speak in tones Scottish. Little Irish about them. My landkin's voice is pigstick to me. Their shared badge of country. All that old Irishness crap promoted by Americans and professors of English Literature. Menace and cupidity. All balls. Ireland and its joys. Kicking in the holiest face you can find. Savagery likes the widespread. Blooding the streets. A curious thing, my country. With its flag, craned and glued to poles. The Trickler. The green, white and the all that glisters. Singing:

> Our Ireland is a lovely place,
> A supergroovy nation.
> Bigotry is her pastime
> Death her occupation.

What is it about Ireland that the Irish love so? What makes them guff on so endlessly about their country? Is it the pain and the poverty, the death and danger? Is it the spite, hatred, treachery, stupidity, vice, inhumanity or the comfortless despair? Whatever it is, we can see that the Irish have a lot to be grateful for.

What can I say about the Irish that the Irish won't deny? What can I add to the long list of platitudinous evocations of that Gaelic shitheap?

I know, I'll tell you a story. A true story. An Irish story. It happened while

160

I was still at school and became something of a cause célèbre in the Lower Sixth common room.

One naughty old night in October, two guys from my school are committing the startling gaffe of walking down the Crumlin Road. (Nasty area. No man's land. Shankill on the one side, New Lodge on the other. Where the different Gods met, i.e. between the shit and the shore.) Justifiably, my two schoolmates are a mite anxious. This is the era of the Shankill Butcher, a staunch anti-ecumenalist gentleman with a penchant for decapitating the papish faithful. Headhunting land is this. So, on they walk, gingerly skipping the tripwires of their fear.

They are stopped by three men who produce big bad guns. Of course. Had to be. As you can imagine, our two heroes fairly wet themselves with terror. This is it, they think hysterically. Hello bullet, bye bye life! The guntoting vigilantes ask our boys whether they are Catholics or Protestants. Here is a tiny, breathless whiff of a chance. A microscopic escape clause. Catholic or Protestant. Has to be right first time. There will be no runners-up award. Our boys ponder madly. There are no locational hints and the gunmen are giving no clues. One of the boys tosses a mental coin and fearfully hazards the fact that they are Catholics. The gunmen look uncertainly at each other. 'Prove it,' says one of them.

JesusfuckingChrist, think the two Malcolmians, we've made it! We've fucking made it! Relief creases their hearts and their ears sing with survival.

They recite the Hail Mary and are both shot in the head. Ho ho ho ho ho.

You'd guessed, hadn't you? Dontcha just love that?! The bastards actually made sure. They fucking checked! The perfect, cyclical cruelty of that moment of hope and sanguine prayer. The heartless artistry of that pause of glad incantation. Clever bastards, you have to admit.

(I only know this story because one of the boys survived. Survived a headshot! Not in great shape, naturally. Paralysed and all that kind of thing. Life in a wheelchair is hardly cosy but, strange to relate, the thing that bothered him was that moment. It drove him insane. That prayer ... that answer.)

Yes, mine was a shitty city, leprous and not too pretty.

Think about killing someone. Go on. Some guy. Some poor sorry sod. Anyone. Think about killing him. Take your time. Think about it. Think about his life, his mom and dad. Think about his children. Think about all the boffing he's done, the breasts he's kissed, the thighs he's creased, all that kind of thing. Think about his toothaches, his constipation, his beerbelly. Think about the books he hasn't read, the people he hasn't met and the places he hasn't seen. Think about his vanity and ignorance, his greed and selfishness. Think about his industry and his kindness, his clemency and tenderness. Think about him buying his unfashionable shoes and his painfully vulgar jackets. Think about his bad jokes and embarrassments. Think about his baby talk and teeth, his flask and sandwiches, his snapshots, his overdraft, his furniture, his handwriting, his bald patch, his favourite meals, his cigarettes, his football team, his dirty socks, his face and his span of years. Think about him. Think about his life.

Think about killing him. Think about that.

What's worth that, eh? Who needs that?

Bye bye Belfast.

*

Oh yes, Deirdre and I faded away soon enough. That little love came to its end just before I left for Cambridge. A good job too. Deirdre was increasingly off her tree in the last sad days of our relationship. Her demands and quirks were ever more extravagant and dislocated. Eventually, she told me who had poked her leading to her little miscarriage. (I hadn't asked.) It was some plumber who'd been gimmicking their bathroom. He boffed her good, apparently – on the bathroom floor, no less! Repulsive, isn't it? Well, the plumber obviously didn't have any rubber love-gloves handy and subsequently Big Deirdre got firmly up the spout. It's depressing little details like this that take the tragedy out of my life. The constant presence of the absurd, the hilarious squalor of the incidental.

I saw Deirdre for the last time over a stained coffee table in Robinson and Cleaver's. On that extremely neutral ground. I had prepared well for the big scene. I had rehearsed the gist of a lot of shouting and ranting. The usual thing – what the trouble with her was and so on. Goodness, was I going to give her a bad time! Of course, when it got down to it, I bottled out completely. Didn't seem worth it all of a sudden. I was free now. Free. This notion hit me with sudden welcome euphoria. You know, I had forgotten how really very young I was. Funny thing. So, I simply smiled and took my leave. I think that this was probably more galling to her than any abusive tirade I could have concocted. I just buggered off. Heavens, it was fun!

I'm hard on Deirdre, aren't I? I'm square and swift in the blame-laying department. According to me, Deirdre was a monster. Cruel, selfish and blindly stubborn. There is a certain amount of truth in this but I claim no innocence on my part. She was bad but no worse than me. I was a casserole of casuistry, spite, conceit and insensitivity. Curiously, under the age of twenty-five, one tends to think that one has a franchise in callous, wilful egoism and irresponsibility. It seems tempered by the sly excuse of one's tender years and poor experience. This doesn't wash. At least, with me it doesn't. I was just a little shit, pure and simple. A rotten bastard.

(My word, isn't all this relentless self-awareness bracing?)

How did we actually get around to that big split? You want to know what caused the ceasefire? You want to hear about that last straw? Of course you do.

Deirdre chucked me, strange to relate. She dropped me and gave me a free transfer. She was boffing someone else (comme d'habitude). She phased me out.

Rich, isn't it?

THREE

Barn Elms. Broad caresses of warmth and sunlight ripple lazily over the sports fields. Gentle rows of polite poplars bend and curtsey in this slight, summerscented breeze. There is a low town-fed hum of early summer boredom. Hot and quiet. The sound of heavy, distant footfalls punctuates the crowdless silence. The bowler runs in hard, nostrils madwide and feet drumming on the drying grass. A sweet crack of satisfaction as the batsman clips the ball smartly off his legs. The deep, glowing pleasure of cricket bat meeting cricket ball with equal repelling force. The little ball zips towards the boundary ropes, high in the air, whining outwards, plopping down thwunk just in front of my feet.

Embarrassed, I throw it back to a bemused long-on.

Yes, I'm watching a cricket match. A cricket match, would you believe! Now, what more idyllic way can there be to spend an idle afternoon in June? The sun is less harsh than earlier and that toothsome little breeze diffuses the worst of my sweaty smells. My headache has further calmed and my bowels are, relatively speaking, still. And I'm watching some cricket. This is fun.

Cricket is a surprisingly important game. It matters oddly, even to an Irish tramp like me. Of all sports it is the most coherent and cohesive. Cricket's dashing, dapper, thoughtful, friendly and encyclopaedic. Cricket glows with summer and shimmers with its ponderous, siesta pace. It's a game of the mind, of the imagination. Of course, the most important thing about cricket is that the Americans don't play it.

The bowler thunders in again, accelerating over the flattened, much-trodden grass. The ball flies straight and fast from a whirling confusion of arms and legs. Batsman's knees hoist into action, pushing forward. The stumps blast noisily apart. There is a muffled cheer from the fielding team and the bowler looks modest in the distance. The air hums its warm song of brightness and anticipation as the batsman shuffles away from the wicket. Gosh, it must be nice to be allowed to throw things at people with impunity.

I've done my boking and I'm feeling the better for it. I was a bit lost for a moment back there. Not quite up to what to do. I felt tired, sick, stupid and even slightly mad. I slipped a little. Just for a moment. I mustn't let this happen. I mustn't think too much about alternatives and similar badgering cruelties. I've done rather well so far and I'd hate to pack it all in after having got so far. Not to mention leaving my poor story in the lurch so. I chirped up doublequick. I'm good at that. (Sometimes.)

I lie back on this grassy bank while the new batsman comes out. The earth seems to sigh and exhale a moist, heated lethargy. In answer, my mind and sense begin to roll and billow into abstraction. Sweat tickles my ears and I travel in dreamy geographies of peace and rest. I feel terribly European.

At first England seemed to me a leavened land of wieldy beauty. A loaf smell to me, the untried child of Turf Lodge. An unseen song of glamour and wealth. On the train from Stranraer to London, I watched the station signs signal to my window the towns and cities of my childhood imaginings. A place to see my books. Contrast. Vive la différence. Ireland and its squalid joys. England and its seedy ploys.

I was awash with yokelism and hickery. In the wonder of London my heart bounded with heady delirium as I trod the streets of all my bookish memories. Covent Garden breathed raffish Restoration scents to me; Westminster Bridge where great crowds still flowed in unfaced streams; Bloomsbury, a museum stamped village . . . and the river, Lizzie Hexam's friend and foe. Other men's imaginings.

Well, as a matter of fact, at first England seemed to me a pile of piss. London, lithe and loathsome. Where was Dickens now? I'd never seen a tart before. Not a proper one. Nor a sex shop. The dirt was different to Irish dirt. Sticky and snobbish both. And lumme was I cool about it! (No, not a whit.) I was a man. Going somewhere.

I was fucking terrified. The city was wholly too vast for my provincial compass. I got lost on the underground and somehow ended up on Hampstead Heath. From up there, the city seemed to lie inert with a grey, torpid malice. The women I saw in London were lascivious and ill-clad in the autumn warmth, returning breastbrowned from topless beaches. Not like the women of Belfast and Ireland. They were gorgeous, fabulous, breathtaking. Faces touched with the well-monied sheen of wealth and artifice. I had not witnessed beauty of this order before. I felt hopelessly parochial as those generous eyes traced my features with marvellous, maddening carelessness. Emblems of desire and unattainability.

The underground was superb. I rode it for happy hours. An unfamiliar, snaky monster of populous indifference. I sat in half-filled carriages and changed lines at will. The station names held the challenge and mystery of old acquaintances newly rediscovered. They filled me with pleasure and furtive excitement. I tried to appear casual. Just like a real Londoner. I was aware of being rustic and unsharpened. Enviously I marvelled at the insouciance of my fellow passengers who disembarked lightly and confidently without glancing at the station signs.

I got lost again and finally extricated myself from this subterranean grip at Turnham Green. I threw caution to the winds and got a taxi to Liverpool Street Station. I would have to take London in easy stages.

It was late in the afternoon when I reached Cambridge and daylight was dimming fast. One's first sight of places like Cambridge is always one's best and fondest. I looked upon that town's toylike perfection. The dim redolence of the past hummed through the tiny grandeur of its decorous narrow streets and gloomy hallowed passages. The soft grey twilight mirrored perfectly the cloistered mustiness of its ancient courts and lawns. The colleges sprawled in the centre of the little town with a frowsy, graceful indifference. My thick heart swelled further. It was all so old. So preserved and clean and perfect. Loveliness tilled my rude Bogleian soil. Cambridge. My victory.

With some difficulty I found my college and rapped with the head porter, a hatless, grey-haired Irishman called Sepulchre. (Honestly!) He was very groovy. Chockful of respectability and humble discretion. I did my man-of-the-people-cum-Paddy-working-boy-made-good routine and he loved me. I smiled my widest, most engaging smiles and we boogied and funked. I always had the common touch.

My name was already painted upon the wall above my door: R. BOGLE. This context gave my funny old name an aristocratic look that it had always hitherto lacked. For the first time in my life I felt that my name was more than a slapstick jumble of ludicrous consonants. It looked grave and weighty up there on that wall. I was chuffed with it. (My name can be more of a handicap than you might realise. I mean – Ripley Bogle. It's hard to live down sometimes. God knows what old Betty and Bobby were thinking of when they named me. Probably of the disadvantages of alliteration.)

My room was fab. Woodpanelled and dark. Its windows looked out on the river to my lasting disbelief. This was wonderful – incredible. I switched off the light and sat staring out at the river and smoking a cigarette. As I stared out across the darkened trees and grass to the night-blackened river, I could scarcely believe the extent of my own joy. This was me, Bogle, the tramp, the waster, the boozer, the slipper, the slider and the fader away. What was I doing here?

So there I sat in that darkened college room, smoking thoughtfully. My rise in life had at last begun and fond hopes and expectations began to rise in my uncertain heart.

'. . . and now we have the answer to last week's Saturday Teaser when you could have won Kim Wilde's new album . . . you lucky, lucky people . . . and the answer was . . . "Count Borulawski, the Polish dwarf who claimed to love the most beautiful baroness in the Court of Dresden." . . . yes, I know – a bit of a tricky one, that!'

A radio belches irritating vulgar noise. Two young women have sat on this grassy bank not far from me. Their radio is loud and their clothes are worse. They glance over towards my harmless, agreeable self and giggle maliciously. Their laughter is shrill and insistent. These girls aren't posh. They're dogs, brutes, harridans. Some of the fielders have noted the uninvited clamour and make vague, inept protesting gestures. The girls giggle further, pleased with the ripples they're causing.

'Wasn't that just tremendous? Later we'll have Rodney in the studio to talk about his new single called "My mother used to beat me". I wonder if he's got the bruises to prove it, eh? Ha ha ha ha ha ha ha hee hee. It's all fun on this Saturday lunchtime. We've just had a call from a listener in Bletchley who says that I misquoted Immanuel Kant earlier on in the show. Well, I'm very sorry, Mr Jenkins, we'll get onto that as soon as possible but in the meantime we'll go to the newsroom for a motoring flash . . .'

The girls start to divest themselves of their vigorous clothing. They strip down to their sturdy underwear, sniggering at me as they undress. Some of the cricketers stare at them in furtive disapproval. I don't blame them. Apart from anything else, these hefty girls' flesh is better left to the imagination. I wish they'd keep it to themselves. If we all had a whip round we might be able to buy them a sunlamp or something. It would be worth the expense.

(Oh, bloody good shot! A veritable square cut. A stroke I could never master. I love cricket dearly but can't play worth a damn.)

One of the girls throws a nasty gesture at me and shouts something incomprehensible. These bootgirls are obviously under the impression that I am deriving some pleasure from the spectacle that they present in their strapping underwear. They are sadly wrong. I wonder if I should go over and explain this to them. Best not.

'Thank you Rob, and now we're going to announce the result of our newest Listeners' Poll. You remember we asked our listeners to tell us all about their very favourite sexual fantasies. This was our first Kink Poll of the year and I'm glad to say we had some very interesting replies indeed and we're able to announce ha ha ha ha ha heee that the most common sexual ha he hee hee fantasy among listeners to this ha ha ha ha station is . . .'

They are prone now, these girls, baking their pale, lardy flesh in this unfriendly blare of heat. So, bless the day! They're stupid as well as ugly and rude. These tarts are really going it when it comes to the social handicaps. Good on them. More power to their troglodytism.

Out. Gotta be! By a mile. Plumb! The batsman walks, gamely not awaiting umpire's decision. Nice to see that kind of thing. The players bunch in celebration. A couple of fielders stray towards the boundary near to where the two brides of Dracula are sunning themselves. They look speculative, sanguine. Oh come on, guys! Not those two. You'd have to be desperate. Open your eyes! Take a look!

They have made their decision now and trot casually over the boundary rope. They meander towards the girls, taking an unconvincing circuitous route. They aren't bad-looking these fellows. They could do much better than this. Perhaps it's a bet or something like that. Yes, I hope so.

' . . . and now we have Dave from Reigate on the line – Hello Dave from Reigate, can you hear me? . . . hello . . . hello . . . ha ha ha ha ha ha ha, it looks as though we're having a few difficulties with Dave from Reigate there – we'll try and get Dave on the line later on in the show. Well, ha ha ha ha hah ha ha ha ha ha ha ha hee hee. [D.J. searches frantically for something to fill the sudden silence . . .] This is the new one from Mick Jagger and Frank Sinatra . . . let's hear it for the boys . . . ha ha ha ho ho ho oh hee hee . . .'

The girls have heaved to a sitting position and they are now talking to the errant cricketers. The sight is depressing me. Some of the other fielders call to their chums. Play is ready to recommence but these two don't seem very interested. They sit down close to the girls and wave their team mates on. There are mutinous mumbles on the pitch. Their abdication has not been well received. Democracy fails and order collapses. The romantic cricketers seem happy enough and look to be progressing well with their conquests. The girls giggle hard and point blatantly at me. One of the men guffaws coarsely while the other, obviously socialist, seems to be making a stab at some kind of egalitarian, excusing comment. They seem to find me funny. I wonder what it is about me that can be so very comic.

Eventually the two cricketers dawdle back to the game, obviously having concluded their tryst with these sun-loving trogs. The ladies' hilarity increases markedly in pitch and intensity, as well it might – they could never have expected this kind of flattery – what with being so ugly and everything. They turn the volume up on their hissing radio as a reminding leitmotif of their raucous presence. Gosh and golly, aren't they chuffed! Their contempt for me seems all the sharper for their erotic victory and their campaign of feeble abuse and profane gesturing does not abate. I seem to be side-splitting now. They swap their cruel jokes with the two cricketing beaux hovering needlessly around the boundary and all is well with their world.

'. . . and now some letters that have been sent in just this very week, one sent in by Gillian Crawley in Slough – thank you for writing Gillian – she says ha ha ha ha ha "I think you've got the sexiest voice on the wireless and I want you to fill me with your babies" . . . he he hee heee – it's all go here on London's favourite radio station. What a girl eh?! Well, Gillian, you naughty little minx, that seems like a good idea to me ha ha ha ha ha ha hee hee ho ho! But in the meantime I'll play the new UB40 track ha ha ha ha ha ha ha ha hee hee heeeee . . .'

The girls start to sing along. Their thin, fag-hoarse voices shrill with energy. The cricketers wink, smile, ogle, nod, titter and smirk. Oh, I'm getting depressed – I'm getting into misery. Give me a gun. Let me do the noble thing. Though not to myself.

—

Can you imagine it? Me at Cambridge! My word, a turn up for the books. What a picture. Come with me. See the scene.

Cambridge, a flat dunned October town. Trinity Street winding narrowly down to Great Saint Mary's onto the broad boulevard of King's Parade, shop and college flanked; a tiny showpiece. A pale academic glimmer in the heavy afternoon, a tinge of library and reading lamps, glowing and distant. Undergraduates traipsing the town streets, aimlessly avoiding the end-of-season tourist dregs. When met, greeting one another with embellished tales of vacations lonely spent. The new university year was heaving slowly into movement, a lethargic countdown. The air wreathed in the old, damp embrace of sky and earth. Cambridge rolling on, college fronts and towns-folk alike indifferent to the shifting generations of youth and promise. Cold in turn to new-blooded freshers and the others, older not wiser.

In the midst of this, Ripley Bogle, hero, walks ponderously the closet gloom of high, tightly squeezed Senate House Passage wheeling his battered old black bicycle at his faithful side. Click of heels and rattle of wheels making his only song, dimming daylight filtering blondly on his hero's paleness.

Lovely, isn't it? Heartswelling. The third and last of my little snapshots. When I was doing good. Hightime.

In charcoal grey, baggy but suave, 1950s Oxfam suit, a dying breed, price – fifteen crinkly pounds in two sweet notes. Floppy white shirt. Unstarched collar sharp against the dark of his lapels and bisected by the fading grey of his ancient spotted tie. Trimly, he steps out onto those elegant twilit streets. Mid-October and the wind is yet warmed. Dreams of kings and fanfares. A progress of triumph and manfulness and all those older things. He steps in brown brogues, a careful mismatch with the darkness of his garb. He whispers to the tune of his footsteps. In the extremity of the second twilight with its lower moon tinging red, his face and hand will irradiate. And all he waits will never come.

Them were the good days, to be sure. By quite a long way. I had what I wanted as well as a little break from anxiety, poverty, shame and the necessity for forward planning. I was at my best back then; at my poshest, cleanest and most attractive. You could have taken me home to mother, believe me. Brings a tear to my eye, it does. All that promise and easy hope. Me thinking I was set fair and straight for happiness. I'd done the hard bit. What else could be left?

But I was soon to find that Cambridge was a disappointment. Its beauty had diverted me at first but even that soon dissolved in habit's grip. Engaging only the eyes, it lacked that Belfast smell of harshness and rough theatre. Short and shallow it pleased. A gentle confectionery.

To me, the English seemed a curious people. Those at Cambridge at any rate. They were polite, charming, ready to accept and eager to include but despite these easy graces, they puzzled me. Paranoiac that I am, I suspected that they had some kind of secret, some unspoken thread which united the strands of their race, class and culture.

Of course there was no secret about the English. A well-hidden characteristic but no secret. I watched as my contemporaries allied themselves to an endless series of societies, clubs and factions. I saw their rapid espousal of any modish current in politics, art, fashion or scholarship and the desperation with which they attached themselves to large groups of their fellows. To be themselves, they needed others. Exclusion was the chiefest of their terrors. The fear of being alone was everywhere, or rather, the fear of being seen to be alone. Unpopular, youths created elaborate fantasies about their out-of-town activities and popular undergraduates made a frantic circuit of dismal cocktail parties, tending their success with careful hand. Incessantly, they talked of their legion acquaintance and decorated their bare walls with out-of-date invitations.

Touched with no other love, they were the rulers of their own aridities. Selfishness and sterile egotism abounded. They didn't mean to be selfish. They were limpets to any body of fellows greater than their own. There was little personality and no soul. These people were almost indistinguishable, one from the other. The nebulous impalpability of ideas and trends was preferred at all times to the brute empiricism of humanity. The tricky area of personality was treated with some trepidation and individuality was rare and largely ignored. They feared human, interior congress. They disliked the notion of people differing from themselves. In one of my epic, universal moments, I concluded with rare intelligence that an Englishman's lack of interest in himself naturally precludes any interest in others. Remote, impersonal, disengaged. Easy pickings for the dark, concocted vitality of the Celt (i.e. me).

There was one surprise in store. Having immersed myself in the glad accounts of idealistic homo-communism of Cambridge in the thirties and the feigned working-class accents of the sixties and seventies, I was taken aback at the extent of the ideological transformation that had taken place. The soft mantle of retarded fascism now cloaked the old town. Dickens had spat teeth at less than this. Not to put too fine a point on it, wankers and dickheads filled every street in a riot of stupidity and power. The Union Society was in the grip of a caucus of actual lunatics and the university Conservative groups spent their time in exposing the KGB's role in British trade unionism and suggesting ethnic repatriation as the only viable solution to the nation's economic decline. Empireless, declining, they were sad, sad folk.

In addition, snobbery and the notions of aristocracy were in vogue once more. Me, Myself, Ripley Bogle, foremost in nature's dukedom, I had difficulty in comprehending the dynamics of aristocracy. Calmly, I looked upon the Sainsburys, the Cadburys, the McVities and the Greek merchants' sons who were included in this code. Tacky newcomers, unfamilied and arriviste. In my hickish innocence I had expected them to be disowned by the elder bastions of the English upper classes but no. They were smoothly, hitchlessly included. They had what it has always taken. Dosh, power and more dosh. Aristocracy. Qu'est-ce que? Nothing. Doesn't exist. Empirically, notionally or otherwise. What makes an aristocrat an aristocrat? Years ago an ancestor clobbered some luckless peasants and nicked all their pigs and chickens. Or some pederast groom was knighted for shovelling the shit of the king's horses. All starts with commerce and servility. Was and is no such thing as nobility. Sons of thieves and stewards. Kings are the same.

Adventitious in creation. Sons of bruisers with big swords and haemophilia. Kill to rule. Power then was based on real power. Who and how much you could kill. Strength of arm and sword. Now, power is only a claim, a code of behavioural practices that distinguishes different groups of people. Pronouncing Magdalene wrong and having no vents in your jackets. Stunning! Only a point of difference. Who's to say which is best? Guttersnipe at king's feast. But then a Cambridge ponce would be just as out of place on the Falls Road. For a little while, that is. Before they strung the poor bastard up. Different aristocracies. Just as jealously guarded was the violent aristocracy of Turf Lodge. Keep out! No interlopers please. I myself had all the attributes for this other English acceptability. Intelligence, charm and.polish (I did. I had it then. All that.) Confidence and poise were mine. I used to wonder what it was exactly that could make a five-foot-two eighteen year old with bad breath, no brain and vigorous acne feel in the merest way superior to an epic form like my good self. Nought else but a superstitious relic of time past; and sift it to its true worth and it is nothing. Too right.

To Webster and myself if seemed that only in England could the estimation of human worth and power be based on something so insubstantial as snobbery and class. (We were wrong, Webster and I, but at least we tried.)

To this intricate, insecure structure old Ripley Bogle posed a problem or two. The difficulty was that, spoilsport that I was, I feared no one's contempt or poor opinion. All these feeble folk feared my unflappability and foreigner's strength. My solitude and lofty disdain for favour seeking. My breathtaking pomposity and unconquerable self-belief devastated them utterly. From whence had I brought this assurance and power? The trim confidence that begets authority. I hadn't been to their school after all. Where did it come from? How could it be?

Upon me they employed their last resort, their most complete weapon – inclusion. They tried to make me one of them. I had an open invitation to their minor little world. They tried to clip my clever little claws. I was pet of the smart set. It was a pity. I was rather looking forward to being looked down on and the nasty scuffles that would have resulted.

But the girls – the girls were different. They were worth the bother – mostly because they were better looking and had bigger tits than the boys. Anyhow, for the most part, I had what they wanted. A conduit to desire. Cutey Bogle, lady pleaser. When I had lived in Belfast, being Irish had not been a terribly distinguishing feature but I soon learnt to milk it for all it was worth in Cambridge. These trim women, weary of the arid youth of their own race and class, saw in proselyte old me a piece of Irish rough. Albeit a very polite and acceptably mannered one. A good thing too, I imagine. The real thing might have proved a little too robust for their tastes.

I wasn't one to argue. This Irishness lark was so obviously a good one that I went to it with a will. I looked for that stamp of clowning Celtism. (From which I was profoundly free. Though only because I left. For what should I have stayed? For school, for priest, for gun? I chose the delight of Albion – daring choice. After all, England owed me a living after taking away my lovely land, my tithe and my tongue. From Cromwell and the Scots Prots to the Long Kesh and the League of Liars. Having no country of my own, I rather thought that I would take theirs. Fair, that seemed – an eyesore for an eyesore.) Thus I, deserter of that snakeless shambles, endeavoured to improve that Gaelic effect. I began to affect something of the air of a Celtic working-class hero ... though I was bloody glad that I was doing it in Cambridge rather than Belfast. Of course, this was all the worst kind of shite. I didn't much like the working classes. (The working classes never do.) But what the hell! It sounded good and suited me well enough.

Some examples of the Cambridge I witnessed. A couple of character sketches. Some people I knew.

Benedict Sparrow was reading Law at Trinity Hall. Where else? He was an extrovert sort of chap who compensated for being only four feet and eleven inches tall and having a face like a plastic bag full of soft shite by the vigour of his moral, political and judicial convictions. He was an Old Etonian as well which he seemed to find very compensatory indeed.

Among other things, this prodigy espoused the reintroduction of capital punishment, the complete dismantling of the welfare state, repatriation for ethnic groups, departure from the EEC and – quite seriously – the immediate invasion of France. Now these notions were not unusual in Cambridge at that time (apart perhaps from that curious twist of xenophobia at the end) and initially they made little impression upon me. It was only when I discovered that Sparrow's grandfather was Lord Chancellor, that his great-grandfather had been Master of the Rolls, that his father was Attorney General, that they had all read Law at Trinity Hall and that the family considered young Benedict to be the most promising of the lot that I began to worry. I was no part of a socialist but I was horrified to chew on the fact that I was encountering future heads of government, law, industry and commerce and they were all already, almost without exception, right off their fucking trolleys.

Another face of Cambridge was illuminated by a young man named

Joshua Swinnington-Booth. Now, Joshua was another Old Etonian but he had changed his name to Bazza Wilkins, feeling this nomenclature to be indicative of his truer nature. Despite the fact that Bazza's father was a proper peer with an ancient seat in the House of Lords, Bazza had a skinhead haircut and wore enormous black boots with huge spidery laces that always seemed to be trying to crawl up his thighs. He only wore denim and had an extraordinary East End accent. All in all, he might not have looked out of place in any South London gang fight, though his combative expertise might have proved rather theoretical in such circumstances. His conversation consisted almost entirely of street-fighting, violent crime, Islamic fundamentalism and the brutalities of various paramilitary groups, though I suspected that he had first-hand experience of none of these things. Those who had generally wanted to forget about it do not trawl it out for the edification of their varsity buddies. This young man spoke with relish of hatred, blood and death. He was also breathtakingly confident and well-informed on the subject of the IRA.

My acquaintance with this interesting fellow ended abruptly one day when, after drinking my entire stock of spirituous liquids, the Honourable Bazza informed me that I was a 'dirty turncoat bastard' who was betraying his countrymen in his pathetic efforts at social climbing. Some of this actually stuck and I lost my rag quite extensively. Unfortunately, the intrepid Bazza couldn't stand straight long enough for me to knock his teeth down the back of his throat.

Another gem was Art Likely, the short-arse American exchange student with the 1950s Brooklyn accent. With all his guff and grumbles about how much better and hipper New York was compared *to* London. His fulsome crap about Central Park, Times Square, Broadway, Madison Avenue, Greenwich Village and all. How he prosed and lauded! With his orthodonty and platform heels. And of course it eventually transpired that he was from Albuquerque and had only set foot in New York twice in his life and one of those was to catch his plane to London. The stage Yank. (In his defence, I must say that it was he who introduced me to the pastrami sandwich, so he couldn't have been all bad.)

Oh, there were others, scores of them, equally awful. Sāndra (Săndra to you and me) Whitsun, the fat, lisping snob-monstrosity who terrorised the good-looking men of the town with her voracious, wobbling sexual incontinence; Vanessa Hampton, the giant anorexic Sloane who pursued my little buns for two fruitless and depressing years; Roger Markham, the public school Zionist who dyed his hair blond and tried to join the Monday Club; Sebastian, the winsome homosexual artist who filled his bath with paint and

174

then scoured Milton Road looking for diminutive wide boys to dunk in it. They were all much of a muchness. Take them for all in all, they were prats. Why is it, I wonder, that it is the cleverest folk amongst us who make the most howling embarrassing mistakes when they are young? Deep, huh?

The one aspect of my Cambridge years that I have neglected to mention is the boredom. My God, the boredom was appalling! The sheer tedium was huge for the majority of us though no one would have admitted it. Perish the thought! There we all were in our poky, uniform and depressing little rooms, free of family and warmth. Sweet nineteen and never been missed. We were all, to our varying degrees quite terrifyingly lonely. With our mainly solo nights, we craved warmth, sentimentality, the merest congress. Can you imagine those lonely nights? Decorated with college infestivity and sounded with the staircase footsteps of those busier and happier. Our society was brittle, frantic, free of much intimacy or reward. We were like baby birds leaving the nest, full of doubt and not much kop at anything useful.

(Loneliness is embarrassing. Especially at Cambridge. It was never mentioned, never confessed. But it was there – in big red letters. For almost all. Apart from me, of course.)

Good old Cambridge! Like it, loathe it, you can never really ignore it. It won't leave you alone. Once it's got its nasty little hooks into you, it doesn't let go. Perhaps that's what I like most about Cambridge. Its sheer doltish persistence.

After a while sunshine gets to be a bore. We passed that stage a couple of hours ago and now the shrill, nagging heat is going too far. My hair ebbs and flows in a sea of scalpsweat and my eyes sting with salty moisture. I walk into slow and dwindling small distance. My steps are weary, uncertain. My back is bent, my head is low, my all is done.

I was enjoying the cricket but had to get offski as those two trogbims with the wireless were behaving in the most insupportable manner. I must confess that I am rather at a loss as to what it was about me that bothered them so. It is rather humiliating to be an object of contempt for folk such as they. I must look worse than I thought. I've been kidding myself obviously. I've fallen. Fallen far. Farther than I would have thought possible. Shucks.

I turn my head and look back at the little scene. The two girls are still sprawled hugely on the grass and I can just make out the white figures of their two fond admirers. It looks dead set, I must say. I can still hear the faint, tinny scratching of their radio. What with the heat and brightness and insistent noise, it makes a rather vulgar little picture. I don't know why but I find it very depressing indeed.

Mustering my cheeriness, I march on with renewed vigour. I'm conscious of smelling rather strongly and having curious patches of hot dampness dotted around my unattractive form. My face is wet with sweat and my gaping shoes emit an almost visible cloud of rot and decay. My eyes are narrow in the slanting sunlight and my mouth puckers and grimaces as I pant for hot oxygen. An old lady is walking her dog near by and I must pass her. My heart sinks with shame as the animal bounds towards this joyous repository of all that's recondite in the smell world. The old lady calls her dog back sharply. She's probably afraid that the mutt will catch something. Looking and smelling like I do, I have a sudden abundance of humiliation. The old lady passes by and try as I might, I cannot prevent my greasy eyes from meeting hers.

And guess what? She smiles at me. Yes, she smiles. She looks at my filth and cess and halo of flies and she smiles. At me and my dirt and my depression. She gives me a little grin. How about that!

A curious thing, life, and curious those who live it.

FOUR

Ordinarily, I'd have missed the point of beauty so extreme – less than paled, the softened eye of comeliness. Laura was beautiful, breathtaking, fabulous, hard to believe. I had it bad for Laura. I had it big and bad and sad for Laura. I was in love, you understand. In it up to my oxters.

Laura is the girl who troubles me still. I pine for Laura, I lament her passing, I miss her. It's in my dreams she comes to me, unbidden and unfound. Through sleeping glass she talks to me, my scene she loves, my proxy and my fool. She didn't love me a whole hell of a lot in past actuality but in these phantasms, she does the bit for me. She loves me inside out. She's nice in dreams. She's very nice indeed.

As I say, the facts don't really justify this kind of sanguine extravagance on the part of my subconscious. Our relationship was chequered. It was candystriped, polkadotted! It's a curious thing but I've always been superb with the women I don't really want. I've been charming, debonair, sensitive, erotic, virile and enigmatic. When a woman I really want comes along I do my best for gaucherie, clumsiness, arrogance and abrasive failure. I never seem to fascinate the girls that should be fascinated. I plough my way through the fainting multitude of adoring Bogle admirers to the girl I love and promptly make a dickhead of myself. It's depressing, it really is.

On arrival in Cambridge, I was prepared and keen to disseminate, to father millions, to make my genealogical mark upon England. I was pleased to find that English women were so much better looking than the Ulster harridans I was accustomed to. They laid me out. I envisaged failure and womanlessness. To my surprise, I was a hit. I got my bims. My women. These girls were posh, gorgeous and firmly pro-Bogle. I was in several kinds of clover. They were all so fucking clever! Coming from where I did, the notion of intelligent women was foreign to me and I was intoxicated by all the kinky feminine genius at my disposal. I studied hard, keen to learn. I'm grateful to them. They gave me a lot. It was a good deal. I got their beauty, humour and tolerance. They got me. I did bloody well out of that little bargain. Where was the equal, automatic share of task and profit in that? I always drove a hard one.

After my juvenile trials with Dear Deirdre I considered that I had the subject of women pretty thoroughly taped up. My attitude on this was another example of the Bogleian verdict on that which he knows nothing about – been there, seen it, done it, forgot about it. Commitment and monogamy had slipped out of my top ten. I was ready for the seductions indiscriminate. Me of the glad eyes and the pointy penis. Fun I sought. Nothing was worth breaking my poor little heart for.

Laura broke my poor little heart almost immediately. It was due to me and my disabilities with beauty. Laura was a girl who prompted need and vigorous desire. I was chanceless in the Indifference Stakes. You know, it's hard, it's so hard not to fall in love with beautiful women. I try on principle and usually manage but Laura roped me effortlessly in. I was trussed and tapered. Gone.

It wasn't what she said or did; it wasn't even the way she said or did it. I don't really know exactly what it was . . . but it was – that much I'm sure of. That, I know. Our first meeting was a gem, a beauty. You would have loved it. Picture this. We see an early October Cambridge party of the garden variety. We see the callow youths doing their desperation, their heady glee and lonely chatter. We see Bogle doing his Irish, his hard-drinking, hard-thinking best. We see the lovely girl. We see that beauty. We see the icy Laura. She is approached, poor girl. He moves in, his eyes wide and smile heavy with liar's content.

BOGLE (*a phantom causing fright*): Marry me.

LAURA: Sorry?

BOGLE (*in ardent cups*): The one evil in the world is cruelty.

LAURA (*astonished*): I beg your pardon?!

BOGLE (*mysteriously*): If I were a fly, would you pull my wings off? (*Pause. The girl is amused and confused but hardly much lured.*) I mean . . . hello, how are you?

LAURA: Ah . . . hello.

BOGLE: I'm Irish.

LAURA: Oh.

BOGLE: Whereas you're not.

LAURA: No, I'm not.

BOGLE: See, I told you.

(*Pause – unsurprisingly*)

LAURA: Is that an important point?

BOGLE: A point of difference.

LAURA: Yes.

BOGLE: At least it's a point of something.

LAURA: Oh.

(Pause. The silence is brief and fragile. He can't afford to take any liberties with it. He ploughs on.)

BOGLE *(after much thought)*: Hey, you wanna come round to my place and scale my kettle some? *(The girl gives a startled shout of laughter.)* Was that funny? *(She is still helpless with laughter.)* Tell me. Why do you laugh?

LAURA: Is that how you chat up girls in Ireland?

BOGLE: I don't chat up girls in Ireland.

LAURA: Why not?

BOGLE: Have you ever met many Irish girls?

LAURA: Not many, no.

BOGLE: You wouldn't understand. *(Pause. He smiles, the charmer.)* That was nice.

LAURA: What was?

BOGLE: When you laughed – that was nice.

LAURA: Thank you. *(She smiles, she wavers and she decides to stay.)* You're a funny chap.

BOGLE *(keenly)*: Do you like me?

LAURA *(surprised)*: Well ...

BOGLE *(passionately)*: Would you die for me? *(She erupts into laughter again.)* Well, would you die for me?

LAURA: Assuredly, I would ... though I mightn't be quite so keen on living for you.

BOGLE: Aye, there's the syllabub!

(Another pause. All her charms conspire against the vigour of his rationale. Her eyes shine on his folly.)

LAURA: You're not very good at this, are you?

BOGLE *(moue)*: Oh dear, and I thought that I had been doing conspicuously well. I was wrong then?

LAURA: Not entirely.

BOGLE: Good. I so much want to shine for you.

LAURA *(amused)*: Oh, you are, you are.

BOGLE *(insistent)*: No, I mean properly. Like you shine for me. Tell me, how do I do that?

LAURA: Well ...

BOGLE: Incident and narrative must form a kind of cold collation. If calm reigns most targets may be achieved without too much heartache. Have pity on me. I've had a bad life – full of badness.

LAURA: I don't understand.

BOGLE (*coming over all wise*): Ah, so much intolerance in the world! You're much too pretty much too young for any of that.

(*Pause*)

LAURA: English Literature. Wrong or right?

BOGLE: Right.

LAURA: You don't seem the bookish type.

BOGLE (*in his stride now*): My literature leads my life for me. My own is empty and female fruitless. Sad, very.

LAURA: Very. (*She smiles and drifts off, unconquered. The boy remains, inspiration fled and misery arriving.*)

Not good, huh? My lines had not improved since the time of Deirdre. I was only good at non sequiturs. I was big on words littered with the fag ends of half meanings and semi-memory. I was trying out for cute incomprehensibility. Setting out for love, I missed the turning point at allure. This kind of thing had washed the subnormal, beastbrained Deirdre but Laura had intelligence. She wasnae impressed.

My first few weeks at Cambridge I spent in trying to put myself in the way of a chance encounter with my fair enslaver. This feeble ploy was conspicuous for its lack of success. We didn't move in the same circles as yet. Our scarce, infrequent meetings were monuments of hilarity and failure. I fucked up constantly. Tongue-tied, limbless and free of gorm, I mucked it up. She eluded me constantly. Alone at night I waved the ragged remnants of desire until they shredded. I drank too much and said too little of merit. I had no kind of a chance. A curious thing. Me always desperate for her presence but only managing gauche misery and inadequacy when actually with her.

In addition, she had a bim, a boyfriend. Greg, he was called. Greg the pukka prat. Greg the runtish, cock-eyed little git. Greg wasn't too keen on me. He thought I was outré, beyond his diminutive pale. He thought I wanted to pork his girlfriend. He wasn't far wrong. The closest he came to perception.

As a matter of fact, I didn't much want to pork old Laura. I was in the grip of one of my pure infatuations. Goodness, I hadn't even tried to estimate what her jugs would have been like! It was love I wanted, not the heat and distraction of rut. I needed the intangibilities of callow, soulful exchanges of polite desire. Laura seemed perfect for that.

Oh, I had it so bad! She dominated everything for me. I was obsessed with her pale image. With some women, it is hard to believe how beautiful they can be. My image of her repeated everywhere, mirrored in all the women I saw. I saw traces of her everywhere. A heartstop sighted in the distance. Never her. All the time, I smelt the sweetness of her clothes and hair. Her halo of pale milky hair. Familiar and feared. A counterpace to my unsteady heart. I wanted her and my poor unlikely need coloured all that I did and particularly, all that I didn't do. I was just a gimp in love.

Without a trace, my confidence dissolved and my resolve departed. My face was heated and my meagre, battered little pulse raced in Laura-fed panic. Her quiet, indescribable beauty glowed in my darkness. I tried to forge some kind of carelessness but my road was never the middle one. The joy and adrenalin of my desire was quashed by my conviction of its impossibility. This was to be a passion unrequited. She was infinitely beyond my reach.

I mooned hopelessly around town, weighed down by my soppy secret. I gimped it up. At one point I worked up a modicum of courage and decided – what the hell – I would make a declaration! She would be flattered surely. They almost always were. So, I climbed the staircase outside her room where I paused for the breath of hardiness. It failed me badly and I threw myself hard down in the hope of breaking a leg. (A state well-known for its erotic appeal.) Two flights I o'erflew before my crunch! Well, smiled I, a little pity goes a long way. And what did I get? Concussion, a sprained ankle and she'd fucked off to London for the weekend! It called for coherent action or capitulation . . . and the most I could muster was fantasy.

Not that I was entirely without my encouragements. One day, early in my second term, deep in winter, I had a stutter of hope. Conjure my hopelessness, my lovelessness and generally forlorn, youthish state. I was abject, depressed, sour with sperm, much unloved. I needed a good day and got it. It was one of those Cambridge afternoons, steeped in gloom and solitude. The weather had been cold and grey all day. It had rained hard and now briefly stopped. The afternoon throbbed unholy boredom in each sparse undergraduate room, driving the university population onto the wet, comfortless streets. They searched for that to colour their monochrome loneliness and vexation. Libraries, matinées, rehearsals and meetings of every kind. All were sought in desperation by the shifting tides of bored youths. Their grey sky was pockmarked with ugly smudges which dropped again cold, glamourless rain onto the softened streets. I myself wandered along past Castle Hill cheerfully. I loved this kind of dun and moistly bitter thing.

A sudden winded, angry squall of rain clattered from the sky, drenching the air and drowning the streaming roads and pavements. Cars slushed noisily and hurried from the diamond-studded downpour, hissing their wakespray in rearward jets. I dived into Kettle's Yard for safety and floodfree rest and fag. I shook my quickwetted head and looked about me.

Poncy little covered courtyard gutted and tarted. In one of the chintzy doorways a poster blared, announcing an exhibition of work by women undergraduates. Oh fun, I thought, oh fucking fun! However, I was feeling listless and not too keen on braving again the sudden enmity of the sky. So, I went in.

It cost me one pound and fifty pence, no less! For this sum, I was given a cyclo-styled catalogue and the freedom to wander round the joint. I browsed aimlessly. It was dull stuff mostly, tampon moods and working mothers, that kind of thing. All pretty rich, coming from these privileged, childless varsity bims. I was just about to bugger off back to maledom when I noticed something in that little catalogue that made my rocky heart stop and start. I read that Laura had three pieces in this exhibition. I zoomed around, eagerly searching.

I looked at her two paintings first. With a sickening lick of jealousy I saw that one of them was a self-portrait. Dark, brown-tinged, très sombre. She still seemed incandescent despite the laboured Rembrandt background. Pale shimmer through the frumpy ochre. And beautiful, very beautiful. I was furious. Others would see this. I stared unhappily at the lifeless evocation of my clownish lusts. The other painting was a landscape. Academic and self-conscious. I was disappointed and relieved at this instance of imperfection. I moved onto the drawing, the last of her pieces.

Abruptly, the blood seeped from my face and my heart thumped hard in my muffled chest. It was a large, highly-wrought portrait of a young man. Framed from the waist upwards, the boy's torso was naked. He had long, dark hair and a frank, arresting gaze which produced discomfort. This was even more open and offering than the self-portrait. Above all, and this was what made my hero's blood stammer so alarmingly, ... it was me! Me. Ripley! Not as I had ever looked but it *was* me. Definitely. Unmistakably me.

So, there I stood, rigid with shock and wild hope, while a middle-aged, midwestern tourist couple moved onto Laura's paintings. Yes! That was it. A test. They would set me right. Americans were good at that kind of thing. I waited until they came to the drawing and then stood slightly to one side as they studied it intently. There was a laden pause as their worried gaze scanned the sketch and they glanced covertly at my smiling face. I detected a tiny Yankee double-take. They looked again at the sketch, harder than before. There was a long silence before their eyes were drawn to me once more. I almost giggled but fought it and watched them struggle through their understandable confusion. There was a brief moment of guilty calculation before I saw surprise and recognition flare in their cheeks. They smiled awkwardly and looked at each other for the confirmation of their unease. They murmured something at me. I smiled disarmingly in return

182

and they moved on, bewildered by all this English oddity.

I was right. There was no doubt of that now. Mr and Mrs Magoo had seen it. They had recognised me. This secret emblem of myself wound wreaths of hope in my mind. I looked at the naked form again and a deep blush tinged my cheek, cutely enough. In truth, I was a little embarrassed by the nudity of this other, pencilled self. Gravely, he stood in that mute, weird appeal. Laura had created this. Conjured it. Must have done. She had no photographs of me. She must have used her memory and sense. Imagined me. The grey, pencil-stroked chest and belly. Fleshed me from her own mind. Committed with her white hands.

Out of the little gallery I stumbled, dazed and ecstatic. The day had changed. Effort gone in the slow slide to evening. The rusty, dampened prospect seemed suddenly vital, pregnant, hope-giving. Happier than before, I walked across Magdalene Bridge, a thick, massy trail of road and pavement over the peppergreen salute of the wallthinned river. I decided that I would find and confront her. With what? Oh anything, anything at all.

Strangely enough, I did meet her quite by chance later that evening. I had just had a couple of hours' worth of kip in Trinity library and I bumped into her outside the porter's lodge. The sky was dark and hard. It was one of those awful Cambridge encounters where both parties stop to talk more in surprise than anything else. When the question of how long to wait before moving on is a tricky diplomatic dilemma. It was always bitterly vexing to be left standing by your interlocutor.

In the darkness I sensed that these thoughts were revolving in her mind. Her greeting was reluctant and edgy. Mine was hilariously nervous. Timidly, I asked how she was.

'Fine. And you?'

'Yes, pretty much the same.'

The pause was horrendous. I continued quickly before she saw her chance to move on.

'Vanessa tells me you've got some paintings showing in Kettle's Yard.' I lied glibly. Blithe could I be.

She smiled briefly, whitely and without encouragement.

'That's right.'

Her reply was disconcertingly open-ended. There was another incomprehensible silence while I wondered what to do. I was flashing at the rising ball outside my off-stump here. Now hold on a minute, I thought, urbane as we undoubtedly are – this is taking sang-froid a little too far. This girl had been sketching my naked tits for Chrissakes! Laura's eyes flickered with sudden life as she asked anxiously

'You haven't seen them, have you?'

Tiny pause now. Worry, embarrassment, hope. I smiled in answer and missed my cowardly boat.

'No, I haven't. I want to, though. Tomorrow perhaps.'

Now, whyever did I say that? Laura was calmly negative in her beautiful, beguiling way.

'Oh, I wouldn't bother if I were you. They're not very good. Really, they're not.'

'Oh,' I said unhappily.

Despite the sad waste of my strong opening, she was still standing there. I took some comfort from this. Obviously, she wasn't reluctant to speak to me. Why stay if she was? I gave her one of my boyish grins.

'Well,' I said expansively, 'isn't this fun . . .?'

Just then the dwarfish Greg came scuttling out of the porter's lodge. He didn't slow when he saw me.

'Hello, Bogle. Can't stop now,' he squeaked.

He put his stunted, unjust arm around his lovely prize and strode off, swaggering with perceptible triumph. He might have been a midget but he was only half a fool. Sadly, I watched as they ebbed unseen into the darkness. She didn't look back. It would have been difficult under the restrictive grasp of young Greg's odious, proprietorial arm. Enemy, bastard, small poltroon!

Rueful Ripley watched her loveliness recede into the lamp-pitted darkness of Great Court. I felt depressed and humiliated. Damn! My big chance. My only real opening and bang! There it was flying over the night trees, waving its little paws! Bugger! And there was me congratulating myself on keeping her waiting. Great! Clever boy. Didn't occur to me that she might be waiting for old Greg. Sappy Bogle. Loser and joker. Their butt. Both were probably having a good giggle. She would be thanking her smooth-chinned lover for rescuing her from the funny Irishman. She would mock my ardour. She had missed anything of import in my reference to the drawing. It had been a fantasy. Coincidence. All balls. I'd made a prat of myself. In front of her. Well, fuck her, I thought in compensatory vein. Or not as the case may be.

(So, I drew little comfort from most of my meetings with the fair Laura. Though I was encouraged to note an antipathy towards me from Greg. His aggression could only be good for me, hinting, as it did, at a certain lack of confidence in Laura's fidelity to him. She herself gave no hope nor encouragement. I was faced with the lure of blind faith and self-belief. And though I wavered a fair bit I had to feel fundamentally confident that she would one day see the inside of my Y-fronts.)

FIVE

London simmers, gently sweating as the huge orb of the fiery sun hangs white and merciless in the low sky. Concrete buildings and pavements shimmer dishonestly in the brightness. Shops hang gaudy canopies over their windows. All of a sudden, the city has a festive, summer air. The sun beats and beats in a spurious, mediterranean masquerade. The pale, mask-like London faces have begun to tinge and reflect the glow of the sun. In hot, sticky little cafés, prudish old women glare venomously at the prevalence of youth and flesh. They console themselves with thoughts of winter, their season. And still the sun falls and spreads its smellsetting rays throughout.

The Serpentine boils and bakes in heavy heat. The water is splashed and striped with light and there are lots of swelling semi-dressed girls lolling on the grass and precariously in boats. Multitudes of ice-cream vendors loudly ply their sugary wares and children's vests are dribblestained with snot, tears and melted lollies. Their plaintive, inarticulate clamour is harsh in this heat and their mothers are running out of sweat and patience. Old folks lounge on ranks of deckchairs and young bloods play desultory games of soccer on sloping grass. They hope to attract the sunbathing beauties. I'm feeling mainly less than up to this.

The day has slowed its march. It lopes now. It danders on, it jazzwalks. Various cassette devices blare differing, tuneless songs. It should be discordant but merges neatly into a heated hymn to this young day; this hot, heavy, slow day. I look at the youths around me. I share their age. I share their suitability to this day. Or I should but don't. I stare with sad longing at the deckchaired oldsters. That's where I should be. I'm not feeling up to this promenade of youth.

Despite all this dusty discomfort this is one of the better places to be today. This health-giving sunshine seems less onerous here than it did in the streets. In the microwave jumble of glass, concrete and dust. In the

185

citystew. Nonetheless, I need a rest. I've had a bad afternoon. I want to watch its death in comfort. A little sit-down is what I require.

I passed out again, you see. I lit out. It was much worse this time. I had a deal of bad dreams. Nasty, depressing dreams. All about things I didn't want to know or learn. What is it with these dreams of mine? Why do they wish me this harm? I didn't invite the bastards. They're free to leave when the fancy strikes them. They never do. What do they want with me? I've got it bad enough already. Where is my auctorial control?

This passing out business is beginning to worry me somewhat. This time loss of mine has been on the up and up in recent weeks. For instance, last Friday I didn't actually pass out as such (I think) but I had a complete memory lapse between noon and evening. I suddenly found myself in Victoria coach station (not somewhere I'd willingly go, poor as I am). I was bewildered and frightened. I had no idea where I'd been or what I'd been doing. This temporal manque both surprised and depressed me. I knew what it meant – more or less. At the very least, I knew that it wasn't good news. I probably hadn't done very much that would be fun to remember – it was just the principle. I'm not sanguine enough about my life to write off the odd bad day here and there. I need all of my days, good or bad.

You can imagine that this kind of thing makes you think a little. I wondered to what I owed this new diversion. Hunger? Exhaustion? Poverty? Boredom? God knows.

Needless to say, my bad dreams were all about Laura. They were very bad indeed. Not a lot of romance to be had. They all came to their squalid, graceless end without resort to pleasure of any kind. Nasty loveless Laura. Hardly fair. When you dream about women, you generally expect some kind of sex, good or bad.

Upon waking from this most recent of my sad little trances, I felt so dreadful that I mosied on back to town. I was no longer in the mood for the metropolitan outskirts. Not in that mood at all. So now here I am, traipsing around the heated Serpentine, dodging the families, the doggies and the joggers. It's hardly ideal but probably the best of my day's swaps. Barn Elms was getting me down.

Now I seek a bench, I seek my sit-down. I want a rest. I can manage one of those, I think. I trundle through the trees, eyes swivelling and feet superblistered. This is deckchair land all right. They charge money for the use of these spindly, rickety seats. So, I can't take one of those. Obviously. I haven't the courage needed to defy the merest deckchair attendant, be he ever so infirm. I slouch grassily past the seated ranks of OAPs, fat businessmen and bored, defiant non-paying punks. I revise my options and try to find a tree against which I may sit. That's it. I find it easily. Midway on the slope backing from the boating lake, it stands in tall splendour, free of satellite chairs. It spreads high above me, leafy, immense and free of charge. I plant my arse amongst its roots and ease my knobbly back onto its yielding bark. I breathe and smile, relieved. My poor feet inflate and my knees click and clack in unexpected luxury. This is the happiness I've wanted.

Contentedly, I watch the boating lake palpitate in the dying heat and the dawdling, baked crowds slip away. The broom of lassitude sweeps me up and cools me off a little. My sweat bubbles and dries. The afternoon fades, tired and grateful. It will be dark soon. Saturday night and fun will be had. Even by me. In a way – of its sort. We know that nights are usually bad news for me and Saturday is especial but I have a feeling that this one will be cool and welcome. Friendly and forgiving. Come. I need a little night.

It has to be said I am feeling appreciably worse – older, sadder and less buoyant than I have felt for a very long time. The asperity of my decline is breathtaking, its projected speed delightful. I was a fool to think that this indigence would fail to take its toll. I'm starting to suffer now. I'm growing replete with jaded beggary. It occurs to me of a sudden that I can scarcely be a quarter of the fellow I claim to be. It's sad. All, I trust, will end in tears.

No, I must not dissemble when it comes to the tale of my deterioration but I must be wary of the hyperbole of intermittent self-pity. It's not that I'm spreading myself too thinly. It's just that there's little left to spread.

This lowslung sun has fallen further and now fringes the lower reaches of the gleaming horizon. Folk shade their eyes from the slanting glare and stand in weird silhouette tableau. The bustle has eased with the heat and the afternoon palls hard. Late Saturday afternoons are always like this. Strange, limbo-like, disaffected. Glamourless and restive, time for the football results and dressing for the night's excesses. It's never much of a nice time. Composed of dust, beer smells and boredom, it used to get me down when I was a kid. It's like that now. The proletarian smell of ironing board, the dust and the flat glad glare.

Just because Laura committed the sin of not loving me doesn't mean that I was entirely without the comfort that women could bring at Cambridge. As a matter of fact, girls would leap on my bones with startling regularity. Mostly without success, it must be added. For some reason I came over all abstemious at Cambridge. I kept refusing to sleep with gorgeous women! Incredible but true. It's well-documented. Check it out if you like.

First there was Vanessa, six foot one, emaciated, supertanned and demanding with her hundred-pound hairstyles. She was a friend of Laura's; pampered and used to getting what she wanted. The wanting of me was easy, the getting of me slightly more difficult. Though not by much. You might deem it undiplomatic to pursue a girl (Laura) by porking her best friend (Vanessa). You would be right. And so I didn't. Pork Vanessa, that is. I did everything but. I beguiled and lured her, I fed her dreams and hopes and made damned sure that she loved me bad. This she did with some alacrity. I had a lot of what she wanted. It is with some wicked retrospective nostalgia that I admit that I broke that rich girl's poor heart. Looking back, it was probably good for her. Didn't someone say that all experience is invaluable, especially pain? Yes, someone did. Me, I think.

Vanessa once threatened to kill herself if I didn't shtup her on the spot. I was flattered but hardly convinced and when I turned her down, she got engaged to an Arc and Anth from Magdalene instead. Suicide might have been kinder.

My brief excursions into the actorly world were also immensely female fruitful. It was through acting that I met the diminutive Sarah. She was playing Ophelia to my masterly Hamlet and was keen to get into my hose though there would have been little room as Gertrude was honouring me with her gymnastic attentions at that time. So Sarah and I had a more or less Platonic situation going. Occasionally, she would discard her garments and present her breasts to me with the words 'God, dontcha just love my tits?' Sarah was really inordinately fond of her small but splendid bosom and, I must admit, with some justification. She would write interminable letters to me mostly complaining about my 'existential otherness' and 'destructive sensuality'. (I kid you not – ask her if you don't believe me!)

My strange accord with Sarah quickly faded to recrimination and hauteur. Sarah's problem was that her intelligence was matched only by her immaturity. I think I might have mentioned this once. It was a pity about Sarah. I liked Sarah. I could have gone for her. It was, sadly, not to be.

I also had a Thespian introduction to Julia. Julia was a swinging legal woman who played Kate to my brilliant, picaresque Petruchio. I actually had a vague affair with Julia. (These things were always *vague* at Cambridge.) Julia was hard, brisk and brilliant. In my early, hickish days, she typified the spirit of London for me – swift, rigid and quick to dismiss. Sex with Julia was akin to visiting the lavatory. Once, with the chivalrous intent of cunnilingual compliment, I began to slide down her ample form when I was yanked up by the hair. She gazed at me in fury and hissed at me, 'Don't you ever,' she spat, 'don't you ever do that!' Needless to say, I didn't. Julia was terrified of tenderness or endearment. Anything less than cautious bitching was an affront to her. The merest acknowledgement of gratitude or affection would send her scuttling for cover, gagging in helpless contempt. Weakness, poverty, imperfection or unhappiness revolted her. They had no place in her plans and could not be considered. With my bulging satchel of inadequacies, quirks and gross realities, I presented her with a multitude of problems which she did her best to ignore. We managed friendship in the end, just about, but romance had to bite the flawed, human dust.

There were others, quite a few others. I was a pretty handsome, sexy sort of person and much came easy to me. I didn't do all the boffing I could have done. I took nowhere near all of my chances. I perfected the regretted refusal. With surplus of sadness I would decline these erotic challenges. I told some awful whoppers. Some huge wobbling edifices of deceit and fantasy to excuse myself. It's curious what crap folk will believe given the chance. Girls don't mind if you don't sleep with them as long as you come up with some spectacular spoofing. Tell them you have cancer, no dick, Mexican gonococcal pharyngitis or an ineradicably homosexual leaning. (N.B. Never, but *never* tell a girl you don't want to sleep with that you have only three weeks to live. She'll be combing your pubes with her teeth in seconds!)

I did all this turning down because I felt that I should keep myself sporadically clear for the gorgeous, remote Laura. In the end it was a point-less exercise for though I slept most of my undergraduate nights alone in my own bed, the extent of my venery was exaggerated and fabricated to ridiculous lengths. According to popular varsity gossip, I only stopped screwing to eat and would sometimes even take a flask and sandwiches to consume on site. Patently untrue, of course, but surprisingly difficult to deny convincingly. And perhaps a myth not entirely unpalatable to my stock of self-regard. So Laura was kept fully informed of my coltish frisk-ings. By God, I wish now I'd done half of the rogering that was attributed to me.

Despite all the tampon tantrums, glaring illogicalities and vigorous lunacies that I endured with my Cambridge women, they gave me a fucking good time. They were all young, intelligent and undaunted by con-sequence. Even the most fraught Cambridge romance was free of the tender humiliation, warped emotion and scarred outcome that bedevils most of the world's love affairs. This is probably because nothing bothered people very much at Cambridge. There was little considered worth raising your pulse for. This was a nice if dull arrangement. Life tended to be pretty civilised when free of trauma. Excess had no part to play (except in my maudlin musings upon Laura).

Thus it is that the little town of Cambridge always holds for me the sweet redolence of blameless sex and sentiment. In fact when I was last in Cambridge, about a year ago, I suffered an erection walking down King's Parade, so pleasant were my memories. On the best of my past imperfect mornings I would rise from the rumpled but crisp bed of some pukka, charming natural scientist, stoke up on twelve o'clock coffee in some dull café, have lunch, smoke a bit, bid a brief but poignant farewell to my lovely boffin and stagger back to my room for a nap or a quick dip into some metaphysics. This was my life and a fucking brilliant one it was and all! I journeyed from idle pleasure to seamless content stopping off at painless ease on the way. I had it good. This was perfectly correct and just how it should have been. After the relentless, nineteen-year shitstorm that I'd just braved I deserved a good time! I called in my debts, I realised my assets, I hedged my bets, I called the shots, I shot the breeze, I made every incomprehensible cliché my own.

The whole thing would have been idyllic – the sudden money, the privilege, the sharp educative women and all that – it would have been idyllic if it had not been for the cruelties inflicted upon me by the evil Laura who seemed perversely intent on not falling in love with me. At one point I thought I'd try a little demonstrable and athletic heroism. I persuaded Vanessa to watch me in the Final of the Colleges' Cup, making sure that Laura would tag along. Soccer was my forte and I felt sure to dazzle and arouse her inexplicably dormant passions. In the event, I did rather well. Fucking well, as a matter of fact. Limberquick, dartsharp, I shone. Trim and tricky, I played a frigging blinder. (If George Best had been half the player I am, he would have made it!) I scored a hat trick naturally and rings round the oafish, lumpen opposition. I spoiled it a bit by getting sent off for taking a swing at their goalkeeper, something that had never happened in the eighty-year history of the competition. I considered this to be the most dashing of my roguish achievements but apparently Laura had told Vanessa that it was a pity that I was such a boor. This was probably the least disastrous of my attempts to impress Laura.

I bribed my way into the First Eight, I wrote poems, I sent her unattributed flowers for which she thanked the stunted, noisome Greg, I brushed my teeth, combed my hair and behaved in the most unreasonable fashion. None of it worked. When I came to Laura's attention it was invariably due to some wild folly or blushing miscalculation. I couldn't seem to strike the note of attractive desperation.

When I looked at old Greg I was bewildered. I couldn't understand it. This dwarf, this prat, this hapless, feckless mediocrity! What could she want with him? I came to the conclusion that I was simply too tall, sexy and clever for Laura's taste. That helped a little. Only a little.

(Oh that Laura! She gave me trouble. She whopped the worst of it into me. Down the treelined space of all my fantasies she walked in beauty on troubled ground, thinking of England and what it had stolen, a splash of ecstasy on my blackened grass.)

Back here in Hyde Park, old sunnybuns has tripped heavily down these airy stairs. A bright but fading segment peeps above the tallest of a distant clutch of buildings. We still have this glare business. The sticky, linear light trails along the earth, slicing sharp shadows through the figures of buildings, trees and crowd. Patches of low rogue glint blind the eye. I grimace in discomfort and shift round profilewise to shade my eyes from this attack. Under a bright adjacent tree I spot a colleague, a fellow mendicant.

He is an ugly, soiled middle-aged man with a vile rash seaming down one side of his face. His hair shines and bubbles in the moistening heat. From the folds of his moth-and-bug-eaten garments peeps a balloon of grey, hairy belly, dimpled and oblong. His face is ragged with disease and dirty beard, his eyes heavy with old debauchery. He is not a man you would necessarily want to have sex with. No indeed! He doesn't look like a nice sort of chap at all. God, I hope he's not a friend of mine!

Embarrassing but not impossible. Indeed, he seems to be eyeing me with something akin to sodden recognition. I could actually be acquainted with this creature. Goodness me, I should not be ashamed of it. Certainly not! Jesus himself was very keen on the destitute and stoutly repulsive amongst us. He was practically a tramp himself! Lazarus was a vagabond. Yes, Big Laz was a tramp and a half. It's cool to know *clochards*. It's chic. It's suave. If old Christyboots could manage it, I should have no trouble.

Catching my eye, he makes an ashy swipe at a smile of amicable bond. His brown, barnacled teeth fail to gleam in his sloppy grin. Yuk. I search my memory uneasily. I look back upon both volumes of 'Vagabonds I have known'. I run through the lists of Paddys, Mickeys, Jimmys, Billys, Jocks and Johnnys. No, I don't seem to find him there and I could hardly forget a scrofulous wretch like him.

Uhoh! He stuttershuffles from under the lee of his tree and stops short in confusion. Oh dear, crustychops here is obviously thinking about approaching me. For all my sudden access of Christlike egalitarianism, I can't help feeling that this would be an awfully bad idea on his part. I'm not looking forward to his society. I turn my head away and try to look as though I'm thinking of something else. I hum a mental tune and pray desperately that he won't approach. I don't want you seeing this kind of thing.

191

I turn back and see him still rooted to his spot, thankfully. I wonder what he could want from me? Money, sympathy, sex? As a matter of fact, now that I think about it, he does seem rather familiar. But how could I know someone like him? He's a bad kind of tramp. A dirty, diseased, greedy kind of tramp. He's the kind of tramp that other tramps wouldn't let their daughters marry. Where have I seen him before?

Oh shit! Here he comes. He has conquered his diffidence and limps towards me with a grisly expression of solidarity hoisted onto his rancid features. His dirty old eyes have caught mine and they aren't letting go. I stare at him with (I hope) undisguised loathing.

'Awright, mate?' he queries solicitously. Wonderful – he's Scottish – just what I need right now! He is much uglier at close range and un-believably foul-smelling, even to a BO veteran like me. Try as it might, my snob nose cannot help wrinkling with disgust.

'Gorrenny smokes on ya?' he growls.

'No, sorry.'

He eyes me with brutal, drunken disfavour.

'Sure about that?' he demands with menace and intent.

Oh, so he wants a little trouble, this monster. He wants to play the punching game. This is a pity. I'm not really in the mood. I have no hatred to spare at the moment. Nonetheless, if it comes to that, I will naturally do my best to accommodate him. I reply in what I judge to be soft, slow tones of guarded threat.

'I haven't got any cigarettes, I told you that.'

He shrugs extravagantly and smiles a green and runny smile. He comes over all friendly and tries to put his arm around me. I skip away quickly but the odours that escape from his oxters make my head swim. He pauses, offended. Tramps are funny like that. They'll try to stand on their dignity whenever possible. Foolish behaviour. There's never much of a foothold here. He speaks again.

'Och, forget about it, friend. Forget about it. Iss awright. I know. You know me. I know all about it. Iss awright. Don't you worry.'

It's exactly this kind of sozzled vagabond that always comes out with exactly that kind of dismal crap. To what regions of absurdity and austere futility must their minds reach for these meaningless mumblings. What do they mean who have no meaning left? What do they try to say when they say this kind of thing? Who asks? Who answers? Who's interested?

'D'ya hear me, friend? You kin tell me. I know all about it. I'm your pal.'

His eyes are glazed with pain and strange intention. He knows what he's talking about. No one else does but he seems pretty sure of his ground. I stiffen my legs and straighten my back, just to let him see how tall I am. Just to let him know precisely what he's taking on. He doesn't seem unduly impressed and glares at me, undaunted. The sun is fully in my eyes now and it does me the favour of rendering this thing's features hazy and indistinct.

'Go away now,' I advise, quite calmly, rather pleasantly. This could be a mistake. As I've hinted tramps can be surprisingly touchy. Still, he's only an old beggar and I'm feeling lucky.

'Ah now, don' be like that! We're pals. Jus' gimme a couple of wee smokes an' I'll be on my way. A couple of fags an' I'll leave you alone. Okay? I know all about it. I know. Isna right? Isna? Me an' you, pal, we're awright. We're just awright! Don't fockin' tell me. I'm not stupid! D'ya think I'm feckin' stupid? Issat what ya think? Issat? Tell me. Issat?'

I've noticed that tramply conversations tend to form a depressing spiral. One can't but help going down with them. You can't glitter in conversation with a tramp. It is impossible to emerge from a down and out dialogue looking and sounding like Oscar Wilde. It can't be done. Aphorism would be misplaced. I'm endeavouring to ask this person to go away now but it's not working. My message is not coming across as forcefully as I would like. I've got myself into an exchange here. A disquisition on motive and outcome. I'm getting bogged down. It's always like this.

'Fuck off!' I posit, neatly. Like I say – hard to shine.

'That's a fuck, at a fockin', don' you try that, pal! Don' you feckin' try that. Fockin' bastard. Didna see ya yessurday wi' a full fockin' packet, ya lying cunt! D'ya think you're feckin' better than me . . . d'ya? Eh? Eh? D'ya think you're berrer than I am? Ah, you're no fockin' good. D'ya know what you are? Yerra cunt! Yerra feckin' cunt!'

I try to smile at a young woman who passes by, giving us a wide berth. I try to look aggrieved, harassed. Bloody tramps! my eyes say. They never leave you alone.

I stare at my interlocutor, my mouth tight with ever-decreasing patience. He too is angry, choking and spluttering in his wrath. His hands work with quick, vicious annoyance. He points and gesticulates, his crusty fingers close to my face. I draw back a little more and notice that the deckchaired respectables are now staring at our little scene with some disapproval. These disputes are always rather drawn-out affairs. They start with the keen hectoring of the supplicant, moving slowly onto a plateau of profanity and abuse, screaming hard into each other's faces and then finally dribble into violence of varying quality depending on age and how petty the discord is.

'I told you already, I have no cigarettes. Now fuck away off before I kick you shitless!'

Oh, this is poor, not very good at all. Very unfrightening stuff. I slipped up there. Encouraged by my feeble taunts, his ire grows apace. He spits thick on the innocent grass. His voice stretches thin with hysteria.

'Ya cunt! Don't you feckin' try that on me, ya wee bastard! Ya want me to break yer feckin' balls for ye? Didna see ya? Didna see ya yesterday? Ya lying cunt! Whoojoo think you are? I saw ya sneak off with that wee tart yessurday, smoking away like the selfish cunt y'are. Wuddn't give a fella so much as a feckin' smoke out of friendship. Y're a cunt. A dirty, fockin' cunt!'

Oh, so that's it. Yessurday? Indeed. This guy obviously noticed me in that rubgrub shameshop of yesterday. He mustn't have liked my flash exit. He saw my shy ciggies. He wants some of that. Well, tough titty! Even if I had some left, he wouldn't have a fucking chance. He's getting on my tits, this fellow. I'm sorry for his trouble but I've got increasing problems of my own. He'll have to go. He really must.

He has noticed my recognition and stands squat before me, his short, smelly legs wide in a square stance of combative readiness. Christ, I almost laugh. I'd rather not hit him but I won't be slow to break his bones and mash his brain if called upon. I feel suddenly better and speak to him with some final elegance.

'Now see here, my indigent friend, you really *will* have to toddle off now. Content yourself that I am tobaccoless. You will find no joy here. If you stay, I'll be under the unwelcome necessity of beating the crap out of you. In short, if you like life, lope off before you lose it!'

This is more the tone. He stops mumbling for a moment and stares at me with sludgy incomprehension in his mean little eyes. I smile encouragingly. I mustn't expect too much from these people. His eyes bulge and his lips tremble with slobbery fury.

'Ya bastard, ya cunt, ya feckin' cunt, ya whoorbag!'

His frothing, champing maw spills buckets of screeching obscenities. His grimy hands form puny fists which he shakes in my amused face. He stamps his feet and yells his silly yells.

'. . . ya cunt, ya bastard, ya dirty, greedy focker! Ya rotten bastard, ya cunt . . . !'

We seem to have moved on to the mad abuse stage here. Next, we'll have the violence, I trust. Some of the deckchair dwellers have moved off already, peeved and muttering. The endless claxon of his hatred continues uninterrupted, a steady, reasonless flow. These people become apoplectic at the drop of a hat. They have a lot of despair to burn off. I'm told that when actors have to cry they usually try to think of the sad things that have happened in their lives, so the best weepers are the hardest livers. It must be something of the same for a tramp. Only easier.

194

'. . . ya dirty, filthy, feckin' whoor, ya cunt, ya bastard! I'm gonna feckin' kill ya. I'm gonna tear yer fockin' dirty head off!'

Yes. Yes, of course. Roll on. Keep it coming you sad troglodyte. You missing link. Tell me all about it. I want to know.

'You're a dead man, ya cunt! You're feckin' dead, ya dirty bastard . . . I'm gonna . . .'

I stick out a cute right jab. It lands nicely on the side of his mouth, sounding a good crunch and slap. He looks surprised for a moment before rocking back onto his heels. His hands fly to his face and his eyes look up at me in shock. I swipe again, my meaty paws rapid and urgent with joy. It swings round to the side of his jaw and thwunks hard upon the bone. He bites the dust this time, falling hard and fast. A low wail escapes from his fisted mouth and he rolls away, covering his head with his hands.

I got pissed off, tired of it. I lost my rag. Hardly admirable, I agree but what can a poor boy do?

He stumbles to his feet, quickly recovered, and gives vent to a brutal squeal of pain and rage. I'm rather taken aback by this unearthly noise and lose a little nerve. This gives him time to scramble towards me with his old arms whirling in attack. A flailing fist catches me hard on the nose and I feel a spurt of wet warmth splash my face. Another wild swipe jabs my throat surprisingly hard and as I gag and choke he kicks me brutally on the pelvis and starts to hammer my back and head. I bend in pain. This is going less well than I had hoped. I had not envisaged this. I feel my shin split and crack as he sends a massive blow into my left leg. Right, that's it! This agony is sharp, shrill and euphoric. The draught I needed. A big mistake. I begin to lose my temper.

Surprise over, pain finished, excess invited and fury here to stay, I recommence my onslaught. I whip the back of my skull into his face and hear a pleasantly moist crunch. I am straight now and he hovers before me with his ruined face steady, targetstill. I whip my arm round and send a huge elbow punch into the exact centre of his bloody visage. He grunts in hard breathloss and stumbles back again, I follow and repeat the process twice, driving him groggily back each time until his back hugs my erstwhile tree. I pause for a tiny breath before punching him hard and straight in the throat. I feel something give way in there and my heart races with mad hatred. I bring my leg high, foot arched and stamp hard at his groin, twice before falling over in disequilibrium.

I roll away, just in case, and leap quickly to my feet, feeling abruptly lithe and full of energy. He is slumped against the tree still, his mucky gob weeping gore onto his chest, his hands cupclutched around his crushed testicles. He chokes and coughs blood and breaths harsh, scraping and wheezing. I waltz in again.

(You see, I should have started it off like this. I never had much of a jab. My combination work was good but my jab was always weak. I was all one hand. Boxing is no use to me here. It's demolition I want.)

My trusty feet come into play here and I try a series of jarring, inhuman kicks into his ribs and hip. He crunches, snaps and cracks audibly and despite stubbing my toe on his thighbone, I am much encouraged. He is prone now. Legs tiring, I opt for a rest, sending one final clubbing boot into the side of his head just to give me some breathing space. I don't want him dishing out any nasty surprises.

Phew! Ooooh! Oh boy, I'm bushed! This kind of thing takes it out of you. He stirs again and I jump up and down upon him in mild frenzy, grinding my feet to kill any pugilistic hopes he might still harbour. After a final series of valedictory stampings, I stumble away, my pulse tumbling with wary distaste. An airy belt of pain appears artfully just below my ribs as I try to fight for my breathing rights. Dear me!

As I pant steadily in recovery I listen to his moans and gurgles and watch as the onlookers try to look away convincingly. Apart from the disaffected punks who have already cheered once or twice, I don't think anyone has enjoyed watching this. The geriatrics scuttle away self-righteously, obviously looking for a policeman. I look back at the messy heap of my opponent. There is a fuck of a lot of blood around the place. I'd better bugger off before the fuzz trundles along. This doesn't look much like the handiwork of self-defence. I might have killed the stupid old bastard!

I check that he's still breathing before moving off as casually as I can. The thing is not to run. I pass through the thick, censorious gaze of the furtive witnesses and strike diagonally across the park. I head towards Speakers' Corner, keeping up a smart and wary pace. My head throbs and my skull itches with pain and irritation. He hit me a couple of good ones, to my surprise. I wipe my nose and find more snot than blood. I run my blind palms over my face, checking on my spurious normality. It all seems pretty much OK. I'll pass – just about.

I walk on the grass, I lurk between the trees. After that little episode, I'm not feeling sociable. I want to get back to the streets before I get arrested.

I don't know what happened to me back there. I went spare. I blew up. Jesus! I really overdid it. That stupid fucking bastard! I didn't want any trouble. God, I hope I haven't killed him. That would be wonderful. Murder! What next? Christ, I really gave it to him. He'll never survive that. I didn't mean to go so far. I lost my rag. I frothed, I screamed, I raged – Hell, I just let it get to me.

The sun has dropped out of sight now and the sky is flat with dimming haze and sunless colour. A little wind has whipped up and it dries my sweating face. I spot a couple of bobbies dawdling down a nearby path and quicken my pace as unobtrusively as possible, then plough on, frightened and depressed. This has been a bad day and it's getting worse. I'm practically jogging by now and have to steel myself to slow to a more natural, less conspicuous pace. I don't want any friendly interest for a while.

Oh no! Jesus Christ, no! It can't be, it can't. No!

About fifty yards in front of me, I see a hunched bloody figure shouting crazed obscenities at me. It's him. Unbelievably, he's come back for more. He clatters towards me while I stand immobilised by terror and disbelief. Lazarus-like, he's tramped on back from the dead. He seems very pissed off indeed and despite his limp and my well-placed additions to his handicaps he moves quickly, scuttling horribly. Help! Not this. Not again!

Ten yards off, I see the glint of his blade. My tired mind jolts into fear. This is a new game. He wants to give me a sharp reminder.

I watch as his stubby, evil arm sweeps towards me clutching its thin slice of steel. I step back quite slowly and my overcoat flaps open allowing the blade to slip and slice neatly along the front of my shirt. A tiny scream of ripping cloth and I'm all cut up. A diagonal, strangely pleasant, warm sting of sensation lights up on my chestflesh and I bellow in fright. By God, he's stabbed me, the bastard!

I should be terrified but I am so exasperated that I have no time for fear. That's it! I'm getting tired of this guy. I swing wildly at him in an access of mad anger. I miss luckily and his knifeswipe swishes past my stumbling face. It was eyebound, that one. He stands to face me, his knife raised. He thinks he has me here. He lunges knifefirst at my stomach. It is an easy task to step aside and deliver a snaphard kick into his ailing kidneys. He swings round, blade high and waves his danger at my throat. To his surprise I ignore the knife and kick him again. In the abdomen this time and very hard indeed. He looks at me as I jump back out of range. There is a tiny, laughable pause before he chokes, crumples and starts to spill thick blood from his already streaming gob. The knife quivers in his hand and I step in to kick it away. Without his weapon, the man bends full and clutches his ruined gut. He moans and slobbers another great splash of blood before sinking to his knees. This is over for him now. His brief business with me is concluded. He keens frothily, glugging and stammering in his own blood. He's run out of argument.

I inspect my wound. It extends thinly from my left nipple, seaming down past my navel. Deeper at the top, it bleeds surprisingly little. A pretty ineffective attempt, it must be said. But still, painful and annoying. Looking at the figure of my enemy kneeling in bloody atonement my impatience returns with renewed vigour. I'm calm and rational but quite disgruntled.

Quickly, I look around me to check that there are no coppers lurking before swinging my foot with all my might full into the bastard's chest. I hear the sound of what can only be several ribs shattering and he crumples backwards surprisingly slowly. Good. I walk around him and kick him in the side of his skull for the second time that day. Better. His head snaps sideways and lolls horribly. I didn't kick him very hard. It isn't easy to really give it to someone on the bonce. Civilisation has seen to that.

I looked down on his plastered, vanquished face. His mouth is open and a tooth lodges in a pool of gore forming in one of the folds of his neck. His breath makes bloody bubbles as it escapes his mashed mouth and nose. It hasn't been much of a day for him either.

A quartet of peevish car horns sing their busy song on Park Lane. Tyres whine as the loser brakes hard and the winner revs off in gross triumph. Traffic seems silly at a time like this, I must say. Very tired, my legs ache and my long incision weeps as I bend down to pick up his knife. The sudden pain annoys me and revives my flagging anger. It's not really a knife. Just a sharp piece of metal with black tape wound round one end. I wonder where he got this. I can't really see him making it. He doesn't seem the artisan type to me. The shoddy nature of this Bogle-slicing implement irritates me further. I grasp the handle end tight and walk back to its owner.

Oh, he is looking very bad. He is looking terrible, awful! It's quite upsetting. This is a big moment in this creature's life. Today spells the end of an awful lot for him. His jaw looks broken, I'm certain a couple of ribs bit the dust, his kidneys can't be feeling too clever and his head must hurt like fuck! In addition, something internal must be in trouble to spew up all that heavy, smelly gore. He has lost a lot of the essentials. Hardly my fucking fault. I didn't ask him to try to kill me.

I tighten my grasp on the makeshift weapon once again. I calculate. I estimate. I choose my spot. Coldly furious and filled with calm hatred, I crouch beside his battered body. Hyde Park and I'm getting no hassle for this! What's happening to the world? As I bend over him, knife poised, a few small drops of my own blood drip and fall onto his breast mingling with his darker, wetter stuff. How's that for fortuitous profundity? I've picked my spot, I've gripped my blade. I'm ready.

As I prepare to stick him like an old pig, the man grunts and slobbers loudly. It is an attempt at speech. I'm surprised he can still manage it. He raises his head and looks at me (I think) through his mask of blood and pain. He tries to lift a hand as his own blade moves against him. He sobs and gurgles in wide-eyed terror and flops back.

I pause, I gather strength and summon ire. I look at him, I raise the knife, I shut my eyes and . . .

And?

I chuck the nasty, smeared thing away from me wearily and stand with slow, sorry pain. Why do that? What's worth that? Who needs it?

I walk away, quickly. My shirt torn, my head sore and my belly wet with blood. The sun has long gone and the late spring day delves into early evening as I put my feet onto the pavements of Park Lane. I look back and see that a small crowd has gathered around my fallen friend. It can't be very nice for them.

These days Oxford Street doesn't shut up in the evening and I find myself plunging into a sudden mass of jostling crowd. Instinctively, the crowd forms a slipstream around me and I am not mauled too much. This is good news as the slightest bump might just finish me off.

The shops glare their pious, backstairs glare and the street lamps hum and pop as they are switched on. They darken the sky and lend sombre weight to this new pain of mine. The faces around me are studious, shopping, hustling, dealing faces. They are young, semi-bright and hard. They billow past me, staring at my wet red stripe of stomach. I button my overcoat and hug my arms tight round my cooling trunk. There is no heat now. The day's warmth has died and my flesh prickles with cold. My heart slows gradually. Calm. Rest. Debrief. I breathe deeper now and pause for nought. The passing people stare still, their eyes hard with contempt. I discover that I am crying. My wet little tears are tripping me. I stop and drift to the inside of the pavement, leaning my head against the sprightly shine of a shoeshop window. They shuffle past me, changing course, avoiding me and my embarrassments. I move my head to wipe my face and notice that the window is now smeared with my blood and sweat. I wipe the window instead and walk again. Snailslow, the sky deepens to dark as I watch. Oh God! Oh Jesus fucking Christ!

*

I think many of my personal problems stem from the fact that I never knew who my father was. My real father that is, the man who paid the halfpenny or whatever it cost in 1963 to shtup my old mother. Surprisingly, I was largely untroubled by any filial calculations until I went to Cambridge. Then someone asked me if I never wondered about it. Promptly, I began to wonder about it.

In a sense I was lucky. I had a wide choice of potential pater and could take my speculative pick. A lot of men have visited a prostitute at some point. It really could have been almost anyone. Soon, every time I saw an attractive or admirable man over forty years of age I would begin my extravagant chronological calculations. My eyes would mist and my throat would swell with tender, sonly thoughts. At one mad point, I even began to notice an unmistakable resemblance between myself and the Duke of Edinburgh. No kidding! That long drop of nose, that straight forehead and flat, rigid wipe of thin mouth. It wasn't so very implausible. You really never know. That pomposity, that snobbery and abrasiveness. 'Daddy!' I cried.

At the time, other imagined fathers included: Richard Burton, Gerry Fitt, Philip Larkin (!), Denis Law, Colin Cowdrey, Rab Butler, Ringo Starr, Bill Shankly, Robert Graves, Paul Schofield, Enoch Powell, Peter O'Toole, Seamus Heaney, Cliff Richard (!!), Richie Benaud, Robert Kennedy, Jean-Paul Sartre, Ronald Biggs, Clint Eastwood, Chris Bonnington, Harold Pinter, Gore Vidal (?), Tony Jacklin, Lord Lucan, Jean Genet, Pele, Anthony Burgess, Robert Mitchum and Pat McGahey, barman in the Sports Bar on the Lower Falls during the early months of 1963.

Sad, isn't it? Rather endearing? I don't know why I bothered really. He was probably just a grimy Irish shit anyway, that father of mine. Why dream? Why bother?

SIX

Sloane Square. Twilight. The sky darkens and swirls above these flatwhite bands of pulsing street lamp. The square of groundlight flouts and repels the blanketed, infinite growth of dark overhead. I sit sad as the people move in crowdstamped hush and hurry and the cars grumble as they swing around the square. Blood seeps bitterly onto my tongue and I see a dart of shining lines at the blurred periphery of my vision. Evening is arriving and I'm ready for night. It's bad. *I'm* bad! I've got to sleep. I'm dying here.

All this locational detail may be relentless but it's what matters most to me. These days few of my dramas occur indoors. I have but a poor memory and my interiors are sketchy. Not that I need them anyway. The vast outdoors is my house and hall. I'm an exterior expert. I'm Prince of the Pavements, I'm the Parkbench King and the cold winds of the outside permanently fleck my flesh. To come with me, you too must brave the air and the wide bare boredom. Yes. Perambulation's the name of my game. I'm an outdoors kind of chap, more or less willingly. It's with purpose, fear and gratitude that I stalk the streets of the city.

This isn't so bad. It's mostly cold and wet and shitty, I admit, but its comforts are also sharp. The focus and range I inherit from all this space steadies me nicely. I can wheel and circle without restraint. The wide uncurtained music of landscape plays for me and I breathe unlimited by wall and roof. I have a kind of freedom. My nights are long and austere, dotted with light and incident. What homedweller could say the same? Quite a few, I should imagine.

I'm trying to find something good to say about having no home and all I can think of is its sporadic and stiffly sought visual appeal. Well, that's something and at least I make the effort.

By God, I'm tired. Terribly, horribly tired. My head is fuzzy with fatigue and my tenantless gut bubbles with nausea. My limbs are liquid and my mind is vacant, reluctant to work, demanding, militant. It hit me about ten minutes ago and I had to sit down so I plonked my arse right here in the middle of Sloane Square. I was plastered to the ground by a great slab of weariness. I just lit out. It was bad but I'm recovering.

You'll be wanting to hear about my wound, no doubt. Well, it's not as bad as it could have been. Seven or eight inches long, it scores raggedly across my ribs from my left tit down to my poor cold navel. It's not *very* deep but there is a little loose flap of flesh at the bottom which stings like buggery. I've bandaged it as well as I can with some cockeyed strips from my shirt. After the fight my shirt was already pretty fucked-up and these newest inroads into its structure have done it no good at all. It flaps wetly on my belly as I speak and exposes quite a lot of my chubs to the cruel, night air. Or at least, it would if I had not buttoned my coat so primly around my new weak spot.

Oh, it hurts. Yes, it certainly hurts an awful lot. A surprising amount of pain is most definitely issuing from that area. For instance, if I'd been asked, I would have declined this new joy. But I wasn't asked and here it is, so to speak. I think it needs stitches. It seems a safe bet. And probably quite a lot of stitches at that. At one point I toyed with the idea of nipping down to Casualty at Guy's or St Thomas's but I bottled out. They'd ask questions and probably fumigate me into the bargain. Those doctors, they're hard on tramps. They don't faff around; they hose the buggers before they'll lay a doctorly finger on them. And once again, I was scared of meeting someone I know. A lot of Cambridge medics do their Clinical at London hospitals. That would be very embarrassing, now wouldn't it? 'There's a stabbed tramp in cubicle four, doctor!' 'That's all right, nurse, I was at Cambridge with this man ... and what are you doing with yourself, these days, Bogle old chap?' I'd blush, really.

(Which reminds me – about yesterday's charitable bim in that soup kitchen I patronised. You remember. Well, I have to confess that I did know her as a matter of fact. She was at Cambridge with me. I didn't like to mention it yesterday. I hadn't got to the better bits of my story. Must have been a shock for the poor girl. Tee hee.)

Anyway, back to my battle honour. Like I say, it almost certainly requires stitches but I'm afraid it's going to have to seal itself. I hope it manages OK. I'm no good with gangrene.

So, what did you think of all that fight business? Pretty revolting, wasn't it? I didn't like to do it, believe me. But, realistically, what choice did I have? Discussion? Surrender? A plea of polite pacifism? Do you really think he would have listened to my effete, decorous reservations? He didn't seem the sweet-reasoned type to me. God, I duffed him up pretty bad. I really whopped him about. I went too far, I suppose. But at least I didn't stab him. At least, I didn't do that. The shape he was in by the end, it probably wouldn't have made much difference if I had. A nasty business. Are you disgusted with me? Disappointed? Outraged? Do you think I overreacted? What would *you* have done? Not that, eh? I hope you still like me. I hope you do.

Of course, on the other hand, what am I saying? Why apologise? The guy cut me. The dirty old bastard sliced me up. You could say that he deserved anything I dished out. I did the right thing. I did the manly deed.

Nonetheless, the incident hasn't helped my day which stumbles on in joyless stamina. I got hot under the collar. It takes time for one's pulse to calm after that kind of thing. I was panting like a rabid dog for about an hour and a half. Mad and sad. I was all a-flutter. I'm calmer now. I've eased off. This violence thing, it's no fun.

When I got my breath back I was feeling so less than fine that I decided to nip over to the King's Road to cheer myself up. That was a mistake. I've had some good times around here but that was then and this isn't by a very long way. Watching this evening's youthful exquisites promenade wasn't good for my morale. Thick-haired and smooth-skinned, they slouched their way into my bad books. They made this youth thing of ours seem so easy, so desirable. With their sharp clothes and enviably choreographed walks, with their chinkless belief and easy confidence, they got me down. So young, so strong, so fucking beautiful! Jesus! It made me cast a new, jaundiced eye upon my own attire. Christ, I've been kidding myself! I look rough. I thought I'd been scraping by but I was badly wrong. Compared to these glittering folk I look like what I am. I fool nobody. My poor, grey, shrinking face and its hat of hair, of thick clot and dirt. My clothes and their fade and stain and fray. My peeling, splitting shoes and their sad glimpse of sockrag. And now my creeping crimson centrestain. My little blotch of blood. I look like the sad news I am.

All day I've been trying not to think about cigarettes. You might have noticed that I've mentioned them less. It was a feeble ruse at its best and the past couple of hours have routed it utterly. After the fight I was gasping badly enough but the King's Road really did it to me, left me desperate for nicotine. The terrible thing was that all these trendy young bastards were smoking away like gooduns. Taking two or three puffs and then chucking two good inches of faultless tobacco onto the pavement! My feeble pride prevented me from picking up these prizes. I might have tried it if it hadn't been for their cool, their youth, their arrogance and my jealousy. I couldn't manage it though. I have only five left and I bleed in need of smoke.

Fat black taxis spill fat white theatregoers outside the Royal Court. The Thespians shuffle inoffensively into the building and I feel another jealous twinge. I'd love to go in there with them. I'd love to sit in that warm and populous dark and soothe my tired eyes in its distant blur of artful stagelight. Watching plays spells dosh to me. I've only ever been able to do it when I've had lots of lolly so all its associations are pleasant, solvent ones. It's an almost purely bourgeois form, let's face it. For all the well-paid anarchist grumblings of all those playwrights and directors and wankers, theatre belongs to the well off. The stalls of the Royal Court are rarely bursting with proud UB40 carriers. So what! What's wrong with the bourgeois and their gentle pleasures? By Jiminy, I'd like a little of that sort of thing now. That stage ease, that theatrejoy. A little prosperity and snooze and then some serious three-handed smoking in the interval. Why for that, I'd sell my soul.

Ah, but why dream? It's no use to me. Let's look at what I've got instead. This illuminated, churning square, the tripping young crowds, the hard cars and their circling noise, the big bad night, my eight-inch wound, my weary despair, my sad old self and story. Perhaps a little dreaming wasn't such a bad idea after all.

Across this square a girl screams loud and sudden. I glance over quickly, fearful for her, much concerned. I see her stand in her slippery white trousers and grey quasi-leather coat. She totters on tall red heels and seems vividly pissed off with what appears to be her beau for tonight. She bellows again, right in his bent face, and his white socks tremble. He makes a wide conciliatory gesture and she smacks him hard in the gob. He looks at her for a moment and steps politely aside, allowing someone to pass. Then he steps forward again and really lets fly at her. She takes it crack on the jaw and zooms groundward, surely dead. The young man runs an exasperated hand through his bleached, bouffant hair before bending down to help his lover to her feet. No! Ouch! Oh, I could have told him that would happen. A swift, sharp red heel bang in the jewels. He slumps on top of her clutching his groin and they writhe angrily on the guiltless pavement. I turn away and leave them to it.

It's certainly getting to be a nasty night. It seems that, come Saturday, our thoughts and deeds turn to violence. To rampage, barbarity, riot and brutality. For a moment there I was going to lay all this at the door of the yob amongst us but after my little adventure this evening I'm not going to get away with that, am I? That won't wash. What does the breaking of the week do to us? It's axiomatic that greater freedom spells greater licence means less restraint leads to abuse but that can't be the whole bit. All that glugging weekend booze certainly lends its anarchic hand but it doesn't explain the frenzy of intake, the mad dash for inebriation that Saturdays lead to. Everybody really slaps it into themselves on Saturday night. No one hangs back. They stuff it all down their necks, hard and fast. They guzzle, trough and slurp. They get too pissed to think and then try to kick the shit out of anyone who come to hand. To mark the end of the working week, so to speak. Christ, these people must have shitty jobs if this is how they celebrate. It's all just revenge, retribution. A spot of fervent grudge reduction.

Saturday's sins are liquid, frothy and come from bottles. Saturday's penance is sharp, bright and comes from cutlery drawers. Saturday's justification, its raison d'être eludes me. Football, supermarkets, furniture superstores, restless schoolkids, fishing? Are these things necessarily worth the sleepy sink of Sunday's repentance? Let's forget about Saturdays. Let's get rid of them, abolish the mad bastards!

I wince in stiffened bitterness as the gory thoroughfare in my belly creases. Its drying edges rub together and cause me what you might describe as some discomfort. I yelp softly to myself and clutch my ribs like a plugged but indomitable cowboy. Mad Bull Bogle gets it in the guts but takes a hunnerd darned Injuns with him to the great fatuous fantasy in the sky. (When I was a kid, I never dreamed of being a cowboy. This worried me. Made me suspect that I was queer or something. The Wild West didn't appeal. I thought cowboys were jerks. Chawin' quid, ropin' steers and talkin' bull all day. And then having to crap outdoors! What a bunch of prats! The Seventh fucking Cavalry shlepping into action in the nick of time. Eight million blood-crazed Apaches suddenly think, 'Aw fuck me, Sitting Squirrel, it's the Seventh Cavalry, let's bugger off before we get bored to death.' And then plucky May-Ann, pin-up of the wagon train who's got an arrow in her tit, gives brave and handsome Captain Bluster a fireside blowjob. I preferred the Indians with their groovy gear, wacky names and pliant squaws. I always thought I'd have made a good redskin. Anything for a shot at John fucking Wayne!)

These pleasant, light-hearted thoughts have done the trick. That stripe of hot pain has dripped away now and I'm only feeling awful again, thank God. Nothing like escapism.

Sloane Square has been a bad choice for my present slump. Not that I had much choice. I had to slump somewhere. Sloane Square is bad because of all these posh youngsters waltzing around. They show me the lunatic rate of my deterioration. At Cambridge I mingled unobtrusively with people like this. Now we inhabit different galaxies and belong to separate species. A minute ago, a little gaggle of gorgeous girls traversed this little middle island in crossing the square to the tube station. They tripped over these stones and slipped past my bench, eager and gladdening to behold. I watched them sadly, without hunger but brimming with disengagement tristesse. Distance pain. They were so clean and young and rich and nice. That was all gone for me. The bad thing was that they looked at me. They chucked a glance my way. They looked at me in that way of theirs. The way I've seen my girls look at cripples, road accidents, insects. The look that means they shouldn't see such things, things that have no place in their world of health and beauty. I've seen that look. And that's how these girls looked at me – with that calm disgust. More openly than usual. They must have thought I wasn't human enough to recognise their expression. Or maybe that look just looks different from this end.

At least the weathery sky is providing some edification. It's a beaut, a real little honey. Late evenings aren't always easy to place on the glamour scale between morning, afternoon and night. But this is definitely the best bit of today beautywise. Thick ribs of dark orange stretch round the sky and the heat has put its coat on. At this time the day breathes. The failures fade and the day crowds upon you jangling its sour merriness. Like oil on water it strands and separates. It hits you hard if you let it. But that you mustn't. You have to remember its lies and crimes and fight it dirty. You have to be hard.

The schools of trendies still revolve around my bench in their wide pavement circle. The cars are fewer but still parp their contribution. The air buckles and drifts, restless and confused. The lights flicker, splay, drip, glimmer and stutter and sweep. I am stiff with dynamic despair. Things have started to go wrong for me here. Oh deary me.

It wasn't long before things started to go wrong for me at Cambridge as well. I was encouraged by all the leeway people gave me on account of my Irishness and hard-boy image. I kept chancing my arm. I pushed my luck, shoved my fortune and jostled my fate. I persisted in going too far. I picked fights, skipped lectures, told lies, got pissed, taunted dons and made fewer friends. I fucked everyone off in a big way. I kept the porters sweet with my laddish, glad-eyed roguishness and was a big hit with the kitchen staff and bedders but the others were growing less keen on me by the minute. At the Boat Club Dinner (I crashed) I chatted up the Master's wife in rough-house manner and got chucked out. On another drunken occasion I made a pass at our dodgy Franciscan Chaplain, Brother Bunting. I chucked up in a supervision on Jane Austen and hit at a cheeky college groundsman for giving me lip. I dashed, I shone, I dazzled. I wazzed around like the big Bogle I was. I must have thought it was funny or cool or attractive – something like that. I was wrong.

I began to hear rumours of anti-me mumblings amongst the dons. The word was that they weren't going to stand for any more of my ostentatious oik hilarity. I was treading on toes and the toes weren't too chuffed about it. Towards the end of my first year things came to a head when I bawled out some freelance scribe from King's for giving me a whole load of crap about my politics. This was supposed to be when we were discussing the Faerie fucking Queene. All those dickless Trotskyists from King's got right up my arse. I lost my rag and told this guy exactly what kind of a wanker he was. It took a very long time.

Anyhow, they pulled me for it. I was hauled before Dr Byron, the Senior Tutor, on a cold and meagre day. The wind blew shrill and elegiac up the draughty old staircase as I thumped on his grumpy old door. Byron's secretary let me in. Like most men, I've always had a kink for the notion of the personal secretary. It always seemed like a neat arrangement to me. The old bag who now looked at me with her fastidious female distaste really nuked that idea. She was a middle-aged, ill-favoured old trout who smelt of hospitals and peppermints. She looked just the kind of wizened old bitch who prided herself on what a very good wizened old bitch she was. There was a fond myth amongst us romantic undergraduates that she was a secret and insatiable nymphomaniac with a pervy penchant for decrepit Cambridge dons. I didn't like to think about it. Her flattened potato face was heavy with aversion as she surveyed my shabby clothes and unshaven chin. (To be fair to her, I was looking pretty bad that day. Another fruitless night of Laura dreams, talking to myself and kissing my pillow.)

She told me icily that I was ten minutes late. She enjoyed telling me. I was glad it gave her pleasure and almost told her what a complicated life I led. Before I could, she disappeared into the other room with a soft, efficient hiss and swish of skirt on tights. There was a pause and I played with my nose for a while. The formidable matron returned and in a voice painted with a finely judged contempt for all things Bogleian, she intoned sepulchrally: 'You may go in now.'

Wow! May I? Horseshit! Hot dang! Aren't I the lucky one? Go in! I most certainly will! Whoop, whoop, wahey!

'Thank you,' I said.

Dr Byron's pad was pretty neat. A cavernous room – massive and overarched. Lots of dark-toned wood panelling and rich, heavy old furniture. Brimming with beauty and sloth and that sombre, venerable academic mustiness you get in period movies. It was much like a film set in general. It had huge latticed windows which filled the room with great sheets of light, a queer kind of dusty, trapped, museumed light. Bookful and boundless. There was a large and suitably faded globe in one corner and a huge spidery telescope blocking the door. Books, thumbed and unthumbed, were regimented neatly on the shelves – a paper palisade of lore and enquiry. Pompous old books, dusty and distinguished, unstained by coffee or jam, not a paperback amongst them. Byron himself was seated at a desk at one of the enormous lucifer windows looking onto the river. He looked up absently as I closed the door and craned himself elegantly out of his chair. His dull ochre tweeds sang a preserved duet with the decrepit atmosphere of the old room. A sage's fustian.

'Hi, Prof,' I said. 'I dig the crazy pad.'

No I didn't. I didn't say anything. Byron spoke first.

'Ah, Mr Bogle!' We shook hands with differing, double-aged grasps. 'Do sit down.'

I dropped my buns into one of his old armchairs and scratched my balls with conscious gracelessness. No point in courtesy if he was going to bawl me out. Byron remained standing.

'Would you like some sherry?'

'Nah, makes me puke. Thanks all the same.'

This was the lark and plan. Shake the smug old shit up a bit. Be good for him. I waited for his fury. There was a tiny silence before he replied with some aplomb.

'Yes, it invariably has the same effect upon me . . . but I'm told that this is what we are supposed to offer to our undergraduates.'

He seated himself gingerly as he spoke. Pacific and overlapped by knee. Undaunted by his élan, I began the business of lighting a B & H, neglecting to ask permission. That, I thought recklessly, would be a discourtesy difficult to ignore. I inhaled deeply and exhaled noisy bluegrey. Arabesques and a couple of cheeky smoke rings completed the insolence of the effect. I glared at him, challenging him through that nebulous curtain of smoke and haze. The old man spoiled it all by saying: 'I don't suppose I might cadge a cigarette . . . ?'

'I beg your pardon?'

'A cigarette.'

Deflated, I gave him a cigarette and lit it for him with a shaking, vanquished hand. Jesus! I was being highly outcooled here. Byron sat a little straighter in his chair and his face twinkled with a dry, powdery beauty.

'I'm not supposed to, you see . . . my doctor's the most appalling old fascist and my secretary seems to regard it as her inalienable right to keep my lungs free of tar while she is in my employ. Her vigilance is startling. Consequently, I never have any of my own and must beg for them where I can.'

He paused, his small head framed by the greylit riverwindow. A portrait silhouette.

208

'Well now, Mr Bogle, you seem to be having one or two little difficulties of late. An altercation with a member of the teaching staff of another college for instance. Yes. And it seems that the gentleman in question now absolutely refuses to teach you. Mmmm. All a touch extreme, don't you think? What on earth did you say to him ... or perhaps more importantly, why did you say it?'

This was safely controversial ground, I felt. My breath was bad but my reasons were good. I looked at the old man as offensively as possible before replying. I felt that I was on home ground here. I breezed into speech.

'He told me that I was wasting my time at university because I didn't do his lousy essay and because I refused to admit that Henry Fielding was a proto-Marxist whatever that is. He told me that I was imbecilic, abrasive and superficial so, being the soul of wit and repartee, I said that the notions of logic and form were a pair of hairy bollocks anyway and added that he was full of shit.'

I smiled, simply, winningly. I felt rather pleased with myself by now. Byron spoke.

'Well, yes ... quite right too, really.'

'Wha? Come again?' I grunted in piggy bewilderment.

The dapper old fraud was smoothly objective.

'You had a certain amount of justification in saying more or less what you did say. The terms erred on the side of overstatement and profanity but the content was fairly plausible. The man was quite obviously off his chump.'

You don't need me to tell you that this was not how I had planned this. Dr Byron blushed slightly. An old hand at this kind of thing, he had at least the decency to feel a little embarrassed by the lack of contest.

'Well, that's enough of that ...' he appeared to recollect something hurriedly '... though of course, I must censure you most severely for your discourtesy towards a member of this university ... but we'll take that as read, shall we? Good. So, apart from this unfortunate business, Mr Bogle, would you say that you're happy here?'

'Well ... I ... ah ...'

'I imagine you're quite aswamp with disillusionment already.'

'Why, yes I am, actually.'

Byron smiled, an angel-framed sage beneath that latticed, windowed sky. All those words and other thoughts in his well-stocked mind. He brought it all to bear.

'Yes, of course you are. Just as it should be. No doubt, you feel that you don't really fit in here or something like that.'

'Well ...'

'You see yourself as something of a misfit, a rebel, I daresay. Which you suppose to be something entirely new in Cambridge.'

His tack chosen and revised, Byron gestured theatrically towards one of the huge windows. He was obviously beginning to enjoy his own performance. He ponced on.

'There have been rebels and misfits in Cambridge for more than eight hundred years, Mr Bogle. Great tedious shoals of them. All varsity rebels to a man.

'I'm afraid the walls of this university will hardly crumble at your advent, you know. Oh really, my dear boy, I've seen such a lot of rebellious undergraduates leave this insidious den of privilege and élitism only to become prominent figures in the very Establishment that they had affected to despise as young men. Our largest bequests come from those who professed to like it least when they were here. It's all tosh. Terrible old nonsense. Will that be your fate? You know, I rather think it will. Like you, they all had that appalling arrogance of youth. Dear me, no one is greater than this university. Goodness no, it is much too old and has seen far too much.'

As the old bloke spoke, the very room itself, that dusty wooden cavern seemed to muster its ancient strength and come brownly to his aid. Bravo! Encore! What price Varsity Rebels? Hardly used. Electric windows and sports trim. Rarsity Vebels. In the rich paled and paling light I heard the reedy hymn of the past, all the legioned history at the old man's side. I felt less momentous. I shouldn't really have been fucking about with all this well-established poshery. It wasn't right and surely they wouldn't stand for it. They'd get the Tradition troops out, the Culture Commandos. I sensed the wide panorama of all those dead guys to whom this room had access and power. All those toff stiffs. I recognised my position of privileged unimportance in this sepulchral chamber. I stared at Byron while I collected my thoughts. Hughie Byron, wee Hugh. There he sat, guarding and ministering to his big worldroom, his archive hut. Nothing to him were other experiences. What life his before all this? *Rien*. Otherwhere and unconscious, he. This wee worldie nothing to him. It enters in the shape of me, old Rippers, old Bogle, unshaven and ill-smelling. We have other bits, other lifeparts. No matter. Not for him and his Larvsity Berels. Those other lifescenes. Remote from him. Lucky bastard. Not his. Others come here. He watches. Others. Girls. Varsity girls. Fruited bodies, things of birth. That they use to unghost the false power of this dead room and man. They are the world he doesn't like. With their traces of rut and blood. Rut in bedrooms, in houses, rut in countries and land. All those girlie kibbutzes. Ho ho. Not for him. Rut and rut. Me, the Kibbutzed rutman talks to Dr Barren. How that? Barbed City Revels. Not rut here. Interdit. Stop that.

Yeah, well fuck him, I thought as his old voice continued to seep dreamily into the fading room. He was dead too and thus he governed. I was being unfair. He was a nice old codger. Like him, I counselled myself.

'. . . believe me, Mr Bogle, you fit in here better than you can possibly imagine. Despite your efforts to the contrary.'

Liked, he paused effectively.

'You know, I find your behaviour oddly reassuring. If a little vulgar. In some ways undergraduates like you are the most fun. Cambridge is the perfect place for you, you know that well enough.'

He smiled rather self-consciously – an old man, his youthless past behind him. His little show was drawing to its end.

'Well, I think that's about all I have to say . . .' he looked without envy or resentment at me, his uninvited charge '. . . apart from suggesting the wisdom of perhaps investing in a razor and some shaving soap.'

I scratched my vanquished, bristled chin. I never much bothered with shaving in them thar days. Some things never change.

'Have you anything you want to add?' asked Byron.

I had a lot, an awful lot. I wanted to spike the old fucker's pompous guns. I wanted to give him a bad time. I wanted to do some showing off.

'No, I don't think so,' I replied gamely.

We both stood, concluding the interview. Byron stubbed his sneaky cigarette out in a flowerpot. He turned his dim old face to that dim old prospect outside his window.

'Things are changing here but neither quickly nor, I'm glad to say, a whole hell of a lot. Much, thankfully, stays the same. Whether you like it or not, when you came to Cambridge you signed yourself up as a member of an élite. An élite, mind you – meritocracy, aristocracy – it matters little. Still an élite. Egalitarians don't come to Cambridge. Not real ones.'

While he droned on, I stared at the lazy grey river, spotted and pock-marked in the growing drizzle.

'When you chose all this, any residue of supposed class integrity dissolved. It will evaporate further. Cambridge will shape you ineradicably in its own mould. As it always does. You will be one of us, or something equally vulgar. You must ask yourself: Is that really such a bad thing? Mmmm?'

He turned his face to mine, all aged and kingly (him not me). His little smile was full of kindness and the promise of future kinship. Inclusion. It made me want to puke. We shook hands again and I moved away from the gentle cocoon of that garrulous room. As I opened the door, Byron's hesitant old voice halted me briefly. He was back in his cosy little corner. The drizzle pattered hard against the great latticed windows now, sounding the wide oaken chamber with muffled, expiring thuds and hisses. Old Byron's moist, geriatric eyes glittered uncertainly in the rainsplashed gloom. He smiled quite sheepishly.

'Oh, I nearly forgot − one more thing, Mr Bogle. If you try anything like this again, you'll be out on your arse doublequick. Within the hour, believe me. Thank you.'

I buggered off while the buggering off was good.

Can you credit that? What a wily old bastard! It will evaporate further. I have to admit, he did the job on me there. He stitched me up, he ran me ragged. I was most surprised to be left standing by an old codger like him. It was good for my humility which was, by that time, growing by the minute.

I wised up a bit after that. The knives were obviously out and I didn't want to lose all my Cambridge comfort. I wasn't that disaffected, that socialist. Also, I certainly didn't want to surrender my only chance of getting a crack at Laura. Things had started to pick up a little in that department and I didn't want to chuck away all my good work. But I'll tell you all that later. There's a lot to come.

Shock is a clinical state that is characterised by a fall in the blood pressure. The sufferer is pale and cold, the skin feels clammy and the pulse is weak and rapid. We have more blood vessels than we have blood to fill them. Usually the body works this discrepancy out on an incentives basis. All the big boys − brain, heart and kidneys, get their big share while the proles − muscle, skin and stomach, have to make do with a lot less. During shock this nepotistic arrangement gets all screwed up and the blood supply gets hazardously socialist, picking its friends without care. Or, in other words, shock is a state of circulatory failure when blood is insufficient to fill the main blood vessels.

There are two types of shock. Compensated shock and uncompensated shock. When compensated shock occurs the blood overdoes its bit and flies madly to the major organs leaving the poor proles almost bloodless. So you get pale, cold and weak. In uncompensated shock the blood can't be fagged and so those big boys get no backhanders. The heart and brain begin to run out of their necessary while your toes pulse and blush with surplus goodies. The latter is a bugger and really fucks you up. The worst thing is you can't see it coming. Your pulse whips up a little pace but there aren't any good giveaways. It sneaks up on you and tears your heart out.

Now, sitting here in Sloane Square with my well-informed hands running over my limbs, I'm pretty sure I'm not in shock. This is bad news. It means if I am in shock that I'm in uncompensated shock, aka an awful lot of trouble. I hope to God I've just missed the shock boat entirely. I can't take the hassle.

The dark is darker. Hello night. The little lights of this place glow with greater strength, shutting out the stars. Streams of late, discarded blossoms litter these pavements, trodden and streetstained like spring's cancelled gesture.

A group of young blacks, three in number, cross the road with jaunty, hipster ease. It shames me that I have known so few black people. They were unheard of in Belfast and Cambridge was scarcely bursting at the seams with mad Rastafarians. It was hardly my fault. Anyway, whenever I've tried to be polite to a black guy I've always been denounced as a guilty liberal, patronising wimp or just a white bastard. They've got a point, I suppose, but I can definitely do without it. These guys want blood. With all this circulatory failure around, I haven't got the blood to spare.

'Hey, nignogs! Jungle bunnies! Why don't you coons bugger off back to the fucking trees. Hey, monkeymen! Wanna banana?'

These intemperate cries spew from a little bunch of white youths on the other side of the square. They laugh harshly and begin a series of monkey calls and ape gestures. They aren't yobs these guys. They're clean-cut, posh, pukka.

'Hey, Kunta Kinte! Darkie dickheads. Fuck off back to Noogooland, why dontcha? Golliwogs! Rubber lips! Sod off, Sambo!'

Their taunts are lazy, speculative, free of much serious intent. The black guys hear them and turn around idly. They gesture provocatively in unison, fingers high and pointed. The white guys increase their shouts but make no moves and the three blacks shrug dismissively before turning round and walking on. It ends as most of the city's little incidents end, without violence or conclusion. The white youths shuffle on, babbling excitedly, congratulating themselves, talking about the ones that got away.

Tut tut. It's not very nice, is it? I mean what's the point? Jungle bunnies indeed. I can't see the sense in bigotry against blacks. I mean they are English after all. They have the same accent as us, they live in the same country as us, they play cricket and laugh at jokes about Bletchley. They're as English as English can be. They're just like us, only black. At least they're not Welsh! They're just black. Simply black. It's no big deal.

I look up at the sky. It looks down at me. The night sky is a funny thing nowadays. What with all these rockets, satellites and space stations, etc. the sky seems lower, closer. Space has moved down a notch. The modern sky is tightly wrapped around its earth, like an orange in tin foil. Soon we will have to crouch under our shrinking coil of moon, and star and junk. Who knows what you'll see when you skywatch these days? Soon, they'll be launching advertising hoardings. Soon. The night has lost its distance, its mystery and appeal. For us, the sky is next door, it's a low ceiling, it's a stepladder. It's a bore.

Talking of bores, my uninvited incision has piped up again. It's making its point here, rather too forcibly, if you ask me. Its point has something to do with gangrene and tetanus. I think my wound's worried about how dirty that nasty old blade was. This has rather preyed upon my mind as well. But short of nicking some antibiotics from somewhere there's not much I can do. I still don't want to hit a hospital. I admit that I should have cleaned it up a bit but I can nip into some public toilet later on. God, terrible isn't it? Infection prophylaxis has never seen it so good. Nothing like swabbing your wound from a toilet bowl. As a matter of fact, I could always piss on it. Uric acid is sterile. But then again, I'd have to have an awful gymnastic dick to be able to piss on my own chest. Nix to that. Oh me, what trials!

I stick my hand through the folds of my coat and am pleased to find that the tawdry bandages on my belly are not as wet as before. They're still not dry but they're getting there. The pain is insupportable but at least I'm not making any more mess. I don't know quite why that should make any difference but it does.

I stand up and my shadow shoots before me and branches into doubleheadedness. I walk towards it but it floats away like the faint ogre it is. I drift across the road through the sludgy sounds of cars and buses. Laughter culls the streets and the people walk quickly, fuelled with drink and weekend adrenalins. Names are shouted out in surprise, incredulity, denial or mockery.

'Jenny! Ha ha, Martin. Micky. Juliaaaa!'

Festivity seems to be everywhere tonight. Young couples amble in grapplestiff, four-legged formation like amorous crabs. Troops of boys and girls outflank each other, do battle, flee and chase to rout. Drinking boys stagger under the weight of their bottles, cans and drams. They are all noisy in their pleasures and will, I fear, grow noisier as night stumbles on. They have a way to go. Just like myself.

And on that way I now go. With my soft limp, my stomachstab and my weariness, I trudge away.

SEVEN

Well, things came to a head with that Laura sooner than I had expected. Since I had imagined that they would never come to a head, this isn't saying much. Anyway, eventually, in the end, things came to a head as things always do, in the end.

May Week. Yum yum! The night of the Trinity Ball. Treble yum! As in every year, that infamous week was dragging its boorish heels with remarkable infestivity. Exams had been botched, rowing had been rowed, balls rolled, drink drunk and the damp, dreadful end was in sight. The town's little streets sweated black-tied prats, boors and rascals. There was much constant noise and little consecutive sleep. Cambridge swelled with end-of-term fever. A doctor was called but there was little hope.

The night of the Trinity Ball. Darkness was arriving late, having all his summer obligations to take care of. The evening was cooling as the sun buggered off, bringing its shine to somewhere nicer. Clouds gathered high and jostled in their conspiracy, ready to piss on any fun they might espy. It would be a cold night and rain looked like a reasonable bet. The usual May Ball quartet – darkness, cold, rain and wind.

The night of the Trinity Ball. Most of third term had been leading to this. I was being dragged along by some halitotic harpy from Clare who, apparently, had the hots for me in a major way. (Who can blame her?) She was called Emily and keen to be a banker. I tried to like her, after all, she had paid for my ticket, but I couldn't seem to manage it. She persisted in talking about banking, finance and the stock market. She was a very boring girl. God, she was dull! She told me that I was a little honey but that if I ran out on her halfway through the night, she'd chop my dick off for me. She was paying, so the terms were hers. I smiled as best I could and tried to be gallant. She wasn't up to much but, like she said, at least she was paying. I wondered if girls got this kind of deal when they were paid for. Quite probably, I concluded.

I must say, I was jolly handsome that night. I looked pretty near my best.

We all have our good and bad days, pulchritude-wise. This was a good one. Unusually for a guttersnipe, I looked like a fucking dream in a dinner jacket. All tall and slim and boffable. And my features had decided to grace me with at least one night's worth of perfect, exquisite symmetry. (I swear I had a dimple in my chin that night! Next day it was gone but it had been there, I promise you.) My cheeks were smooth and my eyes spun their strange, emerald web of allure and enigma. My word, I was gorgeous that night. I was stunning. Grown men fainted with desire as I passed them in the street. I was almost arrested for being too handsome in a built-up area. I was just too dinky for words. You would have porked me on the spot, honestly.

I was glad about this for two reasons. Firstly, I knew that Laura was going to be there and I was pleased that she was going to get a good look at what exactly she was so foolishly missing. Little Greg would make a poignant foil to my startling beauty. The other reason for gladness was that this Emily person was bound to grow intimidated, overawed, aware of the extent of her hubris in trying to date a godlike creature like me and would promptly bugger off before she was struck by lightning or something.

The night of the Trinity Ball. It was all set up, prepared. The scene was set, the players summoned, the action waiting. With the, by now, frankly slavering Emily, I boogied on in there, determined to do my bit for Bogle.

Four hours later. Darkness had fallen. Emily had been effectively faded and I strode through the scene, epicene and alone. The night was disfigured and obscene. Its boundless maw spilled confusion and darkness upon all. The adultered blackness heaved and belched, not dispelled by the meagre corpse candles of the muddy illuminations. The college splayed in sudden ugliness as grubby coronas of orange sprayed their tacky dimness. The old courts and buildings hid amongst the vulgar brightness of canopy and awning. Cacophonic loudspeaker music and the inane thrashings of several dismal student bands filled the air. The grass frothed with undergraduate vomit, corrosive and stinking, a May Ball carpet. The very air sweltered and bulged in effluent, intemperate festivity.

Yes. Mealy undergraduates, yellow with sweat, flexed their odious bodies in a wild cavort of sudden, fragile liberty. Expensive gowns and dresses spilled their skirts onto the trodden filth and were dragged raggedly from one man to another. The dancing was moronic and glassy-eyed. Bottles and glasses splintered under foot, slithering in the pulpy grass. Light and darkness flashed, wheeled and streaked in deleterious symphony. Half-eaten food, lay moulding and ghastly on every table and chair. Take it from me – it wasn't pretty.

Earlier, one agreeable young lady had urinated upon my shoes. At first I hadn't realised what was occurring. I was trotting briskly away from the Evil Emily when I tripped past some bushes. Rustle and scrappy whistle of movement. White, upperclass, feminine bottom pointing backwards out of the shy foliage. Rearward aimed jetstream. Hiss and splash. Onto my kicks. Shined them nicely. Why lookee here! Someone's just peed on me patents. Sick. Very sick. The worst thing being that the owner of the bottom (quite pretty actually) giggled when she saw me. Whatever happened to modesty, shame and rectitude?

Despite myself, I was unruffled by these caperings. I rather relished it all. It looked rather good since I was looking so bloody handsome, treading soberly through the slime and muck and hilarity. It would look so fab, so funky. Bogle the ascetic amongst the sportive excess of his peers. I liked the thought.

I lit a cigarette and stole a bottle of champagne from an unconscious girl lying outside one of the marquees. Ever Mr Solicitous, I checked her pulse before going in search of a quieter spot where I could drink and smoke my way through the rest of the night in handsome solitude.

The scene on the Backs was, if anything, worse than the riot of drunken glee on the other side of the river. It was really very cold by this time but this did not hinder the various undergraduettes who were dancing drunkenly on the riverbank with their dresses round their waists. The sight of their pallid, scant breasts appalled me for some reason. I mean I liked tits but they were shy creatures which thrived in discretion and deserved a little mystery. I felt grim and sourly pure. Strong, Irish and full of shit.

As I trudged towards the dark trees at the very edge of Trinity Lawns I passed through the main body of revellers. They were wilder, emboldened by the greater darkness. They laughed, danced, toppled, sang, screamed and shouted. All were desperate to be seen to be having that good time. Those best years of their life and making them count. And how! The vomit was more of a problem here. (Oh, the bally boke!) In the greater gloom it wasn't easy to avoid its lush and acrid carpeting. Nonetheless in a very dark and relatively pukefree corner, I could see half-dressed couples in various sordid parodies of the sexual act. The night heaved and suppurated in its ghastly celebration and I tried to work out how posh all this could be.

As I plodded away, I noticed a rogue band of stragglers at the fringe of the Lawns. Gatecrashers probably. Well, fair enough, I hadn't paid either. I quickened my pace to pass them. Suddenly my heart trembled in that unpleasant, hair-trigger way of his. Laura. Unmistakably. Her beautiful hair. In a green gown that bared her white shoulders. Three couples, all pissed. Laura staggered drunkenly beside the sawn-off figure of her boyfriend. Loverboy Greg. King of the Cambridge midgets. He obviously was the first to spot me and said something to the others. They all stared in my direction with boozy malevolence and my spirits lifted in the hope of some head-breaking. Greg and the other two blokes stopped and had a little conference. They broke away from the girls and walked towards me with sturdy, laughable little strides. Yes! Yes, please, I prayed. Just give me my excuse. Come into my parlour, boys. Come into my world. Let me show you round.

They came to a halt just in front of me. Poorly menaced, I smiled in affable recognition.

'Hello boys,' I said levelly.

There was no reply. Greg's puggish face was suffused with a pretty damned difficult combination of anger and contempt. He was no trouble but the other two were bigger, more substantial. A slight ripple of amusement trailed its sluggish way across their bludgeon features. I smiled again. All four of us now grinning, monkey to monkey. I spoke.

'Well, I'd love to chat, chaps, but I gotta go.'

''Fraid not,' snapped the brave and terrible Greg. It was trouble that he wanted. Him and his friends. He worked up the courage and eloquence for further taunts.

'You should have stayed in bog country, Paddy. Nobody wants you here.'

Or do they? I glanced over at the girls they had left behind. Ah, so that was it. La femme cherched. I giggled outright, more in joy than amusement. Poor old Greg, poor old sap. I tried to picture what he saw as he faced me there. Me in my beauty – two feet taller, a yard wider and a mile and a half better looking. I wanted to kiss him in compensation. He piped up again, his unchinned voice painted with excitement and intent.

'Didn't you hear what I said? Are you deaf? We don't want you here. You don't belong, old son.'

I crouched to catch the drift of his thin, eunuch's squeal. Terrifying stuff. I started to move away, sniggering in open derision. The tallest of Greg's buddies blocked my way. Very big and very unsmiling, this boy. He looked a little more like it. I winked at him and Greg's voice turned me round.

'You're not going anywhere, Bogman.'

'I thought you said I didn't belong here,' said I in my best finicky manner. Greg's face rippled with confusion. Goodness, it was a giggle. The girls had obviously realised what was going on and they approached us now with anxious faces. They called to their men, asking them to move on, to forget about it. (Whatever 'it' was.) I backed them up.

'Yes boys, why not take a friend's advice. We don't want any trouble now, do we?'

'Shut up,' said Greg.

'Oh, come on, is that the best you can do?' I enquired.

There was something of a pause here while these tough young things struggled with their inspiration. The girls had moved amongst them now and one of them was pulling her beau's sleeve. Laura was staring at me with something I could have sworn was akin to shame. She whispered something to Greg – obviously a plea for pacifism. Greg and his chums, however, seemed reluctant to surrender their chance of kicking the crap out of me. I was glad about this in a way. They must have neglected to account for the gap in expertise in this sort of thing that our different backgrounds engendered. Though there were three of them, I came from the Falls Road and one can only be so much of a wimp if one hails from the Falls Road. I was simply out of their league, nastinesswise. They wouldn't have a chance. Might be good for them. A salutary lesson in the fortitude and persistence of the jolly old working classes. And it would look so dashing, Laura would love it. Hospitalising the boyfriend was the greatest seduction technique known to man.

'. . . please, Greg . . . *please*.'

Her voice was another of the beautiful things about her. She was looking so nice. So pale and trim and fucking adorable! The intimacy in her voice squeezed my gut with jealousy. I looked at them together. It was a crime. Her shining, gifted comeliness and his stunted, brute lack of appeal. I rippled my chin, flexed my teeth and tried to look as beguiling as possible.

At this point I should probably have leapt in, fists flying, eyes flashing and lips puckered for Laura. I should have kicked the shit out of them, obviously, but I didn't. I just walked away. I came to the conclusion that there was no way in which I could glitter romantically so I cut my losses and shimmied the hell out of there before the three stooges changed their minds.

When I looked back their little group was drifting away in its turn. Laura hung back with Greg. He was bent double, regurgitating prodigiously and with some native aplomb. She raised her head and looked in my direction, her hair draped on her pale shoulders. I thought of several gestures I could comfortably make. It didn't seem propitious so I left it out.

Yes. Failed again. Another chance given the short straw. Anyway, was she worth this? There were a lot of cute pukka bims to be had. Who needed her?

Me.

Eventually, I found myself a quiet spot near a little brook where I could ignore the dross of the greater revels. I planted my arse and said hello to the advance party of little drizzle that the sky had just launched. Lit a fag, took a swig and settled down in solitude. Ah, how nice that seems when you're an ego kid like I was! The night heaved and lurched on, crashing to its vigourless end. Me, me fag and me booze, we waited for morning.

It came and found me cold and sad. Having rained, it stopped. Stopped white and clear. Beauty greeted the morning, damply saving the night's sins. The river glistened sluggishly at the soft, apologetic sky. The prospect was littered with the ragged stain of the night's excesses. Canopies lounged, sad and hungover in the morning light, and tents and awnings were robbed of their bogus nocturnal glamour by the watery sun's level gaze. It was very early and various formally dressed couples wandered stiffly along the Backs. They were shoddy, worn and listless, their uneasy unions half pleasing, half shaming. They looked young. The Backs breathed its pompous freedom after its night of subjugation.

And where was Bogle to be had? you might ask. Just where we left him – at the far end of one of the grassy esplanades, hidden by drooping trees, feeding some ducks with one of last night's discarded bread rolls. My back against another damp fatherly tree, a great big daddy acorned. My fingers tearing bread. My mind numb with stolen, easy content. It had been a good night. Wet, cold and dark but pleasant in its way. One of my more enjoyable roofless nights, to be sure.

Embarrassingly enough, I had been thinking about Maurice. The stark, mad night and populous dawn had triggered a touch of profundity. I was stuffed with the delicate meal that regret seems to constitute for the young. I was polishing my miseries. On days like that, crumpled dreams can talk to us when we iron them out with memory.

Abruptly, all my little ducks fled their posts in dumb greedless panic. I heard a voice breathe my name quite softly and I looked up in surprise. Blinded slightly by the pallid sky, I recognised the dress first. Oh wonderful, I thought. Timing, timing is the essence of lyricism. Despite my efforts to the contrary, that vulgar, susceptible heart of mine lurched into my throat at all this enigmatic event.

'Hello Laura,' I managed to say. Pretty good considering my poor extempore showings previously.

She told me that she had been searching for me for ages. She wanted to apologise for all that unpleasantness of the night before. Greg had been drunk, she said. He wasn't like that normally. His work was declining and he wasn't happy. He probably regretted it already. He was confused.

I was inconsolable by the time she had finished. I sobbed wildly, my desperate grief-stricken keening cracking the air. Poor Greg! My God, what had I done?

Well, that's not true actually. I simply smiled and said something sensitive like: 'Ah, who gives a fuck anyway?' As a matter of fact, I just smiled. I left out the dialogue altogether. It hadn't served me very well with Laura up to now. I was trying a new tack. Total silence. I was nervous but sanguine.

It had obviously been something of a rough night for Laura. Her dress was torn in places and her hair was dishevelled. The girl should have presented a squalid spectacle with her torn gown and sottish demeanour but, predictably, I was beguiled. She looked much more gorgeous than usual; her disarray only increased her allure. She stung my senses, the bitch. I was furious. I could see that this wasn't playing fair. By way of counter attack, I invited her to sit down.

'Why?'

'Why not?' I tried – on the off-chance.

And to my extremity of disbelief, Laura Markham moved down our little bank and dropped onto the grass beside me, careless of the rainsoaked soil. She kicked off her shoes and laughed. Well, stap me vitals, I thought, if this isn't actually something like it! I fretted, I wobbled. Lumme! Help me, mother, I'm near to happiness here!

So what was a poor soppy fool to do? Expire of bliss? Write a poem? Rip her knickers off? I did what any good man would do. I clammed up – of course.

For five minutes I sat like an idiot trying to think of something ineffably charismatic to say. Her bare, hairstroked shoulder was touching mine and I could taste her warm, winesour breath. Her hair brushed my neck softly, my blood was in tumult and my opportunist erection was tickling my chin (nothing like a little pragmatic lust in these matters). You know, folks, I was in an excess of joy. We've all had these moments, haven't we? When you just *know*. Yes? When you're suddenly graced with an access of erotic certainty. It had taken its time, true, but erotic certainty seemed mine now. I was *very* chuffed. Christmas had come early and, with any luck, it was going to screw my buns off.

Laura had arrived. She was here! Avec moi. Old Rippers. Big Boges. It looked as though she was going to let me love her. After all my sterling despair. Just when I had let infant Hope run off back to its mother. I was so winded by this immense and complex thought that the most I could manage after those five stunned minutes was:

'You must be cold.'

'Yes.'

Brilliant! How could she resist? At least it gave me the cue for some corny stuff with my dinner jacket. I removed that garment and draped it loosely

221

around those lovely pukka shoulders of hers. I was moved by an unspeakable, facile tenderness and struggled madly to light a cigarette in an attempt to conceal my panic. Her beauty was painful to me, it crushed my heart. I smoked away there, quite calm, my dress shirt stamped white against the red chivalry of my braces. I turned my face to hers and my bright eyes clouded, the cowardly bastards! She smiled at me, inches away from those scummy Irish lips of mine. Who needed conversation? The captious flower of speech obliged. I was left willed but stationary. The rule in these situations is to keep your gob shut and try to look expectant. It worked.

She leant hard against me and kissed me sharply on the lips, hers tightly shut, pushing my head back against my old tree. She pulled away rapidly, her face rigid with anxiety and suspicion, trying to calculate just how that risk came out.

'What's wrong?' she asked thinly. 'Isn't that what you wanted?'

It suddenly occurred to me that Laura had no idea that I was so desperate for those peachy little buttocks of hers. I hadn't considered this possibility. How could she have missed my bovine adoration? Ah, so beautiful and yet so free of vanity! This was ineluctably the bim for me. Now, I had just been kissed by this, the queen of all my dreams, so my voice was a little shaky when I replied with all the trembling intensity at my disposal that yes, that was almost exactly what I wanted.

Please, no laughter, if you don't mind! I can't help it. I was young. Concocted lyricism appeals to us kids. The shoddier the better. Then again, why should I make excuses? I loved the girl. Or at least, I loved her as much as was in my power. Which was more than you might think.

You'll be glad to hear that there was rather less beating around the bush after that. We got down to business, so to speak. She told me how hopelessly besotted with me she had been the whole bloody time, for instance. She felt that she had been monstrously obvious from the start and asked me if I had any inkling of this passion. I said that I hadn't really thought about it. (Ho ho.)

Later that morning, we had breakfast together in a rickety little coffee shop on the Chesterton Road. The mad old biddy who served us was a romantic soul who seemed to labour under the delusion I was Scottish, from Dunfermline to be precise. She told us that it was lovely to see such a happy young couple as ourselves and asked if we were going to marry and all that kind of thing. This was, of course, hilarious and surprisingly good grist to my passionate mill. It's nice the way life sometimes provides its nudging little eccentricities just at the right moment. (You know, I almost slipped the old dear a tenner, so grateful was I.)

Ah, that breakfast was breathtaking, it was ambrosia. But it wasn't anywhere near as good as lunch. And dinner beat the other two all hands down. In short, we spent that day together, as well we might. We simply walked away from Cambridge as we were, she cloaked in my jacket and I gallant and youthsapped in my shirtsleeves. We walked slowly through roads and fields and lanes. We passed entire villages without noticing them. We were intimate, confiding and hilarious. We were young, strong and blamelessly sentimental. And we were, of course, together – unbelievably for me.

My God, I was happy! Fucking ecstatic. Here was me, Ripley Bogle, brother to criminals and scourge of the tasteful, walking through June beauty with this whisper of English woman! It was pleasant to reflect on how well I had done for myself in the end.

Would you believe it but I'm almost sobbing now? Quel jour! The weather, contrary to all its previous endeavour, came out strongly in my favour. The day before had been a disaster but we were graced with sudden sunny warmth and wide, glad light. All the people whom we passed seemed to be on firm orders to be especially gracious to us. We were smiled and waved at, saluted and gently envied by everyone we saw. I think we looked like a groovy pair or so I hoped. All conspired to my purposes. Her words, her eyes, her laughter. Her mouth was a soft pennant of kiss upon mine, her shadow darkened my face. All my cigarettes and plausible, detectable joy. As you can see, I'm rather sentimental about that particular day. Having what I wanted in this world. That seemed to be just about it for me. I burned for her.

Night came when we could walk no further. We were miles away from the little city and exhausted. Night played its part as well. Slumberdarkened to only feel. Prompting that couch we needed. In that summer night of scent and sweat we got there. Dropped on the grass and let the warmth do its work. Couched in the easy night of Cambridgeshire. The mandate truth, fucking in those photogenic fields. Cambridgeshire is a gentle bed. They hoover the hedges, you know, and shampoo the sheep. Oh, I wanted her in all. And got her, I seem to remember. She was a dream I could never have had. A ribbon of joy, quiet and tiredsweet. We stained the grass and felt bad about it. In the shadows. My skin tingled with gratitude as I holidayed on her clear, uncurtained flesh.

I thought I'd made it. I thought I had it all sown up. What more could there be? I smoked the night away while she slept, her head resting on my shoulder (surprisingly painful). We lay in that grass, warm and silent, speculative predictions patrolling my mind. I didn't know what I had done to deserve it but it looked as though I had been sentenced to a term of happiness. I looked at her face as she slumbered. No! No way, I thought, just where is the catch, the clause of disadvantage? How will I pay for this? I was bound to lose it. I'd be pushed back to mundanity with these secret plateaus tucked away in shining pockets. Girls, those girls, they will always go off in the end. They'll turn sour, crap on your bones, dance on your grave and mock your memory. So what, I decided, who gives a toss! A little living in the present seemed the proper notion. Happy in that, I watched as frowsy birds awoke for day, opening up to find our secret pair – a glass that was black to them.

Oh Laura, you did it to me! You really did. Why goodness, love was here, manhood due soon and sincerity just around the corner!

EIGHT

Aaah! Ouch! Ow! Hmmnnhhh! Ooooh!

Midnight. Bloomsbury. Pub bench just outside the British Museum. Cold. Dark. Disquiet.

Oooo! Hmmnnhhh! Ow! Ouch! Aaah!

Ah, hello again. I've just been having a little trouble with my belly button. It's sulking, the sod. And doing quite a respectable amount of bleeding into the bargain. Pain is also prominent in this disagreement and I've been rather startled by the prodigious stock of discomfort my navel seems to hold in reserve. You know, the strangest parts of your body can really surprise you when it comes to dishing out pain. You can never be complacent about threat-free regions. They don't exist. Your body is there to give you trouble and give you trouble it will most assiduously, given half a chance.

My gut is playing me up because of my stab wound. My gut blames me for this. I've tried to reason with my gut but you know what guts are like – I haven't a hope of an objective dialogue. It has, at least, stopped bleeding. This is good as I was growing anxious about how much of the stuff I had left. I'm not sure how much blood I've lost exactly but I'm sure it's more than a smidgeon; a fair amount, not to be scoffed at. It is very stupid of me not to see a doctor about this matter but I'm too tired now. I might do it tomorrow. When I feel a little better.

Even before this well-rehearsed discomfort came out of its short retirement I had been thinking about what a very bad night it has been with one thing and another. Dawdling back from the King's Road was the kind of eye-opener I didn't need. I had nothing left to learn about Saturday nights but I still did some revision. The night has stretched and loitered in debauchery, excess and casual villainy. The city has donned its ragged festive cap. I've seen drunks, faggots, yobs, junkies, tarts, ponces, gits, perverts, tramps, wide boys, posh hooligans, girls, boys and lunatics. They've all been demonstrating the changes that the streets produce in all of us. Madness, wild excess, ferret fear and rodent instinct. Indulging in their rough, escaping horrors. Having their high good time.

I myself have been subject to a wide variety of abuse, mockery, disbelief, contempt, disgust, jocularity, hatred and threat as I limped, shuffled and trudged my way back here. Quite a large number of rowdy young men seemed keen to knock my block off and such like. I stayed out of trouble though. I'm all sliced up as it is and I didn't want to add to my growing collection of battlewounds. I seem to be annoying an awful lot of people these days.

I was proud of my self control (aka cowardice) in avoiding these proffered altercations. I mean, some nights it only takes some fatgobbed jerk to stare at me too long and I'm leaping in there with my little Irish fists flying. On the other hand, some nights I'll travel miles to avoid a scrap – I'll let people taunt me, revile me, gob on me, feel my balls or fart in my face rather than lay fist on flesh. This I call my readiness to adapt.

On the whole I try to steer myself away from conflict. Bottle and head breaking outside nightclubs and dance halls. The simple feral joys of youth. That force and sapling unwisdom. Kick and smash. It's no fun and frequently hurts.

I look around me here in Bloomsbury, upon the museum, the twee little pubs and the comfy, prosperous bookshops. This is more like it. Let the difference be your guide. A little belt of sanity. Doggedly oblivious.

I developed a taste for this kind of gentle ambience business while I was at Cambridge. It was all Laura's doing. Our first few months together were spent in trying to posh me up a bit. She was good at that and taught from a position of well-established expertise. After a lot of intensive civilising on her part she even invited me out to her home in Oxford. I was a little anxious about the whole thing. Her house was fucking massive, like an army barracks practically. My school had been smaller than this. Her dad was dead posh. I can't remember exactly what he was – the King of England or God or something but he was fucking pukka at any rate. She had about fourteen brothers who were all about ten feet tall and incredibly handsome. The whole collection – brothers, sisters, mum and dad were all frankly superb. I felt horribly oikish and malnourished. I can't say I shone much, the dad had been keen on old Greg by all accounts. He was at least a member of the requisite class to poke the old boy's daughter, something I could scarcely claim. He kept asking me about my family. I told them my father, an eminent physician, had died when I was young and that my mother, a well-known minor novelist, had followed soon after and that I had been brought up by my great-aunt, a Polish refugee. I could tell that they had their doubts but they could hardly challenge me openly and at least it kept them quiet.

No, I didn't really show to much advantage on that first terrifying visit but at least the bevy of sisters conceded that I was appallingly good-looking. Laura was pleased enough with my performance. Term had ended now and the apparent success of my visit meant that I could visit Laura whenever I could mitch off work. (I was labouring on a building site in Brixton that summer.) I managed to do this with perfidious regularity. If I didn't make it to Oxford she would come down to my nasty little bedsit in Rotherhithe and bonk the buns off me. She showed me a different London. A precise, attractive, redolent London, full of galleries, theatres and pretty places. Elegant stages from which to conduct the soppy action of my stunned euphoria. After a week of bare-chested ribaldry and laddishness with my boisterous chums on the building site, I would nip back home put on my posh gear, brush my teeth and hose down my language and rendezvous with my own personal child of ease and privilege. It seemed like a nice arrangement.

It was an extraordinary, fabulous summer. London was at its constant best for us. The sun loitered longer than usual and the tourists must have heard we were in town and avoided our delicate, lyrical path. She educated me in the ways of taste, discretion and her kind of life in general. Our days were spent in leisurely witnessing of beauty and varied happinesses, our nights in protracted series of awesomely sophisticated lovemaking. I discovered that sex isn't sex when it is with someone you think you love; that it is something else entirely, something bewildering. I learnt a lot in many ways.

And she was just so gorgeous the whole frigging time! Goodness me, how do girls manage it? Every time I looked at her, I was speechless with startled appreciation. Each tiny movement, gesture and habit seemed part of an elaborate edifice of beauty and intelligence. She was a composition of breathtaking parts. Nothing placeless or disarrayed. The clothes she wore took on something of this. I began to get a tiny glimpse of what garment fetishists enjoy. Her dresses, shoes, skirts and her every kind of tasteful, discreet haberdashery beguiled me on their own account. Draped on her form they transcended the limits of simple clothing and became canvases upon which she painted her heartstopping attractions. White lace, blue silk and all colours of chiffon, wool, and good taste. I had mocked such things before but now I realised that if you plonked them onto the right chick they could be pretty hot shit.

That was the best of my summers (an easy enough choice out of my poor selection). As before, I kept trying to spot the punishing clause in all this unmerited happiness. I feared that I would not be permitted to keep her beauty, her Englishness and love genius all for myself. This wasn't the kind of life and luck I was accustomed to and now expected. What was going on? I fretted endlessly but shucks, was I happy! Now, I knew that gratification was in some part a crime. An enemy to sensibility and resolve. I knew that it was a dangerous and subtle commodity. So what, I counselled; everything but everything has its place. Give gratification a chance. Who knows, it might just come up trumps. I stood up for gratification and it supported me.

I'm told a man will mostly love in others that which he sees reflected in himself. I disagree. A man will mostly love in others that which he hasn't a ghost of a chance of seeing reflected in himself. What do you think?

Love is a tricky thing, requiring good sense when there is a lot of hoping going on. I tried to keep myself in check. I tried to keep my joy driven, directed, marshalled. The trick with this maintenance of reality business was simple. Expecting less than you get. That's the line of thinking that should be pursued. The flaws in this process are many and pressing but if you persist with love-charm vigour then the game might not slip away. And when you see your chance, your tiny aperture of opportunity, then you dive like a goalkeeper and hope for the best.

Laura was one of the daughters of the world. One of those people who life seems to have blessed in a shockingly arbitrary manner. She was good for me. My little dalliance with the good amongst us. For a time, for a very short time, she made me a little like her. She dragged me halfway up to meet her. By jiminy, it was awfully nice up there with all that charm and discernment. I'm grateful for the jaunt.

Lookee here, the monsterblack night has grown windy and the bereaved paper that litters the streets has erupted into a caper of abrupt freedom and madcap flight. Posters flap with ragged insistence and sheets of newspaper roll, billow and climb like ancient bi-planes. The wind whistles, the cans clatter and the litter whispers in rapid disregard. This is a terribly atmospheric thing for them all to be doing. I'd like to applaud but I'd feel silly. For all my beef with the weather, it's always full of fun and games.

I'm very tired now. My eyes bulge, parched and salty. I feel the fumes of exhaustion blowing back through my slowing thoughts. All my clarifying intentions are being undermined and I feel that old, familiarly Bogleian sensation of life slipping away from me. Gamely, I struggle to exert some kind of control. This is difficulty itself, that jarred rheumatic heresy, leaving a picturesque hole in my cleverness. See what I mean? I'm dithering, I'm waffling rather.

The only thing that is actually keeping me conscious is the pain streaming so swiftly from my ripped-up abdomen. Five minutes ago, I coughed hard, trying to produce a sticky little piece of mucus-thick obstruction lodged in my gullet. I got the gobbet out all right but also squeezed another little gush of runny blood out of my palpitating stomach. The darkness from my saltpiece interior. Don't you know. Though the wound hurts like purgatory, it is, by way of compensation, a radiating oasis of heat in the desert of growing cold that the rest of my body has become. Exhaustion really does it to your temperature, it nicks your body's scarf and gloves. Eventually in a humorous culmination of injustice and outrage, exhaustion leaves you too cold to sleep. That's funny, a real giggle.

I've been thinking about Perry tonight. I suspect I've been making a mistake with Perry. Mostly due to the incapacity of youth to communicate with the old and sick. We deem them inconsolable. We feel there is nothing that we can say to make it better. This is wrong. (I think.) Why do the old necessarily need to be consoled? What is wrong with them apart from being old? Age can't really be described as an affliction. Can it?

Perry certainly doesn't need my goofy sympathy. I can hardly try commiseration from a stance as shaky and degraded as mine. He merits more than that.

I'll do better from now on. I'm going to turn over a new leaf, Perrywise. I must start to give him his due and more. I must avoid talking down to the poor old cripple. I'll have to hurry though. I'll have to get that bid in before the hammer falls.

'Yeeeaaaarrghhhcttchkkk!'

Hark! The anonymous cries of London's streets. The flower of discord. Other people and their problems never much to do with you. Distance and other stories. The shouter's part. The boozed-up call of triumph, loss and mad despair. Soon to be answered by its mate distress. Through the space-black air are strung these calls of rowdy disaffection and remorse.

'Yeeeaaaaaaoooooooooooooowww!'

There it goes. Hello there, how ya doing? Me mad too. It bares them less a fool to trill unattributed so. The purest art, I am assured.

'Aaahhhaaawwaaawaaaaayyyyaaarrrghghhh!'

Goodness, a trio no less! There's a lot of vocal grief on the prowl tonight. I hope they don't get together and come round here looking for their trouble.

A tall, plump, bobble-hatted policeman ambles round my corner and dawdles speculatively, discreetly in my direction. I sit a little straighter and even cross my legs in a parody of insouciance. I rub my eyes and prepare my affability.

'Evening,' he says.

'Evening,' I reply.

'Cold.'

'Yes. Very.'

He pauses in his faintly ludicrous hat and height and humour. He shifts his weight rhythmically from one leg to the other and seems inclined to chat. He's old for a bobby – forty-five to fifty and is obviously applying the volume of his wisdom to the question of whether or not I am a tramp. I have my coat wrapped tight around the bloody region of my wound but I'm sure he can't have much room for equivocation on this issue. I must be looking lovely, sitting here. I must be a picture of prosperity.

'How's it going?' he asks lightly.

'Ah ... pretty well.'

'Good.'

'Yes.'

He smiles carefully. His eyes are bright but guarded and I suspect his conclusions have mostly been made by now. The starfish shield on his helmet glints in the flood of yellow street lamp. It's a charismatic arrange-ment and lends a rather epic air to this particular PC. He looks around him, left, right, back, front, in that airy manner peculiar to policemen. His eyes come to rest calmly upon mine and I try to smile in a reassuringly confident fashion. He nods his head in waggish tolerance.

'Good night then.'

'Good night.'

He trundles off in standard chummy copper trim. Wide-legged, shuffling, jocoserious. What a jolly sort he is indeed! These days I might have expected to have been beaten up or shot or something. I'm pleased to see that the traditional peeler yet has his place in London. It gives us tramps a chance. I wonder what he wanted anyhow. Did I look like a criminal? Did I kill that tramp in Hyde Park? Are the rozzers, in point of fact, looking for me? I doubt it.

Nowadays, it's very humiliating to talk to policemen even when they're nice. When I was at Cambridge I used to address them loftily as 'Officer' or 'Constable' or even 'My good man' but I don't think I'd swing that now.

The BM sheds its slim glow upon me and its serried troop of windows merge and buckle in my weary gaze. I read the posters in a shop window. William Etty. George Eliot. *Hampshire Landscapes 1840–1914. Chinese Philosophy*, a history of, by Martin Freeman. *Bodyline*, a troubled tour. Cheilidhe, 18 Lancaster Avenue – June 24. Looks like there's a lot of fun to be had there. Their words and pictures swim into numbness and bewildered repetition. Weariness is a doctrine, a wild and ludicrous system of confusion, semi-memory and kyboshed depth of thought. In its scrambled schedule, order and sense go awry – mundanity delights and fascinates, cohesion appals and simplicity is all but incomprehensible. Exhaustion is stale and fevered. It corrupts perception and blackmails purpose. It undermines the merits of intelligence. It makes you think of silly things.

Near at hand, I hear the celebratory tinkle of breaking glass. Shouts. More bottles bite the splintering dust. Two? Three? Shouts again. Bellows of brutality and fear. I hope my little copper is OK. I trust he's meeting no resistance. The noises die abruptly and the comic wind takes its place. The little flags of litter flutter once more. It's a sly wind, this, parodic even. It's taking the piss.

Wind or no wind, I think I'll be doing a lot of sleeping tonight. My head is ducking, bobbing and lolling into neckless poor suspension and my thoughts keep cutting out on me like playful neon. Tomorrow is Sunday and I'll need most of my strength to pull through that trial. You might have noticed my success in mentioning cigarettes with less implacable monotony today. I've been trying to forget about them. This hasn't been entirely successful but by a supreme and uncharacteristic effort of will I have managed to save three fags until now. This is good stuff but I doubt that they'll see daylight. They won't last the night no matter how much I sleep. I shall have to work something out tomorrow. Touch Perry for a couple of quid perhaps. And Hunger will I imagine show up once more. Yes, He will want some attention. In addition, my newest wound will be making his presence felt in forceful terms. Tomorrow's going to be no kind of good day. I'm not looking forward to it. Well, we'll see how it goes.

On cue, the rain makes its entrance. Ha fucking ha. Dontcha love this? Hi there, rain, you're looking good. My head spots, with tiny, soft-pressing darts of lazy drizzle. The pavement dots and thickens its moist stains. It's a slow, pleasant process. No one's about to hurry here. This rain is not the whole hog, it's an attempt, a half-hearted try. The rain's not too bothered. It switches off as abruptly as it switched on. The weather, Jesus! What did I tell you? The events of climate are going wrong, they're changing policy. Or perhaps this is just something I've never noticed before. I'm not too sure about any of this. You can never tell and I'm awfully tired. Don't rely on me right now.

Laura once told me that she couldn't imagine me living past the age of twenty-five. She told me that I was a faintly tragic figure and that I didn't have much of a place in the ranks of normality and passion-free simplicity. This was at the height of our lyricism and I'd just spent half the night making her sing her orgasm song (a medley actually) so I didn't take this too seriously. Girls are always saying that kind of thing anyway. They try to tell you what they think you want to hear (quite incorrectly usually). Charitably, I tried to disregard this rather hilarious statement. But in my present state, I'm not so sure. Perhaps the dear girl was just about right. When you think about it, I am rather a tragic figure.

Notwithstanding, my innards now conspire to dispel any momentary melancholic grandeur. I belch with rumbling, gurgling acid power. I almost faint on account of the overwhelming odour that suddenly bubbles from my anarchic throat. I cough, choke, spit and groan. Oh, that's terrible, that is disgraceful! I swallow clumsily and almost vomit in disgust. Christ! Only one thing for it. Reluctantly, I drag a precious cigarette from my dwindling pockets and strike my match with mad haste. Bugger! I try again. And fail again. I have three matches left. I wrap my coat around the crook of my shielding arm and try again, my head bent in desperation. The little blot of sulphur spits and hisses and survives. It burns in flickering, sulky fragile life. I smoke. The moist, cheesy fumes smother the revolting cud on my tonsils. I breathe smoke deep and struggle to pleasure. I sit back a little, I ease my knees and pocket my hands. I compose myself.

SUNDAY

ONE

Already the day is humming. Hum hum, it goes. It's a strangely irritating sound peculiar to Sundays. Even in my etiolated unsocial state Sundays horrify me. Sundays strike their dull terror into my soul. Sundays, those Sundays, they make me sweat and gibber with horror. Much that is engaging about Sundays – rest, ease, contemplation and comfort, etc. – its unattainable for the majority of the population. These are restricted pleasures. Sundays! Only vicars, widows and cricketers like them. I've never met anyone who likes Sundays.

This particular Sunday is a very bad Sunday so far, even by the standards of Sundays in general. It hasn't started well. For instance, Perry died this morning. Yes, he did. Well, actually he **may** well have died last night. We can at least say that he was dead this morning – so it's still Sunday's fault. It's a curious thing to say – 'He *was* dead.' As if it was something he had any control over or say in. As if it **was** an act of performance. It isn't of course. You can't *be* dead as such. You are dead. Death's intransitive, perhaps reflexive even. Or is it? It's a difficult area. Grammar can't seem to cope.

Perry's dead. I ask myself how I feel about **this** and I'm not quite sure. I think it's bad . . . what I feel I mean. In fact, I'm quite sure I don't feel good about it. I'm not celebrating. It makes me unhappy, bitter, tired and melancholy. I struggle with my selfishness and find that I liked Perry. I did. I had a wealth of admiration, gratitude and pity for Perry.

(Pity gets a bad press, these days. God knows why but people are usually indignant to find that they are pitied. They don't like it. This is wicked and foolish. Who are we in our egocentric folly to devalue the emotion of pity? I myself would love to be pitied right now. I'd take any charitable offers. Pity is nice. Pity can be beautiful. Think of the last time you felt real pity for someone. Come on, think about it. That weight of selfless solicitude and care. For your child, your wife, your mother or something. See? There, that's not an unpleasant thing, is it? Three cheers for pity. Weakness and

235

disability should be cherished. Given half a chance, weakness is not something to be ashamed of. It's there. Give it room. Let it breathe. Have a little pity on it. I do. I allow my weakness to live, I give it its head.)

Perry wasn't around when I dawdled over to Putney this morning. When I went looking for him at the shack I found a harassed doctor and a quartet of coppers and ambulancemen. They were wrapping old Perry up when I got there so I knew the score immediately.

The coppers quizzed me about him for a while and seemed annoyed that I had got in their way. Anything I told them would spell more paperwork and these two boys were no Nobel prizewinning authors to say the least of it. They were very cheesed off indeed and treated me with scant respect, tramp that I am. Even the doctor was excessively brusque when I asked him how the old man had died. He bullshitted about emphysema for a while before buggering off. They didn't like the look of me and weren't keen on my conversation. I can't say I blame them. It was a depressing scene in that rickety little shack. I'm glad Perry wasn't around to see it.

Apparently, Perry had been something of a cause célèbre with social services down there in Putney and had even been mentioned in a couple of local rags. They called him the Old Man of the River or something revolting like that. Halfway through this ordeal, a local photographer arrived to take some mournful photographs of this dead semi-celebrity. He was very excited about this opportunity for his art and wanted me to pose for him, suitably distressed. I told him to fuck off so he had to content himself with snapping the shack, the coppers and the ambulance. I have a funny feeling the bastard took a picture of me when I wasn't looking. I was too tired to enquire.

I escaped as soon as I could – it was getting me down and the Peelers were growing inquisitive. I managed to bum a couple of fags from one of the ambulancemen. He gave me a box of matches as well. He was a nice man. He noticed my stab wound when I was putting the cigarettes in my pocket and wanted to take me back to the hospital with him. I just about talked him out of it by promising to go to Casualty later that day. I don't think he was convinced but he didn't want to argue.

Before I left, he asked me if I wanted to see it. I misunderstood at first but when I realised he was talking about Perry's corpse I was horrified. No, I didn't want to see Perry! I didn't want that sadness. Not at all. Dead, covered and whipped away as he was, Perry was safely gone. I could manage that quite well. It was clean, unfussy, remote. If I'd seen him, he would have stayed with me. It wouldn't have been just a corpse, a hunk of dead, smelly meat. It would have been Perry. A real thing. Perry was a memory now and I wanted to keep it that way. It was easier. Perry had been here and now he was gone. Simple. Belonging to the faculties of recollection already. In between these trim calculations, there was this corpse thing, this sack of melting flesh and organ. That had nothing to do with me. Nor a great deal to do with Perry anymore.

You know, I cried as I limped back into town. I wept and sobbed hard. Sometimes grief can take its time to hit you but when it gets around to hitting you, you stay hit. Grief's terrible. So sad. The worst thing about grief is the beady eye it brings to bear upon your own pride and self-love. When someone has died, the merest movement, the tiniest gesture, the poorest pleasure, seems like the vilest of selfishness. Like smoking a cigarette in the presence of a lung-cancer victim. Suddenly, you seem to be revelling in that constant alphabet of experience that is lost to the dead. Sky, air, smell and sound appear furtive, stolen from your dead friend. You are loaded with guilt and embarrassment. This is a weird feeling and it really fucks you up if you let it. You mustn't allow this. Catch a grip on yourself. It's not your fault that you're alive. Death is not your responsibility. None of it is your fault. Don't blame it on the sunshine – blame it on the boogie.

Oh grief, what a bad un you are! Grief is the spilt milk of regret. Grief is when you broke the best vase as a six year old and prayed for a miracle of reconstruction before your parents came home. Grief wants the clock turned back. It craves a second chance. Death is not like that. Death is definite, absolute, ineluctable. Death spells the end. The act and fact of dying, the cessation of the vital organs and functions of the human being, the departure of the soul and spirit. Full stop. Grief can't bend those rules.

I'd like to mourn Perry but I don't know how. I'm in the grip of a surplus of sentiment and pain but I don't know what to do with it. I cared for Perry and was grateful for his affection and help but what can I do about his death? I'm ill-equipped to be the old man's mummer. I doubt that he would have expected it of me. I doubt he'd have wanted it if offered. Most folk would probably hope for a better mourner than me.

When my father died I was too young and too stupid to have much of a clue about a suitable reaction. When Maurice died I performed an approximation of mourning. But it was a feeble thing, mainly composed of anger, guilt, hatred, regret and remorse. None of these quick emotions would seem to apply to Perry's demise and I'm too tired and shamed to work on another version.

I think I should talk to his family. You remember that I mentioned his sons. Well, I know where one of them lives. I'll have a wash and try to do Perry proud. Yes. No matter how unfilial, I'm sure Perry's son would want to hear about his old father's death. Of course he would. No one's that callous or that busy. That's what I'll do. I'll freshen up a little and go and chat up Perry's son. Though hardly a harbinger of joy, I'll be welcome. I was Perry's friend and mentor — I taught him everything he knew. The son will want to know. Bound to.

Balls! No chance. If the sons disowned their pauper father while he was still alive, they're unlikely to get the bunting out for his cheesy trampfriends now that he's safely and silently dead. They won't want to know. They don't sound like the guilty types. I'm too dirty and not posh enough to play the part of Conscience. Forget it. They won't be interested.

It's not much of a death, is it? A squalid piece of shacktheatre starring five bored and busy professionals, a callous photographer and a sentimental, procrastinating tramp. Oh, that's bad. Perry wasn't up to much in the eyes and gauges of the world but he deserved more than that. Surely.

A terrible admission. While they were all rooting around outside the shack, dumping Perry into the meatwagon, I nipped inside, rifled around rapidly and nicked his dosh. I knew where it would be and I was right. In his tobacco tin, buried under a thick layer of weed. It was easy. Seventy-five quid! Where the fuck did he get all his dosh from? Seventy-five quid. Christ almighty, it's a fortune! I slipped it into my coat and mosied on out again.

A disgusting thing to do? Perhaps. I'm sure Perry would rather it went to me than get lost in posthumous bureaucracy. He cared about me. You know he did. You saw that. Anyway the crime wasn't in taking the money. No, the crime was in looking for it in the first place.

Another terrible admission. After trudging through my self-disgust all the way back into town, I climbed onto Waterloo Bridge and chucked the seventy-five quid into the river. I threw those fifty packets of Benson & Hedges into the water, I dropped that thousand cigarettes into the Thames. I'm penniless again but at least I've got my dignity. Ha fucking ha! Christ in heaven, the things I do sometimes!

*

Perry told me once that he had dreams about being a young man again. All fit, healthy and big in breath. On waking, the sensation produced by these dreams was so agreeable that the fantasy began to infiltrate his days as well. It moved in and set up house. It was involuntary at first but soon Perry began to daydream about this intentionally. In these fantasies he did not appear as he actually had been as a young man, he appeared as a new, improved version. Taller, stronger, better looking, more intelligent and (you have to laugh) with a larger penis. It was most enjoyable, he said, to have a firm, flat belly and strong thick legs once more. Abundant hair and a smooth face. It was wonderful to be young but these daydreams always made him feel curiously ashamed and ridiculous. For Perry, this longing to be someone else was the most comic disgrace of all. An old man with his laughable pipe dreams and improbabilities.

I told him not to worry and all that kind of reassuring and affectionate stuff. I told him it was no big deal but I began to worry on my own behalf when I started having similar fantasies myself. It was all right for Perry because he was ancient but I was only a kid for chrissakes! I didn't tell him about this. I didn't think he'd have been interested.

TWO

I pull out the first of my fags. I hold it high, close to eye. I recognise my bondage to these small things. I produce that match and with brave, reckless hand I strike. Look. Flame. Fag. Full happiness. I inhale hardily. I, Vlad the Inhaler, smoker of the many! I pull hard, I suck it up. Oh, my gladdening happy Christ! I'm whole again. I'm me again. And out it comes in a straight, clean whoosh of carbons and rejected air. Wheeee!

Rigid in the sky, the clouds weep their gentle stuff. Today is a greyer day altogether. It's warm but the light is throttled by banked, strangling clouds and long finespray drizzle. I'm glad in a way. This is conspicuously more like it. Sunny Sundays are in some ways the least endurable type of Sunday. At least this particular Sunday isn't trying it on or chancing its arm. It is awash with dull, clogged air and slow, trundling crowds, aimlessness and heavy boredom. You could bottle it and call it Essence of Sundays. Ah, but who would buy the frigging stuff? The Americans, no doubt. Or perhaps the Welsh.

Now that I can look back upon it from the vantage point of a couple of hours later, I find it tremendously hard to believe that I chucked those seventy-five smackers into the drink. What a jerk! I could do with that dosh now. I need it now. It would be effusively welcome. Because ... yes, you've been waiting for this to happen, haven't you? ... Hunger has come back to see me. He sent his boys round earlier this morning to put the frighteners on me but like a jerk, I ignored them. Now, the big bossman himself has arrived on the scene. Apparently, Hunger has already heard about the rent I threw in the river and is distinctly unamused by the incident. He has calculated that the filthy lucre concerned would have kept me fed for a month, if wisely handled. Already, just for starters, He has offered to cut my kidneys out and nail them to my ears. I can tell he's upset.

After Hunger's little visit my poor old innards threw a bit of a wobbler. They all clanged and sang and clapped. My belly ballooned and stretched as Pain went to work with its sledgehammers, hacksaws and gelignite. Quite horrible. Thought I was going to split open, that I was going to get one of those compulsory Momus' Glass arrangements. Very unpleasant indeed.

I must do something, that much is clear. I haven't eaten since my big charity binge on Friday and I don't know how much grace my gut will give me. Probably not a great deal if I know my gut. I'll have to get some sustenance PDQ. Having come so far, I wouldn't like to peter out for lack of fuel. I've a lot of unhappiness to get through. I need all the glucose I can get.

Anyway, I'm nearly finished. My story is dragging to its end now. There's not much left. A few concluding details, a couple of inaccuracies to be cleared up. All the business of conclusion. The seal of finality and end. Nearly there.

In the end I got booted out of Cambridge. Or as they would prefer – I was sent down, don't you know. It amounts to much the same in that I was chucked out on my ear. I lost all that hard-won privilege in minutes. I just fucked up. Old Byron said that it was because my work hadn't been good enough, that I hadn't applied myself and all that kind of thing. There was some truth in that but it was far from being the main reason. I think it was really because they didn't like me, those dons. I had put too many people's backs up. I had pissed off one too many. Well about fifteen too many, as a matter of fact. They all obviously considered me a yob. Not the sort of chap they wanted in their college. They slung me out.

Naturally, I was upset. All that comfort and respectability thrown away like that. It had taken an awful lot of bollocks for me to get to Cambridge in the first place. And now, after all my little trials, I was back in the same position I had occupied before I went there. I was on the wrong side of Shit Street once again.

I think the thing that hurt most was that I had completely ruined all the good work I had put into the Laura Problem. I mean, I had got there with the Big L, I had achieved my romantic objectives, I had finally made it and now I was nuking all my fond hopes of erotic permanence. Laura was, of course, furious with me. She thought that it was all my own fault and a waste of talent, etc. She was quite right and bloody cheesed off about it. As was her right, I suppose. Needless to say, she couldn't afford to bask in my new aura of failure and rejection. She had a lot of success to get on with. So, regretfully, sadly, grateful for the brief but good times, she let me know with all her gentleness that it was not to be.

I cried a river as I packed my meagre bags. I was grief-stricken. Destroyed. I'd just lost the lot. My success, my entrée, my opening, and my major bimbo. How could I have been such an arsehole?

On the day I left Cambridge, Laura and I met under a sanguine tree in

Christ's Pieces. It was a very emotional scene. Lots of sobbing, pleading and girlish recriminations . . . from me, at any rate. I was rather enjoying myself, if truth be told. It seemed a noble and dynamic sort of scene, the sort that I should play by rights. I don't think Laura could have seen it like that. She signally failed to come up with the melodramatic goods and didn't cry once. I think my theatrics depressed her. The worst bit was that when I tried to kiss her she backed away and wouldn't let me. Over, she said. Over.

So sad. I turned my sorry sights towards the fine old city of London.

Thus, I wazzed around for a year or so in the metropolis, doing odd jobs – building sites, pubs, cafés – that kind of thing. I got myself a grotty flat in Finsbury Park and led the life of disaffected London youth. Despite the gaping, bleeding loss of Laura, I had a surprisingly good time. I usually had round about enough dosh and though I made few new friends, I even managed to get myself a girl. She was called Jenny and worked for one of those glossy women's magazines that talk about orgasms, G-spots, the New Man and cervical smears. She was very doing-things-going-places was Jenny. A real career woman, you could say. What with me being such a very competent doss artist this could be a pain in the arse sometimes but, generally speaking, we got on pretty well. I liked young Jenny. She was unpleasantly healthy, successful and wealthy but I still liked her. She was intermittently keen on me as well. She really liked going to bed with me for some reason. (God knows why – I was never very good at all that orgasm business. Never seemed to have the requisite time or lung capacity.) Why yes, she certainly enjoyed boffing my poor old bones! She was big on such things as sexual autonomy (!) and unfettered self-expression. I was mystified as to exactly what any of this meant but I suspect that was the casuist justification for some of the revolting things that she used to do to me. I couldn't see the attraction – I mean Jenny was thoroughly boffworthy by anyone's standards and I was already in pretty bad shape by that time what with the fags and booze and cultured indolence and all. Nonetheless, she persisted in knobbing me as much as possible.

All in all, I believe it lasted nearly a year with Jenny. She wouldn't let me move into that swish Chelsea flat of hers and insisted on maintaining her casual rights with other men. Some guy proposed to her. Some middle-aged, balding editor. She accepted on the spot, naturally. She consoled me with the observation that I appealed to her darker side or something like that. I was 'affair material' she explained lightly.

I suppose it was always doomed to failure. I had made no secret of my still-kicking longing for the cruel Laura. So, what did I expect? I pined openly and this annoyed Jenny, strangely, considering the fact that she was busy rogering half of West London most of the time. I mean, what is it with girls? Who do they think they are? Nowadays, if you so much as say a word against women, the feminist SAS come round and bite your balls off double-quick. Girls feel fully free to slag us blokes off all the time but if we try it we're sexist, chauvinist, fascist, Methodist even. What a load of crap! The vast majority of women are full of shit. Just like the vast majority of men, myself included. The bims have gotta take their share of the flak for this. There have been so many times in my life when I have wanted to tell some bird what a jerk she is. Practically every day of my life. But you can't do it. You can do it with a fella and get away with it (if he's small enough). If you try it with a girl she'll kill you, she'll chop you up. We're always hearing that girls are supposed to like men with a sense of humour, that manly laughter attracts women. But if that manly laughter extends to some of the awful bollocks these women come out with then bang! – the end – you wake up in Intensive Care. (Girls can really thump. They can *dig*. I'm told that when a woman hits you are supposed to come over all masterful and dominant, grasp her flailing arms, lift her off her feet and snog her into submission. I can never manage that. I always drop like a stone on the first punch.) Men are supposed to be ever vigilant against their own misdemeanours and grosser traits and then completely ignore the dirty great howlers that the ladies habitually commit. It's hardly fair.

Come on, boys, speak up! Give some of these autonomous bimbos a bit of their own. Criticise, mock, cavil, throw your weight around a bit. Don't let them grind you down. Go gay if you have to. Don't let the tampons get away with it. Show them who's boss.

The trouble with girls is . . .

Risk. Mostly. What you stand to lose. The poetry of diminishing returns. The hazards of erotic investment. Ever had a lot of dosh? Ever lost a lot of dosh? See what I mean? No? A kind of poetry in there. Doggerel perhaps but who's counting?

Those two great joys and two leaden chains. Girls let you see them. They make you acknowledge your net loss. The mismatch of your profundities. The fact that time is absolute, that life is irresolute, death dissolute and that love fails to rhyme, try as you might.

Girls are Love's accountants. They try to balance your books, a hazardous enterprise, seldom fun. They'll work hard but their commission is high, horribly high. Heaven help you if you fall behind!

Actually, the real trouble with girls is that they never seem to love you the way they ought to.

Jenny certainly suffered badly from that little shortcoming. She walked right out on me, only pausing to tell me what a no-hoper I was. Apparently, I was paralysed by my cleverness and my nationality. She told me that I could no longer afford to go on living on the grace of other people's tolerance. It would run out soon. I wasn't going to get away with it for very much longer. I was hardly worth the bother. I was cute but no big deal.

I missed Jenny more than I would have thought probable. Her leaving affected me quite badly. I cracked up a little bit. I even gate-crashed her wedding where I distinguished myself immensely by shouting out in the middle of the ceremony:

'Stop! That woman is having my child!'

Oh boy, was I popular.

There were times, after Jenny's brusque exit, when I actually wanted to die. To stop this diverting story of mine. Goodness me, I desired it utterly, despite the urgent claims of rounded narrative. I didn't really consider suicide or anything like that – I was too handsome and working class for that – but I didn't make any long-term plans. I thought of Laura and the sisterhood of rejection she formed with old Jenny. Christ, what was wrong with me? It must have been something pretty major, quite fundamental. The quickest route to humility is to have the women in your life despise you. My word, the contempt of others really gets your faltering self-disgust raring to go.

With the help of varying amounts of cheap booze I slid into a squelching mulch of self-pity, envy and erudite regret. One night, I got so pissed that I tried to beat my landlord up. A big mistake as his consequent pugilistic skills proved. He kicked me shitless and dumped me on the pavement outside my pad. I was too embarrassed and terrified to go back for my things.

That was just after the New Year and since then I've been more or less as you see me now. Dossed around and tramped it up, clochard-fashion. The winter was bad. It was by far the worst part of my twenties so far. My previous sorties into the world of homelessness had been blessed by temperate skies and gentle months. I didn't have the indigent expertise needed to comfortably survive a winter on the streets. Still, I got by, somehow. Nearly lost a few fingers and certainly didn't have much fun but I pulled through. (The snow nearly got me though. It was a close, close thing with the snow. I don't want to talk about it.)

I saw Jenny a couple of months ago. This is not the coincidence it seems as I had been hanging around outside her flat for days. In the hope of some guilt-provoking cadging. I felt sure I would get quite a lot of quids off her. No chance! When she eventually spotted me one afternoon, she tripped on by before I could limp into range. She pretended not to know me. Though to be fair, on reflection it was probably the greatest kindness she could have done me. After that setback I gave it up and left her to her tubby hubby.

And that's about it up to now. Winter passed, spring failed to happen and now the middle months are here. I'm hungry and wounded and tired but not much else is happening on the life-threatening front. Apart from the cold and wet and heat, these past few homeless months tend to merge into one maudlin gang of reversal and outrage. I've had my little adventures of course. I could hardly fail to have a lot of those since I've been patrolling the outdoors so much. But these don't interest me. They're plausible, predictable, incidental. You don't want to hear about them. Of course you don't.

So, two years ago I was munching pheasant in oaken chambers brimming with the gentry and now I'm licking the lichens off London's lavatory walls. There's a certain amount of vulgar, catchpenny resonance in that observation, don't you think? A smattering of purely adventitious profundity.

You don't agree? No? You're probably right. It's been done before. All old hat. You'd think that, considering all the pain and sorrow my life plies me with, it would at least take the trouble to be original.

THREE

Do you want to hear something wonderful? Would you like a little anecdote? A story, *une petite histoire*? Yes? OK then, fine.

One night a couple of weeks ago I was wandering down some festering main street in south London, unhappily chewing the cold and smoking like a bugger. It was fucking freezing – couple of hours after midnight – the bad part of a cold night. Near the end of that sleepless road, outside an armourplated off-licence, I saw a kid doing much the same as me – just dandering along. He was wearing a shortsleeved shirt and a pair of greasy pyjama bottoms while I almost froze to death in my ragged but thick overcoat. He was barefoot! It was nearly three o'clock in the morning, the place was absolutely deserted and this kid couldn't have been much more than six years old! I'm not normally the soppy type as you might have gathered but this really hit me hard. A fucking toddler roaming the mad old streets at this time of night! I mean to say – it's just not on, is it? Even for childless, sterile, selfish young bastards like myself this sort of thing is hard to swallow comfortably. His smeared face and bluecold hands. And those crusted scarified toes! He was singing blithely enough, the little bugger. Some childishly precocious pop ditty. I could scarcely believe it. So ... what did I do? Talk to him, take him back to where he belonged, give him some dosh, call an ambulance, a social worker, a priest, a camera crew? No! No, I did none of this. I crossed the road and passed by as quickly as I could. I was too scared to go anywhere near him. I had visions of myself taking two tentative, philanthropic steps towards him and instantly being arrested, beaten up, charged, found guilty, sentenced, banged away and then gangbanged with baseball bats in a poky latrine deep in the heart of Wormwood Scrubs. Now, I ask you ... what kind of a world can this be?! What has happened to all of us? I was fucking frightened to help this solo nightkid! I just schlepped on by.

In my defence, I must add that five minutes later I grew so disgusted with my cowardice that I went back to find him. He wasn't there by the time I had retraced my steps. I looked hard for him but he'd disappeared. I slunk away, deeply ashamed. What about that, then? I'm a regular hero am I not? Pretty impressive stuff.

Relax. It was a spoof. Sorry. I was just trying out some epiphany stuff to get the concluding mood going. What do you think? Touching? Trite? Implausible? Anyway, I've nixed it already. It was cute but not quite up to scratch. It's out.

It's easily done, isn't it? This spoofing business. It's a constant temptation. And though it smacks of the Australian picaresque, quite an easy trap to fall into, so to speak. And though I hate to give myself away like this, betray my natural vulgarity and predictability; I am forced to admit that over the past couple of days I have not held the banner of Veracity and Rectitude as steadily as I might have done. It's true. I haven't quite been candid, my honesty has wavered rather. I haven't told you the whole hard truth.

For instance, you might have noticed that I was not exactly expansive in my account of the events surrounding the death of Maurice. That must have set you thinking. I mean it deserved a mention – it's not every day that the friend of one's youth gets it in the neck from a bunch of urban terrorists! Bit of a bloody gap in the narrative, don't you think! Well, I had my reasons. My conduct in this matter was rather ambiguous. I was embarrassed. Shy. I wasn't sure you'd be interested. (As if!)

Well now, soon after his seventeenth birthday young Maurice's involvement in Nationalist politics extended from the theoretical to the more practical issues. In short, he joined the IRA, that silly sausage. He got his grimy little mitts on some hardware. This was, of course, supposed to be a black secret but half the school knew about it within the week. Me? Oh, I was surprised and much perturbed. I was very fond of my Maurice, I didn't want to see him growing any gunshot wounds. I had a serious talk with him. A heart to heart. A discursive, allusive, solicitous slanging match. I tried to tell him all that stuff about guns and bombs and all – how dangerous and adult they were and that sort of thing. I did my best to warn him. I screamed at him, called him a stupid bastard and even hazarded the possibility of my duffing him up. (A rather dangerous notion now that Maurice was a bona fide Provie!)

Maurice did not take this in the manner I had intended and indeed advised me to go and fuck myself. I pleaded, begged, whined and sobbed. I pointed out the moral error involved in the wholesale slaughter of civilians. Maurice pulled me up short at this. His mad eyes cleared and I could tell that he was going to say something that he was particularly proud of. He told me that no civilians would be killed. Only soldiers, policemen, prison officers, the UDR, etc. They were legitimate targets, he claimed.

'Legitimate!?!' I squeaked scornfully.

'Yes. Legitimate.'

'Don't be stupid!'

'They're here. We didn't invite them. What do they expect?'

'You must be joking.'

He wasn't.

'There is a military presence in Ulster that doesn't belong here. The Brits aren't Irish, the Unionists aren't Irish, not properly. What does that make them?' he asked.

'Fucking lucky,' I replied, rather neatly, I thought.

'Yeah, that's funny. That's very fucking funny. It makes them invaders.'

Goodness, I had a fit. I laughed my socks off.

'Invaders? Christ, Maurice! Get help. Watch your grammar here. Your propaganda's slipping and your petticoat is showing.'

'You're a nice fella, Ripley, but you can be a smug bastard sometimes.'

'Aw, stick it up your arse!'

It wasn't much of a rational disagreement, hardly an equable exchange of views. I went home, slept off my anger and resolved to try again the next day. I had thought of something good to ask him, something thorny – difficult. I put a purely hypothetical proposition to him. I asked him what he would do if he was asked to participate in the random elimination of 'civilians'. Not that such a thing could happen, of course. But what would he do in that unlikely event?

He told me that he would simply refuse. No way, he'd say, nix, no chance, sorry – it's just not on.

I think that was when I began to worry about young Maurice in earnest.

Many months passed clumsily by and the rumour was that Maurice was becoming involved in all kinds of dirty doings. Much of this was, doubtless, bullshit of the highest order but it was clear that he was, at the very least, up to a large amount of no good. This depressed me. I knew Maurice didn't have the lexicon of brutality and evil needed to survive in an Irish Paramilitary group and I was sure that it would end in tears. It ended in much worse than that.

Just after Christmas, Maurice arrived at one of my lesser hovels on Indiana Avenue and sought sanctuary with me, his dear friend. He was pale, panting and visibly shitscared. They were after him, he said. I wasn't sure exactly who he meant by 'they' but I could bet my buttons that they wouldn't be friendly folk. He claimed that he was sorry to get me involved like this but that there was nothing else he could do. He said that if I could just hide him for a bit, he would get a boat to England and lie low for a while, or something similarly cinematic. He pulled out an enormous revolver and assured me that it would all be all right if we kept our heads. I swear I almost pissed my pants.

Apparently, there had been some kind of little tiff in the ranks of whatever faction Maurice had belonged to. It seems that my friend had been both vocal and indiscreet in his choice of ally in this disagreement. In the subsequent putsch, his splinter group had been rather heavily defeated and was now in the process of being randomly decimated. Maurice's name was prominent among those due for elimination. He was, in short, primed for the chop. It was dying time.

How did I feel about all this? Fucking terrified, naturally. I was a schoolboy, for chrissakes! I was an infant, a frigging toddler! If someone was coming round to bump Maurice off they would hardly let me off on account of what a nice guy I was. If they found us I would get it firmly in the neck. Why had he come to me? They were bound to check out Maurice's buddies and I'd be near the top of that list. Here was me wanting to go to Cambridge and here was the IRA trying to blow my fucking head off! It was outrageous, insupportable. It was very disagreeable indeed.

Nonetheless, I swallowed my terror (with some difficulty) and promised to aid my old chum. He was, after all, my friend. I couldn't leave him to get all shot up. I didn't welcome this new trial but I had no other choice. Nothing else for it. Maurice knew that before he came.

He couldn't stay with me – that much was obvious, to my great relief. We would have to find somewhere for him to doss until he could sneak offski. We racked our frantic brains for hours that night before coming up with a truly terrible idea.

We spent a sleepless night in my room, icy and talkative with fear. I learnt a lot about Maurice – mostly about how surprisingly stupid he was. He was full of nonsense about the havoc he would wreak with that gun of his in the event of our being caught. I tried telling him that his gun would be no help and that he would be too dead to employ it usefully but he wouldn't listen. He vowed to take a few of the bastards with him. I hoped fervently that he wasn't going to include me in this excursion of his. Life was beginning to look up for me – I wanted to stick around to see how it all panned out.

Next day, we got an early bus to Kilkeel, a fishing village in County

Down. Maurice's dad had a little boat parked in the harbour there and we planned that Maurice should use this for the maintenance of his low profile. The boat was tiny, risible, but it would do in the want of any better as Maurice was keen to point out. I bought some grub and fags in the local grub-and-fags shop and said goodbye. Like the fool he was, my friend was in rather good spirits. I think he enjoyed the gipsy nature of his retreat and it must have been quite affecting to have me waiting upon him in this manner. He was full of plans about how we would meet up in Evil England once I got into Cambridge and suchlike. It was sad for I knew Maurice was going to die. I knew that quite well.

He was grateful to me for risking my neck on his behalf (as well he might be!) and said that despite the fact that there was nothing about me he liked, I wasn't all bad. Though this was obviously culled from the gruff, un-emotional, buddy-bond school of tenderness, I found it rather touching in spite of myself. We said our goodbyes and I buggered off, leaving Maurice with his silly gun and sillier optimism.

The next few days were very bad days indeed. I saw Maurice once for about half an hour and spent the rest of my time in Belfast, studiously crapping myself. My work suffered badly. I found that I couldn't really concentrate on Dryden or Sir Thomas Browne with the threat of imminent assassination hanging over me. I was thrown, rather. I was weak with terror the whole time. It was, as you can imagine, an awfully strange position for me to be in. Normal life, the great flat plain of mundanity is but rarely disrupted by this kind of quick, stiff danger. This was motion picture stuff. Not the kind I wanted either. I wouldn't have minded playing a minor role in a couple of soft porn delights but I didn't want to branch into the violent Ulster thriller genre. I was scared, man!

It's curious to note exactly what constant fear does to one. Hilariously enough, fear does actually have a deleterious effect upon one's digestion – yup, you sure do spend a lot of time on the bog. This is bad in several ways. Firstly, it is not, in essence, a great deal of fun. Secondly, one is consider-ably more vulnerable to terrorist attack in that position. Thirdly, embarrass-ment – few folk would want to pop their clogs while asquat upon their cuckstool. The other thing that constant, mad fear graces you with is a vivid hatred for the passing of time – especially at night. One works oneself up into such a funk that minutes hurt, hours injure and days supply the coup de grâce. You drift into paranoia with some ease. Nights are spent in trying to cajole unpunctual dawn and days are spent waiting for the anonymity of darkness. All your time is filled with horror and weeping exasperation. And it's a cumulative thing – it snowballs, this timely fear. The longer it continues the worse it gets. By the end you'll be chewing your ears with fright.

Of course, in the end, they lifted me as I was walking home from school. I hadn't bargained on this, poor fool. In my room, I was purple with wariness and suspicion but when I was outside I waltzed gaily around, as I thought, perfectly safe. Silly of me, wasn't it?

Three men bundled me into an old Bedford van just outside Coulter's Garage at the top of the New Lodge. They put a bag over my head and told me to keep my gob shut or they'd break my legs. I concurred.

This was at half past four in the afternoon, thin light still dripping from the retreating sky. We must have travelled for hours because when I was kicked out of the van, I could see from under my hood that it was now dark. The pavement was wet and reflected the patched street lamps in its dull grey sheen. For some reason I was suddenly desperate that I should not die in the rain. That I should not lie last on wet pavements, with all my stuff getting all muddy and rained on. I was cold and my trousers were still wet from where I had pissed myself in the van. This had incurred some wrath from my captors, one of whom had kicked me in the ribs for my lapse.

We walked away from the van and turned down some kind of hill. I stumbled often, sightless in that dark. The fellow who had kicked me in the ribs cursed me and kicked me as much as he was allowed, which was really quite a lot.

We came to a house. One of the men knocked on the door and we waited, rather edgily on my part. I heard the distant hoot of some struggling boat. A harbour, that meant. Larne? Derry? Kilkeel? I hoped it wasn't Kilkeel. The door opened, I was shoved inside and we moved through some quite large rooms before I was brought to a halt. A chair was pressed hard into the back of my knees and I sat down heavily. There was some muttering, the sound of exiting footsteps and a voice advised me:

'Five minutes. Stay good and you'll be fine.'

For that five minutes I simmered in wretched terror, my hooded head streaming with sweat and silent, squeezing tears. I breathed hard, my mouth flapping fishily. My eyes stung with heat and sweat and the hood would stick to my mouth and nose as I inhaled. My neck streamed and my hair dripped salt dampness onto my collar. Jesus, for an awful moment I thought I was drowning in myself. Being asphyxiated by my own steam and sweat. Actually, this was all quite handy in that it took my mind off the pressing business of my probable, imminent demise.

Soon enough the hood was whipped off and I was blinded moistly by brightness. 'Fuck!' I said. 'Fuck up!' I heard someone reply. I took it in good part and kept my gob shut while my eyes adjusted to the (quite dim) light.

'Comfy now?'

I mumbled humble assent. There were two of them now. Medium height both, one balding and tubby − the other silent and hirsute with his Sinn Fein glasses and Gerry Adams beard. The bald guy spoke again.

'Well now, son, sorry to take you all the way out here but we have a wee problem and we need a wee hand. I hope you're just the fella to help us out here. What do you think?'

Carefully, with infinite calm, I replied that I didn't know. I winced, awaiting the blow, shot, stab, scream. None came. There was a brief silence. The bald guy smiled quite pleasantly and winked at his four-eyed friend. This worried me. Joviality didn't fit. Where was the cosh or the power drill? These boys weren't comedians.

'We're looking for Maurice Kelly. You know ... Maurice, your wee buddy. Well, we want to talk to young Maurice. We have something to say to him, you see.'

For some silly reason, my faltering confidence had burgeoned rather in those last few minutes and I was able to say with some élan:

'Maurice? He's buggered off. I don't know where he is. Nobody's seen him for weeks.'

There was another pause. My baldy chum wasn't smiling now. His breath issued jerkily, as if he had been trying to hold it back. He closed his eyes briefly and lit himself a cigarette. He didn't offer me one, the bastard. I was growing in ease now. It all seemed a little corny, embarrassingly cinematic. This bollock-head was obviously an amateur, a cowboy. He whispered something to his taciturn friend and turned back to me. He sighed theatrically, massively, as if summoning the last poor vestige of his patience and self-control. I almost giggled.

'Now, don't fuck us about, son. Just tell us where he is and you can fuck off home. I'm not in the mood for a cute cunt like you, believe me.'

Laughable, wasn't it? I leaned back in my chair and scratched my balls. I leered offensively at them.

'I just told you − I don't know where he is. How the fuck am I supposed to know. You're wasting your time ... really you are.'

Ah now, this was foolish. This was horribly misjudged on my part. Quick as a cow, the saturnine beard had produced a large automatic and was pressing it hard against my temple. I heard a click and felt a small vibration in my skull as the gun's workings slithered and shunted, primed for discharge. My bladder did its bit again and I smelt the rising smell of urine once more. The bald guy screamed at me. He was apoplectic − admirably so. He had a lot of anger, this fellow. It must have been quite a chore to keep it in check for so long. This was obviously the role he played in life. The anger part. He was the man who scared the shit out of people. He had only managed to make me wet myself so far but these were early days.

'Where is he, you stupid little cunt? Don't you know what we'll do to you if you piss us off? Have a bit of wit, kid. Tell us where he is!'

Oh man, I had pushed my luck too far and now my luck was shoving back. It was Telling Time, to be sure. No messing around now, it was most definitely time to tell.

Now, I imagine that few of you have ever had a gun held to your head. At least, I hope that few of you have notched up that nostalgic credit. It's a curious experience. Astonishingly odd, as a matter of fact. Especially, if one is, as I was, just an ordinary, everyday civilian bloke who has never envisaged the idea of his noggin one day making a pulpy target for some lunatic marksman. The thing about having a gun held to your head is that – it hurts! Yes, it really hurts. It does you damage. Half the time, the bastards don't have to shoot you in the end. The gun at the head has done enough. With that, havoc has already been wrought, it has all been taken care of. We're always seeing this kind of thing in the movies. The bad guy with the rod and the good guy kneeling, terrified, sobbing, sloshed with buckets of sweat effect. That's a good touch, that sweat business. My word, is perspiration a problem when one has a gun to one's head! A gun to the head sows it up. It kills the soul or something close. Death is a fingerflick away. A tiny trigger reflex and your head gets spread wide across the room. You're gone! Your life is someone else's decision.

This is why the old gun-at-the-head ploy is such a good one. It's unsubtle, barbaric, old-fashioned but it really gets the job done. It's a great incentive scheme. Few folk argue.

So, sitting there with that dirty great cannon stapling my temple, I tried to think of Maurice and all that life of his. I tried to think of friendship, honour and humanity. I tried to think of what this big gun would do to Maurice. I tried to think of how much that would hurt and appal. I tried. But I had that distraction. It was difficult. Very.

I spilt the beans, of course. In a big way. I sobbed and screamed my way to infamy. I told them everything. I told them about Kilkeel, the boat, the gun he was carrying. I told them things they didn't want to know. I just talked and sobbed and begged. I went to work on treachery and accomplished quite a lot.

They asked me to show them exactly where he was hiding. They wanted me to come with them. They told me to take my time, get my breath back and all that. They gave me handkerchiefs with which to mop my tears and cigarettes to smooth down my hysteria. They could scarcely have been nicer.

The car ride to Kilkeel seemed to take for ever. There were four of them now. The driver, a dark-haired man whose face I could not see; the taciturn guy with the beard who sat with him in the front; my bald friend and another man, a nasty-looking giant with a woollen hat and crooked teeth. These latter two sat on either side of me and occasionally directed glib comments to the driver who seemed to be a comic chap, always ready with the quick quip and ready giggle. Despite themselves, they made up a scary little bunch. They weren't really terrorists, these men. They weren't political, idealistic. They were crooks, thugs – they were just bad boys.

It was strange driving along the motorway. I watched the other cars slip in and past and by with longing. Cars populated by couples, families or single drivers. Lots of little lives that lacked this kind of incident and end. Dull, safe, mortgaged little lives. Abruptly, this seemed an exquisite state of being to me. How gladly I'd have swapped places with any of those mediocre, normal travellers, how happily I would have settled down into their motorway drudgery! God, how fucking precious life suddenly seemed while I sat in that car with those four lunatics! How very, very much I wanted to live.

It took us nearly two hours to reach Kilkeel. We travelled slowly, wishing for no attention. The car was parked near a soccer pitch in the middle of the little town and we walked towards the harbour, leaving our waggish driver behind. We walked in loose formation just like any friendly bunch of lads. It looked casual enough but I knew well that I'd be shot like a dog if I tried anything silly.

It was a rotten night; dark, cold and wet. The little road to the harbour glistened evilly, reflecting the straggling lamps dotted along its length at irregular intervals. Down on the little beach the invisible sea could be heard whispering gently to the soft, dark air. It wasn't late but there were few folk abroad. The dying night got me badly. I walked quickly, treading heavily, hoping that my footsteps would take the silence away. It didn't really work.

When we reached the harbour they stopped. The bald guy whispered in my ear. I pointed towards one of the small boats near the outer lip of the tiny harbour. He motioned me on.

I was to board the tiny craft and get Maurice onto the little walkway. I was to inform him that there had been a change of plan and that we had to get back to the city immediately. I was to walk towards my three captors with my friend and wait for whatever it was they were going to do. I knew I was going to be shot but I didn't much care now. I was tired and even rather bored. I wanted it all to be over. I wanted it to stop.

As I walked towards the little boat I glanced back and saw that my little trio of pals were loitering near the dark outer wall of the harbour. They looked full of business. Maurice would never see them in time. In time for what, for chrissakes! In time for what?

Maurice had his gob round a big red apple when I boarded his boat. The idiot reached for his ridiculous gun *after* he had seen that it was me. As a display of vigilance it was less than startling. I sensed myself growing awfully sad. He smiled, chucked the pistol back onto the tiny bunk and motioned me to sit down on the stool he had been occupying. He seemed pleased to see me. He must have been lonely, the poor fool.

'What's up?' he asked.

'Nothing.'

'Good.'

He gave me a cigarette and went on munching his apple. He seemed relaxed. He told me that he figured that since they hadn't caught up with him yet he was probably pretty safe from there on in. He was full of mocking praise for my courage and constancy. Friends were friends, he said. As sure as little white worms lived in big red apples. He laughed a lot at that. Apparently, he had spent most of his dull hours of late in creating useless and incomprehensible aphorisms. He might publish them one day, he said. They were bad enough.

Ah Christ, he was looking so bloody handsome that night. Just fucking superb. It made it harder for some reason. It was a crime against aesthetics, apart from anything else. The boy was simply too good-looking to die. His black, sleek hair, his creased, high concentrate grin and his square, even fucking chin! The entire kit of his facial perfections stood up and bellowed out to me: 'Come off it, Bogle, you can't! You know you can't. We're too perfect. Too great a loss!'

He finished his apple and took my cigarette from me. It was his last one apparently. He asked if I had brought him any more. He was surprised that I hadn't but said that we could get some when we got back to town. He sucked hard and gave the fag back to me. I inhaled slowly, dizzy with grief.

Me? I was numb. I was nauseous. I was on brittle overdrive. My mouth was well controlled, saying those things with some ease. My hands were steady and my brow was dry. But my eyes – my eyes were on their own. I kept thinking 'My God, he must see it! He must know something's wrong. Come on, surely it's obvious?' My eyes were giving it away. They were tipping him the wink.

No, they weren't. My poor old caring eyes were behaving themselves perfectly. They were keeping stum.

Maurice was keen to know why we had to move but he accepted my silence without protest. Lamblike to my slaughter. He extinguished his little battery lamp and I picked up his coat. He took it from me and shoved the revolver into one of the pockets. Before we left the boat he turned to me and said:

'Thanks, Ripley. I owe you one.'

Oh his smile was a picture, a small delight.

'Yeah, sure,' I said. 'Let's go.'

It was going well until our feet touched dry land. The sudden real air revived my flagging morals and I had a brief awareness of the naughtiness I was up to. My sphincter gasped and my bladder thought, oh no, not again. I stared landside, at the darkness of the high harbour wall and could see nothing. Where had the bastards gone? What was going on?

Maurice was already striding inland, towards the little town. My head crackled with panic and terror as I followed him slowly. Waiting to see his body jerk and splay and crumple. After about thirty yards he stopped and turned round. I was ten yards behind him and he waited for me to catch up. His face was open, guileless, tolerant of my poor pace. I neared as slowly as I could. My steps were leaden reluctant. Jesus, surely it would come now. Surely they would do it now while we were apart. No shot came and I drew level with my friend.

'Jesus, Ripley,' he chided gently. 'Get your arse in gear. It's not a fucking promenade.'

His smile was bemused, exasperated. And handsome of course. Oh yes, it was frigging adorable. Him and his smile. Aw, fuck this, I thought, just fuck this!

He didn't hear at first. He stopped again and looked at me in some surprise. My voice was thin, high-pitched. Again, he misheard. His eyes sparkled with dark streetshine as I repeated myself.

'What? I can't hear you. What?'

'Run, you stupid bastard! Run for fuck's sake!'

Still, he stood and looked into my face. I turned and saw a glint in the shadows under the harbour wall. His gaze followed mine and he saw it too. He choked in fear and his eyes swept back to mine, their sheen suddenly gone. He ran.

And where did he run? Away, of course. Towards the sea. Where else was there to run? He sprinted right to the end of the old jetty, right to the edge of the black water. He stopped and I saw his shoulders sag and tremble as he turned back towards me and lifted his arm in an abrupt, airy gesture – abnegation, annoyance or amused despair. He flipped in the air, staggered backwards and folded slowly forwards onto his knees. He looked up again and his neck suddenly sprouted a gout of blood and red flesh. He twisted sharply and dropped onto his face, thudding softly onto the old harbour stones. I heard steps behind me and soon felt the presence of the bald man at my side. Silently, we watched his two colleagues approach the body. The bearded man clutched a pistol with some kind of silencer attached. He bent over Maurice's prostrate form and beckoned towards the bald man at my side. My companion seemed to understand and he gestured towards the little boat. Through sudden tears I watched the two men carry the body into the boat, stumbling and almost dropping the corpse into the sea. I felt a small splash of vomit smack the back of my throat and had to swallow quickly to keep it down. My quiet gagging disturbed my silent captor and he put his fingers to his lips motioning me to silence. I kept my lips pressed tightly together lest my boky breath should escape and give him the smell of my fear.

The other two emerged from the little boat soon enough. The bearded man's eyes were heavy-lidded as if he was drugged or sleepy. He smiled at me, slowly. He produced the silenced automatic from under his coat and pointed it into my ribs. He looked at his bald buddy, smiled again and pulled the trigger, quite gently.

To do them credit, the other two didn't seem to find this funny. The hairy guy obviously couldn't care less and giggled all the more. Personally, I was pretty unperturbed either way for surprisingly my fear had faded and had been replaced by a great welter of weariness and discomfort. I didn't much care what happened as long as I didn't have to put any effort into whatever it was. I know that this sounds like the worst kind of thriller-writer bullcrap but it's true. Like Jacobean tragedy, Fear needs a sense of loss to survive. There didn't seem to be much left that I could lose.

They didn't kill me. They didn't shoot me. They didn't hit me. They didn't even warn me into silence. They weren't stupid and they knew that, as before, they didn't really need to do any of that. They did do something though. They did something devilishly clever. Something quite appalling in its implications for us all. What did they do? Why, they simply pushed me into that little boat, they untied its ropes and they pushed it off, the bastards. They sent me out to sea, me and Maurice.

Actually, Maurice wasn't quite dead. He was pretty close and definitely getting there but not quite bereft of life. This puzzled me at first while I struggled round the joky little craft, helpless with terror. Why hadn't they killed him? But when I calmed down and had a good look at old Maurice I realised that they had killed him, only slowly.

It wasn't so bad for the first couple of hours because Maurice was

257

unconscious and the moon was clouded over. The dark and relative silence (broken only by Maurice's great gobs of dying breath) were easy enough. Soon, however Maurice regained consciousness and started to scream, gruesomely enough. Mother of God, he just wouldn't stop screaming. Over and over, the same bitter, inarticulate cries. Accustomed to Maurice's usual rather stoic outlook this torrent of inebriate agony was doubly unwelcome and it stilled my little soul with the tricky grip of horror and panic. His eyes were open by this time. Wide open and boiling in his bloodied skull. His frantic hands tore at the frayed edges of his wounds, splitting his own soft flesh like a ripe, bloodfilled peach. This wasn't doing him any good and I had to pin his desperate, groping arms to the floor, fighting hard against his insane, livid strength. To do this, I was forced to sit on his shattered stomach and as my friend struggled, his blood pulsed and spurted onto the crotch of my trousers, seeping through that thin cloth and wetting my groin, warm and sticky.

Thankfully, the fury soon ceased and the mad strength ebbed as his screams died away, slowly gurgling in the nameless froth in his damaged throat. Gingerly, I inspected his wounds again, properly this time. One in the neck, one in his abdomen – slightly left of centre and one on the left side of his ribs right smack in the middle of Lungtown. This lung had obviously downed tools almost immediately and his chest was heaving as his right lung struggled to compensate. Maurice was quite definitely having oxygen trouble. I was surprised to find that the hole in his neck was quite small in comparison to his chest wound. It looked awful, ragged, slimy and glistening but had probably done less damage than the other two. It was curious how my friend's blood, so precious and integral to him, had such power to repel me. This, after all, was the very stuff of life. Bathetically enough, this made me feel a fierce and sudden love for the dying man. For he was surely dying now. The ragged, scored gaps in his smooth, precious body spat and dribbled dark, angry gore onto the soiled boards at the bottom of the boat. Yes, he was for the high jump.

It was just about then that I really began to consider the notion that Maurice was no more for this world. I felt bad about it as you might expect but my sentiments on the matter were far from clear. I was troubled with cloudy distractions. Guilt was billed for a starring role but had so far failed to show up. Weariness was there all right, putting in his usual reliable work and Grief was making motions from the wings but the show wasn't going well. Cues were being missed and lines fluffed. We seemed to have lost dramaturgical direction in the seat of my emotions. We needed a guiding hand.

By now, Maurice was very nearly quiet. He was whispering urgently and incoherently, his eyes revolving, searching for some frantic goal. He was venting massive bloody sobs of fear and pain and wasn't looking too good. I stared into his face. His nose was broken and bloody from his fall on the jetty and one of his eyes was puffy and closing fast. I called his name. There was no reply and no recognition. Still his mad eyes swivelled and his hands flapped and clutched. He was somewhere else obviously. Somewhere not very nice by the looks of it. In his monolunged fight for breath, his brain was obviously not getting its full quota of oxygen and this was, doubtless, no aid to the collection of his thoughts.

I left the tiny cabin and stumbled onto the uncovered portion of the boat. I could see the dotted lights of the coast on our right but had no idea how far away they were. We seemed to be drifting away from them at any rate and I wondered how long it would be before we, or rather I, was picked up. The moon had struggled through the gritty sky and was now dumping its paleness on all the waves around me. The sea itself was eerily quiet, easily crowded by the mad creaking of the little boat. I felt an insane desire for a cigarette. It was an appalling thought. Here was my best friend dying in agony more or less by my hand and my thoughts were sharp on my lust for tobacco. I tried to figure just what kind of a bastard I could be and came up with no good answer.

I sat outside for about an hour actively slowing my pulse and breathing calmly. Occasionally, Maurice would cry, or gurgle with particular volume but I ignored it. I didn't want to watch.

In the end I had to slip back into the cabin of course. Even I could not manage inhumanity of quite such proportions. As I opened the crazy little door, the sudden grey draught spun silver shining pain in his dying eyes. He tried to turn his ruined, spattered face towards me but couldn't. His mouth still moved with desperate urgency but there was no sound. I bent over him and tried to placate him.

'You're going to be all right,' I said.

I placed my frozen, slab-like hands into the warm, wet stream of gore still pumping from my friend's chest. I did not abate the flow but at least my fingers revived in his heat. When I removed my hands, he shuddered violently, a great retching spasm of agony. I smelt the unmistakable odour of liquid shite, squeezed from his ripped guts. This was both repulsive and touching. It was bitter to see my friend's strength and youth ebb so easily and squalidly away. It was disheartening to watch the blood spew and belch in great gouts of life. It seemed a surprisingly anarchic business in the end, dying. An arbitrary mechanical breakdown. I felt a great surge of pity and comprehension. Pain wasn't the bad thing about dying. It was fear, sorrow and grief that really got you down.

Maurice gurgled, bled and sobbed for another two hours or so. It ended just before dawn. In the end he seemed to conclude the business of dying very quickly. I didn't really notice until I saw the unsightly grey mucus oozing from the dead boy's nose. To my surprise, I felt no disgust and even touched the face lightly with the back of my hand. I breathed easier now, though still distressingly cigaretteless. It sounds heartless but I was relieved that it was all over. Maurice probably would have been the same. He hadn't seemed keen on fighting too desperately for the last of his life these past few hours. I think he was gladly dead.

I looked at his slumped, crumpled corpse. Like I say, Maurice had been handsome. Maurice was handsome no longer. I tried to think of what women's lips and hands had stroked that dead meat at the bottom of the boat. It seemed a world away. Maurice alive bore little kinship to this butchered, mangled mess of fleshrag and bloodstain. The fact that he made such a revolting spectacle in death made it worse somehow. A trim, elegant death wouldn't have been so bad. Something noble, Chattertonian. This heap of slime and carcass tickled my guilt. It was fitting really. He was my friend, his death was my fault and now his corpse would be my private nightmare. I knew him better than anyone now. I had seen him at his last intimate extremity. He belonged to me. I was sad, distressed and sorry but I had enough pride left to think this quite an impressive claim.

I was tired now and wanted a little relief. I struggled out of the cabin and stood straight in the cold, drizzled air. The rain was heavier now and this sapped my strength still further. The dull plate of the sea washed green, dead waters, flat and limitless around my tiny, beleaguered craft. The icy, gulping breeze stole my harshly issued breath and my ears stung and dripped with drizzle and spray. I didn't like this little boat. The notion of its rickety weight and mass being supported on the filmy, insubstantial essence of water filled me with dread. A tiny, illogical pinpoint on the vast, softskinned flesh of the sea. Its tenancy so fragile, so easily lost. The muddy, unwelcomed sea.

It had been a bad night by anyone's standards. I'd been kidnapped by terrorists, marooned at sea, my best friend had died and I had had to watch him do it. I would be in all kinds of bother when we were found. Police, soldiers, press. I felt rather embarrassed at my new, uninvited importance. It was like getting into trouble at school. You wanted to be small and insignificant. To escape notice and reparation that way. But it was a bit late for that.

I was desperate to micturate. I had been desperate for quite a while now but it hadn't seemed right when Maurice was still alive. I could hardly have asked him to hold on for a couple more minutes while I nipped outside for a piss. He was dead now though and it wouldn't bother him. (I can't help thinking that it wouldn't have made much difference to him earlier. He was pretty busy and all.) The impenetrable softness of the moist sky seemed to be pressing hard upon the sea. I began to feel the ponderous warmth of sleep beckoning my damp, cold limbs. That would come soon and gladly but first I had to pee.

With a heavy heart, I leant over the side of the boat and did it into the sea. You can see why I lied about it.

Now for spoof number two. You remember that when I told you about Deirdre's fabulous miscarriage I claimed innocence of the actual impregnation. Well, that was a lie. It was me really. I had planted that particular bun. Predictable really. You must have smelt a rat or two at the time. I'd been shtupping her from the start (after my initial failure of nerve, that is). The sprog, the mess whatever you want to call it, was most assuredly mine. And what's more the actual termination of the pregnancy, the very abortion itself was carried out by none other than yours perfidiously. It was a nasty business and cost us both some moral equivocation. It must have been a lot easier for her since she wasn't even a Catholic; Protestants had abortions all the time, practically every day. It was no sweat for them. No, it was definitely me that was doing the suffering.

When Deirdre told me she was pregnant she was lamentably vague about dates and estimated durations. I was a little upset, envisaging her father coming round to my pad with the local Chapter of the Orange Order or Klu Klux Klan or something all ready to splash my blood about a little. Something had to done obviously. Abortion was illegal in Ulster so we couldn't nip down the nearest NHS health garage and have the little rascal whipped out there. We had to improvise. I figured that she couldn't be more than eight or nine weeks along her way at the most. I decided I'd do it myself.

And I did. I spent a week in the reference section of the Central Library, swotting up on the joys of baby squashing. I opted for that process known as Dilatation and Curretage (or D & C to us medical folk). The thing would be no bigger than a chickpea, a stunted plum. A quick sandpaper job on the uterine cavity or whatever and she'd be right as rain. She wouldn't even notice it was missing. I had a long straw just in case it proved stubborn.

When the auspicious day arrived she came round to my grotty hovel, whipped her knickers off and leapt on my mouldy bed, her eyes wide with terror and her lips moist with foolish trust. I wasn't one for knitting needles and since I was doing an art A level I actually stuck an artist's brush up her twat. Long-handled, soft-haired variety. Rowney's finest. I rooted around for about fifteen minutes – shoving, poking, plunging, cranking. Medicine was easy. A matter of simple physics. Human salvage. A lot of mucky stuff came out amongst which there were one or two encouraging little lumps. That seemed to be it. I snatched my paintbrush back and advised her to watch out for excessive vaginal bleeding. I didn't tell her what she should do in that event, I just told her to watch out for it.

She was in tears afterwards, big bitter ones. I did my best to comfort the poor girl, naturally. At least she didn't know what I had used. I told her I had managed to get my hands on a canula from a friend who worked in Casualty at the RVH. She hadn't looked to check so I was able to spare her feelings quite comfortably, the paintbrush business might have upset her. Girls are funny about the things they allow up there. (I chucked the brush away when she'd gone. It wouldn't have been nice to keep it after that.)

Would you believe I even tried to roger her before she left? Disgusting! I'd just had my hands up her little haven and my doglike dick let me down by panting for more. She wouldn't let me, thank God! She wasn't in the mood, so to speak.

As a matter of fact, it probably would have been all right if my temporal calculations had proved correct. If she *had* been merely a couple of months gone my amateur efforts might have done the job without too much fuss. Since she was in reality more than five months along her way, I cocked it up rather. Christ, five months! It must have been almost fully formed, recognisably human and bloody huge – football size. And I had tried dislodging it with that barbarous brush of mine! Oh dear.

Say what you like about the dubious spiritual status of the foetus, this was hard, this was tough to swallow.

I presume that this was why Deirdre went potty subsequently. It was good madness material by any standards. My word, me and my Midas touch had done well. Awfully well. The whole thing was horrible; the brush, the mess, the lavatorial rejection, the grief and all; but by far the worst bit was the fact that I had tried to boff her afterwards. God, I wish I hadn't done that!

You can see why I lied about it.

Oh yes, one more thing. In addition to all this, I must confess that I never made it with Laura. No, indeed. That was another little porky. Tasteful, lyrical, evocative but still a little spooferie. No, I never did sleep with Laura. Not in any field or bed or place. I might have had a chance once. I'm nearly sure that she wanted me just a bit, that she cared to some degree. After all, she drew that unposed portrait of me, did she not? Yes, I had a definite, well-taught hope but I never got near her. I missed by a mile. Laura grew to loathe me without that aid, for loathe me, she does. Boy, did she come to hate me! I just pissed her off in a multitude of less intimate, less enjoyable ways. Oh Laura, that girl, she's no fan. No sir.

It was all true up to that episode during the May Ball. I didn't quite walk away from that confrontation with Greg and his chums. And I didn't duff them up. They beat the living shit out of me, actually. It was very humiliating what with Laura present, etc. I didn't spend that night enigmatically waiting for morning. I spent the night in Casualty waiting to get my bashed-up old body looked at. There was no trembling matutinal love scene, no blissful day of walking, no roofless night together, and definitely no knobbing. I just made it up. Sad but true.

FOUR

Well now, that makes it three little porkies that I've told you. Three petits spoofs. It's quite a little list, isn't it? Quantitatively speaking, that's a whole hell of a lot of untruth. And such major plot points too! Tsk tsk. I should be ashamed of myself. Two guilty deaths and an erotic no-show. My my, I've certainly tried it on. I'm sorry. I beg your pardon. It just seemed to happen that way. It was all fear's fault. It was pure funk and shame that led me down that crooked path of deceit. I'm coy about my crimes. They embarrass me. After all, my best friend and my unborn child! It's not very attractive, is it? Hardly admirable. Twentieth-century heroes must be flawed, I'm reliably informed. They have to be deeply, ineradicably soiled by contact with this time of ours but there is a limit ... surely!

It has to be said that the vast fucking majority of us lie like there's no tomorrow (or perhaps because there is no tomorrow). Even the most pious amongst us come out with dirty great wobblers every now and then, occasionally, from time to time. In novels, cheeky little narrators do it all the time. Newspapers do little else. Politicians do it habitually, without blushing – 'No, we aren't dismantling the Welfare State.' – 'There is no such thing as MI6.' – 'South Africa's a wonderful place with lots of sun and jolly little brown people.' The important thing about all this is that nobody protests, no one is surprised ... no one expects anything else! It's a fact of life. It's called objectivity or realism or something like that.

And this leeway extends to all our smaller lives and lies. Think about it. Who honestly expects the truth these days? I don't. Do you? I told you about Jenny's bad boffing habits. Well, when I actually discovered that she'd been screwing the neighbourhood I wasn't very surprised. I wasn't even terribly upset. I was hurt, humiliated and jealous, I own. But it was the actual bonking action not the subterfuge that rankled with me. Indeed, the word deceit hardly occurred to me. I realised that she had done me a good office in not telling me. After all, would I really have wanted to know? No doubt, she thought that she was doing me a favour. She was being kind.

And to some degree, she was. The 'white lie' as an excuse, as a concept, now encompasses the vast panoply of human deceit. More than ever, lies have value now. They are comfortable, quick and painless. They get you out of those tight scrapes and reluctant ties. They spare the feelings of those around you as well as yourself. Lies are the coup de grâce essential to modern life. They are the captive-bolt, the humane killer that gives us all our lifely meat. They're vital. Irreplaceable. Where would we be without them?

Increasingly, the truth is a trembling thing. Shy, tentative and reclusive. What would you do if you met it, if someone actually told you the truth? Me, I'd shit myself. I probably wouldn't recognise it anyway. Oh yeah? I'd say. Really? No kidding? Cross your heart? You don't say! Yes, I'm afraid the sad truth is that I wouldn't recognise the truth if it came up to me wearing a personalised T-shirt, introduced itself, produced birth certificate, finger-prints, dental records and testimony from reliable witnesses. 'Come off it!' I'd say, 'What do you think I am? An idiot?'

But this is not to excuse my lying to you. On that count, you could not be more disappointed in me than I am in myself. I concede that the whole affair was entirely reprehensible and I have no real notion as to why I did it. Like I say, I was embarrassed. I mean, after all, they were rather seamy little details. And I wanted you to like me of course. Yes, I rather believe that was very important. These omissions seem more comprehensible on that point, do they not? With all that harsh veracity around, you might have given up on me much earlier. How could I hope to get away with that little lot? You would have walked away in disgust, made yourself a cup of coffee, had a drink and a fag and slagged me off to a friend. 'Do you know what that guy did? Do you know what he tried to swing? Who does he think he is?' I didn't want that kind of reaction. The idea of that made me shudder. That's why I popped it all out now. This is why I've hoisted it onto you near the end.

Yes indeed, we are most certainly near the end. We're running out of paper space. O cruel leaves! O tyrannous covers! You'd noticed already, I imagine. You've seen it coming. You could hardly fail to do so, I suppose. You have that advantage over me at least. You have that leverage. Use it sparingly, please.

Would you like to know which the worst of my lies was (or rather, what the worst of my truths is)? They're all bad and no doubt you have already worked out your own scales and preferences. Objectively, the worst of them is, of course, the one about Deirdre's miscarriage. It worked the most damage (to her, to me, to it) and claimed the most prize – loyalty, spermless innocence and treasured victim status. In my first version of that episode, I emerged smelling of roses whereas in reality I smelt of death, treachery and botched bog-births. The discrepancy in all the versions of me that emerged was at its widest just there. It was the bit that needed the biggest rewrite. I had no right to pile it on in that instance. I had but poor claims to the state of humanity itself in that episode. But, as I've said before, I really wanted you to like me.

However, the spoof that cost me the greatest loss of dignity and self-esteem was, surprisingly, that fictional Laura boff. I mean, strictly speaking, the other two weren't really spoofs at all. They were inaccuracies concerning actual events, omissions of vital detail. However, the whole Laura business was a complete concoction, an utter fabrication. The epitome of spoofing. This makes it worse. I got nowhere near Laura's buns and she avoided mine. There was no need for that little lie. I was covering no tracks, hiding no crimes. I was just concealing my failure. Evading my own comic futility. Trying to bolster the sad figure I cut.

And many's the time I've sobbed about it in the afteryears. Lovelorn and lostlonely. Always hoping in that unrequited cinegenic way of mine. Nice little yearner.

By Christ, since then I've been awash with every kind of clownish sentimentality. How fondly I have dreamt of our final, fulfilling encounter, a decade hence. A projection. Our paths crossing on sanguine paving-stones. Mills and Boon. Velvet dreams. She comes to me. Ten years older and still desperate for my well-preserved and yet firm little buttocks. Yes, this is it. My fantasy. Slush artist! Me lean, smooth and debonair as would be my right. I've done my best to tease this one out. What was it to be? For me, that triumph and choice. For her, the wrinkled regret of all those wasted years. That detail tickled me. Women age so much worse than men, I was pleased to observe. Me in the driving seat. The final faltering ensemble. Poignant with delay. I've wanted and waited for only that.

I know well that I humiliate myself in this. I know that she neither knows nor cares and I can be damned sure that she never gives a thought to the charming subject of Ripley Bogle ... except perhaps to vilify him in her thoughts. Ah, me she has struck and smote. Irony and confidence have been no shield against her woundstrokes. I'm all cut up. This is rather sad, is it not? Despite my deceit, do you not feel a certain amount of partisan outrage swelling in your little heart? Yes? Good. Why don't you go round to her place and maybe even set up a little demonstration outside there. You know, with chants and placards and that kind of thing – 'Requite Ripley!' – 'Love him, Laura!' That might just do the trick and, at the very least, will get me noticed. Will you do that for me? Thanks, kids. I'll do the same for you one day.

Or should I forget it? It's probably too late for that now. Nonetheless, for her I will make the attempt at whatever the modern word for love is – the word that means selflessness, integrity, tenderness and benediction.

I'm a fine one to talk of integrity and selflessness after what you've just learnt! I'm not sure that my callow obsession with dear Laura even merits the term 'love'. If it hadn't been her, it might well have been someone else, as they say. Perhaps I sought it out. The confrontation, the disavowal and, above all, the waiting failure. Perhaps, that was it. The non-possession. Maybe, the waiting was all. The frotteurism of memory.

Can we call this a love? Unrequited or otherwise. The last of self-regard. Lure of the unattainable. The temptation of the sacristy. All for me she would tremble. The epicene, the cassocked priest. She was never even nearly mine. She was real. She might have been shallow and foolish but at least she existed. Was this what I feared? Ach bejabbers, aren't I the empty man, to be sure!

But anyhow, such considerations are futile now. They are tangential, academic. They have no bearing upon the rest of our mutual progress, I think.

So, come on. We've stuck together through thin and thinner, you and I. Like me, loathe me, revile me, ignore me or whatever suits you best but we must be moving. We have conclusions to reach. Follow me five minutes more. Stick around. Over soon. Let's go. We must make an end.

(By the way – all that business about truth being a tremulous thing, hard to recognise, etc. – it was mostly crap. I can see that already and I greatly doubt that I beat you to that conclusion. Pathetic, isn't it? The price I pay for my youth. Instant revision. It was all bollocks. Take Perry for instance. You never really saw as much of Perry as I did but he was chockful of truth, take my word for it. He was the ignorant epicentre of a whole detonation of veracity and integrity. Perry always told the truth. I tried to ignore this but it was a fact. Always. Perry just couldn't lie. Like those loquacious gee-gees in Swift. He had no conception of deceit. That muscular illogicality, that mean comfort. I hope it helped him. I hope it proved a bonus in that life of his. Do you know, I think it probably did.)

*

Old men tell their stories all the time. It's habitual with them. And old women too. It's accepted. Expected even, given the seal and respectability of the norm.

The pleasures in old folk's stories are, I admit, numerous. For a start, there's generally a lot of it; a great deal of story. That's the main advantage the old have. They have a lot of years there. From their long lives and multitudinous acquaintance they can forge their tales, their epic, winding, dynastic histories. But this is also the problem with old people's stories. They've lived so long that they have to telescope in the interests of brevity. They can dash through a decade in a paragraph. Half an hour about the night they lost their virginity and then a generation is dismissed in seconds. There are gaps, longueurs. Shifts of pace and importance. Bland strands of timestretched narrative and thinned reminiscence.

A youth's story is relatively unusual. Rare. For some reason, we seem wary of hoisting our little snippets upon the general ear. It smacks of precocity, hubris, wilful ignorance. What could we have had in our short lives worth hearing about? Who wants to know? We don't have access to that trunk of years, that big bag of witnessed time. This is our handicap and our strength. Events mean more to the young. We lack the objective splay and pose of sequence. Our past is immediate, episodic, hotly self-obsessed. And above all – visual, pictorial. Comprised of sense and free of much judgement or clouding thought. Our past has that focussed, hard-eyed strength. Detail, accuracy, vividness. This is what the memories of the young possess.

The old reflect from a point of stasis. They have finished the best part of their business with life. Their story seems complete, ineluctable. The stories of the young are told halfway through. They are in grip of change. Nothing is certain. They can take no convincing pose nor draw any real conclusions. That is left to you.

FIVE

Trafalgar Square glistens in early afternoon dampness. Mist has come and straggled groups of figures dawdle and stream listlessly in the Sunday gloom. There is heavy, rank moisture in the air, a defamed secretion from the rotting sky. It settles on and envelops buildings, cars and people alike, an unholy sputum. People's breath forms a verminous spoor which loiters in the disfigured atmosphere, coiling and snaking into evaporation. A diaphanous, maleficent mist spirates around the column, cloaking its height.

The day is idling. After the sleep of noon, the day is groggy and disgruntled. The people here feel this and none as much as I.

I'm replete with the clichéd deaths on which I brood. I've been struggling with the imbalance of my guilt and reparation. I'm awkward here under the mirthless eyes of my ranks of faults. They've fixed me in their gaze and they watch me flounder to make amends. A lament to the dead, a paean to the corpse of the world would be useful. A veritable ghostlist. But I don't have the time.

I turn my ragged face, my pinched, sad face towards this thick of London, the city. There it squats and settles. Waiting. Playing out its list of tales and transgressions. In windowpools and wet reflections the haze shimmers. It eludes and dances to other grasps, not mine.

The folk of Trafalgar Square rotate in all their differing speeds, their moves slowed by the day's sluggish veto. Like lunch-hour liberty, like all crafted ease, their freedom is tainted in this envelope of mist. Cars snake past in noiseless order, their face-filled windows stained by the airy muck. The city isn't glittering.

We all want a chance . . . if not two or more. For revision, for erasure and clemency we crave. Our errors past and future gather in our streets, jostling and officious. They want to be heard. They have any God's number of grievances. They want justice. They'd like a little arbitration.

What will they get?

It has all come to its ripeness – as it had to do. Deceit has no stamina. It never lasts the course. Whoops discovery! The liar's dread. It has come to its squalid, graceless point. Not before time and well behind informed expectation. My sundry other inaccuracies. I've tried to infect you with my stately progress. My sturdy journey to the same point of stupidity and vice. I trust I've failed.

I'm fading here, fading badly, but a little left to say. What's the worst that I've done? In basements and backdoor spaces I've looked for some necessity. In the clutch of pavement and disappointed greed, I've recollected, conjured and evoked. Between success and failure I must dance my dance with hokey poems to cull the worst of my crapspouts. This is precarious and wins me few friends.

See my problem? I'm trying here. Where will I find the words I need? I try. I try very hard. For wisdom and benevolence, for comprehension and resolution. Beginning with the trumpetings of maudlin, I sell myself eternally short. From arrogance to banality, no slouch I. I'm defeated by the glaring casuistry of my race and age. Or something close. All my essays at magnanimity and humility go ludicrously wrong. They dribble, as now, into foolishness. But I try. Believe me. I try so very hard.

My early years were spent exposed to the punitive moral guidance of Victorian novels. In these tomes, the young hero, a likable, well-favoured lad, Tom Jones in a frock coat, sets out from the stasis of his usual life on a journey of supposed maturity. He starts his travels well-stocked with every kind of fault, egoism and mean sophistry. Though fundamentally generous of spirit and good in heart, he has his shortcomings. He enters upon this trail of hardship, setback and trial. He encounters figures imbued with stronger and older wisdoms and they guide him to some degree, knowingly or inadvertently. The journey is punctuated with his errors, his faux pas, his misprisions and his follies. Through these he qualifies to some kind of wisdom. A capricious auctorial wisdom but still wisdom. In short, he wises up and gets landed with the major skirt.

This notion had a profound effect on Ripley Bogle, that queerfated Turf Lodge tyke. Ever since, I've tried to apply this gauge to my own maturity. I've tried to get suss quicker than Arthur Pendennis managed it. It's a simple enough system but hasn't gone too well for me. I seem to get more than my share of cock-ups, disasters, humiliations. Gosh, I think to myself after my most recent fall, fuck-up or brief insanity, wow, I've really cracked it now! After all that I must be incredibly frigging wise, Solomon himself! Hello Maturity, nice to meet you after all this time. But then I go out and make another gaffe, commit another outrage against sensitivity and play the abortionist's role in general. No delay. I'm quite a bit wiser after that, I can tell you. However, there are more sins to be sinned and more wisdom to be got. I have to plough in poor completion. I suppose (wait for it) that my wisdom ball will rolling grow perpetually. I suspect that no one gets to be like those guys in the books at the end. It doesn't seem to be how it works in the cold objectivity of reality. No final settling scene, no pudgy benefactor anxious to dish out the dosh and I most certainly don't get the girl on the final page.

This mightn't sound like much. But it's a big step for me. I'm just a kid — these things confuse and appal me.

I look around this tainted square at the dingy pleasures of England. Like sad eyes in a smiling face, it makes the effort but fools few. The nicest thing about London is that London doesn't care. In Belfast I was fettered like all the Irish by the soft mastery of my country, by its mulch of nationhood and its austere, parental beauty. London will play ball if you make the effort but the city will leave you mostly unmolested. It provokes the pleasant spur of loneliness yet populates your dreams, despair or solitude. In dark suit striped with ancient grey London remains polite but distant. This is admirable behaviour on the part of any city and should be loudly commended.

I'm still doing well with the hunger pangs, by the way. If nothing else, I believe that my fortitude in this matter has been worthy of some approbation. I've suffered relatively quietly in that area. My stab wound has also provided some scope for a certain amount of Spartan silence. Though the manner of its creation will hardly have given a great deal of pleasure, at least I haven't milked that little tragedy in the manner that I might have done. The rest of it has been, I freely concede, a mixed bunch. How has it been for you? What do you think of it all? Ripley Bogle, drawn from Belfast, Cambridge and London, sop to the grime and friend to the dead. I've been around in my own small and concentrated way. I've done my best more or less consistently and I've tried to avoid the grosser pitfalls of my own shoddy destinations. Maurice was disaster, Deirdre was all kinds of catastrophe and Laura the last word in fiasco. Oh yes, I did them all some kind of wrong, some disservice. By report and by actual deed, I sold them short. I feel bad about all this, naturally, but the failure that troubles me most is my failure with Perry. I never hoisted any major vilenesses upon Perry, not like I did with the other three at any rate, but for some reason I can't help feeling that I failed him in some ghastly way. Before and after.

Indeed, I'm failing him now. I can't explain how but I'm quite sure I am. I should really be visiting that son of his or something. I don't even know where the old guy will be buried but I know that I won't be there. No one will be there, barring general priests and loons. This is, patently, not how it should be.

Singing in my darkness and opening my eyes. That's truth's task with me as I imagine it is with most of us, poor bodies that we are.

And my quest? What of that? What can we salvage from the butchered shambles of my acid little history? Why have I come to this? It's a tricky one certainly and I'm wary of committing myself excessively but I think that the reason lies in the story and that the story itself lurks sly behind the cause. Can you see it? I must admit, I can't. Not at all. Not a sausage. Absolument rien.

If there's a sin to be committed, the Irish will take its weight, international altruists that they be. The world did me wrong by making me an Irishman. I've kicked hard but Micksville packs a boot like a donkey. When you think about it, I'm practically faultless – a victim of circumstance, timing and nationhood. It's Ireland's fault, not mine.

I only plead that most vices are misnamed. The sins and crimes we all tote up are rarely promoted with the full vigour of intention. We don't commit misdemeanours as such – we make mistakes. Horrible, deadly mistakes, huge in consequence and implication but mostly mistakes all the same. That's my defence such as it is. Really no one wants to be a bastard if they can help it.

That's it. The end. I'm glad it's over. I was running out of evasion. I've sown up all my pockets and I've nowhere left to put my bullshit. I produce the last of my cigarettes. I take it slowly, savouring the process. My last match flares bright and sudden in the mist and I ignite successfully. My exhaled tobacco breath is indistinguishable in the moist fumes of the coiling, weary air. I sit up a little and press my eyes into gazing service. Empty-bellied, I tremble with meagre content. I smile without reason. Things aren't so bad. Perhaps the situation may be resurrected. After all, I am young. I've done it before. Dragged myself out of destitution. The world could still let me in. Perhaps I should go to Oxford this time. Who knows? Smoking with steady, slow compassion, I begin to make some plans.

The mist flickers around me as I stand. Two buses jerk to an angry halt, inches away from each other's metal throats. The mist seems to lose its silence and the muddy noises of Trafalgar Square begin to grow in timbre and renewed confidence. A ball-bouncing child runs just past me, scatter-ing saggy-arsed pigeons with his cries. His mother calls after him. He checks, turns and almost smiles before pressing on with his urgent, disruptive recreation. I move away, crossing their wake. My belly stretches smooth without complaint and my legs support me with affecting ease. I walk trimly, with some aplomb.

Ian McEwan
The Cement Garden £3.99

'In many ways a shocking book, morbid, full of repellant imagery – and irresistibly readable ... the effect achieved by McEwan's quiet, precise and sensuous touch is that of magic realism' NEW YORK REVIEW OF BOOKS

'A little masterpiece of appalling fascination' DAILY MAIL

'For a first novel, it is a darkly impressive piece of work ... a touch of real fictional genius' THE TIMES

'Just about perfect' SPECTATOR

First Love, Last Rites £3.50

Under Ian McEwan's manipulations, depravity may take on the guise of innocence and butterflies can become sinister. With equal power, he can show a child's life become fouled by the macabre, or distil the awakening sensations of first love, tracing its ritual initiations and infusing them with a luxuriant sensual imagery.

'A brilliant performance, showing an originality astonishing for a writer still in his mid twenties' ANTHONY THWAITE, OBSERVER

Günter Grass
The Rat £4.50

Through the thoughts of a caged female rat we learn the history of the
world from the rat perspective, interleaved by Grass's narrator with tales
old, new and fantastical of the protagonists of earlier writings. The result is
a chilling insight into what the future holds: the human race stands
condemned by wasteful consumerism and an urge for self destruction, to
be supplanted by its logical successor in the evolutionary chain: the rat.

'Grass has written an apocalyptic novel which goes further than any of his
work in plumbing the dangers of our nuclear age; the book is dark, bitter,
witty and somehow warming. It asks the obvious fundamental questions –
Who controls the world? Who controls the imagination? – but, instead of
anguished romanticism, does it with the realism of its own convictions and
the convictions of its own imagery.' NEW STATESMAN

'The narrative is seamlessly welded together and lent power by the brown
rat that the author has been given for Christmas ... Reading his prose, as
always superbly translated by Ralph Manheim, is like being wakened from
the sleep of reason by acid rain.' NEW YORK TIMES

'Massive and magnificent' THE DAILY TELEGRAPH

'A magnificently organised howl of anguish.' THE INDEPENDENT

All Pan books are available at your local bookshop or newsagent, or can be ordered direct from the publisher. Indicate the number of copies required and fill in the form below.

Send to: **CS Department, Pan Books Ltd., P.O. Box 40, Basingstoke, Hants.   RG21 2YT.**

or phone: 0256 469551 (Ansaphone), quoting title, author and Credit Card number.

Please enclose a remittance* to the value of the cover price plus: 60p for the first book plus 30p per copy for each additional book ordered to a maximum charge of £2.40 to cover postage and packing.

*Payment may be made in sterling by UK personal cheque, postal order, sterling draft or international money order, made payable to Pan Books Ltd.

Alternatively by Barclaycard/Access:

Card No.

Signature:

Applicable only in the UK and Republic of Ireland.

While every effort is made to keep prices low, it is sometimes necessary to increase prices at short notice. Pan Books reserve the right to show on covers and charge new retail prices which may differ from those advertised in the text or elsewhere.

NAME AND ADDRESS IN BLOCK LETTERS PLEASE:

....

Name————————————————————————

Address————————————————————————

————————————————————————————

————————————————————————————

————————————————————————————

3/87